CW01545402

THE HOUSE ON THE CLIFF

VICTORIA SCOTT

Boldwood

First published in Great Britain in 2025 by Boldwood Books Ltd.

Copyright © Victoria Scott, 2025

Cover Design by JD Smith Design Ltd

Cover Images: Shutterstock

The moral right of Victoria Scott to be identified as the author of this work has been asserted in accordance with the Copyright, Designs and Patents Act 1988.

All rights reserved. No part of this book may be reproduced in any form or by any electronic or mechanical means, including information storage and retrieval systems, without written permission from the author, except for the use of brief quotations in a book review. This book is a work of fiction and, except in the case of historical fact, any resemblance to actual persons, living or dead, is purely coincidental.

Every effort has been made to obtain the necessary permissions with reference to copyright material, both illustrative and quoted. We apologise for any omissions in this respect and will be pleased to make the appropriate acknowledgements in any future edition.

A CIP catalogue record for this book is available from the British Library.

Paperback ISBN 978-1-83561-712-0

Large Print ISBN 978-1-83561-711-3

Hardback ISBN 978-1-83561-710-6

Trade Paperback ISBN 978-1-80656-014-1

Ebook ISBN 978-1-83561-713-7

Kindle ISBN 978-1-83561-714-4

Audio CD ISBN 978-1-83561-705-2

MP3 CD ISBN 978-1-83561-706-9

Digital audio download ISBN 978-1-83561-707-6

This book is printed on certified sustainable paper. Boldwood Books is dedicated to putting sustainability at the heart of our business. For more information please visit https://www.boldwoodbooks.com/about-us/sustainability/

Boldwood Books Ltd, 23 Bowerdean Street, London, SW6 3TN

www.boldwoodbooks.com

For Raphie and Ella: Remembering many wonderful holidays together in beautiful Cornwall, and my shrieks when you persuaded me to join you in the sea.

PROLOGUE
JOHN

21 July 1966

It's several hours after lights out when John's bare feet meet the cold lino beneath his bed. He pulls on his wool dressing gown and a pair of darned socks and tiptoes past the blanket-ensnared forms of the three other boys who share his dorm. *They* might have surrendered to sleep, he thinks, but he hasn't. His guilt won't let him.

It's almost midnight. The moon is shining brightly through the narrow room's towering windows, which have no curtains to ward off the light or the dark. The glass panelled door of their dormitory, scarred at its wooden edges with scrapes worthy of a wild animal, creaks in protest as he pulls it open inch by inch. He turns around to check for movement in the beds, because he doesn't want anyone to know where he's going. None of them have stirred. He'd like to say they're sleeping the sleep of the righteous, but that, he thinks, would be entirely incorrect.

Seconds later, John is standing in the hallway outside. It's almost pitch black, save for the light of a solitary, bare bulb hanging down from the ceiling at one end of the corridor, and moonlight filtering through a small sash window at the other. He's relieved, but not surprised, to find it quiet. At this time of night the monks will all be in their cells, including Father Crispin, their headmaster; the Amadeus house matron, Mrs Turner-Smith, will be in her room on the floor below; and even though he's heard that their housemaster Mr Lee regularly drinks whisky until the BBC closes down for the night, he should be safely locked away in his private quarters, not roaming the halls looking for sleepwalkers and errant boys.

John walks down the corridor towards the middle of the wing, where there's a winding staircase which spans the whole height of the creaking Victorian building, from its basement full of storerooms to the top floor. It once provided rooms for servants but now houses poky single rooms for sixth-formers instead. He walks down the stairs and pauses for a moment in front of a huge window, which is left open at least an inch all year round. The staff at Hallows Abbey seem to believe there is something magical about fresh air, even if it's both damp and freezing, as it is for most of the winter. Tonight, however, it's a warm breeze that's blowing through the gap at the bottom of the window, and John stops to inhale the combined scent of salt, seaweed and algae. There are many things he dislikes about Hallows, but its location, perched on the cliffs on Cornwall's windswept northern coast, is definitely not one of them. The sea might lash both the school and its inhabitants, but to him, it feels like home.

He continues his journey downwards, stopping at the ground floor, which is well lit, with rows of bulbs blazing. From here, he knows he has the riskiest part of his journey to contend with. To get to where he needs to be, he has to walk past the door to the housemaster's rooms. If he is indeed up drinking late, there's a chance he might hear him. John holds his breath as he passes the door. He's glad he decided to do this journey only in socks.

Once this hurdle is overcome, however, he relaxes. Now he only has to open the heavy door in front of him – click, clunk, goes the hinge, but it's only a little noise, so it shouldn't wake anyone – rush through the covered walkway that connects the main school building and the abbey, and then push another wooden door, which he is relieved to find open. He walks through it and pushes it shut behind him.

He stands for a moment, letting his eyes adjust to the darkness of the cavernous abbey, the spiritual centre of both the monastery and the school.

Ahead of him, there is a solitary candle lit in a jar by the altar, and John walks towards it, passing row upon row of upright wooden pews and walking on stones marking the resting place of generations of Hallows Abbey monks. There are quite literally bones beneath his feet, in the crypt. The thought of this usually gives him pause, but not tonight. Tonight, he has other things to consider.

He arrives at the altar and immediately falls down on his knees. For this is where he knew he'd needed to come, when he'd realised he was unable to find an answer just lying there in bed, so pathetic, so *irrelevant*. He'd known at that moment that it was God, and only God, who could help him now.

He lowers his head, places his hands together, and begins to pray. His prayer isn't one he knows by heart or one prescribed by the church, but instead a reel of questions, questions to which he does not know the answer. They emerge with surprising force.

'Can I help you?'

John is wrenched out of his trance-like state in an instant.

He's not alone here after all, then. *This is bad*, he thinks. *Really bad. They'll expel me for this.* Students aren't allowed to wander into the abbey after dark. He turns around and can just about make out that there's a monk standing next to him. It's not one of the teaching monks, though, so he doesn't know his name. But he's clearly part of the order, because he's dressed in their robes.

'Oh, hello... Sir.'

'Hello.'

The monk doesn't sound angry, and John is relieved. He tries to examine his face, to see if he looks cross. The solitary candle's light is too weak, however, and it's only really illuminating one side of his face. It's impossible to make out the details.

'I'm sorry. I wanted to come here to... pray. I needed to do it here. I'm sorry, I'm not explaining myself very well.' John realises he's gabbling.

'I see.'

There's an awkward silence.

'I'll go now. I... I'm sorry.'

John decides the best approach is to leave, before he has to give the monk his name. *Perhaps he can't see me properly either*, he thinks. *Maybe the light is so bad, I'll get away with it.*

'No, don't go.'

'Why? I know I'm not supposed to...'

'This is God's house. Everyone who needs to be here should be here. Who are we to try to impose our own rules on how it is run? Please do not let me interrupt you.'

John nods, but in reality he just feels incredibly awkward. He can't run off now, can he? But the monk is still standing beside him, and it feels strange to pray with someone else there, someone else listening, even if the questions he's asking are only in his head. He decides to pretend to pray for half a minute and then head for the exit. This is all too awkward for words. He closes his eyes, places his hands together and does exactly this. He counts to thirty in his head, opens them and turns to leave.

But there is no monk beside him when he turns.

'Hello?' he calls out, tentatively, quietly. 'Hello? I'm going now.'

There is no reply.

The old monk couldn't have walked very far in thirty seconds, John reasons. And he'd have made a noise moving off, certainly. And even if he had walked away, why hadn't he answered him when he'd called out?

And then, as he's pondering where the monk could possibly have gone and what on earth has just happened, the candle on the altar flickers – once, twice, three times – and then it is extinguished. The church is plunged into absolute darkness.

And then fear rips into John's soul, because the candle is sitting in a tall jar. It can't possibly have been blown out naturally, by a breeze.

In that moment, he is absolutely certain he has just communicated with something supernatural. Something evil. In God's church.

And so he runs, no longer caring if he's heard, not caring at all if he collides with pews or trips over flagstones, absolutely determined that he needs to get out of this place, out of the abbey and into the corridor and back up the stairs, and then back into his dormitory.

Finally, he returns to his bed with huge relief, his chest heaving, his body shaking, and his brain wired. Astonishingly, none of his room-mates wake.

He is unusually pleased to be in their presence. As he yanks his sheets over his shaking body, he closes his eyes, willing oblivion to come and take him. Because he cannot begin to think about what the encounter he's just had might mean for *his* soul, for *his* future, for *his* decision.

Help me, God, he thinks. *Help me. What on earth am I to do now?*

PART I

PART 1

1

AMANDA

August 2024

'I knew we shouldn't have taken the A303.'

It's almost thirty degrees, and their car's air conditioning has given up trying to keep the heat at bay. They've had to lower the windows for fresh air, but it's not working because they're in stationary traffic and the road surface is a sufficient temperature to cook bacon. Amanda is sweating so much that her legs have stuck to the car's fake leather upholstery and there are semicircles soaked into the cotton beneath her breasts.

'The M4–M5 junction would have been worse,' says her husband Mike, reaching down to pick up the can of warm Diet Coke they're sharing, and taking a swig. 'Mind you, at least we no longer have kids with us. Do you remember that time we were going camping in Bude, and we blindly followed the satnav and it rerouted us through a completely bumper-to-bumper Bristol? Jules was potty training, and you ended up having to get her out of the car to have a poo beside a pub garden full of drinkers.'

'Oh, yep,' says Amanda, laughing. Well, she laughs for a bit, they both do, but then they sit in silence for a moment, because the memory is bittersweet. Those days of early parenting were often challenging, as they are for most, but now that Julia and Luke have left home, memories of their childhood are tinged with the kind of nostalgia that bites rather than comforts.

Luke is nineteen and brimming with the enthusiasm and confidence of someone on the cusp of anything and everything. He's about to go into his second year of a Physiotherapy degree at Bristol. Julia, meanwhile, is twenty-one and after three years of ambivalence studying Psychology, is about to embark on an MA in Film in London with her boyfriend Tom, who she met volunteering at a film festival last summer.

Both of their children are happy young adults, on the verge of an exciting future. And yet... And yet Amanda has been harbouring a hope that one of them might have taken some time out of their summer of partying, part-time work and travel to visit their parents. So far, however, they seem to have preferred their rented student accommodation to the family home. Or what *was* the family home, Amanda thinks, correcting herself as a lump forms in her throat. They don't have one now. Well, not one big enough for a family, anyway.

They haven't seen either child since Julia's graduation in July. WhatsApp messages since have been sporadic; mostly pared down, evasive responses to Amanda's increasingly probing questions. She's delighted they're both following their own particular stars. Of course she is. But she also misses them desperately. And she suspects Mike does too, although he doesn't say so.

* * *

It takes four more hours to travel the one hundred and thirty-nine further miles to their destination, a journey that ordinarily should take about half of that. Amanda and Mike pass the time hopping between radio stations, asking the satnav to try to find them a better route, and talking about the new challenge they're both taking on.

Mike is the one who's been appointed deputy head, of course, so he's the one with the actual job, but Amanda has been his wife long enough to know she is absolutely part of the package. When you take a live-in job in a boarding school and you have a spouse, that person will also have their daily life dictated by the establishment. The school decides where you live, usually in a small flat or house on site. This is a perk, of course, but it has also meant they've always lived in someone else's place. They've invested the money they've saved on housing into a rented flat in Bristol, which provides an income stream but none of the comfort of a home.

The school also decides your holidays and which parts of the weekend are your own. They also insist on your free labour to perform an unlimited number of duties such as: theatre set design and construction, birthday cake making, cricket catering and open day planning. Amanda has done all of these in the twenty-plus years Mike has been teaching in the private school sector, most of them schools with boarders. It's a bit like being a vicar's wife about fifty years ago, Amanda thinks, except the accommodation is usually less spacious.

As they turn off the A30 and drive along the network of ever narrowing roads that lead to Hallows Abbey, Amanda catches glimpses of azure in the distance, coupled with the undeniable smell of the sea. She is immediately transported to holidays long ago in this part of England, when the children had been small, their budget had been just as tiny, and they had spent long sunny days on the beach and long wet days touring dusty National Trust houses.

It would be so wonderful if actually living in Cornwall could help me recapture some of the magic of those times, she thinks, aware of course that living somewhere will always be very different to the suspension of disbelief a holiday provides, and that the children are no longer children, and also, not here. But still, she thinks: the sea. *I will be living by the sea, and I've always wanted to do that.* And this thought is just enough to keep her homesickness for their little terraced house in London, their home for almost a decade, at bay for a few more hours. She has promised herself she will not cry today. Or at least, not in front of Mike.

'There should be a sign around here somewhere,' he says, peering at a thick, tall hedge with intent. 'I remember it from the interview. Yep, yep, here it is.'

They arrive at what appears at first to be just more hedge, but then slowly reveals itself to be a narrow gap leading to yet another narrow lane.

There's a large wooden sign sitting atop a somewhat wonky pair of wooden posts. The gold paint that reads 'Hallows Abbey, a Catholic boarding school for boys aged 13–18' is faded, and the blue paint is flaking. 'One of the first things I'm going to do is fix that sign,' says Mike, and they both smile as they turn into the lane.

At first, Amanda thinks someone's moved the sign for a prank, because all she can see is hedge, the very occasional windswept tree and the crest of a grassy hill. But then they reach its peak, where fields give way to moorland, and the sight that greets them on the other side makes her gasp. She already knew that Hallows Abbey sat on its own on a headland, but nothing has prepared her for this: the windswept moor ending abruptly at the edge of sheer cliffs on three sides; the school buildings, sports pitches and abbey, which together resemble a small village; and just a short walk along what looks to be a perilous coastal path, the skeletal remains of a tin mine and its engine houses, silhouetted against the sky.

'I know,' says Mike. 'Quite something, isn't it.'

'It feels... like it's not quite real.'

'Yes. You wouldn't know it was here, would you, if you hadn't turned down the road? I know some parents say the isolation puts them off sending their kids here. But it can also be a strength, I think. If you can't get a mobile phone signal, the kids aren't going to watch stuff they shouldn't on their phones. And if you do it right, you could foster a real sense of community here, of being in it together, of being part of nature.'

'Is that what you said in your interview?' she says, with a smile.

'Pretty much.' Mike laughs. 'I do believe that, though. I think maybe we all need to step away from modern society for a while. It's pretty crazy out there.'

Amanda understands what he means. She knows that social media has the capacity to turn ordinary people into monsters, and the dark underbelly of society had been visible even in the fairly affluent area of London they'd been living in. But even so, the capital had charmed her easily. It had charmed all of them, in fact. When the kids had still been at school, they'd spent weekends and holidays wandering around the Tate Modern with Julia and then stopping for frozen yogurt at Snog or visiting HMS *Belfast* and the Imperial War Museum on repeat with history-mad Luke.

Despite London's reputation for unfriendliness, Amanda had managed to make connections with many people over the decade they'd been there, the longest she and Mike had ever lived in one place. She'd been secretly delighted every year he hadn't announced a plan to move somewhere else. She'd adored the group of friends she'd made at the allotment they'd rented, the part-time job she'd had in the school office organising external exams, the mums she'd got to know at church on Sundays, the women she'd rowed with at the local rowing club. *And now I'm starting all over again*, she thinks, and tears form in the corners of her eyes. She wipes them away quickly, hoping Mike won't notice.

'Right, I think we need to follow this road to the right,' he says, turning at a small roundabout in front of an enormous four-storey Victorian building. 'That's just one side of the main school building. It's got a big quad in the middle of it.' Amanda notices a statue of a monk in the middle of the roundabout, resting on a high plinth. He sees her looking. 'That's Father Richard, who founded the Credans, the order who run the school.' To their right is the entrance to a large church, which is connected to the main building by a covered walkway. 'That's the abbey, obviously,' says Mike. On the other side of this is a three-storey building that looks to be at least a couple of hundred years old. 'Next to it is the monastery, where the monks live. It's the oldest building on the site, built in the early 1800s. The abbey was built at about the same time. The school followed about fifty years later.'

They drive past two smaller, two-storey buildings which are identical to each other. These look to have been built in the thirties. Between them is a walled enclosure, with a wooden door in its centre. 'That's the monastery's walled garden. They grow all sorts, I think, and some of the food is used in the school. And either side of it are the other boarding houses. There's one more that shares some of the main school building, Amadeus. They're all named after Catholic saints.' *Same old, same old then*, thinks Amanda. Pretty much every school he's worked at has had houses named after saints. Male saints, of course. *Just once*, she thinks, *just once it would be great if they could think about doing something different, like picking impressive people from history, perhaps, and maybe even women? Goodness, that would put the cat amongst the pigeons.*

Amanda is well aware that her views on women and female priests are at odds with Catholic doctrine, and she keeps them to herself. But she still thinks them. It's a tiny rebellion, admittedly, but it's her only option. She can't speak out about that or about any of the other thoughts she has about Catholicism, or indeed, faith in general, for fear of affecting Mike's career in Catholic education.

'And here we are,' says Mike as they pull into a parking space on the other side of the main school building. It's reserved for the deputy headmaster. She sees a flicker of triumph and satisfaction ripple across her husband's face. She knows that this promotion means a great deal to him. She's doing her best to feel the same about it, because heaven knows, that feeling is going to have to sustain her through a lot. She takes a deep breath, pastes on a smile, opens her car door and steps outside.

It's the salt she smells first, and then the seaweed. Then she feels an unmistakable dampness on her skin and hears the roar of the waves crashing onto the rocks below the cliffs. Despite the fact it's high summer, the Atlantic Ocean is still making its presence felt today. She wonders, with a flash of dread and awe, what it will be like here in a storm.

'It's this way.' Mike has already lifted one of their suitcases out of the boot and is trundling it down a path towards a side door with a keypad lock next to it. Amanda follows him, noticing that a black and white cat is strolling nonchalantly across the grass to her left.

'Who owns that?' she asks.

Mike shrugs. 'Don't know. Must belong to one of the housemasters.'

'Isn't somebody here to meet us?' asks Amanda, realising that the animal is the only other living being she's seen since they drove up. She's used to schools being empty during the holidays, of course, but there's usually someone around all the time, like grounds people carrying out maintenance. But there doesn't seem to be anybody here. Then she looks upwards at the building they are about to enter and sees the shape of someone – she's too far away to make out their features – standing behind one of the large sash windows, staring out to sea. She almost waves, then realises that would look weird because she doesn't know them, so she keeps her hands by her sides.

'Oh, no. Well, the new headmaster, Father Paul, is here all the time, because he's part of the order. I think he's probably in his office at the moment. He's got his hands full, I think, because my fellow deputy head,

Brother Bede, who's in charge of pastoral rather than academic welfare, applied for but didn't get the headship. He's an old goat. Stuck in his ways. Always tricky. But yes, I think most of the residential teaching staff are on holiday. There's a caretaker somewhere, I think, but I said we'd be fine settling in by ourselves.' He fishes out his phone, consults his emails, and taps a code into a keypad, and the door buzzes. He pushes it open. 'Now, flat three. That means the third floor, I seem to remember,' he says, beginning to climb the stairs. Amanda sighs inwardly. These old places never have lifts.

As she walks up, she checks her watch. It's 4 p.m. She'd thought the removals company was supposed to be here by now.

'Have you had another text saying when our stuff's going to arrive?' she asks, trying to huff and puff silently. She hasn't rowed since June and her fitness has already abandoned her.

'No. But I suspect they were stuck in the same traffic as us. They'll get here, don't worry.'

They've had to shed a lot of their possessions to come here, because they're downsizing to a two-bedroom flat. Amanda thinks about the weeks she's spent packing, sorting and throwing away, crying quietly over paintings made with paint-covered fingers, cotton-wool and card decorations for the Christmas tree, wooden train sets and half-naked Barbie dolls. 'It'll be plenty big enough for the two of us,' Mike had said when he'd returned from his interview here, his eyes pleading with her not to be too upset. She had nodded and tried to smile.

When they reach the third floor, Mike lifts the mat that's sitting in front of the door, locates a large Yale key and uses it to unlock the door.

'Ta-da.' He pushes it open. They both walk through into a narrow hallway decorated with that brand of rugged, shiny cream paint entirely reserved for public buildings, then down the corridor stopping at each doorway, taking in a small double bedroom, an even smaller single bedroom, a functional bathroom, and then a reasonably sized living room, with a kitchen through a door on the right. The place is empty of furniture and, Amanda notices with relief, clean. It smells of polish. She walks over to one of two large sash windows. Both have an uninterrupted view of the sea. She looks to the left and sees nothing but grass and sea, and then to the right, taking in the silhouette of the chimney and engine house of the old mine just along the coast. She notices the paint on the outside of the window frames is flaking. The sea air must really take its toll on the buildings here, she thinks. 'What do you reckon?' he says, with a face like a child showing a parent their homework.

'This view's lovely,' she says, meaning it. She can see the relief on his face.

'Yes, it is, isn't it. I know you've always wanted to live by the sea.'

'Yes, I have,' she says, pulling him in for a hug. She feels her well of enthusiasm refill as his energy blends with hers. 'I love you, you know.'

'And I love you too,' he says, pulling away more quickly than she would have liked. He seems on edge, she thinks. Understandable, however, given that he's beginning a new, senior job. 'Now, I'm going to check out my new office. Do you want to come?'

'No,' she says, still staring out of the window. 'You go and get settled. I think I'll make myself a cuppa, and then I'm going to go and explore. I'm really glad I brought the tea things in the car.'

* * *

Mike doesn't need any encouragement to leave their empty and really rather poky flat in search of his new place of work. He heads off after a few minutes. Amanda doesn't mind. In fact, she's incredibly relieved to be alone after a long and emotionally difficult day. At least with him gone, she doesn't have to put such a brave face on it. She considers walking around their section of the school building, to see if she can locate the fellow resident she very nearly waved at, but changes her mind. What she needs, she thinks, tearing her eyes away from the view of the sea, is some fresh air. She grabs the keys, locks up and heads out.

The first place she wants to investigate is the walled garden. She's already missing her allotment, and she wants to see what lies behind the door. She exits the building and walks around to the far side of the complex, to the sheltered space between the two separate boarding houses. She pushes the door, wondering if it's locked, but is glad to find it isn't.

She steps inside and is immediately hit by the blended scents of warm earth, ripening fruit, lavender and rose. To her left, espaliered apple and pear trees are trained against the garden's walls, their branches heavy with fruit which is just beginning to blush red and gold. Opposite, raised beds host courgettes, tomatoes and runner beans which are galloping up canes. And in the far corner, there's what looks at first to be a summer house, but as she approaches it, she hears the unmistakable sound of chickens, clucking, cooing and rustling. It's a large triangular wooden structure, about ten feet tall, its back resting against one of the exterior walls. It has what looks to be a living space above on a platform, and an area for feeding and freedom of movement below. There are two chickens at ground level, but she's taken aback to see one of them is missing most of its feathers.

'What happened to you, little one?' she asks.

It cocks its head a little and looks her straight in the eye, as if to say, *I could ask the same of you.*

Yes, fair enough, she thinks. *I'm wondering that myself.*

She completes a tour of the rest of the garden, noting how well tended it is. The monks must be great gardeners, she thinks, comparing this bounty to her very small allotment. She decides to ask who's in charge in here when she meets the monks. When she's had her fill, she leaves and heads for the coastal path, because the sea is a siren she can never resist.

There's a strong wind blowing and Amanda's frizzy, thick, highlighted hair whips frantically at her ears and shoulders as she opens a gate in the school's boundary fence and heads towards the cliffs. A few metres beyond it she reaches what she knows is part of the South West Coast Path, a six hundred and thirty mile national trail from Somerset to Dorset via Cornwall and Devon, which hugs the sea. It's a popular challenge for keen hikers, but today this section at least is quiet. Amanda crosses it and walks as close as she dares to the edge. There's no fence at the end of the cliff, and her cursory Google searches about the area have told her that every year, several dogs and, occasionally, their owners, are lost over the side, some of them, if they're lucky, rescued, injured, from a ledge beneath.

Amanda leans over just far enough to see the waves thrashing rocks smoothed by centuries of storms and surging into the granite cliff and its caves below. Then, she feels herself sway and her knees lose some of their strength, and for a moment she imagines what it might be like to fall forwards and tumble into that water, to succumb to its force, to lose all awareness of upwards, downwards, breath or suffocation. She pulls herself back with a start and retreats to the path, her heart hammering in her chest. When she is safely back near the fence, she allows herself to feel a very different sensation: of life, of survival, of renewal. She knows it's just the adrenaline, of course, but it's the first time she's felt this in a long while, and its return is welcome.

When her heartbeat has returned to normal, Amanda sets off north-east, in the direction of the old mine buildings. They're now casting a shadow inland as the sun inches towards the horizon, after a day of warming the grasses, moss and earth that cover this wild stretch of coast. The resulting scent, the heady perfume of high summer, is intoxicating. And it's not just the smell that's enveloping her, but also the noise. There's the rhythmic thrashing of the waves, the chirping of crickets and the cries of gulls wheeling overhead. As Amanda's legs and arms find their own rhythm, she feels a lightening, as if the cloud she has been carrying around with her for months, perhaps even years, is beginning to loosen.

She would dearly love for it to leave her completely. It's been weighing heavily on her for far too long now, she thinks. Around a year, at least. She does need to try to worry less. Her GP in London told her that. Her grown-up children can look after themselves, after all. And her mum isn't around any more to be worried about. Her death last year, at eighty-six, had been sudden but not shocking. Dementia had been eating away at her for years. They had all been expecting it. Her sister Emma even more than her, she suspects, the guilt about that period of their lives seeping back in, unbidden.

Amanda stops. There's a sign beside the path. It's a wooden arrow, with 'To the Beach' etched into it. Beneath it, there's an official sign from the council warning of uneven pathways, potential landslips and steep steps. Amanda walks over to the sign and peers down, wondering if she should give the path a try. She hadn't realised there was an accessible one so close. She can just make out a sandy cove below, but she's surprised by how far down it looks. It could be two hundred, maybe three hundred feet below, she thinks, realising that perhaps going down a potentially dangerous path by herself might not be the most sensible plan. *I'll come down here with Mike*, she thinks. *We will do it together.*

She turns and continues along the path, and she's about to take a path forking right, towards the old mine buildings, when her attention is taken by a brass plaque attached to a large rock to the left of the path. It reads:

> Dedicated to the memory of the ten boys from Hallows Abbey, two members of staff and two crew aboard *The Towan*, which departed from the cove beneath this site on 10 July 1966, never to return.
>
> 'He who goes down to the sea in ships, who does business on the great waters—these have seen the works of the Lord, and His wonders in the deep.'
>
> (Psalm 107)

Amanda takes a step back from the plaque, as if its proximity will infect her with the grief indelibly attached to it. What a terrible, *terrible* tragedy, she thinks, and then as soon as she thinks this, she realises she wants to know more. Who were those boys? she wonders. Who were the teachers with them? And what on earth happened? Why did the boat just... disappear? She resolves to ask Mike about it.

She's about to head towards the old mine when, for the first time that sweltering afternoon, Amanda feels cold. She hadn't expected to need a coat or a cardigan today, but she hadn't accounted for the chill brought by the sea breeze. She decides it's time to return to the school. Perhaps, she thinks, the removals van will have turned up by now, and she will be able to begin the process of unpacking their belongings and establishing a new home, somewhere they can both retreat to in comfort, in new and unfamiliar surroundings. She's achieved this before, more times than she'd like to count, but doing it this time, for just two of them, feels like rubbing salt into a wound. She knows the kids are happy at university. It's not them she's worried about. It's her. Not being needed, not needing to care for others, is turning out to be a major challenge to her self-esteem. Because without it, who is she? What is her purpose? She is approaching the age at which society starts to ignore women. She's no longer the future. In fact, she's rapidly becoming the past. Or *past it*, as she might have once said, dismissively, about a steely-haired schoolmistress with the nerve to wear red lipstick.

As she reaches the school boundary and opens the gate, she turns towards the sea and closes her eyes.

Please help me feel better, she thinks, as the wind blasts her skin. *Please help me feel more like myself. Please help me find a way forward,* she adds, before opening her eyes, turning, and walking back towards the school buildings.

Then a strong gust of wind hits her back, propelling her forwards. Unlike the wind by the cove, this one feels warm.

2

THERESA

September 1965

'There, there. It'll be all right. Just take a moment. It'll pass.' Theresa rubs the boy's back as he retches into an orange plastic bowl. Thirteen-year-old Victor isn't vomiting any more, but his body, wracked by the twin agitators of separation from his family and anxiety about this strange school with its dark corridors and rigid rules, is not quite ready to let go.

Before she'd started the role of school nurse at Hallows Abbey just a month previously, Theresa's nursing experience had not yet revealed the very real link between the health of the mind and the health of the body. She had been taught at nursing college in Dublin that all physical symptoms had physical causes, but she now knows this to be categorically false. She has changed enough sheets and held enough sick bowls in front of perfectly 'healthy' boys to know that extreme unhappiness can lead to headaches, vomiting, diarrhoea and a chronic lack of appetite. The only relief is that the initial, acute period of homesickness usually passes within the first few weeks, as the boys adjust to the parameters of their new life. She's told some boys adapt to it completely, rarely writing home and shrugging nonchalantly when their parents come to pick them up for half-term. She suspects, however, that most simply learn to hide their pain.

'Miss Murphy?' Another boy has arrived at the sick room door. It's John, another new arrival. He's about five foot six, skinny, with dark brown hair in a neat side parting. He's a year late starting – he's fourteen rather than the usual entry age of thirteen – a scholarship boy, parachuted in, she's heard, from a local parish, on account of his ability. And, she suspects, something else. It is clear to Theresa that John's home life is far from the idyll many of her other charges are lucky enough to experience. When he is weeping and retching, it isn't his home life he's pining for, she suspects, but his childhood. There's a haunted look in his eyes. A look she knows well.

'What is it, John?'

'I've a headache.'

'All right. Just take a seat over there,' she says, pointing to a wooden chair over in the corner. 'I'll be with you in a minute.'

'I think I feel a bit better, Miss Murphy,' says Victor, finally raising his head out of the sick bowl.

'That's excellent. Do you feel well enough to make it back to bed?'

'Yes.' His face is blank and pale.

'Good lad. Take the bowl with you, and make sure you take sips of water, little and often. You've lost a lot of fluid.'

'I will. Thank you,' he says, getting up gingerly and walking slowly towards the door. He turns when he reaches it, and Theresa realises with a start that he is most likely seeking a hug or some other kind of physical affection, the kind he would normally receive from a parent. Then, she sees the flash of realisation in his eyes that this is absolutely not what he can, or should, expect here. He turns away swiftly to hide his embarrassment and walks towards his dormitory. She wonders whether she should have called him over and gathered him up in her arms. She knows it's not school policy and that she'd probably be castigated for it, but what, she thinks, is the point of being a nurse if you can't offer human comfort?

'Miss?' asks John. Theresa realises she's been away with her thoughts, and turns back to the slightly older boy.

'Oh, yes, sorry. Let me fetch you an aspirin.' She finds a glass and a tablet, then pours water into the glass from the tap over the sink in the corner of the sickroom. She returns and hands it to him.

'Thank you.'

'Not at all. I'm sorry you're feeling unwell.' John doesn't reply. He just stares into his glass as if he's wishing it's a portal he could escape through. 'Are you feeling sad, John?' she asks, hoping the fact he's come to her means he wants to talk. He nods vigorously. 'Do you want to talk about it?' His eyes dart towards the open door. Theresa understands and gets up to shut it. 'There,' she says as she sits back down. 'There. No one's listening. Can you tell me what's up? Take your time.'

'It's the other boys. They... hate me.'

'Oh come now, that's not true.'

'It *is* true.'

'They're just getting to know you. It's difficult, arriving when they all know each other already. They just need time.'

'I'm not like them.' He almost spits the words out.

'What do you mean?'

'I'm not... well off. My family aren't. I don't talk like them,' he says, in his gentle, lilting Cornish accent. 'I... don't look like them, either.'

'Don't be daft. You all wear the same uniform.'

'I know. But mine's second-hand, from the school, and my shoes are apparently wrong.' Theresa looks down at John's feet. His black lace-ups look fine, she thinks. 'I know they look all right, but the boys tell me they were supposed to come from some shop on Regent Street. Mine came from Clarks in Truro.'

'Oh, I see.'

'Yes.'

'It's tough, being different,' she says, and her mind is immediately transported to another time and place: a convent school in Ireland a decade earlier, where she is being punished for opening a school window and waving at one of her neighbours and his friends, who had been passing by. '*Slattern*,' Mother Mary-Anne had screeched as she'd brought the ruler down onto Theresa's upturned hands. '*Slut*.' The bruising and swelling had made it hard to hold a pen. Her father had told her she'd deserved it.

'I want to go back home. Back to my old school,' says John.

'I can imagine... It must be so difficult being—'

'I hated that place,' he interrupts her. '*Hated it*. But it was still better than here.'

'Oh, I see.'

'Do you?'

Theresa wonders how she'd have fared at a different school. But they were all pretty much the same then, in Ireland, she thinks. Nowhere else would have approved of her wayward nature, either. But she doesn't think he would benefit from hearing this.

'Yes. I do.'

'I just can't... *do* this place. I don't know the words to use. They have stupid names for everything. I keep getting them wrong. And the monks...' He looks thoughtful. 'I thought they'd be like my old priest, you know, interested in talking about things I'd been reading, about the questions I had, but they are so... cold.'

This, Theresa does know about. She'd thought that perhaps the nuns at her school had been an unusual breed of particularly icy humans, and that English men, in the form of monks, might be better. She had been wrong, of course. Bar Father Crispin, the headmaster, who is almost unnaturally kind, many of them, in her experience, are every bit as cruel and unfeeling as the nuns who'd taught her. A large part of her role seems to be mopping up the terrible mess they are making of their students' minds.

She now wishes she hadn't taken a job in a Catholic institution at all, but it had been the only way to get her father to agree to her leaving Ireland, still unwed. Mind you, she thinks, who's to say this sort of behaviour is limited to the Church? Now she's managed to escape her childhood home, she realises her horizons are incredibly small. This year, she has decided she will change that.

'Not all of the teachers are monks. And I think that amongst them there are some reasonable...' she says, before John's withering expression interrupts her gallant attempt to cheer him up. He's clearly having none of it. 'Yes, well, you know you can always come and see me if you need to.'

'Thank you. I do feel a bit better when I'm in here.' He starts to sip his dispersible aspirin.

'Grand.'

'How long have you been working here, Miss Murphy?' he says, after a slightly uncomfortable pause.

'Not long. I arrived over the summer.'

'Why did you come? I can tell you're not from here.'

'No, no, as you can tell, I'm from Ireland. I wanted to travel.'

'So you came here?' says John, his eyes wide and his tone mocking. 'To one of the most godforsaken parts of England?'

Theresa can't help herself. She chuckles.

'Shhh, don't let the monks hear you say that. And I think it's rather lovely around here, actually. It's so beautiful, and the weather is so much nicer than home.'

'If you say so.'

'I love the sea. And I love the moors.'

'Fair enough.'

'Don't you love the sea, John? Didn't you grow up around here?'

'Yes. But I don't know if I love the sea, exactly. It's always been part of my life, but... I respect it, I suppose. It's always scared me a bit, to be honest. My father thinks that makes me a pansy. But whatever.'

Theresa hears the distant rumble of the waves crashing onto the rocks below the cliffs.

'I can quite understand being scared of it,' she replies. 'But your father is wrong. It doesn't make you less of a man.'

John shrugs. 'He thinks everything I do makes me less of a man.'

'Well, perhaps it's just as well then that you're here now, away from him. And you will settle in, in time. I'm sure you will.'

John knocks back the last of the aspirin and hands the glass back to Theresa.

'We'll see,' he says, his voice artificially light. 'Thank you for listening, anyway. I'd better go back and do some more prep. I don't want a black mark for handing it in late.'

'Fair enough, then. I hope you feel better soon.'

'Thank you, Miss Murphy,' he says, opening the door and walking through it. Unlike Victor, he doesn't make the mistake of waiting, pining for a parent's embrace.

3
AMANDA

September 2024

At 5 a.m., the piercing call of a seagull wakes Amanda from fitful, dream-laden sleep, her limbs strangely unrested and a sheen of sweat clinging to her skin.

She hasn't been sleeping well for over a year. She goes to bed absolutely exhausted, but finds her mind refuses to shut down, and she's alternately hot and cold, unable to settle. Some nights, the itching all over her skin, dry but apparently impervious to all moisturisers, drives her to distraction.

Mike, on the other hand, was not woken by the gull. He'd eventually made it to bed just before midnight, completely spent after a very late meeting with the senior leadership team ahead of the new term, firefighting last minute staffing issues.

This meeting had been just the latest in a series, all apparently urgent, all far too long. Mike says it's down to the zeal of the new headmaster, Father Paul, who's come in from another of the order's schools fired up with ideas that he's insisting must be put into practice immediately – something the other deputy head, the curmudgeonly Bede, is resisting with all his might. Poor Mike is stuck in the middle, and it's making for some epic battles. And then of course there are the usual financial struggles all private schools are facing at the moment, as well as Mike's own ideas for change, which she knows he's been working on, quietly. She doubts that either of the other men have given these any attention so far.

In her more optimistic moments before the move, Amanda had thought Mike's new job at Hallows might mean they'd get more quality time together. In fact, now they no longer have to focus on their children, she'd secretly hoped for a period of renewal in their marriage.

How wrong she was. The reality of Mike's long-held ambition for leadership turns out to be servitude. In the few weeks since they arrived at Hallows, it's become clear he is now owned and managed by the school, more than ever in his career. Living in a flat in the largest school building is a huge part of the problem. He is far too available. Someone is always knocking on their door, and every minute of his day seems to be accounted for. Any flicker of interest in Amanda, any chance of conversation about something other than Hallows life, is shut down by a bell or an email pinging on his phone. If he makes it out of his office in the evening, he falls asleep on the sofa next to her, and she has to wake him when she's heading to bed. They have not been sexually intimate for two months. She wonders whether they ever will be again.

Amanda decides to get out of bed and leave him sleeping, knowing that the school bell outside their front door will wake him up at six thirty anyway. It's the first day of term today, and she knows he'll need as much rest as he can muster.

She eats a quick breakfast of muesli and milk, and then, noting the golden light of the dawn, decides on a whim to go outside. She pulls on an old cotton summer dress and a pair of trainers, grabs her keys and heads out into the very welcome wilderness beyond the school's boundary.

Once there, she feels the breeze on her skin and instinctively raises her arms into it, as if she's inviting it to bless her. As she is warmed by the sun's first, gentle, rays, she closes her eyes and imagines she's young again, ripe with potential, ideas and options. Brimming with sex appeal, too, the kind that causes men to do a double take when you pass them in the street. Why hadn't she appreciated how great that had felt, when she'd had it?

Those days are long gone. Now, she knows she would struggle to get someone to look at her if she ran naked down the high street screaming hallelujah.

She opens her eyes, lowers her arms, pauses for a moment in order to process this momentary time travel, and then continues along the coastal path, in the direction of the access to the cove.

She's standing at the top of these steps, wondering how long it would take to get down to the beach, when a tall, slim woman in her sixties or thereabouts, wearing a bright pink sarong and with long silver hair thrust into a topknot, emerges from them.

'Oh,' Amanda says, and then, obeying that unique British instinct to apologise for one's own existence, says, 'sorry.'

'I didn't mean to startle you,' says the other woman, slightly out of breath. 'I don't usually see anyone around here at this time of day.'

'No, well, it's pretty early,' says Amanda. 'I'm not usually up at this time.'

'Oh, I am, most days. It's the best time for a swim, before work. And I hate crowds.'

'You've been swimming? Down there?'

The other woman laughs. Amanda notices she's wearing what looks like a bright green swimming costume under her pink sarong. She also sees she has a tattoo of a butterfly on the upper part of her right arm. Her skin is tanned and unapologetically wrinkled. This woman, she thinks, is not one for covering herself up. Amanda is impressed.

'Yes. It's not that far, honestly, once you've got used to it. And it's so gorgeous down there, so private. I've occasionally risked doing it without a costume.' There's a twinkle in her eye. 'Are you going down to the cove?'

'I was thinking about it.'

'The tide's coming in soon, but you'll be all right for about an hour. Any more than that and there won't be much beach left.'

'How long does it take to get down there?'

'Oh, nothing really. About five minutes down and ten up, depending on your fitness.'

'Oh, great. I might give it a go.'

'I take it you're not local, then? Is this your first time down here?'

'Oh, I'm new here. But local. Very local. At the school?'

The woman breaks into a broad smile.

'Oh, are you? How fab. I work there too. I'm the school nurse. I don't live on site though. I have a house in the village just the other side of the peninsula. Are you a teacher?'

'Me? Oh, no. I'm married to the new deputy head academic, Mike. Sorry, Michael. Michael Chapman?'

'Ah yes, I heard we had a new one coming in. It's all change at the top this year. Well, welcome. That's wonderful. I'm Rosie.' The woman holds out her hand to Amanda, who shakes it.

'I'm Amanda. Mandy. It's really nice to meet you.'

'And I you. Look, I'd best go and shower and get dressed for the day. I'll be seeing you around.'

Amanda watches Rosie set off along the coastal path. She walks with poise and gives off an air of nonchalance, like she genuinely has zero interest in what anyone else thinks about her. Amanda wishes desperately she could feel the same way about her own body, which currently feels like a battleground, home to innumerable warring parties. *How long will I have to wait until I feel like her?* Amanda thinks. *If I ever do?*

After Rosie walks out of view, Amanda decides she will walk down to the cove, despite her concerns about the climb back up. As the other woman had said, it proves to be an easy descent, and within minutes she's on the beach below, which has a concrete jetty jutting out into the sea to the left, and steep cliffs behind her and on either side. She gets out her phone to take some photos and ping one to Mike when she notices there's no signal down here. That's not a surprise, however; there isn't much of one on the cliffs, either.

Her shoes removed, her toes hugging soft golden sand, she peers up at the rock faces which surround her. They're jagged and irregular, with several ledges providing homes to nesting seabirds and enterprising, hardy plants. She notices what looks like a cave over on the left, level with the beach, and walks over to it. Its entrance is sandy and she walks inside for a few metres. It goes back surprisingly far, at least another twenty. The slippery rocks that are dotted along the ground suggest it floods, but the rubbish that's strewn here and there tells her it's also sometimes used as a shelter, or perhaps even as somewhere to hide. She considers exploring further in, but then remembers Mike doesn't know where she is, and she thinks better of it.

Returning to the beach, Amanda looks up and realises Rosie is right – it *is* incredibly private here. The beach is completely invisible from above, and she wonders if anyone would hear her if she shouted for help. She sounds a quick note – she's a keen amateur singer and has been co-opted into several school choirs at Christmas – and hears the echo bounce off the granite, as if there's someone else with her singing a duet.

Then a sharp, unexpected gust of wind comes in off the sea. Amanda shivers and rubs her arms to try to warm up. It's much cooler down here. As it's west facing, the sun won't reach here until lunchtime at the earliest. And then she thinks about the absolute darkness of the abandoned tin mine, whose tunnels might be beneath her feet right now, and beneath the sea, too. She wonders if they ever flooded. The thought makes her feel uneasy, so she walks to where the sea is lapping the shore and paddles in the cool water for a few minutes. She spots a shiny white shell and puts it in her pocket. She will leave it on the windowsill of their bathroom to remind her that their new place, despite its problems, is surrounded by the ocean. Then she checks her watch and decides it's time to return to the real world.

As she climbs back up the steps slowly, pausing at regular intervals to get her breath, she feels full of that particular excitement of discovering a new place. It had been so elemental down there, with just the seabirds for company. So refreshing to be so separate from the normal noises of everyday life. Even though her heart is beating ridiculously fast from all this exercise and she's probably bright pink, she feels energised.

Back on the school grounds, she punches the code into the keypad and climbs the stairs to their flat with excitement rather than her usual dread. She's desperate to share her new knowledge with Mike. She wonders if he'd like to walk there together tomorrow morning, before school. However, when she enters the lounge and finds him ironing his shirt with one hand and scrolling through messages on his phone with the other, she can tell he's not in the mood to talk about anything.

'You OK?' he manages, in between scrolls and swipes.

'Yes, fine,' she says, wondering if he's going to ask her where she's been. After all, she never usually goes out at this time of day.

'Good. The first parents are arriving at eight thirty,' he says, sounding as if he's answering a question.

Amanda turns and heads into the bedroom. She needs to change out of her sweaty clothes, but mostly she just needs to let out her frustration. Getting into an argument with Mike would be a mistake. He needs her support at the moment, and she knows he has zero bandwidth to deal with her emotions. So instead, she throws herself down onto the mattress, gripping the bedding so hard she's afraid it might rip. Then she opens her mouth wide and imagines a primal scream soaring out of it. It's nowhere near as gratifying as actually screaming, but it's all she can do in such a confined space with her stressed husband just feet away.

After Mike departs to begin the process of welcoming more than fifty new boarders for Year 9, Amanda decides to continue the dull, frustrating and emotional task of trying to unpack the remains of their pared-down belongings. This is how she's spent most of the days since they arrived, interspersed with cooking, cleaning, scrolling through Facebook (to feel closer to her friends) and Instagram (to check on the kids). She's also driven to the supermarket in Redruth on several occasions, an activity she is pathetically grateful for. The peninsula the school inhabits is beginning to feel a bit like an open prison. She misses the real world. She knows she can't continue this daily routine much longer before the isolation and the boredom consume her.

At eleven, she sends what she hopes is a breezily non-desperate WhatsApp message to both Julia and Luke asking if they'd like to come down at some point to visit their parents' new pad. She attaches some pictures of the cove, hoping to tempt them. Neither responds quickly, however, although the blue ticks tell her they've both seen the message.

Then, at about twelve thirty, the responses arrive. Almost, she feels, as if they've been conferring. They're jolly messages, saying how lovely the beach looks and asking questions about the new flat and school, but they both say they're too busy with work and study to come. Cornwall is a long way away, they say. They need a clear week to visit, and they just don't have one at the moment. Perhaps reading week, Luke suggests, along with a smiley face emoji. He promises nothing, however.

She checks. Reading week is almost two months away.

Amanda misses them both desperately. There is no use pretending otherwise when she's alone. She sobs into the boxes and the old photo albums and the chipped crockery and then decides that enough is enough.

What she needs, she thinks, is something to do. Something meaningful. She'd thought she'd need more time to settle first, to set up home properly, but she'd been wrong. She needs to be busy. Mike's suggestion of an admin role in the school, something she had rebuffed just a month ago, is now actually seeming appealing.

Amanda ceases her eternal sorting, dresses in smart jeans and a nice shirt, applies her make-up with unusual care and leaves the flat. When she pulls the door closed behind her she feels a rush of adrenaline and a sense of purpose.

A few minutes later, after wandering around the site and asking a few boys for directions, she finds the school's administration office. It's in a small modern building adjacent to the main block. She pushes the door open and enters. There are two women in the large open office, both tapping away at keyboards. She's not surprised to find no men in this office. All of the schools Mike's worked at have been run behind the scenes by a team of capable, clever, underpaid women. In her experience, however, they are usually more friendly. Neither of them looks at her when she opens the door.

'Hello?' she calls out, wondering if they're wearing headphones, and so didn't hear her enter.

'Good morning,' says the woman who's sitting furthest away, finally looking up from her work. Amanda estimates her to be in her late fifties, with grey, poker-straight hair held back from her face with an Alice band. 'Parents need to send all enquiries via reception,' she adds. 'I thought this was communicated to you in the headmaster's summer newsletter.'

'I'm not a parent.'

The other woman, who is considerably younger than her colleague, is still typing away, apparently unaware of the conversation.

'Well, teachers are supposed to make an appointment...'

'I'm not a teacher. I'm Michael Chapman's wife. The new deputy head?'

The woman's eyes narrow. 'I see. What can I do for you, Mrs Chapman?'

Not feeling quite so brave now, are you, thinks Amanda.

'Mike – Mr Chapman – suggested I should come to see you about any work you might need doing. I have extensive experience of exam timetabling, roster management and database maintenance from my post at our last school—'

'I see,' says the older woman, interrupting without apology. 'Well, thank you for letting me know. I shall bear you in mind. We are absolutely fine at the moment, however. Aren't we, Miss Store?'

'Oh. Yes,' replies the younger woman, who seems surprised to be spoken to. Amanda decides this must be a miserable place to work.

'OK,' says Amanda, feeling a mixture of relief and frustration. Clearly this office is nothing like the hive of activity, laughter and friendship that she left behind in London. She wouldn't want to work here anyway. And yet she knows this room also probably represents her only chance of paid work in the vicinity.

Her marriage to Mike straight out of university and their decision to have children early meant she never did anything meaningful with her history degree, which had been very interesting, but which hadn't equipped her for any specific career. Then like billions of other mothers, she'd discovered that finding a job flexible enough to accommodate parenting responsibilities was incredibly difficult, particularly because Mike's profession was what economists called a 'hungry job', one that meant he could never be reliably around to help her. She'd ruled out following him into teaching as an option a long time ago, after a disastrous month spent working as a classroom assistant at one of Mike's schools. It had taught her that she had no natural authority and that a classful of children had the capacity to become a beast of mythical proportions. Teaching, she thinks, is a wonderful option for those who are good at it, but that most certainly is not her. And so she'd settled into admin roles in schools, a job which was flexible, restricted to school hours and terms, and which she'd enjoyed, by and large. This is the first time her offer to work has been rebuffed, however, and it stings.

'I'll let Mr Chapman know if we need anyone,' the woman adds. This insinuation that Amanda is not a person in her own right infuriates her.

'Don't worry,' Amanda replies, breezily. 'I'll see if any of the local schools need help.'

Amanda knows that the nearest secondary school is about ten miles away and that the local primary school only has two classes, but she'll be damned if she's going to be forced to be grateful for any crumbs this woman can throw at her feet.

'As you wish.'

And with this, Amanda is dismissed. She turns on her heel and marches out, taking large gulps of air as the door swings shut behind her. She feels as if she's been slapped. Tears threaten to form and she shakes her head, urging them to stay hidden. She can't afford for any students or teachers to see her crying. She has to maintain the illusion that Mike is married to a solid, dependable, unshakeable team player. She smooths down her hair and clothes and sets off at pace back to their flat. Their *horrible* flat, she thinks, and then tries to dismiss this thought, knowing that if she goes further down this path she'll definitely start to sob. She's turning a corner around the main school building when she hears someone call her name.

'Mandy?'

Amanda turns, and sees Rosie, the school nurse who she met on the cliffs, is about ten feet behind her.

'Oh, hello again,' says Amanda, trying to put on her bravest face.

'Are you all right? You look...' She can see Rosie is struggling to find the right word.

'You're going to say tired, aren't you?' says Amanda with half a laugh. She feels unusually relaxed with Rosie, and it feels right – not to mention good – to let down her guard a little. 'I am tired, as it happens. I haven't slept properly for ages.'

'I was going to say bothered,' Rosie replies. 'You look... annoyed.'

'Ah, yes. Well, I am annoyed. I've just been into the admin office.'

'I see. You've encountered Mariam Newton, then.'

'Oh, is that her name? She didn't even introduce herself.'

'Yep. And Miss Newton is enough to make anyone cross. What were you trying to get her to do? You weren't asking her to process an unauthorised form, were you?' asks Rosie with a twinkle in her eye.

'Haha. No. Actually, I was there about a job. Mike suggested I might be able to work there part-time. I realise I need something to do that isn't unpacking and cleaning.'

'Oh goodness, you don't want to work there. There be actual dragons.'

The two women laugh, and Amanda feels some of her frustration begin to lift.

'So I've discovered.'

'But if you'd like a job, I was just about to advertise for someone to help me out in sick bay. Just during school hours, sticking plasters on cut knees and reassuring anxious boys that they'll be OK. That leaves the actual medical care to me. Do you fancy it?' Amanda is taken aback, and doesn't respond immediately. 'Sorry, that probably gives you something to think about...'

'No, no, I'd love to. That would be great. But you don't know me at all. Don't you want to interview me? To see if I'm suitable?'

Rosie looks her up and down.

'Oh, I'm assuming, given your previous work in a school, that you're DBS checked?' Amanda nods. This is a standard police check that all organisations caring for children require of their staff. 'You just need to formally apply. I can send you a link to the form. I always think, anyway, that you know when someone's capable of empathy and care. They exude something intangible. And in my experience, it's self-selecting work. People leave the job of their own volition if they're not suited to it, anyway.'

'I'd love to. Give it a go, anyway. If I'm rubbish at it please feel free to tell me.'

'Wonderful. That'll save me all that time interviewing people. I'll get the ball rolling paperwork-wise and we'll get you started as soon as possible.'

* * *

'I still can't believe how rude Miss Newton was to you,' says Mike, as they both brush their teeth in preparation for bed. 'I mean, she's got a reputation as a bit of an old bag, but she's been all right with me so far. Well, nicer than Bede, but that's not saying much.'

Poor old Brother Bede. Mike mentions him a lot. He was recently passed over for the headship, which went instead to fellow Credan Father Paul, a few years his junior. Being leapfrogged in this way has made Bede very angry, and he's been taking it out on everyone, but most of all Mike, who, because of his civilian status, is an easier target than Paul. Mike's handling it well, Amanda thinks, but she knows it must be quite wearing to put up with so much passive aggression every day.

'Well, at least I won't have to go back to her and beg,' says Amanda, washing her toothbrush under the tap and placing it in a little mug on the windowsill. 'Thanks to Rosie.'

'Yes, that's a real stroke of luck,' says Mike, before he takes a swig of mouthwash and gargles.

Amanda is already tucked up in bed with a book when he comes into the room. As Mike sets about taking his dressing gown off and then lathering on the face cream she bought him for his birthday, she examines him. He has dark circles under his eyes and it looks like the muscles around them are contracting, like a drawstring bag closing, and the muscles in his jaw keep flexing, suggesting he's grinding his teeth.

'Thank you so much for being here for me,' he says, leaning over and drawing her into a hug which goes on for slightly longer than a perfunctory goodnight. When he pulls away she sees a flicker of something in his expression, but whether it is sadness, gratitude or a mixture of both, she is unable to discern.

'Mike?'

'Yep?' he says, picking up a book from his bedside table.

'Can I ask you about the boat tragedy? The Towan?'

'What about it?'

'Just what happened. I saw the memorial plaque over by that cove I was telling you about.'

'Oh, right. I don't know much, to be honest, but I do know a bunch of kids went out on a boat trip with a couple of teachers – they were the winners of a competition of some kind, I think – and they never came back. It's a pretty dark part of the school's past. You could ask some of the older monks about it, maybe? They might have been here then.'

'That's a good idea. I will.'

They don't speak much after that. He falls asleep almost as soon as they turn out the light, and Amanda drifts off soon afterwards. Her early start and emotional day have tired her.

* * *

She doesn't remain asleep for long, however.

Because someone is crying. Sobbing, in fact.

It must be one of the new boarders, she thinks, and the thought that they're by themselves, roaming the school buildings ridden with homesickness, tugs at her. She can't leave them alone out there. *That little boy needs comforting*, she thinks. *The poor, poor thing.*

Amanda looks across at their digital alarm clock and sees it's half past midnight. Then she checks on Mike, who's still asleep, apparently undisturbed by the noise. She considers waking him, but decides against it. He's never been great at getting back to sleep. So, she inches the covers back and tiptoes out of bed. Then she puts on a fleece over her pyjamas, slips on a pair of trainers she's left at odd angles in the hallway, grabs her keys and her phone so she can use the torch, and heads out of the flat.

When their front door closes behind her, she stands still in the corridor and listens. At first, she can only hear wind whipping up the staircase. She's noticed the door at the bottom is badly sealed. But then there it is again, the sobbing. It's coming from the main school teaching area, which is part of their building, the two sections separated by a fire door secured with a keypad lock on the school side. She goes through this door and enters a corridor lit only by the dim green light of fire exit signage, with doors leading to classrooms running down on each side. *What on earth is a student doing out of their boarding house at this time?* she wonders. The fact he's obviously managed to get past alarmed doors without being intercepted by staff is a major concern. She'll have to tell Mike about it in the morning. The housemaster has some serious questions to answer.

Amanda sets off down the corridor, shining her phone torch through the glass panel in each door. Every time, however, the boy's crying seems to be coming from some distance away, and her cursory checks reveal only a series of rectangular rooms furnished with neat lines of shiny desks and utilitarian chairs. *Where is he?* she wonders. Perhaps he's going back towards his boarding house, as she's heading towards him. She really hopes that is the case. She'd much prefer him to be safely tucked up in bed and asleep, rather than out here feeling wretched. As she reaches the end of the corridor, however, and pushes open another fire door, she can hear his cries getting louder. She follows them round to the left and realises she's standing outside the door to the boys' toilets.

This makes sense, of course. If you were looking for privacy and somewhere you felt safe, the loos, with a lock on each door, would be the place to go. But now Amanda has a dilemma. It would feel wrong, going into the boys' loos, even though this student absolutely should not be in there at this time of day. She stands outside for a minute, just listening, hoping he will calm down. Unfortunately, his agony is not abating. If anything, the crying is getting worse. Eventually, she can't bear it any more.

Instinctively, she pushes the door open a crack and calls out, 'Hello? I'm Amanda. Are you all right?' This is a silly thing to say, she realises, given that he's clearly far from all right, but she doesn't know how else to put it.

The child does not respond, but she can hear what she thinks is sniffling.

'I'm not one of the teachers,' she continues. 'I'm just married to someone who works here. You won't get into trouble.' She pauses to see if he responds, but he doesn't. 'Come out,' she urges. 'Come out and we can talk about it. Everything always seems so much worse at night. It will be OK, I promise.'

There's absolute silence now. The sniffling has stopped. But certain now that a boy is inside and that he's deeply unhappy, Amanda decides to break with social norms and steps inside the room. Then she turns on the light, hoping that this will encourage the student to come out, now that his whereabouts have been discovered. But it doesn't. So she goes along the row of six toilet stalls, pushing each door open gently, and checking behind. Nothing. There's nothing and no one there. When she reaches the sixth door, she is sure she'll find it locked, but she pushes it open with the same ease as all of the previous five. When it's fully open, she looks all around the cubicle, above and below, just to check that someone hasn't just climbed under or over its sides to evade her. But there isn't enough room beneath to crawl under, and when she emerges from the cubicle, there definitely isn't anyone in any of the other stalls. She's alone.

And then Amanda feels a twinge of fear. Because she definitely heard the crying, and it had definitely come from this room. She'd *heard* it. But if that's the case, she thinks, what had been making the noise? It can't have been a student. Perhaps it's dodgy plumbing, she thinks, seeking to reassure herself, to soothe her jangled nerves. Yes, that's common in Victorian buildings. That must be it. She will ask Mike to call a plumber in the morning.

And then, as she's about to leave the room, there's a clatter. Her eyes dart towards the far corner, by the room's only window. Amanda runs over, determined to catch the boy who has been leading her a merry dance. But it's not a boy. It's a black and white cat, the same one she's seen wandering around the school grounds, and as she watches, it jumps down from an open fan light onto the floor and saunters over to the door that leads into the school building, waiting to be let out.

Relief floods through her. That must be what it was, then, thinks Amanda. A cat. She has been searching the school building in the dead of a night for a needy, very shrill cat. She laughs, and every laugh seems to push her earlier fear further and further away. Shaking her head at her apparent insanity, she turns the light off behind her and walks with purpose back through the school building to their living quarters.

As she enters the code into the keypad and pushes the door to their section of the building open, she hears the wailing begin again. But this time, she decides not to investigate.

'Bloody cats,' she whispers to herself. 'Attention seekers, the lot of them.'

4
THERESA

18 December 1965

It's the first Saturday after the end of Theresa's first term at Hallows Abbey and she is feeling demob happy. Her first few months at the school have been exhausting, both mentally and physically. She's on call twenty-four hours a day and although she's usually able to sleep undisturbed, she finds her senses are heightened at night and she often finds it difficult to settle. The boys' health issues are also more difficult to treat than she'd imagined. There have been plenty of grazed knees, of course, but she's also had to counsel many of them, realising that she might be the only person in the school they feel safe confiding in.

It's a bright, cold day, the first after what has felt like an interminable stretch of rain, and Theresa is determined to make the most of it. She's planning to catch a lift with one of the kitchen staff, Anna, who, like her, is staying at school over the Christmas holidays. They're heading into Porthgerran, the nearest village, just along the coast, for its monthly outdoor market, hoping to pick up a few treats and decorations to make their school lodgings feel a little more festive.

To say Theresa is looking forward to it is an understatement. She hasn't been out of school since half-term. Whilst in theory she could walk beyond Hallows' boundary, there's simply been nowhere to go. She realises this makes her no more free than the boys. In fact, it has meant her life has been as confined in England as it was in Ireland, where the convent school and her home had been her twin prisons. Theresa pulls on her coat, picks up her purse, looks out of her window at the crystal-clear sky, and heads outside to meet her friend.

The drive to Porthgerran is short. This is a relief, as Anna is as large as her Morris Mini is bijou, and the tiny single-track roads to the village are essentially an obstacle course, full of tractors, vans and, in one instance, astonishingly, a goat. Theresa feels like kissing the ground when they pull up safely beside the quay, where fishing boats await their next departure in orderly moorings, their rigging clinking in the gentle breeze.

'I've got to head to the post office before it closes,' says Anna, pulling on a blue woollen coat with big plastic buttons. Theresa knows her new friend writes to her parents, who live in North Yorkshire, often. 'And then to Woolworths. Do you want to come with me?'

'Oh, no. Don't worry. I'll just wander around the market.'

'All right. So shall we meet by the war memorial in an hour, then? You can't miss it.'

'Yes, that sounds fine. Let's do that.'

Theresa is quite relieved when Anna walks away. Not that she dislikes her – in fact, she appreciates the other woman's brand of honesty and keen sense of humour – it's just that she wants to experience complete freedom for a little while, going wherever she wants to go, with her own money, not doing anyone else's bidding.

It's easy to tell where the market is due to the chorus of shouting salespeople. 'Fifty flying saucers for a shilling,' someone yells. 'Get your fresh turkey here, folks,' shouts another. Theresa follows these sounds and finds herself in a large village square which is packed with covered stalls selling everything from fresh vegetables to furniture. There's a brass band, from the Salvation Army, she thinks, judging by the uniforms, playing carols next to a Christmas tree that must be at least ten feet tall. It's adorned with a string of coloured bulbs, and there's a golden star at its peak. Aside from the noise, Theresa's nostrils are assaulted by a vast array of different smells: the salty tang of fresh fish; the rich aroma of freshly fried sausages; the cloying sweetness of fruit being sold off cheap, before it turns.

She wanders slowly from one stall to the next, buying a bag of boiled sweets from one, and some silver tinsel from another, which she plans to hang over her bedhead. Then she spots a stall selling mince pies, and her mouth waters, memories of her grandmother's baking flooding back. She'd been quite young when Grandma Edie had died but she still remembers the warmth of her home and her hugs, in stark contrast to the house she'd shared with her parents, which had been consistently cold, both in temperature and emotion.

She approaches the stall and pays for a pie, which is presented to her in a striped paper bag, and walks over to the railings that divide the marketplace from the harbour. She pulls the pie out of the bag and inhales it, the familiar combination of spices instantly transporting her into the festive season.

Then everything happens very quickly.

Something large swoops down, so fast that initially she's not even sure what it is. It snatches the mince pie from her hand.

'What the? Oh my...' she says, yelling in frustration at the sky.

Then someone laughs.

'Got you, didn't he?'

Theresa turns to see a man standing at the railing, laughing. He's in his thirties, she thinks, tall with broad shoulders. He has a handsome, chiselled face, dark hair with a slight wave in it, and a closely clipped beard. He's wearing well-worn jeans and a thick woollen jumper which is grey, with flecks of blue in it.

'Yes,' she says, miserably. She's hungry.

'That was our Harry.'

'Harry? A seagull called Harry?'

'Yes. Why not? I've got names for all of 'em.'

Theresa wonders whether he's having her on.

'You spend a lot of time here, then?' she asks.

He shrugs and turns so he's leaning on the railings, facing her. 'You could say that.'

'Do you work at the market?'

'Oh, no. Although they're selling some of my catch today.'

'You're a fisherman?'

'Yes. We'd called it a *pyscador*, though. In Cornish.'

Theresa notices the way his trousers cling to his thighs. It's not something she usually notices.

'Oh. I see.'

'You're not from around here.'

His Adam's apple moves as he speaks. His voice is deep, gravelly, and there's an inflection of humour in every word. She feels something stir inside her.

'Yes. I suppose that's fairly obvious, given my accent.'

'Yeah, and the fact you held your mince pie out for the birds.'

Theresa laughs in embarrassment.

'Guilty as charged.'

'I shouldn't worry about it,' he says, walking over to her bench. 'I've just bought one myself. Fancy sharing?'

'Oh,' replies Theresa, flustered both by this offer and by her proximity to this rather attractive man. 'Really?'

'Really,' he says, and his dark eyes sparkle. 'I'm Trystan, by the way.'

'I'm much obliged, Trystan. I'm Theresa,' she says. He holds her gaze for just a little too long. She blushes and looks away.

'Theresa,' he says, sitting down next to her. 'That's such a pretty name.'

5

AMANDA

Late September 2024

Amanda pauses in front of the mirror she's hung in the hallway to check she looks vaguely presentable. She knows she's only going as far as the nurse's room, but she's always taken pride in her appearance, and today feels like the sort of new start that deserves an effort.

She's chosen a pair of black trousers (crucially, for her unpredictable, bloated tummy – with stretch) and a loose red shirt, and she's wearing flat black patent pumps on her feet. Yes, her clothing looks professional, she thinks. Her face, however... When, she wonders, did her eyelids begin to droop? And surely those crow's feet at the corner have grown at least a centimetre overnight? She's applied her make-up as best she knows how, but you'd never even know she was wearing eyeshadow at the moment, and her foundation is making the skin around her eyes resemble crazy paving. This is not the reflection she saw in her twenties, or even, frankly, in her thirties, even when she was knackered from bringing up two kids. No, she knows this is undeniably the reflection of a middle-aged woman. Amanda runs her hands through her hair, which has at least an inch of regrowth at the roots. She spent more than half an hour taming it with straightening irons this morning, and it already looks frizzy. She lets out an involuntary sigh, grabs her keys and phone and shuts their front door.

It takes her about ten minutes to locate the room, which is on the ground floor of the main building, next to the library. She knocks and waits.

'Come in,' says Rosie from behind the door. Amanda enters. 'Oh, don't you look lovely.'

'Oh. Thanks.' Amanda beams. Not only is this sort of compliment rare as hen's teeth at the moment, but Rosie is the nicest person she's met at Hallows Abbey and she feels genuinely pleased to be back in her presence.

Rosie checks her watch. 'Also, you're early. Excellent.'

'Well, I didn't have to come very far.'

Amanda looks around. The nurse's room is actually two rooms, connected with a door, which is currently open. She can see that there's a single bed in the other room, currently unoccupied. Rosie is sitting at a desk, on top of which there's a computer, a phone and a large notebook. On the table behind her there are various tools of her trade. Amanda recognises a blood pressure monitor and an otoscope for examining ear canals. On the wall is a large, locked cabinet, which she assumes is where the medicines are stocked. In the corner to Amanda's right is a sink. At the end of the room is a large sash window, through which she can see one of the boarding houses, Wenceslas, on the other side of the road.

'Absolutely. Well, welcome to my humble abode. Not that I actually live here, of course, but it feels like it sometimes. Now, let's start with a cup of tea, shall we, before the first boy arrives to keep us busy? Someone always creeps along to see me after registration, keen to avoid double maths. Take a seat, and I'll put the kettle on.'

Amanda sits down in the chair that's presumably reserved for visiting students, beside the desk, while Rosie walks over to a table beside the sink. She fills a kettle and turns it on.

'So, who do they go to when you're not on duty?' she asks.

'Oh, they're the responsibility of their house's matron out of hours, unless they're really poorly, in which case they call a doctor. It used to be that the school had a nurse on call almost all of the time. They had to live here, on site. Thankfully they changed that more than two decades ago.'

'Yes. Living here is quite...' Amanda realises she is about to be too honest.

She doesn't want word getting around that she's been Bede moaning about the accommodation they've been given.

'It's OK, I know,' says Rosie. 'I know a few of the women employed as matrons here. It's odd, I think, living where you work, or in your case, where your husband works. And this place is... how do I put this? Stuck out on its own peninsula, miles from the nearest town... It's its own little world, isn't it? It's definitely not the *real* world, at any rate. It can feel quite discombobulating, I reckon.' The kettle boils, and Rosie puts tea bags in two mugs and fills them with hot water.

Amanda thinks about the unease she's been feeling ever since she arrived. Is it simply because Hallows Abbey is so isolated and such an odd institution, she wonders. *Is that it?*

'How long have you worked here?'

'Oh, about a decade now,' says Rosie. 'Milk?' Amanda nods. 'Yeah, so I used to be a practice nurse at a GP surgery in Redruth, but I fancied a change before retirement. It's a slower pace here. Mostly it's just patching up sports injuries and working out when they need to see a doctor for antibiotics. But there do seem to be more and more mental health problems now, though. More than ever before.'

'Homesickness?' Amanda thinks about the pale, sad faces she's seen on the younger boys in the past couple of weeks, since the term began. She doesn't want to even think about how it would have felt to have sent their children away from home at thirteen. 'Oh yes, that.' Rosie places a steaming mug of tea down next to Amanda, and sits in front of the desk, swivelling to face her new colleague. 'But so much else besides. I wonder, you know, if it started with Covid, when they were isolated from each other and from society for so long. There's so much anxiety about. Self-harm. Depression. Not just low mood for a bit, but persistent low mood. The kind that the doctor needs to see them about. The school does have a counsellor for the boys, but he's getting so booked up now, they are having to wait weeks to see him sometimes.'

'Goodness. I didn't realise it was this bad.'

'Oh, I'm putting you off working here now, aren't I? Don't listen to me. I'm just moaning. The boys are lovely, and most of the time we have a laugh together. I'm just... upset for them, really. It's quite unnatural, isn't it, to spend so much time away from their families. And although there are some female teachers and a lot of the non-teaching staff are female, there's such a strange imbalance here. I don't think it's just that though, or even just this school or single-sex boarding schools, to be fair. Other school nurses I know say the same thing. This generation sometimes seems so damaged. But why, that's the thing? What's happening to them to make them feel this way? I wish I knew.'

Rosie picks up her tea and blows on it, her eyes unfocused.

'My husband thinks it's social media. The stuff they see on their phones.' Amanda picks up her own mug and takes a sip. 'He's been reading up on this theory about, what is it...' She's momentarily forgotten the word. This happens a lot these days. 'Yes, *rewilding*, that's it. A theory about letting kids reconnect with the outdoors, with nature. Getting them away from their phones and doing things with their hands that doesn't involve scrolling. He's just starting a club for boys who are interested in getting outside more, actually.' This rewilding idea has been an obsession of Mike's for some time, and this new club is the only way he feels able to introduce the idea to the school. Both Father Paul and Brother Bede have steadfastly ignored his suggestions of introducing it more widely, to Mike's intense frustration.

'Is he? Well, he may have a point. That may be part of it. I've definitely had boys in here saying they've hurt themselves doing crazy weightlifting stuff in the school gym, trying to emulate some of the beefcakes they see on those video apps. And others who say what they've seen has given them nightmares.'

'Like what?'

'Oh, violence, generally. Some of it is incredibly graphic, and there's just no warning. It just pops up there on their feeds. But once they've seen it, they can't unsee it. Some of them come in to me actually crying. Sometimes quite big boys, you know, sixth formers. Just crying.'

There's a pause.

'I heard someone crying the other night, you know.'

'Did you? In the school? One of the boys?'

'Yes. Or at least, I thought it was. It was quite loud. Late. After midnight. I could hear it from our flat. I was a bit worried, to be honest.'

'I can imagine. But how on earth could you hear someone crying from there? The boarding houses, even Amadeus, in the main building, are quite separate. Had someone slipped out?'

'Yes, I thought so. But when I searched around looking for them, I couldn't find them. Not a soul.'

'You couldn't find them?' Rosie's eyes widen.

'No. It gave me a fright, to be honest. I thought I'd been hearing things. Until I went into one of the toilets, you know, one of those at the end of a teaching corridor.' Rosie is listening, mouth wide, as if spellbound. 'I didn't know if I should go in there, you know... it being for the boys. But it was so late, I figured it was fine. No one should have been in there. So I pushed the door open.'

'And was there? Anyone in there, I mean?'

'Yes.'

Rosie looks like she might have stopped breathing.

'It was... a cat.'

The older woman bursts out laughing. 'You had me there, Mandy, you naughty woman.'

'What did you think I was going to say?'

'Oh, you know—' They are interrupted by a knock at the door. 'Ah, here we go. First customer.'

Rosie gets up and answers the door. A few muffled words are exchanged and a boy enters, a young teenager. The skin around his eyes is puffy.

'Come in, then. This is Mrs Chapman, Hector. She's just joined the medical room team.'

'Hello, ma'am,' says the boy, sticking to the naming convention she knows Father Paul has introduced at Hallows Abbey. *Sir* for male teachers and other staff, and *ma'am* for females.

'Nice to meet you, Hector,' says Amanda, standing up so he can sit down.

'There's a chair next door you can bring in, Mrs Chapman,' says Rosie. 'You can observe this morning and I'll teach you various bits and bobs as we go along.'

And so begins Amanda's first morning of paid work at Hallows Abbey. It passes quickly, far more quickly than in her previous admin job, during which she had at times felt like a child waiting for Christmas as the clock had moved achingly slowly towards 5 p.m. Here, there is a steady flow of boys to see. So many at times, in fact, that she has to put a chair outside the consulting room so they can wait to be seen. Their needs vary, from headaches to stomach upsets to twisted ankles and accidental cuts during design and technology classes. Rosie shows her how to clean up minor wounds and apply dressings, and how to set the other room up for boys who need to have a lie-down, usually while they wait for the matron from their boarding house to come and collect them. It's involving work, making use of Amanda's mothering skills as much as any medical ones, and she's surprised to find she really enjoys it.

Before she knows it, the lunch bell sounds.

'Right, that's us off for an hour,' announces Rosie. 'Shall we head to the staff dining room?'

'Yes. I'm starving.' And she is, actually, properly hungry, not just bored hungry, which is how she feels most of the time when she's stuck in the flat surrounded by boxes.

'This way.'

Amanda follows Rosie down a network of corridors lined with framed portraits of old monks, interspersed with the occasional crucifix or a statue of the Virgin Mary. The walls are mostly covered with scuffed and scraped wood panelling, as if the school's inhabitants are passengers on board a cruise ship well past its sailing date. 'Here we go.' Rosie pushes open a heavy, panelled wooden door and they enter a noisy room that smells of boiled brassicas and roast chicken. Amanda looks around quickly to see if Mike is anywhere to be seen and is relieved when he isn't. She wants to get to know Rosie better, and if her husband was here, she knows he'd join them and they'd have to make polite conversation. She's keen to find out more about the school and what makes it tick, and she knows Rosie wouldn't tell the truth in front of someone from the leadership team.

They queue at the serving hatch to collect their lunch – as the smells suggest, it's a roast, heavy on the braised cabbage – and take a seat at the end of a long wooden table which is next to one of three large sash windows running along one wall.

'It's not exactly haute cuisine, but it's edible and it's free,' says Rosie, tucking in. 'Which is something. And of course, there's nowhere to go out and eat here for bloody miles, so it's Hobson's choice really.'

Amanda picks up her cutlery and begins to eat.

'Yes. I'm still adjusting to how far away we are from everything. We used to live in London and of course I could pop out at any time of day and get pretty much anything within a five-minute radius. Now I have to drive for miles just to buy loo roll.'

'Yes, it's a different way of life here, make no mistake. I mean, particularly here, at Hallows. I live in a village, as you know, and although there's just a post box, a pub and a visiting library van, it's nothing compared to this place. It's like you walk into an invisible time portal when you drive off the main road and head up over the hill.'

'That's exactly it,' says Amanda. 'It feels... alien here.'

'It definitely has a unique atmosphere.'

'It's... creepy, don't you think? Or is that just me?' Amanda is thinking about her encounter with the cat, and how she'd almost convinced herself, for one crazy moment, that she'd been hearing a ghost.

'Oh yes. Mind you, any old buildings can be creepy, can't they? Particularly when, you know, you get sea frets and whistling winds... it's all set up for it. But rational explanations don't work for everyone, of course. The stories some of the boys tell me have to be heard to be believed.'

Amanda's head snaps up from her lunch plate. 'What stories?'

Rosie smiles. 'Oh, the usual. Headless monks. Ghostly former headmasters hell-bent on revenge. Beautiful singing maidens luring ships onto the rocks. All stuff dreamed up by the bullies to scare the more gullible boys.'

'You don't believe in ghosts?'

'Nah. If there was something in it, science would have proved it by now.'

'You're not a person of faith, then? Despite where you work? I know the Church tends to believe in spirits...'

Rosie laughs. 'Shhh, don't tell anyone. I mean, of course you don't absolutely need to be Catholic to work here, but I don't boast of my atheism, obviously.'

'Fair enough. I'm not too sure what I believe most of the time, either. And between you and me, our kids are pretty similar. But yes, please keep my secret. I don't want to get Mike in trouble.'

'My lips are sealed. Anyway, going back to ghosts, I have heard one story a couple of times. It seems to be something of a favourite. The boys tell me an old monk appears to people when they're upset. He's not scary, apparently. Not toothless or about to scream or missing a limb or anything. Just an old monk.'

'And do you believe that?'

'I'm not sure when the last sighting apparently was, because it all gets a bit Chinese whispers, but I'm inclined to think they're confused, and it's actually a real monk they saw. There are a lot of them here, after all. The older ones all blend into one a bit.'

Amanda has only seen the non-teaching monks at a distance during church services so far, but from what she's seen, she tends to agree.

'I suppose so,' says Amanda, chewing on an unexpectedly solid roast potato. 'It does sound a bit unusual, anyway, doesn't it? Ghosts are usually, you know, spooky.'

'Yes, it's rubbish, I think. But people definitely enjoy scaring themselves with ghost stories. They've been doing it for millennia. It's part of human nature, wanting to give ourselves a thrill, thinking about things that are beyond our comprehension or control.'

'You've clearly thought about this,' says Amanda.

'Ha, I've had many years on this earth. And my job has made me a keen observer of people. They are endlessly fascinating.'

'I get that.' Amanda picks up a plastic jug of water from the table and pours herself a glass. 'Oh, by the way, I wanted to ask. Just along the coastal path from where we met, there's a memorial to a group of boys from this school, who went missing at sea. I wondered if you could tell me about it. Mike doesn't seem to know much.'

'Ah, yes. The Towan. It's such a terribly sad story. A group of Hallows boys and two members of staff went out on an annual boat trip, with two crew. Something to do with a poetry competition, I think. The weather was fine when they left, but there was an unexpected storm and although the boat, a local one named after a beach in Newquay, should in theory have been able to cope with the swell, it didn't. It went down with all hands. A few things from the boat washed ashore in the days and weeks that followed, but their bodies were never found.' Neither woman speaks for a moment, allowing the symphony of clicking cutlery and animated chatter to provide a burst of normality, as their minds process the horror and grief of this event almost six decades earlier. 'People are still talking about it, you know. There was a podcast made a year or so ago by some crackpot conspiracy theorist, who claimed that the boys hadn't died at all. She suggested they'd been taken by a visionary teacher to a futuristic commune and changed their identities. It was all completely bonkers. But people love a mystery, don't they.'

'They do,' Amanda says, not wanting Rosie to think she's mad, even though she's making a mental note to look this up. After all, Hallows Abbey is her life now, and she wants to know as much about it and its history as she can. 'So they never found what caused it, then?'

'Not with 100 per cent certainty, I think, no. But there was an inquest, and several things came to light. There was some suggestion that one of the teachers involved might have been suicidal. I remember that – that came up in the podcast, actually, but they dismissed it. And then there was just the mundane stuff, like the weather and the condition of the boat.'

'Not finding those bodies must have been particularly hard for those poor, poor parents.' Amanda feels tears forming, partly for the boys who were lost, and partly, to her embarrassment, because of how much she misses her own children. Who are, of course, alive and well, but not with her. A tear wends its way down her cheek. She brushes it away with her right hand and carries on eating, hoping her new friend and colleague hasn't noticed.

'I know,' says Rosie, looking at her with concern and sympathy. 'I know.'

6

THERESA

January 1966

It's 11 p.m. when Theresa opens the door of her sparsely furnished single room in the main school building and tiptoes down the corridor. She's dressed casually in black slacks and brown jumper and her winter coat, aware that the frosty, clear night outside has bite.

Not that the temperature bothers her. She's so desperate to get to her destination that she has to stop herself from running there. She *would* run, frankly, if there wasn't a chance of discovery. Although she's an employee and not a student, eyebrows would certainly be raised if she was found to be out of her bed at this hour. She's supposed to be on call at night in case one of the boys is sick, for a start. However, she is absolutely prepared to risk it tonight.

Five minutes later, she wedges one of the external doors open with a stone so she can get back in later – she doesn't know the code for the door – and sets off towards the path at the top of the cliffs, gulping down the fresh sea air as she strides away from the school. She feels its claustrophobic atmosphere drift away from her as she does so, and her excitement builds as she anticipates what lies ahead. This is what she left Ireland for, she thinks. This is how it feels to be free.

The moon is unshielded tonight, and the old mine's chimney is casting its shadow over the heath beyond. The moon is just bright enough, in fact, to reveal the outline of the person who's standing in front of a large wooden door at the foot of the adjoining wheelhouse. When she sees this, Theresa abandons all attempts at nonchalance and starts to run. She arrives at the abandoned building out of breath and with beads of sweat forming on her forehead, but she doesn't care at all, because Trystan definitely doesn't.

She runs straight into his arms, and he wraps them around her. She revels in their warmth and strength, just as she'd done, shockingly, on that bench by the market just before Christmas, and twice since, over the school holidays. Not as often as either of them would have liked, unfortunately, due to him living in shared lodgings with an angry landlady, and also because he's out at sea a great deal. But when they can, they meet, and when they do, it's absolutely the best feeling she has ever felt. She can't quite comprehend how or why he seems to love her, but he does, and it's both the most extraordinary relief that someone feels that way about her, and the most extraordinary source of joy. In fact, it feels like armour.

'Oh my goodness it feels like it's been forever,' she whispers breathlessly into his thick jumper. He is at least eight inches taller than her modest five foot four.

'I know exactly what you mean.'

His voice is dark and warm. And so is his mouth, which meets hers with magnetic force. For a moment her entire world is reduced to his lips, his tongue, his hands and her enraptured body, which her brain has now surrendered control of. She's never taken any illegal drugs, the kind that are apparently freely available now on the London scene, but she feels as she imagines she would if she did; her nerves are heightened, her heart is racing, and she is flooded with euphoria.

Then, as she luxuriates in her pleasure, a memory of home flashes into her mind. She knows what she's doing now is against every rule she was ever taught by the local priest, by her teachers at school and by her father. And of course if the monks at Hallows Abbey knew about it, she'd be sacked in an instant. And yet, breaking the rules these men – and let's be honest, whoever enforces the rules, the source of them is always men – have imposed upon her, doesn't frighten her at all. In fact, she's revelling in her rebellion. She wishes, actually, that they could bear witness right now, seeing her being loved, enjoying the body God gave her; that they could watch her soar.

'Are you all right, Theresa?' Trystan asks. 'You seem... distracted. Have you changed your mind?'

'No, I'm fine,' she replies, with force. She refuses to let her past dictate her present. 'In fact, I'm brilliant.' She smiles up at him in the darkness, and he returns it. 'Shall we go inside?'

* * *

An hour passes and they part, promising to meet again in a week's time.

Theresa walks back slowly towards Hallows Abbey, absorbing and acknowledging the new sensations in her body, while trying to avoid thinking about the awful withdrawal she knows she will experience until she can see him again. Because she is as addicted to him as her father is to alcohol.

She wishes desperately that he was able to come to see her more. She wishes, in fact, that her contract didn't insist that she lived in the school. What it would be, she thinks, to be able to lie on a bed with him, instead of on a pile of abandoned sacks on a dusty concrete floor. *One day*, she thinks. *One day, we'll be together, and we'll fall asleep together in the same bed and wake up the next morning and I'll make tea and we'll eat breakfast, and we'll be able to hold each other all day if we want to, every day. And—*

Theresa's train of thought is interrupted by a light. She's standing at the gate at the boundary, and she can see it shining from a window in the main school building, possibly, she thinks, in one of the classrooms. And then she panics, but not because of the light, which of course could have been left on accidentally, but because of the silhouette of someone standing in the window.

Someone's seen me out here, she thinks. *Someone is awake, and they've seen me.*

Theresa acts instinctively. She picks up the pace and walks to the school as quickly as she can. On the way, she comes up with a cover story. She'll tell whoever it is that she thought she'd seen a student outside after dark, and she'd gone to find them, only to realise she'd been mistaken. She thinks they'll believe her. She has a good reputation in the school. The boys and the staff trust her.

She's relieved when she finds the stone is still there, propping the door open. She removes it and walks up the stairs two at a time, keen to locate whoever this is, to deliver the explanation she has ready. When she's on the correct floor – the third – she makes her way to the teaching corridor she thought the person had been in. She expects someone to be waiting in the corridor for her, or for them to be behind each door she tries. But there's no one. Just room after room of empty classrooms full of wooden desks with slam tops and half-crumbled chalk and dusty board rubbers. She goes down a floor and searches the identical corridor below, but draws a blank here, too. She stands in the darkness by an open window, wondering where they could have gone. *Perhaps I was mistaken*, she thinks. Perhaps it was a different part of the school, or maybe it was simply the moon reflected in a window, and not a light. Shadows playing tricks. Yes, she decides. It's either that, or whoever it was hadn't even seen her, and had gone back to bed. After all, she realises, once you've got the light on inside, it's almost impossible to see out of a window in the dark.

This rationalisation calms her. She realises how tired she is. She has to be up early in the morning. She walks quietly and carefully back to her room, has a quick wash in the sink in the corner and climbs into bed, pulling the sheets and blanket over her. She drifts off to sleep quite quickly, but not before she's said her nightly prayers and also considered and then batted away the nagging, haunting image of someone watching her in the darkness.

7

AMANDA

Late October 2024

'Are you ready yet? It starts at nine thirty.'

Mike is standing by the front door. No doubt, she thinks, checking his watch, like a bouncer who's about to finish his shift.

'Yes, nearly.'

This is a lie. Amanda is currently yanking a dress off over her head. It's an old dress, one she used to wear for her job in the office at his previous school, and she'd reached for it without thinking when searching for something to wear to Sunday mass. It had been an old favourite, and so she'd been disturbed to discover this morning that it no longer fitted. It was straining around her upper arms and disturbingly pinched around her waist. She'd looked – and this hurt her to admit – puffy. She wonders how she's managed to put on so much weight in such a relatively short amount of time. She hasn't made any huge changes to her diet that she's aware of, and aside from a habitual nightly glass of wine, she isn't drinking heavily, either. But her middle is undoubtedly more round. As she grabs a grey wrap dress from her wardrobe – a very stretchy size fourteen – and puts it on, she wonders if these changes in her body might be behind Mike's apparent disinterest in her recently.

It can't be just his job, can it? Even though there's no doubt that Mike's new role is taking it out of him. He's working far more hours than anyone would think reasonable. He falls asleep in front of the television every night, and snaps at her all the time. This is new behaviour, and it's upsetting. But he's exhausted, frustrated and worried. She knows that. In rare moments when he's been up for a chat, she's gleaned that apart from Bede's general disgruntlement and the constant arguments between him and headmaster Father Paul on policy, the school is also having money troubles.

It's far from full. In fact, the number of boarders has been dropping steadily for at least a decade, and the cost of running the pension scheme for the teachers and the recent increase in National Insurance contributions for staff is eating away at its profits. Well, actually, more of a loss than a profit now, and this gaping financial black hole is something that Father Paul is understandably obsessed by. Mike often has to eat breakfast in the staff dining room, where the headmaster holds impromptu meetings over his cornflakes and yogurt. Mike cannot miss these. If the church does pull the plug on the school, his job will go up in a puff of smoke. Amanda does understand the politics and importance of what's going on, but that doesn't make its impact on her any easier to bear. The fact is, she misses her husband. She misses him very much.

'I'm here,' she sighs as she walks into the hallway and pulls on a pair of black low-heeled court shoes and lifts her black woollen coat from the hook on the wall. She resents the fact that she's expected to attend mass every Sunday, pretending that she's a devout Catholic. She converted to the Church to marry Mike, but she's never really felt like she belongs. Her roots are firmly in the questioning and doubting, Church of England style of things. As she suspects Mike's might be these days, too. But that's yet another thing he doesn't talk to her about.

'Good.' Mike opens the front door and sets off down the stairs at pace. Amanda tries to match his speed but fails spectacularly. She hasn't worn heels for a while and her balance seems to have deteriorated. Her right foot slips on a step and then her whole body follows. In a split second she falls backwards and finds herself descending the concrete stairs on her bottom, which, despite its current padding, hurts like hell.

She considers swearing, which always seems like a terribly naughty thing to do in such a holy environment, but then her shame and frustration and sadness find another outlet. She starts to cry.

'Oh... Mandy. Oh... here, let me help you up.'

Mike heard her fall then, from the landing below. Of course he did, she thinks. The impact probably generated an earth tremor detectable as far away as Truro.

She looks up at him. He appears agitated rather than concerned and is holding out his hand. She's about to take it and dust herself off and try to hobble into chapel, when something inside her snaps. She could pretend she's feeling fine and go and smile at the other staff, monks and the boys at church (whose attendance is also mandatory) or she could just stay here. She could stay here and not have to put on a brave face for anyone today.

'No.'

'You don't want my help?'

'No,' she says, through her tears. 'I can't face going there today. I just can't. You go. I'll be fine. I'll make myself a cuppa.'

'Don't be ridiculous, Mandy. You're my wife. They will wonder where you...'

'Oh, sod... the bloody headmaster,' she says, momentarily forgetting his name. She forgets names a lot at the moment. 'Sod the lot of them.'

'Mandy!'

'Really, Mike? I've just fallen and hurt myself. Don't you care?'

'Of course I do. But you'll be OK in a bit. We can pop back up and get you some ibuprofen, that'll help...'

Amanda has stopped crying now. Her indignation has extinguished her tears.

'Bloody ibuprofen! Can't you see that it's about so much more than some bruises? Haven't you noticed how I look? How... different I seem? Can't you tell I'm not feeling great? Or don't you even look at me any more?'

'God, Mandy,' Mike says, looking around as he does so, no doubt checking there's no one around who's hearing this embarrassingly public marital argument. 'Let's get you home. Perhaps it's best you go back to bed. You're obviously not feeling well.'

'Finally. You've noticed,' she says, hauling herself up to standing without her husband's assistance. She begins to walk back upstairs slowly and carefully, using the banister for support. Mike follows behind her, judging correctly that she does not want him to offer his arm or his hand. He opens their front door and she hobbles inside, taking a right into their bedroom. She pulls off her stupid shoes and throws herself down on the bed. Mike wanders in behind her.

'Look, I'm sorry that I seem a bit... distracted.' Amanda glares at him. 'You know how it is at the moment. If I'd known what a terrible state the school was in before I'd arrived, I'd probably never have taken the job.'

'Oh, don't be ridiculous. Of course you'd have taken it. It's a promotion. The promotion you always wanted. You'd have taken it if it was in the Outer Hebrides.'

Mike looks pained.

'Don't be like that, Mandy. I know you're feeling... not great, but we made this decision together, to come here, didn't we? You wanted to come, too.'

'Did I?' says Amanda, remembering the conversations they'd had about it, when Mike's face had been shining with excitement, and she had felt simply unable to quash his hopes. You can't do that when you love someone. You have to let them chase their dreams, even when you know the price you're going to pay for them.

'You said you did.'

'Well, yes.'

Mike sits down at the foot of the bed.

'Look, Mand, I can tell you're unhappy. I know it's a lot, asking you to move here, so soon after your mum's death, and of course the kids leaving home has been a big change...'

'This is not about Mum. It's about me. About moving me to somewhere I don't know anyone, without anything to do, and expecting me to be fine.'

'I do miss the kids too,' he says, absent-mindedly running his hand over the duvet cover, as if he's trying to iron it. 'But you've got a job now. That'll help.'

'I just... want them back,' she says, remembering the hugs they'd both used to give her in the morning in the kitchen, the silly chats they'd have in the car on the drive home from school in the evening, a mixture of terrible lunches, awful homework and amusing teachers. She misses all of it, even though a lot of it had driven her to distraction at the time.

'I know. But they're adults now. They need to do their own thing. We need to do our own thing now, too.'

'Do we? What's that, then? Work ourselves to death? Never see each other? Because that's how it feels.'

Mike winces.

'It'll be half-term soon. We can go and see the kids, if you like. We could combine seeing Jules with a trip back to see our old friends in London?'

'If Luke and Jules can spare us the time.' Their responses to her messages are becoming even more sparse. Once every other day, at most.

'And then it'll be Christmas. We can invite them here.'

'Where will they sleep, even if they both want to come?' Amanda asks. 'We don't have room.'

'I don't know. One of them can sleep on an air bed. Or we can ask the monks if we can use their guest accommodation.' She sees him check his watch.

'What time is it now?'

'Twenty-five past.'

'You can still make the service if you go now. Just tell them I'm ill.'

The truth is, Amanda just wants to be alone. She knows she's in no mood to try to explain her unexpected rage and her profound sadness, and Mike is too tired to listen properly.

'Really?'

Mike clearly agrees with her.

'Yes. Just go. I'll see you later.'

He grimaces.

'I've just remembered... There's the lunch after... the one we've been invited to at the monastery. Do you still want to come to that?'

Amanda sighs. There goes the quiet lunch à deux she had been hoping for. She knows it's important that she shows her face, however. And she is also curious to visit the monastery, to meet these monks who run this school. She wants to ask them about the boat tragedy, to see if any of the older monks remember it. And she also wants to find out how she can access the walled garden again. She's tried to visit it several times since she'd discovered it, but it's been locked. She wants to know who keeps the keys.

'Yes. I'll come. Just give me this hour or so to get myself together.'

'All right. If you're sure.'

'Yes. I'll be fine.'

Mike leaves quickly, and when the door shuts behind him, Amanda exhales slowly, imagining that all her frustration is contained within her breath. And then she swears, loudly and repeatedly, while thrusting her middle fingers up in the air in the general direction of the monastery, the monks and her husband. This show of defiance is cathartic. She feels her heart slow down a little, enough for her to sit up. She sits there for a while, looking out of the window. It's a stunning autumn morning outside; the sky is cyan and clear, and there's dew on the grass below. *I should try to walk on my ankle before it seizes up*, she thinks, acknowledging privately that it isn't even that badly injured. It was her pride that had really taken a beating. She knows instinctively that being outside, away from these walls which seem to be closing in on her, will make her feel better. She changes quickly, grabs a thick coat and sensible shoes, and heads out of the flat.

* * *

There's a gentle breeze blowing in. Amanda breathes it in and then turns, letting her face absorb a few rays. It's a very different sun now to the one they'd baked beneath during their arrival in August. It's spent most of its time hidden by clouds recently, and even when it does emerge, its power is weakening. Such a difference in just eight weeks, she thinks, knowing that this season signals a descent into darkness which will only begin to reverse in January. It's a thought she doesn't relish.

She turns and walks up the coastal path. She's decided to walk down to the cove, hoping she'll be alone down there, even though it's a weekend. It's so far out of most people's way, she often finds it empty, except for the odd fisherman or walker.

She's about to descend the steps to the beach when she spots movement out of the corner of her eye. She turns to look. Someone seems to be walking around the old mine buildings. Her eyesight isn't what it used to be, but she can definitely make out a human shape, and she gasps when she sees them pull open a door and walk inside. She knows the dilapidated buildings are unsafe – the school issues stern warnings to students to steer well clear. Not to mention the fact that there are large 'Keep Out' signs affixed in several places. You just can't miss them. Who could be going in there, she thinks, and why? Unable to contain her curiosity, she abandons her plan to walk to the cove and instead turns and heads towards the mine. If it's a student up to no good, she reasons, she needs to find them and send them packing before they injure themselves. That roof, she thinks, looks like it could fall in at any second, and heaven knows what state the floor's in.

She picks up the pace and reaches the buildings within a couple of minutes. Rosie has told her that the site had closed in the fifties, relatively late compared to many of the county's tin mines. She'd told her that the mine shaft was apparently covered at the surface and subsequently is believed to have collapsed, but that many tunnels remain underground.

Amanda hasn't been this near the complex before, but she realises the buildings look even more decrepit up close. The empty engine house and its accompanying chimney are still standing, but she sees that chunks of stone have fallen off the structure, and the salt from the sea has eaten away at wooden window frames and doors. She can also see that it's still fairly easy to get inside the complex, despite several large signs stuck on doors and windows warning people not to do so. Someone has placed some metal barriers around it at some point, but many of these have been pushed over by the wind, and no one has bothered to right them.

Amanda clambers over one of these and heads for the door she thought she saw the person enter. She sees that it was previously padlocked, but that the lock is broken. *Has this just happened?* she wonders. *Or has it been like this for a while?* It's impossible to tell. She hesitates for a moment and then decides to pull the door open. If there's someone in here who doesn't know the dangers, she reasons, she needs to tell them the risk they could be running.

The old door's hinges scream in protest as she pulls it open wide enough for her to lean in to take a look. There's very little light inside, despite the bright sunny day. What windows that remain are small, very dirty and over-grown with weeds. The light that's seeping into the room through the doorway illuminates air thick with dust motes and a stone-flagged floor littered with what look like old sacks.

'Hello?' she calls out. 'Hello? Can you hear me?'

No one responds. She stands stock-still listening for any signs of human life, but the only sounds she can hear are the cries of seagulls overhead, the waves crashing on the rocks below, and inside, the rustle of dried leaves rolling along the floor, propelled by the breeze she's letting in.

She thinks for a moment. Should she venture inside and investigate further? But then she considers the possibility of rotting floorboards and roof joists, and the lack of proper lighting, and decides against it. Her phone torch would be insufficient, and going somewhere dangerous without telling anyone where she is would be the height of stupidity.

She decides, on the balance of probability, that she must have been mistaken. Or if she did see someone, perhaps they're hiding, because they're up to no good. And she'd definitely be no match for a frightened teenager who's trying to stay hidden. She decides not to risk it. She will leave them to it, if they're in there at all. Perhaps, she thinks, she might come back with Mike, to see if there's any evidence of human activity here, any sign that students have been getting in, or if there's anything illegal going on the police might need to know about.

Mike, she thinks, shutting the door and climbing back over the fencing. Mike, who will almost certainly not have time to do this with her, not with his management role and the new bloody rewilding club he's set up in what miniscule amount of spare time he has. How, she wonders, as she makes her way back to the coastal path, *how* are they going to find their way back to each other? If, she realises with a jolt, they ever will?

***

An hour later, Amanda has painted on a brave face and is seated at a long wooden table next to Mike. And she's grateful for that, because everyone else at the table is a monk. The only other people who are not part of the order are the kitchen staff, who are bringing in steaming plates piled high with a Sunday roast, depositing them in front of each diner. Although they all make vows of poverty, she sees this does not necessarily translate into a life lacking in rich food.

There are twelve monks sitting with them. She knows three of them – Father Anthony, the current abbot, Father Paul, the headmaster, and Brother

Bede, the deputy head pastoral – but she's surprised that the rest are so few in number. She'd assumed, given the size of their living accommodation, that there must be at least thirty of them.

'Is this all of the monks?' she whispers to Mike, before thanking the waiter who's just placed her meal down in front of her.

'Not quite. Some of them are too old to come out of their cells, so food's taken to them. And there are a couple who aren't generally seen in public, so to speak.'

'Why?' she asks, but Mike isn't able to answer, because the abbot, who's sitting a couple of seats down at the top of the table, begins to say grace.

'Bless us, O Lord and these Thy gifts, which we are about to receive from Thy bounty, through Christ our Lord. Amen,' he says, and the rest of the monks chorus it with him. Amanda mumbles along with them, even though she doesn't know this version of the prayer. When the grace is said, there's a clattering of cutlery and the monks dive into their food. No one speaks for a good minute, and Amanda suddenly has a tremendous urge to fill the void. She has never liked silence.

'Thanks so much for inviting us,' she says to the abbot, while cutting up a roast potato. She hasn't spoken to him at all so far, except for a brief word or two after mass on Sundays. Father Anthony is a kind-looking man of about seventy. He's sitting at the top of the table, two people away from her.

'Not at all,' he replies. 'We should have invited you before. I apologise. I did ask Father Paul to arrange it before now, but I think things have been very busy for you all.'

Amanda watches the headmaster out of the corner of her eye. He appears not to have heard this criticism, or if he has, he's deliberately ignoring the abbot. A moment later, he starts a conversation with the monk sitting next to him. Mike seems to be listening to it, Amanda notices.

'It's lovely to meet you properly, anyway, Mrs Chapman,' says the abbot. 'Are you settling in well?'

'Yes. It's a real change, from London,' she answers, aware that Mike is listening.

'It must be. Although, that's what I like about it.'

'I wanted to ask something, actually, and I'd better do it before I forget,' she says. 'About the walled garden. I went in when we first arrived, and it's amazing. But it's been locked every time I've tried to go in since then.'

'Yes, sadly, we have to do that, or the boys use it as a hideout for smoking and vaping.'

'Oh, I see. That's a shame.'

'Are you interested in gardening, Mrs Chapman?'

Amanda nods with enthusiasm. 'Yes. I had an allotment in London. I miss it, actually.'

'I see. Well, I'm sure we can get you in. *Bede*,' he says, raising his voice to get the attention of the deputy head pastoral. 'Can I ask that you show Mrs Chapman around the walled garden? And perhaps furnish her with a key?'

Bede, who has so far tried to avoid talking to anyone, looks put out.

'Of course.' He looks like he's sucking a lemon.

'Perhaps this afternoon?' says the abbot.

'Yes. Yes. Of course,' replies Bede, before turning to reach for a water jug to refill a glass that is more than half full.

'How's your lunch, Mike?' asks Father Paul, taking advantage of a lull in conversation to talk directly to his new deputy head.

'Lovely,' replies Mike, raising his voice so he can be heard.

'Great. We had to fire the last chef, you know. He just wasn't up to it. But this new one is much better.'

Several of the catering staff are still in the dining room, and Amanda sees the expression of the one nearest to her flicker, before their poker face is restored. Whether they knew their previous boss had been sacked or not before this statement is unclear, but if they didn't then they certainly do now.

She wonders if Father Paul is aware that he's just been incredibly indiscreet. She's only met him a couple of times in passing, but he seems, frankly, to be rather pleased with himself. On balance, she thinks he knows he just said something inflammatory, but he doesn't care. That's the sort of arrogance you'd only find in a white man in a position of power, Amanda thinks, recognising it as another of her rebellious thoughts. Embracing her rebellious streak further, she decides to try to talk to Bede, who is quite clearly not looking forward to giving her a tour of the walled garden.

'How long have you been with the order?' she asks him across the table.

'It must be about fifty years now, I suppose,' replies Bede, who appears taken aback to be asked this. 'I was a young man when I took holy orders.'

'So you missed *The Towan* tragedy, then? I saw the plaque on the cliff. I wondered if anyone here remembered it. But you must have arrived in the seventies.'

Bede raises an eyebrow.

'Yes. Not many of us here remember it. There's old Dominic, of course, but he's unable to leave his room now. He's completely lost his mind, poor soul.'

'Oh.' The memory of her mother's battle with dementia looms large. 'Did you arrive here before Father Paul, then?' she says, changing the subject.

'Oh, yes. Long after our esteemed headmaster,' he says, softly.

Amanda sees a strange look shoot across the monk's face and wonders if there are rules in the monastery banning sarcasm.

* * *

Amanda has been reading for about two minutes when Mike begins to snore. She turns over and sees that he is still holding a book – *Rewilding Childhood* by Mike Fairclough – despite the fact he's clearly fallen asleep. She gently removes it from his grip and turns his light off. He doesn't stir.

She reads her own novel, *Small Pleasures* by Clare Chambers, for another half an hour before the sentences start to become senseless and her eyes begin to close. She places it down on her bedside table and turns out the light. She lies there on her back and thinks over the events of the day: the argument she'd had with Mike, who seems oddly changed; the person she may or may not have seen at the mine; the awkward lunch with the monks; and finally, the visit in the afternoon to the walled garden, which had started frostily – Bede had not wanted her there, as she had assumed – but had ended with the giving of a key and a truce of sorts. She is to be allowed to go there whenever she wants, and has been told she can take produce, and feed the chickens, if she so wishes. This last thought brings her unexpected happiness.

She closes her eyes and expects sleep to come quickly.

But it doesn't. An hour later, she is still tossing and turning, checking the digital alarm clock every few minutes in case she's somehow been asleep and unaware of it. Eventually, she decides she needs the toilet. She finds it impossible to drop off if her bladder is calling to her, so she reluctantly pulls the covers back and gets out of bed. She grabs her dressing gown from the chair in the corner – the school is trying to save money on energy by waiting to put on the heating until half-term – and walks out of the bedroom and into the hallway, heading for the bathroom.

Then she hears the crying.

It must be the cat again, she thinks. She shrugs it off and goes to the toilet. But when she comes back out of the bathroom, she stands still and listens. It sounds more human than cat, she decides. Definitely.

She doesn't stop to think any more. This time, she decides, if it's a student, I'll find him. And if it's that bloody cat, I'll let it out. She finds her slippers and keys and leaves the flat, heading at pace through several locked doors towards the school classrooms. The sobbing sound seems to be getting louder as she walks down the empty corridor on her floor. It must be coming from the same toilets, she thinks. Why does that cat choose to jump in this window, anyway, if it can't get out?

She reaches the toilet door and pushes it open. She turns on the light, expecting to find the cat wandering about the place, but she can't see it. She notices, however, that the crying has stopped. *Where are you, you nutty thing?* she thinks, opening each toilet stall in turn. But there's no sign of it. The cat, she concludes, must have climbed out of the window, just as she was entering. *You'll be the death of me, you bloody animal*, she thinks, turning off the light and closing the door behind her, keen to return to her warm bed as soon as possible. She's about to set off down the corridor when she collides with something, someone, in the dark.

'Oh my God,' she yells, feeling herself ricochet off whatever, whoever, it is. A surge of adrenaline runs through her.

'Mandy?'

'Mike. Oh, thank goodness. I thought...'

'What are you doing out here? I heard you leave the flat and I followed you...'

'I was... I heard someone crying.'

Mike reaches for a light switch, and the teaching corridor is flooded in neon light. Amanda blinks.

'Crying? Here?'

'Yes. I thought a boy had got out of Amadeus and was hiding in the loos, crying.'

'And was there anyone there?'

'No. There's no one in there. And the crying's stopped. I think it was a cat. But there wasn't one in there. It must have climbed out the window.'

'Let's just go and check again,' he says. 'Just in case there is a student in there.'

'Yes, sure,' she says, following him into the toilets, where he checks every stall to make sure the room is empty.

'No, nothing,' he says, and he's about to turn the light off when she notices it. Her face must be a picture, because he stops and asks her, 'What is it? What's up?'

Her blood runs cold.

The window isn't open.

There's no way a cat could have found its way into this room tonight, she realises.

No way at all.

'You really didn't hear the crying?'

'No. I could just hear your footsteps.'

She wonders whether she's losing her mind. Hearing things. But she heard it so many times, didn't she? Over and over again. And it had got gradually louder.

'I don't understand.'

'You must have dreamed it. Maybe you sleepwalked?'

'I don't sleepwalk.'

'Well, it must be something like that.'

'What if it was a ghost?' she says, blurting the word out before she can change her mind.

'Don't be ridiculous,' he says. 'They don't exist.'

'How do you know that?'

'I just do. Come on, let's go back to the flat. We both need our sleep.' He pulls the door open and gestures for her to leave.

'Why won't you take me seriously?'

'About hearing phantom voices? Come off it, Mand. That's crazy talk.'

'What if... What if it's a ghost, trying to tell me something?'

As she says this, Amanda is thinking about the shipwreck, and about the boys who never returned. About the mystery that surrounds the boat's disappearance. What if it's something to do with that? What if they're calling out to her?

'Bloody hell. What's up with you at the moment, Mandy?'

'That's a good question. One I think you should be spending more time trying to answer.' The anger she'd felt this morning before mass returns. *Why doesn't he care more about how she feels?* she thinks. Why hasn't he noticed she's struggling?

But of course, Mike is exhausted. His eyes are fighting to stay open. She knows this isn't a good time to talk this through properly. So she settles for glaring at him, stomping past and refusing to talk as they walk back to the flat. Even though she's not talking, however, her mind is racing.

I'm going to find out more about that boat accident, she thinks. *I'm going to find out if there's any truth to the rumours and the conspiracies. And perhaps if I do that, I'll find answers that will bring me, and maybe this phantom boy, if he's not just a figment of my imagination, peace.*

8

THERESA

March 1966

It's late at night and there's a biting wind barrelling in, making the driving rain feel like thousands of tiny needles capable of puncturing skin. Theresa, however, is oblivious to it. She's wearing a raincoat, but hasn't zipped it up, and its hood is down. Her hair is saturated and there are streams of rainwater running beneath her clothing, gently warmed by her skin.

Because she is on fire.

The hour she has just spent with Trystan, like every such precious hour, felt like alchemy. Their different bodies, their yin and yang, had fused and created an experience that now, basking in the aftermath, she is unable to remember clearly, because she's not entirely sure she was fully conscious. She felt, and still feels, high. She turns her head into the wind and rain and breathes in slowly, feeling the chilled air fill her lungs and expand her belly, and as she exhales she imagines her breath is a force field, their mutual force field, which will keep her safe and happy until she sees him again. It simply has to.

Theresa holds the gate that marks the entrance to the school grounds carefully as she opens the latch, aware that the wind risks blowing it hard into the fence, possibly even taking it off its hinges. When she's safely through, she pushes it shut firmly and begins the short walk to the main school building, removing the pebble she'd placed in the door frame and entering the hallway with a mixture of relief and regret.

Her right leg is about to touch the first step when a voice makes her freeze.

'I saw you. I saw you, with him.'

The staircase light is off and her eyes have yet to adjust to the darkness. For a moment, she has no idea who's talking. She doesn't even know where this person is. Are they above her? In front of her? Behind her?

But then she recognises his voice.

'John?'

'Yes.'

John. The awkward fourteen-year-old scholarship boy, the one who's being bullied by his peers for his accent and his unfashionable shoes. She has seen him regularly in sick bay over the past few weeks, far more regularly than she'd normally expect, even for a bad case of homesickness. John has found a different reason to come to see her each time: a headache, a stomach ache, a paper cut, a painful ankle. She is beginning to suspect he has a crush on her. It has happened before. After all, she's one of only a few female staff in the school, and she's young and as far as they know, unattached. It's not unheard of and she knows she needs to discourage it. But she feels sorry for him. She feels, in fact, a kind of kinship with him, as a fellow outsider. And so she's allowed him to continue coming to see her. She can see now that this has been a mistake.

'What are you doing out of bed?'

Normally, this would be enough to prompt a pupil to scurry back to their dormitory with their tail between their legs. But John, it seems, is not a normal pupil.

'I could ask you the same question.'

Theresa's eyes adjust to the darkness, and she sees that he is standing at the top of the first flight of steps. She joins him there so she can look him in the eye. It felt wrong, him being up there, looking down at her. She knows she shouldn't have been out after dark, but she's also an adult, a fully grown adult, and she will not take any of this rubbish from him.

'I thought I saw someone out in the grounds, so I went to check,' she says, reverting to her planned excuse.

'No you didn't. You went to the old mine, and you met him there. I saw you.'

'Don't be ridiculous.' Theresa decides to front it out. There's no way John could have seen who she was meeting, she reasons. It's far too far away, and far too dark.

'I followed you.'

This stops Theresa in her tracks. It had occurred to her that someone from the school might see her leave and decide to investigate. But a fellow member of staff, *never* one of the boys.

'You shouldn't have done that. That's against school rules. I could have you suspended or expelled.'

'But you won't. *You won't*, because I know what you were doing, and I know who you were with. I could tell them. You'd be sacked if they knew. You're a single woman. A single woman employed in a Catholic school. They won't tolerate it.'

Theresa ponders this. They had shut the old door firmly behind them to keep out the weather. There was only one window in the room they were in, and it was high up and filthy. No one could see anything through that. He's bluffing, she thinks. He must be.

'No, you won't.'

'I will, if I have to. I'm here to tell you, you have to stop it now. You mustn't be with him. You mustn't.'

Theresa is frightened. The vulnerable teenager she thought she knew has become a threatening man, apparently transformed by the twin shields of knowledge and darkness. He seems to know her secret, and he's right, she could get sacked for this. But what, she wonders, will he want in return for his silence? All sorts of thoughts fly through her mind, and none of them are good. He's young, but he's taller than her, for a start. She realises he could easily overpower her, if he wanted to. She decides that the only option she has is to try to placate him.

'Okay,' she says, her voice artificially light, as if she's talking to a toddler. 'I'm listening.'

'He's not right for you, all right? He's not. He's... wrong. You mustn't see him again.'

John sounds less certain now. He's jealous of Trystan, she realises.

'I understand. I won't see him again.'

'You won't?' She can just make out his expression. He seems to be pleading with her.

'I won't.'

'Good. Good,' he says. She sees his shoulders drop. He sounds like an awkward boy again.

'So are we all right? We both agree not to speak about meeting here like this ever again?'

Her heart is in her mouth while she awaits his reply.

'Yes. Ye-es. As long as you promise.'

'I promise.'

'OK.' He turns, clearly about to walk away. But she has something she wants to ask him first.

'Before you go, John. It was you, wasn't it? It was you, watching me a few weeks ago? From a classroom? I saw a light.'

'No. It wasn't me. I don't know what you're talking about.'

He doesn't say anything further. Instead, he simply slips away, the leather soles of his slippers muffling his footsteps as he makes his way back towards his boarding house.

Theresa stays rooted to the spot, her heart beating fiercely and her breathing shallow. She has always known that discovery was possible, but after almost two months of getting away with it, she'd begun to feel invincible. The realisation that someone else at Hallows Abbey knows her secret is disturbing. Will John keep her secret? Or will he use it as leverage over her? And also – if it wasn't him, who was it who had been looking at her from that window?

9

AMANDA

December 2024

December is one of the quietest months for a gardener in the northern hemisphere, but that doesn't keep Amanda out of the walled garden. She's increasingly finding herself drawn to the space, busying herself with sweeping up leaves, taming wayward branches and feeding the chickens. The latter is a job she does every morning before work, and one she does not regard as a chore.

One of the other monks helping in the garden, a forty-year-old called Albert – who seems wary of Bede, who cracks the whip widely and grumpily – has explained that they're rescued battery farm chickens. This makes sense, of course. Chickens kept in those horrible places are often so traumatised, they don't have normal plumage. Since hearing this, Amanda has made a special effort to be nice to them. She talks to them every day, and she's given them names that even she can remember. The fluffy one is Molty McMoltface, and the almost naked one, Fluffless Fran.

The weak winter sun is just rising over the horizon as she enters the garden and walks over to the henhouse.

'Here you go, Molty,' she says, throwing pellets down. 'Come on, don't let her take it all, Fran.'

The two mangey-looking hens totter towards the food in the dim morning light, and she watches them peck at it for a minute, enjoying their apparent contentment. Her meditative moment, however, is interrupted by the sound of someone singing. Her experience of choirs tells her it's somewhere in the middle of the vocal range, and could be either a woman or a male tenor. She scans her immediate surroundings, wondering if one of the monks has entered the garden without her realising, but she can't see anyone. She walks up to the garden entrance and opens the door, but notices that the singing is far quieter here than in the corner by the henhouse. She's about to set off around the perimeter to see if someone's singing around there, unaware she's close by, when it stops. She decides not to continue searching. She doesn't want to embarrass whoever it was. She returns to the chickens, puts the lid on the feed box, and strokes Molty's remaining feathers gently through the wire mesh.

'Aren't you lucky, Molty,' she says, her voice gentle, 'to have someone serenade you while you eat your breakfast?'

* * *

'Can you carry these firelighters and the matches? And I'll carry the kindling?'

'Sure,' says Amanda, taking the bag from Mike as they make their way down the stairs and out into the cold, clear evening. It's only five thirty, but it's already so dark outside, they can see the stars.

'It's going to freeze tonight, I think,' says Mike, as they walk around the building towards the walled garden.

'Just as well you're lighting a fire.'

'Yes. I've told them to wrap up warm. But most of them seem to think it's a sign of weakness to wear a coat, so...'

'They'll learn.'

'Have you got the key?'

'Yep,' replies Amanda, fishing in her pocket for it. It's still there after her visit here this morning. Mike takes the key and unlocks the door, and they walk through in the direction of the far left corner, where he placed a metal fire pit this afternoon, and surrounded it with upturned wooden boxes and a couple of camping chairs he'd found in the school's storage sheds.

'What time are they coming?'

'Should be here in about ten minutes. The club starts at half past. Then we have about an hour together before supper. Just pop those down there.' He points to a spot beside one of the chairs. She does as he asks.

'How many have signed up?'

'I got about fifteen last week.'

'That's pretty good going.'

'Yes, I thought so. Particularly because these are the sort of boys who don't usually take part in stuff. They're not interested in choir or chess or drama. They typically make a thing of refusing to join in. So the fact they're coming is a win in itself.'

'Do you think the fact you're giving them toasted marshmallows and Nutella for dipping has anything to do with it?' Amanda smiles.

'Probably. Will you help me light it in a sec?'

'Sure,' she replies, checking her watch.

'What time do you have to get going?'

'The restaurant's booked for seven. I said I'd be at Rosie's for half six.'

'Ah, you've got about half an hour, then.'

'Yes. Happy to stay. It's a beautiful night for it.'

She tilts her head back and gazes up at the vast expanse of sky above them, an intricate tapestry of countless constellations. Even the clearest nights in London didn't look like this. The light pollution had always made the sky appear the same yellowy shade as the streetlights. Here, she can make out strings of satellites skirting the atmosphere, and planets millions of miles away.

And then she sees it. A streak of silver streaming across the sky.

'A shooting star,' says Mike, who's also been gazing at the heavens.

'Wow,' says Amanda. 'That's amazing. I've never seen one of those before.'

Mike reaches out his hand for her, their instinct being, as always, to enjoy these moments together. But then the gate to the walled garden opens, and he springs away from her.

'Are you in here, sir?' asks one of a group of boys who've just entered.

'Yes. Come over here, Jack,' replies Mike, already several metres away from Amanda, busying himself laying kindling in the fire pit.

The boys arrive. They're aged between fourteen and seventeen, she thinks. She recognises one of them, who she'd treated for a calf injury after rugby training a few weeks previously. Rosie had told her afterwards that he's been suspended twice. Once for smoking on school premises and once for truancy.

'All right, ma'am,' he says, noticing her.

'Hi,' she replies, and he smiles briefly before walking up to the fire pit, where Mike's currently placing firelighters.

'Can we help you with that, sir?' says one of the others.

'Yes, you can, George. There's a pile of seasoned logs over there, against the wall. Could you bring a few over?'

More boys arrive. Amanda takes a seat and watches them work together, building the fire high, before lighting it under supervision and monitoring it as it smoulders, then burns. As it catches light, their faces are lit by the flames, and she sees focus, interest and smiles. All things she suspects are absent in double maths on a Monday morning.

'Shall we crack open the marshmallows?' asks Mike.

There's a general mumble of agreement, and a scrum forms around Mike as he digs into his bag and distributes the treats.

Amanda checks her watch.

'I'd better go,' she announces, standing up and forging a path through the boys to her husband, who she can see is in his element. 'I'll see you later.'

He looks up and smiles but doesn't kiss her goodbye. She supposes this would be too embarrassing in front of the boys.

'Yes. See you later.'

***

'Will you pull my cracker?'

'That's a bit forward.'

Rosie breaks into a paroxysm of hearty laughter, and Amanda does too. Her friend's bawdy sense of humour is infectious.

'Seriously, Rosie, you should come with a prescription,' says Amanda, who is enjoying a night off from being the wife of the stressed, prickly deputy headteacher. Instead, she's making the most of an opportunity to spend the school's miserly £15 per head contribution to festive get-togethers at Pronto Pizza in Redruth, where a large group of matrons, assistant matrons and the medical team are getting slowly blotto on a complimentary glass of Prosecco and a great deal of house white. They're sitting at a long thin table, and Amanda and Rosie are opposite each other at one end.

'My several lovers have told me this,' Rosie replies with a wink. Amanda almost chokes on her garlic mushroom starter. 'Haha, I got you there, didn't I?' she says. 'It's only one lover. And I've been with him for ten years. I don't know if that counts.'

'I didn't know you had a partner. I thought you said you'd had enough of marriage after your divorce.'

'I didn't say I was married, did I? I don't even live with him. And there's a lot you don't know about me, young lady.'

'So it seems,' says Amanda with a smile. 'And less of the young. I'll be fifty soon, you know.'

Rosie raises an eyebrow.

'In four years. Stop wishing your life away.'

Amanda feels a lump form in her throat. The truth is, she thinks, she *is* doing that. Because there's not much in her current phase of life that she's enjoying, except perhaps her new job, and the daft chickens. She wants to fast-forward, although where she'll be in four years, she has no idea. Except she hopes it isn't here, in a tiny flat with a husband she hardly sees.

'You know, you give me such hope,' says Amanda. 'You live such a brilliant, full life, and I know you don't tell me your age, but you did let slip the other week that you'll be receiving your pension in just a few years...'

'Ah, yes, well I discovered the secret to eternal life a while ago.'

'And that is?' says Amanda, refilling her wine glass.

'Not stopping. Honestly, if you stop work, your brain freezes. So I've kept going. Oh, and swimming in the sea, of course. I'll be having a dip in there, come Christmas Day.'

'Will you? Bloody hell.'

'Why don't you join us? You and Mike? Or are you going somewhere else for Christmas?' Amanda pauses, and Rosie notices her reticence. 'Sorry, have I said something stupid?'

Amanda feels tears threaten to come, so she gulps down some wine to try to hide it.

'No, of course not. It's just this will be our first Christmas by ourselves. We've never had big family Christmases. Mike's relationship with his parents is pretty dreadful and both of my parents are dead, and my sister Emma and I only really get along on a need-to-know basis. It's generally just been the four of us, and that's been fine. But now the kids have other places they want to be. Luke's got a job in a shop and he's only got Christmas Day itself off, so he's going to spend the day with friends. And Jules has got a boyfriend and she's going to spend Christmas Day with his folks. We'll see them afterwards, of course – we'll go on a road trip after Christmas and visit them both – but it won't be the same, not having them with us.'

'I can imagine,' says Rosie. Amanda sees a flicker of sadness in her usually jolly disposition and realises what she's said.

'I'm sorry. I know you don't have kids and I know I'm really lucky to have them at all...'

'Honestly, don't be. I've had many decades to get used to my reality and I've had, and continue to have, a brilliant life. It's fine. And just because I'm not a parent, it doesn't mean I can't imagine what it must be like to miss them when they fly the nest.'

'No,' says Amanda, digging into her food to hide her embarrassment.

'At least you're going to see them. That'll be nice, won't it.'

'Yes, it will be,' she replies, shovelling the remainder of the mushrooms into her mouth. Then she stares at her empty plate, unable to think what to say next.

'I think it's about more than just the kids leaving though, isn't it?' says Rosie.

'What do you mean?'

They both pause as a waitress removes their plates.

'I mean that I think you've got more going on than a mid-life crisis.'

'I suppose Mike's stressful new job hasn't helped.'

'Not having the full support of your life partner must be tough.'

'Yes. And I mean, I have to be *his* support, obviously. And that's fine.

We've always done that for each other. But it's like he's not there for me any more, you know? Not at all.'

'I don't envy him, or you. I hear on the grapevine that enrolments are down,' Rosie says, lowering her voice. 'I mean, boarding is definitely going out of fashion. That much is clear. If the school is going to survive, it'll mean job losses and big changes, won't it. And your husband will have to work with Father Paul and Bede on that. It won't make him popular.'

Amanda nods. This is pretty much what Mike has been telling her every evening, when he's had enough energy to do so. She knows he'll have to make those decisions before the end of this school year, and she also knows that any bad feeling against him will inevitably impact on her, and her job in the school. They all know who she's married to, after all.

'No, it won't. But it's not just Mike's job, you know, or the kids leaving, or even our move here. I just don't feel... myself.'

'How do you mean?'

The waiter brings their main course, a fairly meagre plate of dry turkey, roast vegetables and chipolata sausages wrapped in pancetta, a half-hearted Italian twist.

'I used to be so confident, you know. So capable,' says Amanda when the waiter has departed. 'I know it makes me sound big-headed, but I was. I was independent, always planning something. I had lots of get up and go. But in the past year or so I just feel so... anxious. My work with you has helped, because it's got me out of bed in the morning, but when my brain isn't otherwise occupied it's like I'm a teenager again, over-thinking everything. I feel paralysed by anxiety sometimes. For example, I went shopping in Truro the other weekend and I was so overwhelmed being in an unfamiliar place with so many people that I had to take refuge in the toilets in Marks & Spencer. And you know I said I heard someone crying, but it was a cat? Well, I heard them again, but I searched everywhere. No cat.'

Amanda takes a deep breath and waits for her friend's reaction. She had thought this latter admission might make Rosie laugh, given her disbelief in the paranormal, but instead she's looking at her with concern.

'OK, well, that's made my mind up. You need to see Frances.'

'Who's Frances?'

'My counsellor. She lives near me. She's brilliant.'

'Oh, I see.'

'She's very good value. And she's worked wonders for me. I'll WhatsApp you her number.'

Amanda has never seen a counsellor, but even she admits that she's in need of help. *Why shouldn't I give it a try?* she thinks. *Something just for me. A rarity.*

'OK, I'll give her a call after the holidays.'

'Good. And the other thing you need to do is make an appointment with the GP. You have registered with one down here, haven't you?'

'Oh, I wouldn't want to bother them with...'

'Don't be ridiculous, child. This isn't London. The GP in Porthgerran usually manages to give appointments on the day to everyone who needs one. And you seem to me to be in need of hormonal assistance. Not that I'm a doctor. But I know the signs.'

'HRT? But I'm still having periods.'

She's seen a few social media posts about the perimenopause, but she's mostly ignored them because she's still pretty regular.

'Yes, well, I had them until my mid-fifties, on and off, but I had a rough old time of it for a long time before then. And of course it's part of my job as a nurse to keep up with all the latest research, and we all know a lot more now about the impact of perimenopause on women. No one ever spoke about it when I was going through it, but we do now, and it's so much better for it. Lots of women are staying on HRT well into their seventies.'

'Do you really think this might help explain how I've been feeling?'

'Well, I'm not sure. You've got a lot going on. And as I say, I'm not a doctor and you'll need hormone tests and whatnot, but yes, I do think it's possible. I was wracked with insecurity for a lot of my late forties. I used to think I was incapable of speech, some days. I could barely remember my own name.'

'That sounds familiar.' When she'd been working in the walled garden with Brother Anthony last week, Amanda had forgotten the word for wheelbarrow and had had to describe it as 'that thing with one wheel and two handles'.

'So, will you go? To the doctor.'

'Yes, I will.'

'And will you come with me for a dip on Christmas Day?'

'I'll think about it,' Amanda replies, laughing.

'Let's drink to that,' says Rosie, picking up her glass. As Amanda does the same and their glasses clink, an unexpected wave of optimism catches her. Yes, she thinks, I'll do these two things, as soon as I can. It's time, she thinks, or actually, well past time, to sort herself out.

10

THERESA

Easter 1966

Theresa stares in the mirror. She's in the ladies' loos at The Smuggler on Falmouth's seafront, and she's grinning at herself like a Cheshire cat. This is partly due to the volume of cider she's been drinking, but mostly due to the anticipation of what's to come.

Tonight, you see, they are finally, finally getting to spend the whole night together. They've made love plenty of times before, of course, but this night away, taking advantage of the school's Easter holidays, signals something new and very exciting. And because it was his idea, she knows it signals Trystan's intent to make things serious between them.

She realises her lipstick needs redoing, so she pulls out her favourite Revlon red and reapplies it carefully, while also checking that the black eye wings she spent ages perfecting with her kohl pencil remain intact. When she's finished, she puts her lipstick back in her handbag and stares at herself for a few seconds more. She sees an independent, fashionable, confident young woman looking back at her, a far cry from the frightened, vulnerable version of herself she has grown accustomed to seeing. She pulls her shoulders back, smooths her hands down over her red turtle-neck jumper, black miniskirt and knee-high boots, and walks back into the bar.

The scene that greets her is somewhat different to the one she had left behind to visit the toilet. She'd left Trystan sitting alone in a booth. Now, however, two other men are sitting with him. She doesn't know either of them. She notices also that there is now a collection of shot glasses on the table, some of them empty.

'Ah, Theresa, there you are,' Trystan says, loudly so the whole pub can hear. 'Come and meet the lads.'

Her heart sinks. She doesn't want to share him with anyone, least of all these two men, who have apparently been drinking for quite some time.

'Hello,' she says, sitting down next to Trystan, and opposite the men.

'Nice to meet you,' says the one on the left. He's slurring his words. 'Ah, Trys, you've definitely got yourself a pretty one here,' he adds, and she sees his eyes check her over like a vet examining a heifer.

'Yeah, those boots are made for... shagging,' says the other, making a crude reference to Nancy Sinatra's 'These Boots Are Made For Walking'. All three men burst into a fit of outrageous laughter, as if he's just shared the funniest joke they've ever heard. Theresa squirms and crosses her legs, pressing them together tightly. She resolves to turn the radio off whenever she next hears the song played.

These two men, she is told, have worked with Trystan in the past. Arthur, on the left, and Pasco on the right, engage in wild banter and drinking games with her boyfriend for two horrible hours.

Theresa doesn't contribute to the conversation. Indeed, she is not invited to. Instead, she only answers questions directly posed to her, and even then only in hushed, reserved sentences, designed to dissuade interest. Eventually, she can't take it any more.

'Shall I get you some more drinks, gentlemen,' she asks, realising that this will give her reason to escape.

'T'would be much obliged,' says Trystan, handing her a handful of crumpled notes. 'Three pints of black.'

She extracts herself from the booth and walks up to the bar, where she orders the drinks from the barmaid. She takes a seat on one of the bar stools and looks around. The rest of the bar is quiet, with only a couple of patrons dotted around.

'You all right there?' the woman asks, as she pulls a glass from a shelf behind her and begins to clean it with a towel.

'Me?' answers Theresa, taken aback that she's talking to her. The time she's spent with Trystan and his friends has made her feel invisible. 'Oh, yes. A bit tired, I suppose,' she replies, not wanting to tell a stranger the truth. She is tired, that's true, but she's also incredibly uncomfortable. This is not the night away she'd imagined.

'He likes the booze, does Trystan.' Theresa notices that she seems to be preparing the drinks order with elaborate care. She's not even got as far as filling the glasses.

'You know him?'

'Yes. He's been in here quite a lot, over the years.'

'Oh, I see.'

'You're not local?' the barmaid asks.

'No, no. I'm from Ireland. I work at Hallows Abbey.'

'Ah, do you? That's a nice school, isn't it?'

'Yes,' Theresa replies, not wanting to tell her that most of the boys seem miserable and the monks give her the creeps.

'I wouldn't have thought I'd see a nice girl like you sitting with those reprobates.'

She's staring hard at Theresa now, and she still hasn't poured the beer. Theresa feels duty bound to defend her boyfriend, but she can't help but agree that she wouldn't mind if she never met Pasco or Arthur ever again.

'I—' she starts, but she doesn't get a chance to continue.

'Any chance of those beers now, Jenna?' shouts Pasco from the table.

'I'm afraid it's closing time now, gents,' says the barmaid, ringing a bell that's resting beside the till. Theresa shoots a glance at the clock on the wall and sees that it's half past ten. There's half an hour until closing.

'Nah, itsssnot,' yells Arthur.

'It is, I'm afraid. I have to clean up after and it's Sunday tomorrow.'

She hears a few grunts of annoyance from the other drinkers, but one by one they slurp what's left of their drinks, put on their coats and leave.

But not Trystan and the gang, however. They still have most of a pint left to drink each and they seem to be sipping it slowly, giggling like small children.

Theresa gets off the bar stool and is about to go back to them when the barmaid whispers, 'Tell them you're not feeling well. You can come behind here with me. I've a quiet room back here. We can talk.'

For a brief moment, Theresa hesitates. She abhors liars and she doesn't want to upset Trystan, and she also doesn't particularly want to chat to another woman tonight. She's here to be with her boyfriend, after all. But she also cannot bear to be in the company of his two 'friends' for a moment longer. And so she makes a decision.

'I'm not feeling great actually, love,' she says to Trystan. 'Can we go back to the hotel?'

This prompts loud sniggers from Arthur, so much so that he appears to be choking on his beer. Trystan, however, appears to grow a conscience.

'Oh, right, yeah,' he says, extracting himself from the booth. Theresa breathes a sigh of relief that her ordeal will soon be over. Out of the corner of her eye, she sees Jenna turn and busy herself buffing glasses. Theresa feels a bit bad she rebuffed her offer of a chat. It was kind of her, she thinks. 'Well. I'll be seeing you, lads,' Trystan says, finally standing up. He reaches for his coat, which he's slung over a nearby table. Theresa walks over to be with him.

'Enjoy your... break,' says Pasco.

'I hope it's... rewarding,' sniggers Arthur.

'Let's go,' says Theresa with a fixed smile. There's some backslapping and shaking of hands to be done first, but a few minutes later she is delighted to be out in the cool air, the welcome darkness hiding her embarrassment.

It's only when they are out of the pub that Trystan puts his arm around her, and they walk together up the high street and through a succession of narrow, steep paths to the bed and breakfast they'd left their bags at earlier that evening.

When Trystan finds the key the landlady gave them in the depths of one of his many pockets, he inserts it into the door and they walk up the two flights of stairs, her tiptoeing, him stumbling. They enter a small room on the front of the property, which looks out over the road rather than the harbour. It's furnished with a double bed, two bedside tables, a wardrobe with a wonky door and it's lit with a single bulb hanging from the ceiling, covered with a pink tasselled shade.

'Well, it'll do,' she says. It's not the hotel room of her dreams, definitely, but she knows his budget is small and she's grateful for the privacy. She opens her small suitcase to retrieve her washbag and nightie. It's pink nylon, bought especially for this evening, and she strips off and changes while Trystan walks down the corridor to the lavatory. When he returns, she's already tucked up in bed under the blankets.

'Well, what have we here,' he says, grinning at the sight of her, and she melts. And for the next few minutes, it's all as she'd hoped it would be. Well, almost. He smells rather too much of beer, but he's hers again, now he's away from his laddish friends. The room is warm, the bed is passably comfortable, and for once, she's not worried that anyone is going to catch them. This time, she is able to really luxuriate in the warmth that comes with being wanted.

* * *

The day dawns brightly, and Theresa is awake to see it, because she has barely been asleep. Before coming to Falmouth, she had imagined sharing a bed with Trystan to be the height of romance. However, sharing a bed with him had not been like she'd thought it would be. Trying to sleep on an exceedingly small section of mattress – Trystan, after all, is a big man – had proved almost impossible. The continual sound of cars passing on the road outside also hadn't helped.

She has grown used to the relative silence of Hallows Abbey, and the splendid luxury, she now realises, of her own bed. At 6.30 a.m. there's enough light to read, so she pulls out the paperback from her bag and begins to read. At seven forty-five she realises she'll have to wake Trystan if they're to make breakfast, which the landlady had told them she stopped serving at half past eight.

She shakes him gently, but he doesn't stir, so she resorts to poking him in the back several times until he wakes.

'Good morning, beautiful,' he says. 'Did you sleep well?'

'Fine,' she says, deciding not to dwell on it. 'But we need to be up. We need to get breakfast.'

'Yes, of course,' he says, sitting bolt upright.

'Would you like a cup of tea?' she asks, noting the portable kettle, tea bags and UHT milk which is sitting on a small table in the corner.

'Yes, that would be grand.'

She starts to walk over towards it.

'Don't worry. I'll make it,' he says, springing out of bed like he's had the best night's sleep in the world.

Theresa sets about making herself presentable for the day. She dresses and brushes her teeth in the sink in the corner and then drinks the tea he's made for her while he puts his clothes on and visits the toilet down the hall. When he returns, they walk downstairs and into a high-ceilinged room packed with small melamine tables covered in plastic mats, playing host to little pots of cutlery, and a small metal basket containing tomato ketchup and brown sauce.

They are shown to a table for two by the window and the sight of sunshine warming the table lifts Theresa's spirits. The waitress takes their order for two cooked breakfasts with tea and toast and heads off to take it to the kitchen. The teenager had seemed entirely disinterested in whether Theresa and Trystan were really married, or by their obvious age difference, and this nonchalance buoys her mood further. *We obviously appear suited*, she thinks, looking out over the view of the road and the busy harbour beyond. *That's good.* And when she examines Trystan's rugged face, she sees that last night's excesses seem to have left him surprisingly quickly. He looks more like the man she knows, and she feels her heart swell. She reaches to take his hand, and he readily gives it, looking into her eyes with an intensity that makes her feel weak. Yes, she thinks, *this* is who he is. He's not that silly performance she witnessed last night in front of his friends.

When the food comes, the change in mood in both of them is palpable. There is teasing and laughter, and yes, flirting. Flirting of the kind she remembers at their first meeting by the harbour in Porthgerran. She looks around the room occasionally at the other diners, and they all seem so grey in comparison, so dull. She feels like a peacock proudly displaying its feathers in a field full of pigeons, and she isn't the slightest bit embarrassed about it.

When they've finished eating and it's time to return to their room to pack up before checking out, she gladly takes Trystan's hand. He leads her up the stairs and opens the door of their room with a flourish, and she knows that this time, this lovemaking, will be slow and relaxed. They don't have anywhere particular to go. They don't have to check out for several hours, and they will make the most of it. He pulls her to him and they kiss passionately. And then, as she's unbuttoning his shirt, it slips out.

'When we live together, we can do this all of the time,' she says, with a beaming smile.

His face and hands fall.

And the mirage she's worked so hard to conjure falls with it.

11

AMANDA

Christmas Day 2024

'Are you absolutely sure about this, Mand?'

It's seven thirty in the morning and the sun is limping upwards, setting the scene for another crisp, clear but depressingly short spell of daylight. Amanda is however grateful that they now have the shortest day of the year behind them, and that each day is one small step forward into the light.

'Yes. I am.'

They are in their bedroom. Like her, Mike is wearing his warmest coat along with an old pair of tracksuit bottoms and a bobble hat. You wouldn't know, she thinks, that he's got his swimming trunks underneath all that.

She's genuinely impressed he's got this far. When she'd first suggested they join Rosie and her friends for a Christmas Day dip he'd thought she was having him on, but over the past few weeks she's dropped it in conversation at regular intervals and eventually worn him down. She suspects he's doing it out of guilt, realising that this rare exhibition of enthusiasm from his wife after such a difficult few months is something to harness and encourage. After all, his decision to take the job here is the reason they are experiencing their first Christmas without the kids since they became parents, something she has tried very hard not to point out. There's no need to do it, anyway. It's such a glaring fact it's like there's an elephant permanently sitting in the middle of every room. So yes, he feels bad about it all, she thinks, and so he's agreed to come and jump into a freezing sea with her before Christmas morning mass to try to make amends.

'Well, let's go then,' she continues, and they walk out of the flat and down the stairs. Mike opens the door to the outside. As he does so, a chill surges through it, and Amanda shivers and pulls her coat tighter around her. She wonders whether she's really capable of going through with this after all. If she can't cope with a cold breeze in her clothes, how on earth will she cope with the Atlantic in December? However, she refuses to let doubt rule her today, of all days. She has always loved Christmas and she's determined to make today memorable for good reasons. It helps that she's been feeling a lot better recently, following the GP visit Rosie nagged her to make and the resulting prescription of HRT.

She'd felt a little light-headed on it at first, but over the past week she's noticed she's been sleeping better and last night she had felt desire for the first time in months. Not that she'd acted on it, because they'd been kept busy with a special Christmas Eve dinner with the monks and afterwards, midnight mass, but the fact she'd felt it at all feels like a breakthrough.

Mike sets off at pace towards the steps that lead to the cove, in an attempt, Amanda suspects, to warm up. She has to do a light jog to keep up with him.

'Sorry, love. I just want to get this over as soon as possible,' he says, with a twinkle in his eye. She's glad to see it. Although she's been wrapped up in her own worries, she has noticed that he's often looked like he's had the weight of the world on his shoulders. She knows that poor mental health runs through his family, and so she's watchful. It's good to see him look mischievous for a change.

She smiles at him and they both run to the top of the path and walk down the steps carefully but quickly. As they near the bottom, she hears the unmistakable sound of Christmas carols. At first she thinks Rosie has somehow magicked up a choir to entertain them, but then she spots a small group of people sitting on camping chairs, surrounding a small portable speaker.

'You made it!' Rosie shouts, getting up and running over to her friend and embracing her. She's wearing a Dryrobe and a bright red and white Santa hat. 'And you came too, Mike,' she adds. 'How wonderful.'

'I couldn't let my wife head off alone, this day of all days,' he says. 'Although I do think you're all barmy.'

'Oh yes, undoubtedly. Come over here and I'll introduce you to my merry band of nutcases.'

They walk over to the little group. Amanda sees that they are all female, and definitely all north of forty.

'Everyone, this is my friend and colleague Amanda – Mandy – and her husband Mike. He's deputy head of Hallows Abbey.' The women all nod. 'Now, let me introduce you. So, this is Rachel,' says Rosie, pointing at the woman on the far left. 'She's a veterinary nurse, and mother of two grown-up kids and three very naughty greyhounds. And this is Sandra,' she says, pointing to the next woman along. 'She's a primary school teacher, she's ace at crochet, and she spends her free time, such as it is, skippering the RNLI lifeboat at Newquay. And last but not least, this is Ellie. She's the elder stateswoman of the group. She won't mind me telling you she's eighty next birthday. She has two ex-husbands and one very patient wife.'

Ellie winks at them both.

'Shhh, Rosie, don't you go making me sound like a strumpet,' she says, looking not the least bit perturbed.

'Right, introductions over. Shall we have a quick drink and then get to it.'

'Excellent,' says Rachel. 'I put the turkey on before I left, but I don't trust my daughter to baste it at the right intervals.'

'We won't be too long in there, don't worry,' says Rosie, dipping into a large bag for life and pulling out a Thermos flask. 'But before we go in, we need fortification. Normally we have coffee in here,' she explains for Mike and Amanda's benefit, 'but I've got my special hot punch today instead. It's got a bit of fruit juice in it but to be honest it's mostly rum.'

Rosie hands out plastic mugs, opens the Thermos and decants an inch or two of the steaming liquid into each cup. Amanda takes a sip and the punch fizzes on her tongue. She swallows and its warmth coats her throat and seems to spread throughout her body.

'Right, everyone, knock it back. Let's go.' Within seconds, Rosie's thrown off her robe, revealing a neon pink swimsuit, and she's racing across the beach towards the waves, her water shoes kicking up sand in her wake. Then the women on either side of Amanda and Mike do the same, and they are suddenly alone as the others whoop and holler when skin makes contact with the icy waters.

'I'll do it if you will,' says Amanda.

'Oh, go on then.'

They pull off their layers as quickly as they can, sitting down to remove their shoes and trousers, and then stand shivering together for a few moments, the sea breeze whipping around them.

'Oh my God, it's freezing,' says Amanda.

'You can say that again.'

'Oh, sod it,' she says, setting off towards the sea, aware that if she leaves it one minute longer, she'll chicken out. She doesn't even check whether Mike is following her. When her right foot enters the water, she finds it impossible to breathe for a moment. Then she gasps, and her teeth chatter as she reaches knee depth, then thigh. It's always at this point that her nerves fail her, even in the summer months. She pauses. She's about to back out, in fact, when Mike arrives at her side and plunges himself head first into the Atlantic's embrace. She realises she can't change her mind now. She takes a deep breath and falls backwards, the freezing water feeling like needles running up her spine. She yells. But it's not a yell of pain, but rather one of exhilaration. It's a yell of defiance against the biting cold, and against everything that's been holding her down and back, against her hormones and her age and her isolation. The other women are yelling around her also, and there's laughter, too; gleeful, belly-aching laughter. Mike is doing the same, and she realises with a start that she hasn't seen or heard him laugh for months.

When the initial shock of the cold subsides, it's replaced by a strange sensation of warmth. For a minute or so, Amanda's world is reduced to the rhythm of her strokes, the sting of the salt, and the roar of the waves. It is a communion with nature, a moment of pure, unadulterated freedom. She has always been drawn to the sea, lured by its raw power and beauty. But this, this is different. It's a test of will and spirit. This feels like a baptism.

'Right then. Enough, I think,' says Rosie, and her friend begins to wade back to the shore. Amanda and Mike watch the others follow suit, but they remain submerged for a minute or two longer.

Mike turns to her. 'I'm sorry, Mandy,' he says. 'I'm so sorry.'

'I know,' she says, realising that he really means it.

Later, when they have drunk more rum punch, dried themselves and pulled on their clothes with some difficulty, Amanda and Mike say their goodbyes and head back up the steps, aware they have to be dressed for church within an hour.

When they return to the coastal path, Amanda gladly takes the hand Mike offers. She feels the warmth of it spreading to hers and then it seems to transfer directly into her nervous system, making her feel effervescent. There's just no other word for it. She giggles as this unexpected wave of joy runs through her and he turns and looks at her in surprise, before pulling her close and landing a kiss on her lips.

'Merry Christmas, love,' he says, and she knows with certainty that for today at least, her husband has come back to her.

12

THERESA

May 1966

Theresa is passing one of the dormitories after breakfast when she hears it. It's a repetitive thud, followed by what sounds like a stifled yell. She acts immediately. She throws open the door.

'White! Shill! Blair! Stop it now!' She runs over to the end of the room, where there's what looks like a heap of clothes beneath a window. When she gets there, the heap reveals itself to be a boy. The three other teenagers scarper. 'John?' she says, lifting his right hand, which is covering his face. His eyes are bloodshot, and he's obviously been crying, but she's relieved to see that his face at least has escaped the kicking. 'Where does it hurt?'

Slowly, painfully, John pulls himself up to sitting.

'Everywhere,' he says with a whimper.

'Oh, John. Let me get you to the medical room...' she says, holding out a hand.

'No, it's all right. I'll be fine in a minute. There's nothing you can do for me in there, anyway.'

'I could give you an aspirin and find you a hot water bottle. And you could have a break from here, time to gather your thoughts.'

'What will I do when I gather them? Hit them with them?'

She is surprised by his anger. His very evident crush means she's used to him treating her with exaggerated respect, accompanied by doe eyes.

'Come now, John. That's not like you.'

'Well, maybe I need to get tougher. That's what they say, isn't it? That you need to fight bullies head-on?'

Theresa abandons her attempt to get him to stand up, and instead sits down next to the window, a few feet away from him.

'They do say that, yes. Although I'm not at all convinced that you should meet like with like when it involves violence.'

'Fair enough,' he says, sniffing. He still has his back to her.

'What prompted it?'

'Oh, the usual. You know the school's annual poetry competition? The theme this year is the World Cup. Well, I was asked to read my entry for it in class. But I did it in my silly accent, apparently.'

'It must be special, to have been chosen to be read out.'

'Well, that wasn't the consensus.'

'Does this sort of thing happen a lot, John?'

'The beating?' he replies, turning around to face her. 'No, not that often. But stealing things from my bag, desk and bedside table, spitting on my plate and whispering when I walk past – yes, all the time.'

'You really do need to report this to the headmaster. He would do something about it.'

'No, he wouldn't. I appreciate your concern, Miss Murphy, but those boys are stars on the rugby pitch. They're heading for the headmaster's first eleven. And they were unbeaten last season. He'd far rather get rid of me, I assure you.'

'That's not true. I'm sure of it.'

'Whatever you say.'

Theresa realises she's not even that certain she's just spoken the truth. Their headmaster is known for his love of sport, and she knows bullying in the school is rife. And despite his strange fixation with her, she desperately wants to help this confused, lonely boy, because he reminds her of her younger self.

'Look, just promise me one thing,' she says.

'What?'

'The next time this happens, you at least tell me about it. And for goodness' sake, come to the nurses' room now so I can check you over.'

* * *

Two hours later, Theresa pulls on her coat and heads out to the car park, where her friend Anna is waiting to give her a lift into Porthgerran. Anna's heading to the monthly market again, but Theresa has other business to attend to, business she simply cannot put off any longer.

The journey to the fishing village is mercifully quick, because Anna's driving has not improved in the five months since Christmas. Theresa is once again relieved to arrive safely. She wastes no time in stepping out of the car, arranging to meet her friend an hour and a half later, and heading off on her own in the direction of the market.

Except this time, she's not going to spend her time shopping. This time, she's on a mission. She eschews the stalls selling exotic fruit and children's toys and instead heads for the nearest pub, The King's Head, which is just off the main square. She pushes the door open and is relieved to see a woman behind the bar. She knows that pubs are masculine spaces but drinking dens in fishing villages are worse than most. Still, she'd have entered even if she was the only woman in the room, because she needs to find Trystan.

She hasn't had a letter from him since their ill-fated night away together in Falmouth, and this silence and her powerlessness in the face of it is driving her mad. She knows they parted on bad terms. She realises now that mentioning living together at that moment had been a mistake. She should have let him raise the issue first, and her unseemly jumping of this particular gun had caused him to bolt. Trystan, she realises, is a traditional man, and her attempt at circumventing the usual way of things upset him. He'd barely spoken to her during their bus journey back to Porthgerran, and he's not been in touch since. Not a single letter from him has been delivered, a marked change from before, when she could have expected to hear from him several times a week. She's been checking the pigeonholes at least twice every day, and she's sure that the receptionist, who's in charge of distributing their mail, has noticed.

And so she is here, in the village where he has lodgings, trying to track him down. She doesn't want to confront him, mind you. Men, she knows from the magazines she reads, do not like to be chased. Instead, she's hoping to find out where he's staying at the moment, so that she can write to him and explain. She has a whole letter composed in her head and he simply must read it, she thinks. He must.

She lets the door of the pub swing closed behind her as she walks swiftly up to the bar, painfully aware of the hush that descends, and the several pairs of eyes that are trained on her, as she does so.

'Hello,' she says, when she reaches the bar.

'Hello, love. What can I do for you?' The woman behind the bar is about fifty, with black and grey hair in a neat beehive. She's wearing a tweed jacket with a frilly white shirt.

'I was hoping you could help me with something,' Theresa replies. 'I'm looking for someone.' The men who dipped their voices when she came in have not yet resumed their conversations, she notices.

'Oh right. I see,' says the woman, obviously, Theresa thinks, a bit put out that she isn't ordering anything to drink. 'Come round the side. It's quieter.'

Theresa follows her into an area separated by a frosted glass partition marked 'dining room'. There's no one sitting in it. Obviously this pub is not somewhere people flock to eat.

'Look. My husband says all sorts of things to young women. I'm sorry if he's been up to his tricks again,' says the other woman. 'How much are you needing?'

'I'm sorry?'

'For the... difficulty you're in?'

And then the penny drops.

'Oh. No. It's nothing like that. Nothing to do with your husband at all, in fact,' Theresa replies, her face colouring from the embarrassment of being mistaken for someone in 'difficulty'. She's from Ireland, after all. She knows what that means. Her mother and aunts have muttered that phrase many times about a girl who's been sent off to a mother and baby home in a distant town, only to return several months later, a lot thinner and with a haunted expression.

'Oh, I see,' says the woman, shifting from foot to foot and inhaling sharply. 'In which case, I apologise. Ignore what I just said. What can I do for you?'

'I'm wondering where my boyfriend is currently living. Trystan... Trystan Trevelyan. Do you know him? And if so, do you know where he is? I have a gift to drop off at his lodgings...' This isn't true, of course. She has a letter to drop off. But she doesn't want to make it sound like she can't even communicate with him. She wants to sound spontaneous. Thoughtful. Not desperate.

'Trys? Yes, I know him.'

'Oh great. Do you know where he's staying at the moment?'

The other woman looks distracted, as if she'd rather be back behind the bar than helping Theresa with her quest.

'Trystan doesn't live in Porthgerran,' she replies after a pause.

'Oh, I know he doesn't have a permanent place here.'

'No, I mean, he doesn't live here. He drinks here a lot, yep, I grant you that, but he doesn't live here. I'd know if he did. And I haven't seen him for a week at least.'

Theresa is sure the woman is wrong.

'Ah, OK,' she says, deciding that going along with what she's told is probably the easiest course of action. 'Never mind, then. I'll ask around a bit more.' She starts to walk away.

'Try Truro, darling,' she says, as Theresa pushes the door open. 'Ask in pubs there. If he's there, they will know. And I say that with certainty.'

13

AMANDA

January 2025

A thick cloak of frost is enveloping the north Cornish coast, after a chilly night with a sky clear enough to see the finer details of the galaxy. Amanda's dawn dip this morning with Rosie and the other girls had been very difficult to begin with but absolutely brilliant afterwards, when they'd sat on the beach all wrapped up, gazing up at the heavens. Nevertheless, she is looking forward to being back indoors, in the warm.

'Come in. I've got a fire in,' says Frances.

Amanda smiles and walks inside. Frances' house feels cosier than Santa's cabin, and Amanda is relieved to be able to remove her outer layers and follow this friendly faced woman into the room she uses for counselling.

Frances is a little younger than Rosie, Amanda thinks, so in her early sixties, perhaps. She's also a little more conventionally dressed. She's wearing a pair of blue jeans and a grey polo-neck jumper, but a pair of long drop, sparkling earrings suggest a seam of vivacity within. Her face is delicately made-up with a sheen of light pink on her eyelids and the kind of nude lipstick that it takes a lifetime to find. She has the sort of demeanour you warm to immediately.

'Do take a seat. I'll just pop and make us a drink. Tea? Coffee? Water?'

'Tea, please. Earl Grey, if you have it. Black.'

'Coming up.'

Amanda walks over to one far side of the living room, where two high-backed leather armchairs each face the fire, which is blazing in the grate. She sits down and looks around her, taking in the red gingham curtains and the matching cushions which are scattered over the chair she's sitting on and two sofas in the far corner, which frame a large flat-screen television. A poinsettia blooms on the windowsill, still in its Christmas pot. The room has a homely feel, and it's perfect for this house, which is an old worker's cottage.

'How old is this place?' Amanda asks when Frances comes back into the room bearing a tray of steaming drinks.

'Oh, at least two hundred years old, we think. It was built for one of the farmhands on the local estate. The big house, as it were, was demolished decades ago, but this house remains. Thankfully.'

'How long have you lived here?'

'Going on thirty years now. We bought it when the kids were small.'

'Wow. I can understand why you stayed. It's so beautiful. And the views...'

Amanda had actually stopped for a few moments when she'd parked her car outside the cottage, because the view had been so spectacular. This house, on the outskirts of Porthgerran, seems to be perched on the edge of a hill which gives way steeply, with fields below plunging down to the sea. Hallows Abbey was just visible across the other side of the creek, sitting as it does, unshielded, on its own peninsula.

'Yes. It's difficult sometimes to get any work done. The view seems to change every time I look out of the window. That's why I counsel in front of the fire. It's pretty, but it's not too distracting.'

'A good idea.'

'Yes, I think so.' Frances places a mug of tea on a coaster on a table between them, and they both sit down. 'Now, before we begin, Amanda, I wanted to ask first of all, whether you've had any form of counselling before.'

'Oh, no,' says Amanda, sipping her tea. 'Nothing. Never.' Frances raises an eyebrow. 'Sorry, I didn't mean to sound proud of that. I'm not pretending to be perfect or anything. It's just I've never felt... like this before.'

'Like... what? Can you describe what you mean?' Frances asks, gently.

'Lost.' Neither of them says anything for a moment. Amanda stares at the fire. A log spits and wheezes. 'Even though I'm beginning to feel more at home here in Cornwall, I feel… like I've lost myself.'

'What have you lost?'

'My identity,' says Amanda, still staring at the fire. It's far easier to bare her soul when she's not looking at someone. 'You know, I was a mother. I was… needed. I was a wife.'

'You're still all of those things, though, aren't you?'

'Well, I'm still married. But most of the time now, it's like we're strangers. Or flatmates. We had one decent day together in the past few months, Christmas Day it was, actually, but apart from that it's like he's possessed by something, like he's someone else.'

'Why do you think that is?'

Amanda pauses.

'I honestly don't know. Stress, I think. The job is hard, harder than either of us thought.'

'Tell me about your role as a mother.'

'Well, our kids have now both left home. My youngest, Luke, quite recently. They're doing very well. Really, very well. So well they barely even send me messages now.'

Amanda thinks about the days they spent with Jules and Luke after Christmas, each of them in their own chosen city, living busy lives brimming with promise. She doesn't blame them for not wanting to come to stay at Hallows. She wouldn't have wanted to do that either, at their age. But it still hurts.

'That's definitely a difficult stage. I remember how I felt. But they will come back.'

'Will they?'

'Oh yes, they will. Not in the same way, of course, but they will always come back. If you want them to.'

'I do. Very much.' Words are powerless. They can't capture how much she wants them to come home.

'Let's return to your marriage. Why do you think things have changed with your relationship? And has this been going on a long time, or is it a sudden change?'

'Oh. Well, I think our relationship used to be quite good. I mean, the early flush of obsession fades, of course, but we've been best friends and, you know, lovers and partners in crime for a long time now. We've been together for more than twenty years. We met at university. And until we came here, I never doubted that we'd go the distance. But now... now, I'm not so sure.'

'How long have you lived here?'

'We arrived at the beginning of the academic year. My husband came here for a promotion. He's a deputy head now. And I understood why he wanted the promotion. But it was a big deal, leaving London. We were so happy there.'

'But you did it, for him.'

'Yes, I did. And I've done that so many times. We both graduated and unlike me, Mike always knew what he wanted to do. He went straight into teacher training and after that, got a job miles away from where we'd been at university, which was Surrey, by the way. I'd been feeling quite content in Guildford. We were renting a two-room flat and I'd got a job working at a local theatre and I felt, you know, happy. But then he got his first job at a school in Rutland. He'd grown up around there and his brother had died and he thought his parents might need him, but that didn't really work out – his relationship with them is difficult and his father is quite unstable – so we kept on moving. After I fell pregnant for the first time, well, I've been busy rearing our children. Who I adore, by the way. Absolutely adore...' Her voice catches as she feels emotion surging up through her chest.

'But now they've gone, and you've suddenly got a lot of time on your hands.'

'Yes. Although I've started a new job...'

'But even so, I expect those evenings and weekends feel different.'

'Yes.'

'Do you think there's a chance you're seeing your husband differently because of that?'

Amanda puts down her mug.

'I suppose so, yes. I mean, we've had someone else at home with us for such a long time. But I don't know... it does feel different between us, more different than I'd have thought it would. It's not just that we don't know what to say to each other – he just doesn't seem present any more. Like even when he's with me, he's not.'

'You said he is finding this new job hard?'

Amanda nods.

'Yep. I think that explains a lot of it, to be honest. The school is... Sorry, is what I say in here confidential?'

'Yes, of course. I know you were recommended to me by a mutual friend, but I would never break a confidence someone shares with me in here.'

'OK, good. Yes, well, the school is struggling for numbers. All boarding schools are these days. Except, you know, Eton. And this one is so isolated. It's not like there's an obvious catchment around here. The new headmaster is very driven and Mike always seems to be in meetings with him. And then he spends hours after he's supposed to have finished work poring over spreadsheets and sending emails. He's exhausted.'

'Well, that would certainly take its toll on anyone.'

'Yes. And I know that. I think I just resent that we came all this way for a job that he's finding so hard. Don't get me wrong, I *am* growing to love this place now... I enjoy swimming with Rosie's group and I've been gardening at the school and I really like my new job, but – oh, Mike is so different now. Things were better between us when we were in London. Well, mostly. I suppose even then I could see that things were changing.'

'What do you mean by that?'

'Between us. They were definitely shifting. And also... I... I felt different. Oh God, it's so hard to explain.'

'How old are you, Amanda?'

'I'm...' Amanda pauses, because for a brief moment she doesn't actually remember her age. She has to calculate it from her birth date. 'I'm forty-six.'

'I see. That's an interesting time, for a woman. A difficult time, for many.'

Amanda finds she needs to do something with her hands. She picks up her mug again and takes a sip before replying.

'Yes, I know. I thought I was too young for the menopause. But the GP put me right on that.'

'Ah. So, you've been to see a doctor?'

'Yes, Rosie made me go.' Amanda smiles, thinking about her friend and colleague's gentle and repeated insistence, and obvious concern for her welfare. 'They've given me HRT. I've been on it for a few weeks.'

'How are you feeling?'

'To be honest I felt quite spaced out at the beginning, but it's settling now. The progesterone is helping me sleep, I think, although the dreams are weird. But it hasn't fixed how anxious I am. And it hasn't fixed my terrible memory. The brain fog. Some days I just feel so helpless, as if everything in my life is disappearing down a sinkhole and I'm powerless to stop it.'

Amanda feels a tear form in the corner of her eye and begin to wend its way down her cheek. Frances reaches over to a table behind her, picks up a box of tissues and holds it in front of Amanda.

'Take one. In fact, take several.'

'Thank you,' she answers, dabbing at her eyes and wiping the tear away.

'I'm not a doctor, but I do know from my own experience that peri-menopause is tough,' says Frances. 'In some ways it's much harder than the actual menopause, which, to be accurate, is what we call the time after your periods stop completely. In peri, your hormones are all over the shop. Sometimes you've got masses of oestrogen and you feel like you could conquer the world, and other days you've got hardly any, and you want to become a hermit. And then on some days, the rage... Oh my God, the rage consumes you. I don't know about you, but I think it's the unpredictability that's hard.' Amanda nods vigorously. 'But the good news is that it's pretty great once you're out the other side.'

'Something to look forward to, then.' Amanda manages a smile.

'Absolutely.'

* * *

The abbey clock is chiming eleven when Amanda pulls into their parking space and walks up the stairs to the flat. It's a Saturday morning, and Mike is busy running supervised homework sessions over in the teaching rooms. Today, she's quite glad he's not home. She enters the bedroom and lies down on the bed, face up. The counselling session has brought a lot of feelings to the surface, and she wants to be alone. In fact, she needs to be alone, to process things.

Hearing Frances' own experience of the menopause had been a surprise, but also a balm. She's done some research of her own into the peri-menopause since being prescribed HRT, but hearing the older woman describe her own experiences so accurately felt validating. She realises that she may not actually be losing her mind, and she hopefully won't have to deal with feeling like this forever. And her marriage, therefore, may not be in the doldrums forever, either. Perhaps Mike's behaviour hasn't been that off, she thinks. Maybe her hormones have made her see problems where there aren't any? Frances says there is joy to be found on the other side, and she decides she'll cling to this. Hope is everything.

When her breathing regulates and her mind starts to calm, Amanda checks her watch. It's 11.15. She has an important video call scheduled for half past. She gets up off the bed, checks her face in the mirror, makes a cup of tea in the kitchen and then heads to the table in the lounge, where her laptop is waiting. She boots it up and replies to emails and peruses Facebook while she waits.

The call comes through exactly on time.

'Hi,' says the young woman, who seems to be sitting on a bed in what looks like a student hall of residence.

'Hello,' replies Amanda. 'Thank you so much for agreeing to talk to me, Joanne.'

'Oh, no worries. I don't have lectures today.'

Definitely a student, then, she thinks.

'Great. I just wanted to start by saying congratulations on the podcast. I really enjoyed it.'

'Thanks.' The young woman's face lights up. 'It's done so much better than I expected.'

'Is it your first one?'

'Podcast? Well, my first series. I'm studying journalism and we've done stuff for assignments but this was more of a labour of love. It's getting me noticed, though, which is great.'

'That's wonderful to hear. It's a great listen.'

'So you said in your email that you're working at Hallows Abbey?'

'Yes. I moved here with my husband last September.'

'How interesting. I tried to get current members of staff to talk to me for the pod, but I had no joy.'

'Oh, there are all sorts of rules here about not talking to the media.' Amanda hasn't told Mike she's talking to Joanne for exactly this reason. He's told her previously that the old headmaster and the abbot had both deeply disapproved of the podcast, much of which they labelled as 'irresponsible gossip-mongering'. But actually, it's this Amanda really wants to talk to her about. Joanne's research has thrown up several lines of enquiry which she simply can't get out of her head.

And that's not the only thing she can't get out of it. The other thing is those cries she heard, the ones Mike had dismissed as nothing. They are haunting her. There's a small part of her addled brain that wonders whether those cries were made by the ghost, or maybe the soul, of one of the lost boys. She knows this is an outlandish suggestion. She doesn't even believe in ghosts. But what, she thinks, what if it was one of the boys who died? And why is it only she who can hear their cries? Why couldn't Mike hear them, and why didn't any of the other people who live in the main building hear them and investigate? She wonders whether there's something she's supposed to find out, some secret that will help find answers to what happened to those boys. And she's hoping Joanne will be able to help her.

'Yeah, I know. Those sorts of rules make making podcasts quite tricky.'

'I can imagine. But you still found out some interesting stuff,' says Amanda, trying to hide how keen she is to find out more. She doesn't want to appear desperate. Or mad. 'You also investigated those stories about one of the teachers?'

'Oh yes, we did. I found out that Sean Milner, the school's head of English, had been diagnosed with cancer just before the trip.'

One of Joanne's podcast episodes had been dedicated to trying to find out more about this man. She'd discovered he was recently divorced, and had been told his cancer was probably untreatable. She'd also found out he had some sailing experience. The episode had stopped short of suggesting he'd committed suicide by scuttling the boat and taking the children with him to the bottom of the sea, but only just.

'Do you buy that theory? That he actually, knowingly, killed everyone on board, just because he wanted to end his life?'

Since she'd heard this episode, Amanda hasn't been able to get this horrific idea out of her head. She knows it does happen, of course. There is the famous example of the German pilot who was losing his sight, and flew his passenger jet into a mountain, and of course the terrible cases of parents killing their own children before they kill themselves. But she just can't imagine how anyone involved in teaching and caring for children could consider doing this. But if it had happened, perhaps this is what this lost boy is trying to tell her? It's a possibility she can't shake.

'Honestly, I don't know. It's not likely, I suppose, but it's an option.'

'They discounted it at the inquest, didn't they?'

'Yes, they did. But the whole thing was over in a day, and they didn't have any physical evidence to go on. They never recovered the boat. Or any of the bodies.'

This is true, of course. But even in her heightened state, Amanda is inclined to believe a coroner's opinion than wild accusations against a man who was probably just a great teacher with a horrible health condition.

'That was the other thing I was going to ask you about. I know that the absence of bodies gave rise to another conspiracy theory…'

'Can I stop you there. It's not a conspiracy theory that the boys were abducted. It's a genuine theory.'

Amanda is taken aback by the young woman's insistence. She has doubts about the official story about what happened, of course, otherwise she wouldn't be talking to Joanne, but despite this, she isn't gullible. She knows these things are minority opinions. It would seem, however, that Joanne doesn't.

'You genuinely think there's a chance the boys were taken to some kind of cult and are still alive there now, with changed identities?'

'It's possible,' says Joanne, sipping from a large tankard of what Amanda assumes is water.

Amanda thinks that it's also possible they were abducted by aliens, but it's not at all likely, either. She's beginning to side with the abbot's point of view that the podcast was full of lies. But still, she wants to ask one more question before she ends the call.

'Was there anything you heard about that you decided not to include?'

The young woman raises an eyebrow.

'There was one theory I wanted to feature, but I couldn't find any witnesses and it all seemed to be hearsay.'

Amanda's pulse quickens.

'I spoke to a couple of men who'd been students at Hallows in 1966 and they kept talking about this rumour that'd spread through the school after *The Towan* sank, saying a beautiful woman had sung when the boat was leaving the cove, and that this woman, like the siren women of Cornish legend, had somehow tempted the boat onto rocks later, causing it to break up. I mean, even if you believe in the supernatural, this sounds mad, but some of the boys saw the boat leave and heard this, apparently. Not that I was able to track them down, though. And because I couldn't find out more, I didn't use it.'

Amanda's heart sinks. She doesn't believe in singing mermaids. She thanks Joanne for her time and pushes the lid of the laptop shut. She sits there for a while, trying to reconcile what she's just been told with this strange feeling she has that she's meant to find out something about the accident. Could there be any truth in any of Joanne's wild theories? She doubts it. And yet she can't quieten the cries she heard. They keep on playing in her mind, day and night. How, she wonders, will she ever silence them?

14

THERESA

Early June 1966

The sun is setting on the most glorious summer's day they've seen so far this year, but Theresa has been impervious to its beauty since it rose, and actually, even before that. She's been so preoccupied, in fact, that even an unpleasant outbreak of a highly infectious vomiting bug and a lower fifth's dislocated shoulder haven't been enough to bring her out of the purgatory her mind is currently imprisoned within.

Because Trystan has been in touch.

After more than a month of radio silence which has caused both painful over-thinking and self-flagellation, he has finally sent her a letter asking to meet her tonight.

Despite her deep yearning to see him again, she's not sure whether to be happy or concerned about this turn of events. She knows they parted badly after their night away at Easter. It's obvious he was upset by what she now knows, after a lot of introspection, was a wildly inappropriate suggestion that they should live together. Why, then, she wonders, has he changed his mind? Has he missed her such a great deal, that he can no longer stand it? Because that's how *she* feels. Their separation has made her ill, both in mind and in spirit. She has little appetite and is struggling to sleep, and her colleagues have asked her several times recently whether she's unwell.

The other possibility she can't bear to consider, however, is that he simply wants to meet so that he can officially break things off with her, for good. And it's this possibility that is haunting her nightmares and her waking hours. Is she less than twenty minutes away from finding out he doesn't love her any more? she wonders. *And if I am*, she thinks, getting up from her dressing table and checking her appearance in the mirror, *if I am, how on earth will I deal with that?*

Theresa makes her way down the staircase and out of the side door, leaving a pebble in the door frame. As she does so, she thinks of John – her strange, sad admirer – and his insistence that she stop seeing Trystan. She wonders briefly whether he might catch her again this time, but then dismisses this thought. This is the first time she's gone out to meet Trystan from school since Easter, and she doubts John has the staying power to watch for her from a classroom window every single evening. He must, she decides, have given up by now.

A light breeze caresses her as she walks across the grounds towards the gate and then the path beyond. Its gentle force is in stark contrast to the tumult inside of her, the combined force of her devotion and her fear. And her doubt, of course. She still doesn't know where he's living. She didn't take the advice of the pub landlady and travel to Truro to try to scour the pubs, because frankly she doesn't know the city at all and she has no idea where to start. And anyway, she's going to sort it all out tonight. She's going to ask him to be straight with her. Her working hypothesis, after much thinking, is that he's probably between lodgings, struggling for work and embarrassed. It's hard, she knows, to be a man and out of a job. Lord knows, her father took a similar loss very badly.

Her heart leaps when she sees Trystan's familiar outline standing outside the old engine house. It takes all of her willpower to stop herself from running to him. She has missed him so very, very much. She longs to feel his arms around her. To feel needed. Loved.

As she approaches him, she examines his face. Even in the twilight, it's obvious that he's pleased with what he's seeing. She's very glad she spent the time making such an effort this evening. She's wearing her miniskirt, which she knows he likes, and her hair is up in a very on-trend beehive. She feels gorgeous, and the way he looks at her, the way he pulls her in tight, bending to kiss her with passion, tells her he agrees. They don't even speak; as ever, she thinks, there is no need to. He leads her wordlessly inside, lays her down and she offers herself up to him, gladly, feeling again, for the first time in months, as if her place in the world is secure.

Afterwards, they sit together up against a wall a few feet away, using his coat as a blanket beneath them. Their legs are entwined. Trystan pulls out a cigarette from a coat pocket, and lights it.

'Want one?' he asks. She shakes her head. Her father smokes, and she has no desire to emulate him in any way.

'I've missed you,' she says, emboldened by what they have just done.

'And I you,' he replies, with a wink. 'I'm really sorry it's been so long. Work has been a bit mad and...'

'I'm sorry about what I said about moving in together,' says Theresa, aware he's just making a polite excuse to spare her blushes. She needs to get the words out that have been running around her head since Falmouth. 'I know I... jumped the gun.' Trystan eyes her through a cloud of smoke, a smile spreading across his face. 'I promise to take it slower now. I know that's what you need.'

He leans over and kisses her passionately. He tastes of tobacco.

'I've been meaning to ask you something, actually,' he says, when they finally part.

'Oh?'

'I've heard that your school needs a boat, and skipper, for an outing for some prize-winners, or something? That's the word in the pub, anyway. I was wondering whether you could put in a good word for me?'

Her heart sinks, because a small part of her, perhaps even not that small, had been hoping he was about to suggest another night away, or even that they begin talking about – considering, maybe – their future together, properly. But then she chastises herself. Be sensible, she thinks. Why would a man who baulked at the idea of living together two months ago suddenly be up for that? She feels once more like the little girl who had worked exceedingly hard at school, but whose stellar school report was overlooked in favour of a note from a Sunday school teacher saying that she was 'wayward'.

She should know by now that there is a very big difference between her hopes and her reality.

'Yes, they want to charter a boat for a trip for the winners of the annual poetry competition. The usual company can't do it this year.'

'Yeah, that's it. So will you? Put a good word in for me?'

His expression suggests he's desperate. She knows he's short of work. How can she say no? She simply can't. Because she loves him, and she wants to help.

'Of course I will. But do you have a boat? At the moment, I mean?'

'I have access to one, yeah, no bother.'

'What boat are you working on currently?' Theresa tries to sound disinterested, but of course this is high up on her list of need to knows, after her strange encounter with the landlady at that pub.

'Oh, I'm here and there.'

'Are you still between those lodging houses in Porthgerran?' Theresa decides she has to persist. She has to, to quieten the rumbles of uncertainty she's at risk of being shaken by. 'If so, I could ask around the staff at school, see if anyone's got a room they could rent to you more permanently. If you need one...'

'I'm fine, thanks. All sorted,' he says, taking another drag on his cigarette before tipping his face upwards and exhaling. He watches the smoke rise towards the ceiling, as if he's seeking divine enlightenment.

'Oh, OK.' She considers letting things lie, before deciding that she absolutely has to know. She has to.

'It's just when I was last in Porthgerran, I asked around to see if anyone had seen you, and they said you weren't living there any more.'

Trystan stops smoking and stares hard at her.

'Why on earth did you do that?' he asks, his voice sounding uncannily like her father's, when he'd been reaching for the long wooden ruler he'd kept by his bureau. Her body and mind react to this question now as she had to his then; her guts churn and every hair in her body pricks up, ready for whatever hell is about to follow. But then something strange happens. She sees his face change rapidly, and all of a sudden he is her Trystan again, the man she knows.

'I was... missing you,' she says. This is the truth, of course. His absence in her life had felt like a physical pain.

'Oh, I see. Well, yeah, I moved away for a bit, you know... I had a boat in Falmouth I was working on for a while. That's why I was out of touch. But I'm back now.'

This explains why the barmaid knew him in Falmouth, thinks Theresa. This makes sense.

'Back in the lodgings house in Porthgerran?'

'Yeah.'

All thoughts of asking him about Truro disappear in an instant. Because he's being himself again and she knows a question like that will make her seem needy.

'Oh, that's good.'

'So you'll ask the headmaster or whatnot to contact me about the boat?'

And then Theresa has an idea.

'Yes, although I'll need an address for him to get hold of you. And a phone number, if possible.'

Trystan pauses.

'Yeah, good point. Look, I'll write an address down for you. It's my sister's place.' He pulls a scrap of paper out of his pocket, scribbles on it and hands it to her. 'She'll pass it on to me. She lives in Truro.'

15

AMANDA

February 2025

Amanda is in bed and asleep when she hears a very loud noise.

She is having one of her new disorientating, hallucinatory dreams and for a moment she thinks the monster of her nightmare is trying to burst in. A second or two later, however, she realises someone is hammering on their front door. She turns over and taps Mike on the arm to alert him, because he doesn't seem to be awake.

'Mike. *Mike*. There's someone trying to get in.'

Then Amanda is aware of other noises. Despite the thumping on their door, she can also hear the shrill scream of wind whistling through their windows and rain hammering on the glass. It sounds wild out there.

Mike throws the covers back and gets out of bed swiftly. She admires both his ability to sleep and his ability to function immediately, apparently transitioning with ease from sleeping to waking. By the time she's come to terms with her position in space and time, he is opening the front door. The racket stops abruptly.

'Mike. Thank God. I thought I was going to have to go and get the skeleton keys. I need your help. Urgently...'

Amanda is still pulling on her dressing gown in the bedroom, but she doesn't need to see their visitor to know who it is. It's Father Paul, the headmaster. Mike's boss. Mike's manager. Mike's keeper.

'What's up?' Mike asks.

'I've just had a visit from the head of St Anthony's House. He was woken about twenty minutes ago by an alarm going off. It was for one of the house fire exits. Then he did a check of the house, and some of the boys are missing.'

'How many boys?'

'About four. But that's not all, I'm afraid. When I was outside doing a cursory look for them, I saw there was a window open from one of the Wenceslas dorms. There are some boys missing from there, too. I've woken the other housemasters and asked them to check. But I think we can assume they aren't alone.'

'Oh. That's not good. Let me pull some proper trousers on,' says Mike, hastening back into the bedroom and grabbing a pair of tracksuit bottoms from the bottom of a pile of clean washing that's sitting on a chair in the corner. 'Some boys have absconded,' he says as he does this. 'Paul has asked me to help find them.'

'I'll come too.' Amanda is awake now, and she knows there's no way she'll manage to sleep, thinking of the boys out there in this wild weather. She pulls out a jumper, a pair of jeans and some socks from the same pile and throws them on. About a minute later, she joins her husband and the headmaster in their hallway, where the two men are discussing a plan of action. 'I've got the caretaker and one of the housemasters driving up the road towards the village. I've asked them to keep me posted on this,' Father Paul says, holding a walkie-talkie. 'It's the only way, given there's such an intermittent phone signal here. Oh, hello, Amanda.' Father Paul looks perturbed. Whether this is due to the presence of a woman, or an unpleasant reminder that his hard-working deputy head actually has a wife who he should really be allowed to spend time with, or the fact that he doesn't want more witnesses to this situation, she can't tell.

'Hello,' she says, ignoring his response and reaching for her thick winter coat and a hat. She doesn't care what he thinks. She hands Mike some similarly warm outer clothing and the torch which they keep beside the door, in case of power cuts.

'Thanks,' he says, smiling at her. She wonders whether he noticed his boss's tone and is trying to balance it out.

'Well, let's set off, then,' says Father Paul.

'Yes. Let's,' says Mike, holding the door open for his wife.

They all jog down the stairs – even Father Paul, who isn't in the best of shape – and are outside within minutes.

'Where shall we go first?' shouts Mike over the wind, which is whipping at their coats, salty spray stinging their faces. The school building is behind them, most of its windows dark. In front of them is what remains of the school grounds, and then beyond that, the coastal path and the cliff face. She thinks about the treacherous drop that's only metres away, and panic threatens to take hold of her, even though she knows it is incredibly unlikely that a group of boys who are used to walking on the coastal path would fall off it, even in the dark.

'Well, there aren't too many options,' shouts Father Paul in response to Mike. 'Let's head out to the path and see.'

Amanda shivers, not from the cold, but from her unease, which is growing by the second. The headmaster sets off, and they follow. Father Paul is at least ten paces ahead of them, his flashlight cutting through the darkness. She can only see Mike's face in the shadow cast by their own torch, but he looks worried.

They decide to head to the old mine buildings first. Up close, they look even more derelict. The recent wild weather has further eroded their industrial heritage. Opportunistic weeds have been blown away, revealing holes in the roof; the metal security fence panels – or at least, those that remain upright – are scraping against each other, sounding like squealing animals caught in traps; and a small and sparse tree, one of the few which have managed to spread their roots widely enough to survive the windswept weather up here, has fallen against a far wall. Father Paul pulls at the wonky door like a man possessed. Its rusty hinges groan and its wood gouges out the earth beneath as it opens. Paul scans the space with his torch. When they reach him, they do the same, but there's no sign of the boys. The building is empty.

'They might have gone down to the cove,' says the headmaster. He heads off in the direction of the gate without waiting for either of them.

'Do you really think they have? In this?' Amanda says to Mike, leaning in so he can hear her. 'What if the tide's in?'

'I'm sure if it is, they'll have just turned around and come back up,' says Mike. Amanda knows he's just trying to reassure her.

The wind whips and howls around them as they make their way down the steps to the cove, which the storm has made unusually slippery. She is relieved when they reach the bottom and find that the tide is still out. Images of their bodies floating in the sea have been invading her mind. They stand on the beach for a few moments and look around them. It's hard to make much out. Their torches only pick up frothy waves and shifting sands.

'Let's try the cave,' shouts Father Paul, his voice carried back to them by the wind. They follow him towards the entrance, aware that if the boys have come down here at all, it's the only place they could reasonably be.

They walk into the cave entrance and immediately the noise of both the wind and the rain is deadened. It sounds like a distant warning in here rather than a real and present danger. At first, Amanda thinks the damp, dark space is empty, but then she sees a flicker of light, at the exact same moment as Father Paul shouts, 'Here! They're in here.'

Amanda and Mike scale slimy rocks and heaps of seaweed to reach the inner part of the cave, about fifteen metres from the opening.

The scene that greets them is macabre.

A group of boys – Father Paul's torch light reveals ten of them, one by one – are sitting in a circle, all wearing their winter coats on top of what she suspects are pyjamas. There are candles in jars dotted around them and two mobile phones are balanced on the floor, lighting up a large piece of paper, the kind you'd be given for an art project. On it are the letters of the alphabet, and words, too, in each corner. Then she hears glass clinking against stone, and she sees one of the boys slip something into his pocket. Amanda knows immediately what they've been doing, because she and Mike did something similar once, back when they were young and stupid. These boys, she knows, are trying to contact the dead.

Things happen very quickly from this point on.

The boys start to pull at the paper, tearing it into small pieces, as the three adults approach. And then one of them bolts. He's about fourteen,

Amanda estimates, and he's sprightly on his feet. He's past them and heading out of the cave before any of them can stop him.

'Don't even think about it,' says Mike to the others. None of them dare to speak. 'Before we march you all back to the school and call your parents, and find wherever Williams has run off to in the vain hope of getting away with this, can someone please tell me what on earth you think you're doing here?'

Mike and Paul keep their lights shining on the group, and occasionally a boy stares right back at them, startled, like they are in the midst of an interrogation with a rogue foreign power. In the absence of speech, they listen instead to the whistling of the wind as it finds its way into the cave, and at the distant roar of the waves. And then one boy speaks up.

'We were trying to contact them,' he stammers, his voice barely a whisper. 'The boys on *The Towan*. We wanted to find out where they are. What happened. Like, you know, they say a siren called to them from this cave.'

Amanda expects Father Paul to come right back to him on this, telling him not to be ridiculous. She knows that the Catholic Church absolutely abhors any kind of spiritualism. But he doesn't say a word. There is a very uncomfortable silence.

And then Mike says, 'Let's get you all back to school, and we can talk about it there, in the warm.' He sounds remarkably calm. Certainly calmer than Amanda feels. She's jittery. Understandable, of course, given the dreadful weather and such an injection of adrenaline when she should be asleep, but also, she thinks, because the supernatural has found its way into this eerie place. Her own unexplained experiences at Hallows Abbey are suddenly writ large in her mind.

The boys spring up one by one, responding positively, it seems, to Mike's suggestion. A chance to get warm must seem appealing at least, she thinks, although who knows what punishment Father Paul will have in store for them afterwards. Amanda looks over at the headmaster, interested to see how he's reacting to Mike's intervention.

But he isn't even looking in their direction. Instead, his eyes are fixed on a spot on the rock face opposite, near where a lit tea light is still flickering. And as the boys file out with Mike, he doesn't move.

'Father Paul?' she says, concerned. They will need several adults to escort the boys back to school, and she's also worried that the headmaster is having some kind of seizure. She's met him many times since they arrived last September, and he's never behaved like this before.

'Yes?' he answers after a pause, his eyes still apparently trained on the rock face. She can't see his face in any detail, and wishes she'd brought her own torch.

'Are you coming?'

'In a minute,' he replies. 'You go ahead with Mike. I'll follow.'

And so she has no choice but to leave him alone in the cave, and return to the wild weather outside, to bring up the rear of Mike's slow, silent and dogged parade of errant boys.

16

THERESA

4 July 1966

The sun is beating down on Hallows Abbey, and the Atlantic is shimmering under a relentless blue sky. The air outside is heavy, thick with the scent of dry grass and the brine of the sea, and indoors, it's almost unbearable.

Theresa decides to leave the window of her room open to try to encourage a breeze. She shuts her door and walks down the corridor towards the hall where they hold their assemblies. She hears some boys talking. She doesn't need to listen too closely to know what it's about: the World Cup is just days away, and anticipation is surging through the school like an electric current, making the air crackle. The boys have been swapping predictions about England's chances at breakfast, lunch and supper, full of rebellious hope. When they're released from lessons, they surge outside and act out the goals they expect to see, running in exaggerated arcs, kicking imaginary balls into goalposts as if they're actually there, on the pitch at Wembley. Many of them have even entered the school's poetry competition this year because it's celebrating the World Cup, even if they despise their English classes. Partly because the prize is an afternoon off school, and a boat trip to boot.

A boat trip, she now knows, which will be skippered by Trystan. He wrote to tell her, to thank her, two weeks ago. He'd also arranged to meet her a few days later, and it had been a wonderful reunion. It had felt as if they'd gone back in time, back to the early days. She is so pleased she has been able to help him find some work, even though she knows it's just one trip out. He won't say where else he's working, but she suspects he's not in regular employment. Things must be tight.

'Now, boys, I know there's been great excitement about this...' says Father Crispin, the abbot and headmaster of Hallows Abbey, when the school is assembled in the hall. A flutter of excited whispers sweeps across the assembled boys, sitting in neat lines, legs crossed, on wooden floorboards. Only the sixth formers are allowed the comfort of chairs at the back of the room. 'It is my great joy to announce the winner and runners-up of our special World Cup poetry competition. I know you worked hard on your entries and that you all want a spot on our special boat trip. Unfortunately, there can only be ten winners, as you know, so without further ado, I'd like to invite Mr Milner, head of English, to announce who's going to be going on the trip.'

A thin man in his late forties with a moustache and a neat side parting climbs onto the stage and walks over to the microphone.

'Thank you, Father Crispin,' he says. 'Now then, let me retrieve the list.' He pulls a folded piece of paper out of his pocket. 'After much deliberation, the English department has decided,' he says, unfolding it slowly for effect, 'to name John Stark of Amadeus House as the overall winner of this competition for his excellent poem "A Cup of Summer". We are also going to award the nine runners-up places on the boat trip to David Blakeley, Stephen Ainsworth and William Woodward, all from Wenceslas, and then from St Anthony's...'

As he reads out the names of the rest of the boys, Theresa searches the crowd for John. She finds him after a minute, sitting halfway back. He's not smiling, however, despite this wonderful news. If anything, she thinks, he looks scared.

'Now, John, if I can ask you to come up and read your poem for everyone?' the teacher says.

John takes several tortuous seconds to show any sign he might be about to move. And yet he does, slowly and painfully, looking to Theresa as if he is heading to the scaffold and not to receive praise. She realises how he must be feeling. Last time, when he'd read his poem out in class, the boys had bullied him for it. And now he's going to have to read it in front of the whole school. Winning this will only make the bullying worse, she realises. Poor, poor John. 'I have a copy here for you. Here you go.' Mr Milner hands an A4 piece of paper to him and retreats. John walks slowly towards the microphone. It's so silent in the hall, Theresa can hear herself breathing. And then he begins to read, in his lilting West country accent:

> I can't bear the weight
> of the classroom.
> Outside feels brighter—
> this Cup, it's lighter,
> this hope that England will rise.
> There's talk in every corner,
> faces alive with certainty—
> I listen from the sidelines.
> I watch games in my head.
> I imagine the glory.
> And yet, it's not just
> the game I long for—
> It's the shared breath,
> the silence before the roar,
> the thought that for once,
> we might be more
> Than we are.
> It might not be ours,
> this fleeting glory.
> But for now,
> there is hope,
> and the thrill
> of a summer story
> yet to be written.

No one moves for a moment. There is absolute silence. And then, one by one, the staff start to clap enthusiastically, and most of the boys follow. There are even cheers. Theresa looks over at John's year, wondering if his tormentors, the boys she caught hitting him, are clapping, too. She locates them. They are whispering to each other, cupping hands over ears so their words can be heard over the crowd. She can imagine what they're saying, and she suspects they aren't exchanging words of praise. Back on stage, however, John is smiling, and she thinks it's genuine. Probably relief, mostly. It was a good poem, she thinks. He's a very clever lad. He deserves his scholarship here, of that there is no doubt.

* * *

The school morning proceeds as normal, but in the afternoon, it's the inter-house sports competition. It's always a great way for the boys to blow off steam after the end of the summer exams, and a last hurrah before the trunks come back out of storage in a couple of weeks and their parents come to collect them for the long summer holidays.

Theresa, however, is grateful that she's required to be in the medical room, and not beside the athletics track. Her instinct now is to want to be alone. She just can't bring herself to pretend to be excited about one boy beating another in the 100 metre sprint.

When the rest of the staff go outside after lunch to watch, Theresa heads into the abbey, gambling that the competition will take a while to get going, and that therefore no one will need her help for half an hour, at least.

It's much cooler in the church than in the rest of the school building, and she's relieved to find it empty. She walks to the front, and, acting on muscle memory dating back to her childhood, genuflects and enters a pew in one smooth movement. She kneels down in prayer. It's not the sort of prayer she was taught to say as a child, however. It's more like a free-form, one-to-one conversation with Jesus. She asks for him to help poor John feel happy and accepted. She asks for Trystan to find stable employment so that they can be together, properly. And she prays for her family. Even her father. A few minutes later, she stands up, genuflects and walks back out of the church towards her rooms. It's when she's passing the boys' toilets that she hears the crying, and she knows immediately who it is, because she's heard it before. She pushes the door open a crack.

'John?'

The crying stops abruptly, but no one replies.

'John? I know you're in here.'

There's still no reply, so she pushes the door open, confident that all students are supposed to be out on the sports field. She doesn't see him immediately. She walks along the toilet stalls, pushing each door open gently. And then the door at the end of the toilet stalls creaks, and John walks out.

He looks a state. His face is red and blotchy, but it's his nose that she notices first. Blood is dripping down his face and neck and onto his shirt.

'Oh, John. Was it them again? Was it the same boys?' He nods wordlessly. He's not even looking at her, she notices. 'You need to tell the headmaster. Something needs to be done.'

'No...' he says, still not looking at her. And then, all of a sudden, he roars, 'Nooo...'

Theresa takes several steps back.

'No. No. No...' he yells. She sees his fists clench and his whole frame stiffen, and it's then she begins to run.

Because she's seen behaviour like this before.

She knows where it leads.

17

AMANDA

February 2025

'Mandy? Mand? Can I come in?'

Amanda glares at the locked bathroom door. She retreated in here an hour ago, just after 5 a.m., fed up to the back teeth with tossing and turning. She's lying in a bath which is now going cold, but she isn't planning on coming out any time soon. She's exhausted, frustrated and definitely, *definitely* angry.

She hasn't been sleeping well for some time, but these days since the incident with the missing boys at the cave have been her worst so far. Not because she's been massively upset by it – after all, no one was hurt – but because the incident has set off a series of events that seem to have swallowed Mike whole.

For reasons no one quite understands, the absconding of the students has sent Father Paul into crisis. He's having what Mike describes as a mental breakdown. A response, Amanda supposes, to the incredible pressure any headteacher must feel when things go wrong. She's sympathetic about that, of course, but what she really wants to do this week – today, in fact – given that it's half-term, is to go on the trip they'd planned to London. To spend time together. To mooch around in the Airbnb they'd booked, to walk in the local park, to grab a coffee from the independent shop on the corner, to see their old friends, to have a long-promised lunch with her sister and most importantly, to see their children for a trip out to the theatre, as they'd planned, with great difficulty, around Luke and Julia's respective schedules. But now – now Mike is having to stand in as interim headmaster while Father Paul is off work, and so his leave has been cancelled. In fact, she suspects he might even be pleased to be put in charge. And the fact that her extreme disappointment is a product of something that seems to be benefitting her husband has sent her into a rage she cannot contain.

'It's locked,' she answers, enjoying this statement of the obvious.

'Yes. I know. Look, Mand...'

'Yes?' she answers, running her hand, its skin bloated with water, over her face.

'I know you're having a tough time at the moment.'

'Yep.'

'I know I moved you down here against your will, and I know your hormones have been giving you hell.' Amanda nods along to this, even though he can't see it. 'And look, I know us having to cancel our break together is bad. It's grim and I won't let it happen again.' She raises her eyes to the ceiling at this. She's heard similar promises before. 'But I don't understand why you won't go by yourself?'

Amanda feels a surge of emotion as she remembers the experience she had a few weeks ago, when she'd driven to Exeter on a Saturday afternoon to see an old university friend. She'd thought nothing of it. She has been driving since she passed her test first time at the age of seventeen and has previously driven herself and her children all over the country to visit family and friends with confidence. But this time, on this journey, she had suddenly found herself acutely aware of her own speed, the speed of the drivers around her, and the potentially devastating metal weapon she was in charge of. Her heart had raced, so much so that she could feel it; then she'd found it hard to catch her breath, and her chest had tightened. It had felt like someone had been trying to asphyxiate her. She'd had to pull over onto the motorway hard shoulder to try to regain her composure and had eventually managed to complete the journey in the inside lane, barely hitting fifty-five on the speedometer.

She hasn't told Mike about it. She hasn't told anybody about it, in fact. She's too ashamed. She can't quite believe that she, an apparently independent, strong woman, can suddenly be afraid of driving. It seems that she is, however. And that's why she doesn't want to drive to London by herself. She's petrified the same will happen again.

'It's a long drive,' she says, finally. 'And I'm already really tired.' This is at least true. She feels like a zombie.

'Well, how about we buy you a train ticket?'

'But aren't they hugely expensive, especially when you buy them on the day?'

'Yeah, probably. But don't be daft, we've got plenty of money now I'm in this job. I'll go and book you one now. If you want me to.'

For the first time since the early hours, Amanda softens.

'Yes please. Thank you,' she says, hauling herself out of the bath.

* * *

It's early evening when the train creeps into Paddington Station, past rows of terraced houses built for labourers but now worth at least half a million pounds each; past concrete overpasses and canals lined with houseboats with smoke snaking out of metal chimneys; past graffitied warehouses redeveloped into artists' studios and luxury loft apartments with a view of London's bright knots of rail. With every familiar sight, Amanda's heart grows more full. *I'm back*, she thinks. *I'm back home.*

Half an hour later, the District Line is packed, and Amanda is forced to stand in a sweaty corner with her hastily packed wheely bag. And yet even this doesn't dull her excitement. The familiarity of this experience, uncomfortable as it is, is reassuring to her. She used to take this line all the time when they lived in the city. Then the recorded announcement sings, 'Ravenscourt Park,' and she squeezes past her fellow passengers and onto the platform. When the train departs, she follows everyone else up some steps and through the barriers at the ticket hall. They'd lived a few stops away from here, so this station and this area are new territory for her. When she emerges from the station, she pulls her phone out to consult the Airbnb confirmation email for the address. She finds it and is about to open the maps app to help her find her way to the apartment they've booked when there's a swift movement out of the corner of her eye, followed by a tug and a whir.

In less time than it would take her to swallow, someone has ridden past her on an e-bike and snatched her phone. They are already several hundred metres down the road and turning right.

Amanda can't even find the energy to scream for help, or for them to stop. She just tumbles down to the floor, raging against the world.

* * *

'Oh my God! So what happened next?'

It's the following day, and Amanda's sister, Emma, has come to visit her at the rental apartment, rather than going out for lunch with her, as they'd originally planned.

'Oh. It was dreadful. I just fell to pieces. A nice woman who worked in the tube station heard me and called an ambulance. It was so embarrassing. They had to sit with me for about an hour, eventually diagnosing a panic attack. They said I should see my doctor about anti-anxiety medications. And I just felt like the biggest time-waster in history.'

'You poor thing. Did the police come?'

'Oh, yes. They did. They called Mike for me, actually, and then they helped me get here and then they took a statement. They were very caring. Not that they'll be able to do anything. Apparently, there's an epidemic of this sort of thing at the moment. Organised gangs. They target tourists, people off their guard.'

'Dreadful. Was it insured?'

'The phone? Yes. But it's just a total pain. It's so discombobulating being without your smartphone, especially so far from home.'

Amanda thinks about their little, wild corner of Cornwall and feels an unexpected pang.

'But you've got a temporary solution now?'

'Yes. I took the police's advice and bought a cheap brick phone and a pay as you go SIM, so at least everyone can contact me until I get my replacement.'

'Well, that's something, I suppose. But I do feel for you. It must have been awful.'

Amanda eyes her sister. She and Emma, five years her senior, have always had what Amanda would refer to as a need-to-know relationship. They've never been openly hostile with each other, but she would not describe them as friends. They're too different for that. And in recent years, since their mother's descent into Alzheimer's and Emma's de facto role as a carer, entirely due to her proximity and Amanda's lack of it, things have been what you might even describe as *frayed*. And since their mother's death, their shared grief hasn't helped mend things. If anything, Amanda just feels more guilty she wasn't around enough.

'Thank you. It hasn't been great.'

This, of course, is an understatement. When the police had finally left and she'd managed to persuade Mike she was all right and that he didn't need to immediately drop everything and come up to see her, she'd had a quick shower and got into bed. She'd been so tired she'd expected to fall straight to sleep, but she hadn't. She had lain awake for hours. She'd been alert to every sound, and being London, there had been many: police sirens; drunken revellers; fighting cats; mating foxes. She had realised, with a start, that these noises were no longer her nightly lullaby, and that she now felt, unexpectedly, like a stranger in the city she'd once called home. And she'd actually thought, lightly, jauntily, as if acknowledging it properly it would mean she'd have to think more about it: *I miss the sound of the sea.*

'So you're set up now, and able to enjoy your break?'

'Oh, yes.'

In truth, this feels like a long time away and Amanda is now really not sure how she's going to fill her time, apart from the trip out with Julia and Luke. They've already said they'll come to collect her from the flat for that. The thing is, going out on her own now feels very frightening. But she has no intention of telling her sister that.

'Great. Now, shall I heat up the lunch I brought?'

Amanda checks her watch and realises it's half past one. She'd registered that Emma had entered with a bag of food and she remembers saying thank you, but she doesn't even remember what there is, or where she put it.

'Oh... Sorry. Let me.'

'No, it's fine.' Her sister stands up and pats Amanda on the knee. 'I'll sort it.'

Amanda takes a moment to get herself together, before following Emma into the flat's tiny galley kitchen.

'Thank you for this,' she says, arriving to find her transferring a quiche to a baking tray and laying salad vegetables out on the counter.

'Oh, no problem.'

'So... how are you doing?' This simple question has triggered anger in her sister in the past – a symptom of her very real burden, of the toll caring had taken on her. Even when Amanda and Mike had lived in London, the journey out to rural Sussex to see their mum had taken about two hours, and so she had never been able to take on a regular caring role.

'I'm all right. Getting used to all the free time I have. It's very strange. I might even go back to work. Jim suggested it. He says I've got too much time to think.'

Emma had been a local TV journalist for years, until she'd had several failed rounds of IVF in her late thirties, and decided she needed to take a break for her health. Fortunately, her husband Jim is a very well-paid surveyor, and she has never needed to return to the workplace to make ends meet.

'That might be a good idea,' says Amanda. 'I felt a bit lost until I got a job in the medical room at Hallows. But I really enjoy having the structure. What will you do?'

'Oh God, I don't know. Not journalism. Well, not in a newsroom, at any rate. I don't think I could face it.'

This surprises Amanda. She's always thought of Emma as the confident one, the one who has talent and a plan. She knows that not being able to have children must have taken a toll on her, but she never asks about it. She knows if Emma wanted to talk about it, she would.

'Fair enough.'

'I miss her, you know. I miss Mum,' says Emma, her eyes filling with tears.

'Me too,' says Amanda, slightly startled. 'I did appreciate everything you did for her, you know. I really did. I wish I've been able to help more...' Amanda finds that she is also crying.

'Oh, Mand,' says Emma, abandoning her food preparation and wrapping her arms around Amanda.

They stand together in silence for a moment, as Amanda gulps down her tears.

'Sorry,' Amanda says as they part. She sits down on a stool by the breakfast bar and dabs her eyes with a tissue.

'Don't be,' says Emma, resuming her task at the chopping board. 'I know it's been tough for you. Mike told me.'

Amanda's head snaps up. 'He did?'

'Uh-huh. He called me this morning actually, to check if I knew about the theft of your phone, but also to tell me how difficult you've been finding things.'

'Oh.' Amanda is conflicted. She's glad he's concerned about her, but also annoyed he's told her sister. He *knows* they're not close.

'Don't be cross with him, Mand. He's just worried about you. He thought talking to me might help. He asked me about my experience of the menopause. Women who share the same genetics often have the same experience.'

Amanda looks at her in surprise. 'Oh... I see.'

'And I had a bloody awful time of it, to be honest. And from the sounds of it, you're having similar. So I've also bought these,' she says, pulling out a box of chocolate truffles from the shopping bag on the counter. 'And this,' she adds, placing a bottle of Prosecco beside it. 'So I think we're all set for a very therapeutic afternoon.'

* * *

'Well, that was absolutely wonderful,' says Amanda. 'Thank you so much for coming all this way to see it with me, darlings.'

'You know how much I love classic musicals, Mum. You can't keep me away. And also, you paid.'

Amanda lands a playful kiss on nineteen-year-old Luke's cheek and takes the arm he offers her. Twenty-one-year-old Julia, meanwhile, walks alongside them as they head in the direction of Covent Garden.

'What next?' Julia asks.

'I dunno. Cocktails?' suggests Luke.

'On a student budget?' says Amanda with a wink.

'Well...'

'I'm only kidding. I'll pay, if you find us somewhere to go that doesn't play music so loud I can't hear myself think.'

Ten minutes later, they are ensconced in a booth in a dimly lit, plushly decorated bar tucked down a dark side alley which would have given Amanda palpitations if she'd been walking alone, but she'd been flanked by her children, and they had felt like armour. She has ordered a Long Island iced tea and is sipping it slowly.

'So, tell me, both of you. What have you been up to since Christmas? How are Bristol and London?'

'Oh, I've been working shifts in our local corner shop, mostly, when I haven't been studying,' says Julia. 'And wondering how on earth we're going to continue paying for our flat after the MA's done, given the cost of renting around these parts.'

'I wish we still lived up here,' says Amanda. 'You could have lived at home.'

'Yes, I could have.' Julia says this with a smile but without enormous enthusiasm, and Amanda understands at this moment that her daughter has taken one more step away from her. It's a process of separation that begins so slowly that you don't really notice, she thinks, until incremental steps that start in toddlerhood become gigantic leaps. One minute you're desperate for some time alone to go to the toilet, and then in what feels like seconds later, you're desperate for someone to actually need you. 'How's Dad?' Julia asks, as if trying to make up for what she's just said.

'Oh, you know... Like he was at Christmas, really. Still working too hard.' Amanda picks up her drink and takes a sip. 'I think he's loving the challenge. But it's just... a lot. He's very tired.'

She doesn't want to tell them how much she's worrying about him. Although both Luke and Julia are legally adults, she doesn't want them to worry about their dad. That's her load to carry, not theirs.

'Well, Julia might not have any, but I've got news,' says Luke, and Amanda is glad of the distraction. 'I've got a boyfriend.' His face lights up.

'Oh, that's wonderful.' Luke came out to them both when he was fifteen. He'd been nervous about their reactions, but she's proud of how both she and Mike reacted. They'd always suspected he was gay, anyway. And thankfully, their own personal brand of Christianity is far removed from that of the older generation, or the monks at Hallows Abbey, for that matter. She and Mike believe that love is love, wherever you find it. It's taken a while for Luke to find someone special, however. This is his first proper boyfriend. And she knows that her son is like her. He's always pretended he was fine having fun and being independent, but at heart, he needs to feel loved.

'You kept that quiet, little brother,' says Julia.

'I don't tell you my secrets. You've always been rubbish at keeping them.'

'Fair enough.'

'So, tell me all about him,' says Amanda. 'What's he like?'

'Oh, he's... He's lovely. He's called Ben.'

'Is he fit?'

'Julia!' chides Amanda with a smile. But she's enjoying the banter. Goodness, how she has missed the banter.

'Yeah, but is he though?'

'I think so,' replies Luke.

'Is he a student, too?'

'Yeah. He's doing architecture. So I'm hoping he'll be able to keep me in the manner to which I've become accustomed.'

'Sounds very sensible,' replies Amanda. 'Seriously, Luke, I'm delighted for you.'

'Thanks, Mum,' he says, grinning. 'And I wanted to say, I'm so sorry I didn't come to see you and Dad at Christmas. I had to work around it, as you know, but I had the opportunity to spend the day with Ben instead and I'm so sorry... I took it. I've been feeling guilty for months.'

Amanda gulps down a lump in her throat. Partly because he's acknowledging her secret pain, but also that he's just moved another step away from her, just like his sister.

She looks at him, however, and she simply can't be sad about it. He is radiating joy, and Julia, sitting next to her, looks equally at ease with her place in the world. We've brought up two fabulous humans, she thinks. Two brilliant people. And she knows they love her. She can feel it. They don't live together any more, and most likely will never again, she thinks, but this love, this *brilliant* love – it'll always be here, she realises.

'Oh don't be,' says Amanda. 'We don't have much room, anyway. Although you can always stay in one of the guest rooms at the abbey. And the beaches are lovely. Did I tell you I've joined a sea swimming group? I actually persuaded Dad to get in the sea with me on Christmas Day.'

Both kids snort with surprise and delight, and Amanda enjoys filling them in on the good bits about their new life: her new job, her new friends, the joy of living by the sea. She doesn't mention the other things, of course: the tough emotional time she's been having; the difficulties she and Mike are having communicating and connecting; the strange things she thinks she's seen and heard; the terrible night when the boys were found in the cave and the headmaster's subsequent strange meltdown. She doesn't want to put them off coming to see them. If they ever do.

'It sounds amazing down there, Mum,' says Julia, when Amanda's finished her summary of their new existence. 'I'll come down soon to see it for myself.'

'Yeah, me too,' says Luke. 'Can I bring Ben?'

Amanda wonders idly what the monks would make of a gay couple, and then decides she simply doesn't care.

'That would be wonderful,' she says. 'I can't wait.'

18

THERESA

10 July 1966

July tenth, nineteen sixty-six dawns bright and clear. Theresa pulls back her bedroom curtains and pushes her sash window further up, so that she can lean out. The air feels lighter today, less cloying, after several days of oppressive heat. She takes in the swooping seagulls, the swaying grasses and the gentle peaks of undulating waves on the sea, and inhales the salty air, still slightly cool after the sweet relief of the hours of darkness that have just ended.

This is the sort of morning that fills her heart with joy. She loves the warm, light months when the baked earth scents the air with sweet grass and the sun imbues her with its energy. And today is made even better, because later this morning, the man she loves will bring a boat to the dock in the little cove beneath the school to take the prize-winners out on their trip. She knows she won't be able to talk to him, or to acknowledge they know each other, but she is planning to go down to watch them depart. Just seeing him will cheer her.

After a perfunctory wash and tidy up, Theresa dresses and heads to the dining hall for breakfast. The corridors are unusually busy for this time of the morning; there's a gentle hum of chatter from the boys, some of whom are readying themselves for their trip out to sea.

Ahead of her, she sees Stephen Ainsworth, one of the prize-winners. The fifteen-year-old is lolloping along – his uneven gait the result of hip issues only spotted when he was a toddler – in the direction of the dining hall.

'Well, hello, Stephen.'

'Oh, hello, Miss Murphy. How are you today?'

Stephen is a lovely lad, she thinks. Always well behaved, always respectful. And from what she hears, quite the scientist. The head of chemistry waxes lyrical about him over lunch.

'I'm well, thank you, Stephen. Are you excited for your trip?'

'Oh yes, rather,' he replies.

They walk together companionably to the dining hall, where he bids her a polite farewell. He heads over to one of the student benches and sets about assembling his breakfast of tea and toast.

Theresa takes a seat in the staff area, next to an unsmiling young teacher of Latin called Brother Benedict, who has obviously decided he can't abide to eat breakfast with his fellow monks at the abbey. Today, she's grateful that he's not much of a talker. She pours herself some cornflakes and milk and sits back down, observing the boys as they enter the room. The youngest of them tend to come in packs, wary, she suspects, of the risk of being picked off by the older, bully boys. The older ones are more likely to come in alone, their age, height and experience imbuing them with a semblance of invincibility. A few minutes later, she spots another of the prize-winners, Christopher Taylor, come in and head straight for the fruit juice. He pours a large glass of concentrated orange and heads over to Stephen, who looks pleased to see him. She hasn't had cause to see Christopher much – unlike Stephen, he's never really needed medical attention – but he seems quiet and she knows from the other staff that he's bright. All the winners of the competition are bright, of course, she thinks. They all wrote lovely poems in celebration of the World Cup, all of them now adorning a cork noticeboard on the main corridor. John's has pride of place, as the overall winner. She thinks about the graffiti someone scrawled over it yesterday, changing the title 'A Cup of Summer' to 'A Cup of Jizz'. It was taken down and replaced as soon as it was spotted, but enough of the boys saw it to ensure the whole school has heard about it by now.

John, Theresa notices, is not at breakfast. *Is it because of this?* she wonders. She hopes not. Her own upbringing makes her feel concerned for his welfare, despite his strange behaviour and his outburst the last time they met.

He'd written her a note afterwards, apologising. He'd pushed it under her door. It had been short and tidily written. He hadn't tried to explain his behaviour away, but had just expressed, in his habitual, beautiful prose, his profound sadness at having upset her. And now that she's had time to think about what happened, she realises she overreacted. He's never been violent towards her or anyone here, she thinks. It's always been the other way around. It's just Daddy, she thinks... His behaviour has made her too sensitive to things like that. He's affected how she feels about many, many things.

Theresa finishes her breakfast and walks towards the door, stopping at the table where Christopher and Stephen are sitting.

'Are you excited, boys?' she asks.

'Oh yes,' replies Stephen.

'Even better that we're able to miss double Latin,' replies Christopher.

'To be honest, I'm more excited about the boat trip than I am about the World Cup,' says Stephen. 'The truth is, I'm not that into football,' he whispers, with mock concern. 'I'd rather read a book. But don't tell anyone.'

Theresa laughs, her first laugh in some time.

'I won't tell. Have a wonderful trip,' she says, tapping Christopher, who's nearest, briefly on the shoulder before she leaves the dining hall. Then she heads to the medical room for what she hopes will be a quiet morning.

* * *

At about midday, Theresa hears the school's heavy front door close, and footsteps walk around the side of the building, past the medical room. A few seconds later, through the windows, she sees a gaggle of boys and two teachers – she recognises them as being from the English staff – walking excitedly down the side of the school, in the direction of the coastal path.

She's glad that John is with Christopher and Stephen for the trip. They are definitely not brutish, bullying boys.

About twenty minutes later, the bell goes for lunch. She locks the room quickly and heads outside, in the direction of the coastal path. She checks her watch. It's twelve thirty. Hopefully, she thinks, she'll be in time to watch them leaving.

She leaves the school grounds and jogs along the path. When she reaches the top of the steps to the cove, however, she pauses. Staff have been told not to come here, in case it prompts the boys to head there too. It's a normal teaching day for most. She can't risk being seen and having to explain why she's there instead of the lunch hall. So, she stands as close to the edge of the cliff as she dares and watches and listens intently. She hears the distant sound of calls which suggest the boat might be casting off. She thinks one of them might be Trystan's. She glows with pride, thinking of him taking charge, of the passengers looking up to him, relying on him. A few minutes later, *The Towan* makes its way out to sea, dancing on the waves. As it does so, she hears what she thinks must be a bird crying overhead. It has a distinctive, plaintive song.

When the boat disappears past the headland, she turns and walks back to the school. She needs to eat some lunch before work begins again this afternoon.

After a disappointing meal of spam fritters and baked beans, she returns to the medical room. There are no boys waiting for her, so she spends some time filing medical records and cleaning the equipment. Then, she looks through the window and notices a tree which is behind one of the boarding houses. It's a beech tree, she thinks. A windswept, bedraggled specimen, and slightly brown after a lengthy spell of dry weather. It's now moving in the breeze, and she's relieved that there's a breeze at all, given how stifling the weather has been of late. And then she sees there are clouds forming. Only small clouds, however. Nothing that will ruin the beauty of the day.

An hour later, however, the windows in the medical room begin to rattle. Theresa looks at the tree and sees that it's now bent over, as if it's leaning on a stick for support. One of the monks scurries past, his habit billowing in the wind. She notices that the once small clouds have now exploded into dark grey towers.

Minutes later, rain starts to fall, with such intensity that it starts to leak through the putty that's holding in the panes of glass on her window. She stares at it in wonder. It's been so long since they had any rain. She's glad for the plants and the grass, but sad for the students on the boat trip, who must, she thinks, be drenched by now. She doubts they took raincoats with them.

A few minutes later, the rain stops, disappearing as quickly as it arrived, although the wind continues to blow fast and hard. She's not surprised: everyone who lives at Hallows is used to the strange weather the sea and the moors are able to conjure together. It's part and parcel of life on a peninsula.

At four thirty in the afternoon, Theresa is in the process of locking up her room for the day when she hears a familiar voice speaking to the receptionist who sits in the big hallway by the school's front door.

'What time did Mr Milner say they'd be back?' asks Father Crispin, the headmaster and abbot.

'He didn't. Well, he said they'd be back for tea. But that only started half an hour ago. Perhaps he meant supper?'

There's a pause.

'I wish I'd organised this myself. If I had, we'd know when to expect them.'

'I'm sure they'll be back soon, sir.'

'Hmm. Yes. Can you call the boat company?'

Theresa freezes, because she knows Trystan is the skipper of the boat, and she suspects he didn't acquire it through a proper boating company. What if he's taken them somewhere he shouldn't have? she wonders. What if he didn't understand how long they had allocated, and he brings them back too late? What if the school gets angry and refuses to pay him?

'I'll see if I can find their number, sir. Mr Milner gave it to me a while back.'

This is a surprise. Trystan has never given Theresa a phone number. Perhaps he gets work messages via a friend, she thinks.

'Good, good. Well, you call them. And look, I'm going to head to the cove to see if they've come back already. They may be just offshore, not able to come in, due to the tides or the wind. Can you send Rob, the janitor, down to help me? He's in the RNLI. We might need his advice.'

Theresa hears the headmaster leave at speed, the large oak door slamming behind him. And instinctively, she does the same, not stopping to talk to the receptionist, who passes her on her way to find the janitor.

It's only when she turns the corner that she realises how strong the wind is. Theresa finds herself leaning into it as she walks towards the school's boundary, and the coastal path beyond. Just before she reaches the gate, the janitor rushes past her, followed by two other men she thinks work in the school kitchens. She picks up the pace.

By the time she reaches the top of the steps that lead her to the cove, she's struggling to stand. She has to brace herself on the rock face as she descends. When she reaches the bottom, she sees the three men standing on the shore. As she approaches them, she sees they're all looking at something on the sand by their feet.

When she gets closer, she sees what it is.

It's a torn school blazer, drenched and dirty, and on the pocket is the Hallows Abbey school emblem.

PART II

PART II

19

AMANDA

March 2025

Amanda is making a cup of tea in the medical room when her new phone vibrates in her pocket. She pulls it out and sees it's a WhatsApp message from Mike.

> Emergency visit from Ofsted. Unannounced. Will be back home late. Don't wait up.

Amanda's been around education for long enough to know that a visit from the schools' inspectorate is never a stress-free experience. She also knows, however, that some warning is usually given for an Ofsted inspection. A sudden appearance is very unusual. She types a reply.

> Today? Don't they usually give more than 24 hours' notice?

Mike replies immediately.

> Yes. But this is about the incident in the cave. Someone's told them about it. So they're coming to investigate our safeguarding.

Amanda's heart sinks. She knows the school's financial situation is teetering on the edge, and that a bad Ofsted inspection could tip it over. All that's needed, really, is something that causes parents to lose faith with the school and it'll fail. And that would be particularly awful, she thinks, given how much effort Mike's been putting into turning things around, especially as the headmaster is now off sick. No one's seen him since that terrible night in the cave. Mike is now effectively running the school.

And the effort he's made since they arrived is now starting to bear fruit, she thinks. He's been fostering confidence and community, helping boys who've been struggling turn themselves and their studies around. He's spent several hours after school every week, on top of his normal workload, running his 'rewilding' club, and from what he's said, it's been getting results. And of course, if the school closes, he will lose his job, and they'd have to move again. And then she acknowledges for the first time a strange new feeling; that, despite their poky flat, she is growing to like their quiet corner of Cornwall. Maybe even to love it.

Her recent visit to London had left her somewhat deflated, because the city hadn't been the panacea for all ills she'd hoped it would be. In fact, she had concluded, as her train had raced through the Berkshire countryside on its way west, that she had felt like a stranger there. Even visits to old friends had simply highlighted how much they'd moved on without her, just as her life had done the same without them. In fact, in the absence of Mike, Luke and Julia, London had just felt like the crowded, confusing, exhausting metropolis it is. It no longer holds her heart, because it turns out that her heart isn't in buildings and busy streets, but in people.

Oh God, Mike is going to be utterly devastated about this, she thinks, dumping two tea bags in the bin and walking back into the other room, where Rosie is sitting at her desk.

'Ofsted have turned up,' she says, placing a mug of tea in front of her friend.

'Now? Without letting us know first?'

'Yes. Emergency safeguarding visit, Mike says. To do with the boys who went down to the cove.'

'Heavens. That's not good. Is he worried?'

'I don't know. I haven't spoken to him. But I know there's a lot he'll need to do and I know how hard he's found previous inspections.'

Rosie takes a sip from her tea and looks thoughtful.

'Look, it's almost the end of teaching time, and it's been quiet here today. Why don't you head up to his office and see if he needs some support. I know you've worked in school admin and he might want someone to talk to who isn't bloody Bede...'

Amanda smiles at her friend, who seems to know her better than she knows herself.

'Thank you. That's a great idea.'

Amanda leaves the medical room and walks up two flights of stairs to the management offices. As soon as she arrives on the corridor, she can sense nervous energy. Admin staff who usually work in a separate building are up here, crowding into a small room which is adjacent to the headmaster's office. She recognises Christina Newton, the caustic woman who'd given her the brush-off when she'd gone to see if she'd be able to offer her any work. She's in the midst of an intense conversation with another, younger woman, whose back is to Amanda. The door to the headmaster's office, meanwhile, is closed. On the right further up is Brother Bede's office, and his door is open. She can see him slumped in front of his computer screen. On the other side of the corridor is Mike's office. His door is slightly ajar, and Amanda can see the back of her husband's coat slung at an angle on a chair. She knocks.

'Come in.'

She walks in. Mike is sitting back in his chair, rubbing the back of his neck vigorously. He always does this when he is stressed.

'Oh, Mandy. Hi.'

'I came in case you needed help. Are you OK?'

His eyes dart towards the open door. He gets up and closes it, and sits back down at his desk, passing Amanda but not stopping to kiss or hug her.

'Umm... not really. It's all gone a bit mad here.'

'Yes. Are they here already?'

'Yes. They're in the boarding houses. And then they're coming up here to look at all our safeguarding policies and paperwork.'

And then Amanda sees it. It's not just stress on her husband's face. It's fear.

'What's up?' she asks.

He pauses, blinking several times as if he's trying to wipe away the nightmare that's currently dancing around his mind.

'It's my club. The rewilding club. I've heard them suggesting it's linked to the incident in the cave.'

'But you said it was a mix of boys who went?'

'Yes. It was. But the ringleaders were in that group. I knew that. Of course they were. They're the difficult boys, aren't they? Anyway, they're sniffing around it, checking my paperwork.'

'Do you know who tipped them off?'

'No. But word is...' he says, staring pointedly in the direction of Bede's office. 'He's never liked me. Or Paul, come to that.'

'Are you sure that's what's going on? I mean, your club obviously has the naughtiest boys in it. That's the point, isn't it? And you've done such good things...'

'Oh God...' says Mike, his head in his hands.

'Look, it'll be OK. Shall I stay with you? We can work out a plan together.'

He looks up at her, his expression unreadable.

'No, we can't.'

'Sorry?'

'We can't, Mandy. This is my job, and my situation to sort. You can't help me.'

'But I've always...'

'Not this time.'

'What? Why?'

'I don't have time for you at the moment. Let's speak later.'

And then she feels the rage again. It bursts out of her like a vicious serpent, and once it's out, there is no way she can contain it. She knows in the back of her mind that he's going through a very stressful time and she should try to be patient, but the disrespect he's showing her at this moment feels like the tip of an iceberg. He refused to believe she'd heard those cries in the night. He cancelled their family trip to London for his job. He went to mass rather than staying to help her after she was injured. She decides that she's had enough. How dare he suggest she's not knowledgeable or capable enough to be able to help him.

'I am not a student who can just be dismissed,' she says, sensing the heat of her own breath.

'Look, Mand. That's not what I meant.'

'Of course it's what you bloody meant. You're far too important now to need your silly little wife, aren't you?'

'Oh Christ, Mand, I don't have the time for...'

'Exactly. You don't have the time for me at the moment. Like you said. Not just today, but generally now. Am I right? Not now I'm almost invisible to everyone except other women of a *certain age*. Do you look at me and wonder where your wife went? Well, let me tell you, I've thought about you almost every day since we moved here. I've done nothing but think about you and how stressed and tired you are. How overwhelmed. I've worried about you constantly, even though I hate our minuscule flat and I miss our kids more than I ever thought possible.' They stare at each other in silence for a few seconds, their battle lines clearly drawn. Then Mike opens his mouth as if he's about to speak, but he decides against it. He simply looks away, at his computer screen, and stares at it fixedly. 'Right, well. I'll go. And I'll be out when you get back later. Whenever that is.'

Amanda turns on her heel and slams the door behind her, not waiting for Mike's response. And then she flies back down the corridor and the stairs, buoyed up by her own rage.

'Rosie,' she says, as she re-enters the medical room. 'Rosie, I need your help.'

* * *

'So he said he didn't have time for you?'

It's two hours later, and Amanda is sitting in Rosie's cosy sitting room in a cottage in a village a couple of miles inland from the school. She's nursing a large glass of red wine.

'Yep. And I just... blew up. I couldn't help myself.'

'I really don't blame you. Not on top of everything else you've been telling me about.' Rosie is sitting on the opposite end of the sofa. She leans over and holds out an open bag of crisps, and Amanda takes a handful.

'Do you think I overreacted?' Amanda asks. The fog of her earlier rage has begun to clear, and she's realising her reaction wasn't at all rational. But then, she thinks, he's never spoken to her like that before, has he? He was so off-hand, as if she was an irrelevance. 'Maybe it's just these damned peri-menopausal symptoms...'

'Well, you have every right to be angry, if you ask me,' says Rosie, gulping down a mouthful of wine. 'They can't get away with blaming everything on our hormones. If my ex-husband had spoken to me like that... well, he did, I suppose. That's why we're divorced.'

Amanda feels a tug somewhere inside her and fights a wave of nausea that races through her. *Divorce*, she thinks. *We can't get divorced. Not Mike and me.*

'He's been so stressed since we arrived,' she says, feeling suddenly defensive. 'He's so on edge. I mean, it's a big job. Bigger than either of us had imagined. The school is in a precarious state. Sorry, I shouldn't really be telling you this...'

'It's all right. No one who's worked at the school for a while could be at all surprised. I mean, that's why they had the shake-up at top, appointing the new head and bringing Mike in. They couldn't let Bede take over. He's part of the problem.'

Amanda nods. Mike's told her that Bede has consistently refused to go along with changes he's suggested, and even Father Paul's ideas. There have even been shouting matches in their meetings.

'He's almost unrecognisable from the man I knew, you know,' she says, tears welling up in her eyes. 'Mike is... Mike used to be... different.'

'In what way?'

'He was... caring. He's sensitive. Not that you'd know it to see him in action at school, of course, but he's always cared deeply about his students, his colleagues, me, our kids... He went through a lot, growing up. Things weren't easy at home.'

'Oh... I see.'

'Yes.'

'You don't have to tell me anything. It's OK. I know I'm another member of staff and...'

'It's all right. You're my friend, and I trust you.'

'Thank you.'

'The thing is, Mike never really got over his brother's death. He had an older brother, you see – Olly. Five years older. He idolised him. But he committed suicide when he was seventeen. It hit Mike very hard. His parents, too, and that was awful for Mike. It's like Olly's death was a massive earthquake. Olly's death split the family up, and they've never got back together. Mike and his parents have been shouting at each other across the resulting fault ever since.'

'Goodness. I had no idea.'

'No. He hardly ever talks about him, even with me. But I know Olly is on his mind a lot. He was a troubled boy, Olly. That's partly why he's been working so hard with the boys here, with the rewilding club... I think his brother's experience... It fuels him.'

'I see.'

'But now this... this issue with Ofsted. I think it could destroy him. He's worked so hard for this, to get where he is. And now it might just tumble down around him...'

'It might be OK, you know. The Ofsted inspection. I'm sure he had all of the required paperwork in place.'

'For the club, maybe. But if the school is doing everything right then how did all those boys get out without being spotted, so late at night?'

'They're teenage boys. They'll always find a way.'

Amanda takes another sip of wine.

'I suppose so.'

'One thing is certain. There's nothing you can do about the Ofsted situation now. Mike, Bede and Paul – whenever he comes back to work – will have to sort it themselves. You need to look after yourself. You're going through a tough time. It's hard enough moving locations, starting a new job and having your kids leave home. It's even harder when you're going through the perimenopause, and your hormones have no idea what they're doing at any given time.'

'Isn't that the truth,' says Amanda, grabbing another handful of crisps. 'Thank you so much for letting me stay here tonight.'

'No problem,' Rosie replies with a smile. 'What are friends for?'

20

THERESA

10 July 1966

'Call the RNLI, Rob,' shouts Father Crispin into the raging storm. 'Do it now. Run.'

The janitor doesn't need to be asked twice. He's halfway up the steps and racing back towards the school before Theresa even starts to process what might have happened. She watches him disappear over the top of the cliff and then turns her attention back to the headmaster and the two other men, who are now pacing up and down the shoreline and along the jetty, searching the water at their feet. She sees Crispin bend down and pick up the sodden blazer and run his fingers over it, as if he's checking its authenticity.

'Can you see anything?' he shouts to Theresa, turning towards her. She's taken aback, because she hadn't thought he'd noticed her. 'I've left my glasses at the school. Can you see anything out there? A boat?'

There's pleading in his voice, like that of a small child asking for a treat.

'Oh, umm...' she replies, loudly, not containing her surprise. Then she scans the horizon, looking for anything that looks unusual. But all she can see through the spray is grey wave after grey wave, rolling in ever increasing arcs, relentlessly barrelling towards the shore.

'No. Nothing, sir.'

Father Crispin doesn't reply. Then the two men who've been combing the shore return from their forays empty handed. Theresa sees them all exchange words, before they turn and head towards the steps.

'What are you going to do now?' she asks as they pass her.

'We're going to look from the top of the cliffs,' Father Crispin shouts. 'And then,' he says, leaning in so she can hear. 'And then, we are going to pray.'

* * *

The hours that follow will be etched into Theresa's memory for the rest of her life. The ever-growing crowd of both staff and students at the top of the cliffs, standing there in defiance of the storm; the sight of the RNLI lifeboat from Newquay, making slow, painful, dangerous passage around the headland, seemingly tossed around in the waves like a toy; the storm finally ending, giving way to an achingly beautiful sunset; and then the RNLI boat returning to base, finding nothing but a single floating lifejacket and one size eight lace-up shoe. After that, the crowd drifts back to the school buildings, none of them aware of what time it is, whether they are hungry or thirsty, or even where they're going and what they'll do when they get there.

Theresa returns to her room on autopilot, and it's not until the door is closed that she allows herself to consider what seems to have just happened. Up until this moment, the possibility that those precious boys, John amongst them, and of course their teachers, might be lost, and not just them but... Trystan. That thought has not been granted lodging in her space. But now... now that she's alone and the boat remains unaccounted for, that soaking-wet blazer haunts her. Did it somehow end up separated from its owner? she wonders. Is that boy still alive, trying desperately to float in that violent sea? Perhaps he took his jacket off? And if so, are they all still alive? But if they are, how are they coping without those life jackets?

And then she remembers the RNLI boat sailing past the headland, empty after hours of searching, and that vain hope begins to fail her. And another dreadful image comes into her mind, of a keel of a boat lingering for a moment above the surface, before sinking with an apparent grace so discordant from the maelstrom around it, taking all on board with it.

And... Trystan. Trystan at the helm. *Oh, Trystan.*

She falls forwards onto her bed and weeps, openly and without caring if anyone hears her, for both the man she loves and those poor boys and men, who only wanted a nice day out. The boys and men she'd seen leaving, full of joy and excitement, only at lunchtime.

Half an hour later, there's a knock at her door. Theresa pulls herself out of bed with some difficulty and goes over to the sink and quickly splashes water on her face. Then she answers the door. It's Michelle, matron of Amadeus House.

'Oh, hello, Theresa. I'm sorry, did I wake you?'

'No... No. It's OK.' Theresa realises with a start she can never tell anyone how well she knew the captain of the missing boat. It must be her secret, she thinks. Her own private grief.

'Oh, good. It's just I've had a sick boy with me all day. And he's asking for you.'

'I see. Who is it?'

'It's John Stark.'

'But I thought he was on the boat trip? I thought...'

'Oh, no. He was too poorly. He woke up with a migraine, I think. I mean, he won't talk to me much, but then, he never does.'

John is still alive, thinks Theresa, relief flooding through her. The fact that one life has been saved from this horrible, horrible accident, fills her with unexpected joy and relief.

'Give me two minutes to clean myself up, and I'll be with you,' she says, a burst of energy pulsing through her. She runs to her mirror and brushes her hair, ties it back neatly, pats her face dry and changes her uniform, which is soaking wet from the hours she's spent outside. 'Does he know about the... incident?' she asks, as she does this.

'The boat going missing? Yes. I told him. He heard boys talking about it in the corridor. Some of them were crying.'

When Theresa is ready, she follows Michelle through the network of corridors and through a series of locked doors into Amadeus House.

'He's in here,' says Michelle, pushing open a door on the ground floor. Theresa knows this is the house's sick bay, used to accommodate any boys who are off school and in need of additional care.

'John?' she says as she enters. For a moment, she can't see him. Despite the long summer evening, the room looks out on a bare brick wall, and so it seems like twilight in here. Then, slowly, as her eyes become accustomed to the semi-darkness, she makes out his outline in the bed. He's curled up in a foetal position, with only his nose and the top of his head visible under the covers.

'I'll leave you to it,' says Michelle, before retreating. She shuts the door softly. Theresa understands from her quick exit that she has found looking after John something of a struggle.

'John, it's me. Miss Murphy. Mrs Turner-Smith told me you wanted to see me.' She hears snuffling under the sheets, but he doesn't say anything, so she tries again. 'What's up? Do you want to tell me? Is it about... the boat going missing? Are you worried about your friends?' Still no response. She decides to sit down on the edge of the bed and wait until he's ready to talk.

She spends the next few minutes trying to shake off at least some of the horror of the day. She knows there's no way she can tell anyone at school about her relationship with Trystan, and so she needs to put as brave a face on things as possible, despite the gnawing ache she feels inside. And then she thinks of the boys, of Stephen and Christopher, of their wonderful bright young brains, the futures they had ahead of them. Because surely they must have passed away, no matter how many prayers everyone in the school has been saying. Surely they have, given that terrible, almost biblical, freak storm. She looks around to try to distract herself and takes in the room's sparse furnishings: the porcelain sink and mirror in the corner, the upright plastic chair, bare bulb hanging from the ceiling. What a room to go to when you're poorly, she thinks. Most children are able to convalesce in their own bedrooms, with soft toys, books and trinkets around them and regular visits from their mothers, mopping their fevered brows. This room, she realises, feels more like a prison.

'Miss Murphy?'

The sheets rustle as John pushes himself up in the bed.

'Yes?' she says, turning towards him. His nose is red and his eyes are puffy. *He looks like I feel*, she thinks. She waits for him to speak again.

'I want to confess.'

'You need a priest for that, John. Not a nurse.'

'I know. I know that. And I will. One day. But for now, you're the only person I trust, and I just can't bear it. I just can't...'

She waits for him to continue. It takes at least a minute for him to speak again, but she knows he needs to say what he needs to say, in his own time. She spent her entire childhood not being listened to, and so she understands well the power of being heard.

'I should have been on that boat.'

'I know that, John. But you have been spared. You felt ill, and weren't able to go, and that means you've been spared. And oh, I'm so glad. I thought you had gone... with the others. I thought...'

Theresa feels a wave of sadness sweep over her. She almost reaches out for John's hand, but stops herself just in time. John is still the strange boy who has apparently been obsessed with her. She needs to maintain her professional role, no matter how devastated she feels about Trystan's – she pauses while she considers the horror of the word she's now thinking of – death.

'Yes. I told Mrs Turner-Smith I had a headache.'

'And did you?'

'No.'

'Why? Didn't you want to go on the trip?'

John rubs his eyes.

'No, I didn't.'

'But you won a prize, John. And the other boys...' She pauses, the image of Christopher's happy smile that morning appearing in her mind without warning. 'The other boys were nice boys, weren't they? Not the bullies.'

'Yes. But that wasn't why I didn't want to go.'

'Why then?'

'Because I heard who they'd got the boat from.' There's a terrible, ugly pause. Theresa tries to process what he's saying. She knows that John had tried to insist she didn't see Trystan. But he can't know his name, she thinks. And he had only seen him at a distance. How could he possibly know what he was called? And how could he have connected the man she'd met at the mine with the man who'd been hired to take the boys out on a trip? She realises she needs to play this carefully. She's not sure how much he knows.

'You know somebody from the boat company?' she says, maintaining her ignorance.

'I do, yes.'

'Who, John? And why wouldn't you get on the boat?'

'Because the man who took them out – he borrowed a boat from a mate. Without permission, I reckon. That's his style. And I know he's about as unreliable and unsafe as they come.'

'I don't understand.'

'That's why you're here. I want to tell someone. I *have* to tell someone. I knew, you see, that my father was skippering that boat. Trystan. Trystan Trevelyan.' Theresa's stomach lurches. She had absolutely no idea Trystan had children. And then a new, horrible realisation sweeps over. If he omitted to tell her that, what else did he fail to tell her? 'There was no way in hell I was going within twenty feet of him,' John continues, unaware of the devastating impact his words are having. 'Not after what he did to my mum. She loved him but he cheated on her all the time. Some of them weren't much older than me.' He doesn't look at Theresa as he says this. 'He's very good at pretending, but he's a liar. And a drunk. He left us. That's why I changed my surname to my mum's, so I could disown him. And why I didn't want to go on that boat. I couldn't risk the other boys finding out we were related. They think badly enough about me as it is. So, I pretended I was ill.'

'Oh, John.' Theresa is dumbfounded. She had absolutely no idea. How could she have? And then she joins up all the dots. A wave of nausea sweeps through her, so strong that she retches, and she has to try to hide it with a cough. He's married. Or at least, he was. He might still be. So she's been having a relationship with someone else's man, hasn't she? And worse than that, a father.

'It's OK, Miss Murphy,' he says, sitting up further in bed. 'It's OK. I won't tell them about you and him. He used you. He uses everybody.'

Theresa turns to look at this boy, this wise old man in a young man's body. She realises with a jolt that she has been misjudging him. It hadn't been jealousy at all that had motivated him to keep an eye on her on her visits to the mine, had it? He had been trying to protect her. And if she'd done what he said long ago, and cut off contact with Trystan, she wouldn't have endured the terrible pain of finding out for herself about his duplicity. And here he is, wracked with guilt because he survived, when his friends didn't.

'Oh, John,' she says once more, and this time she pulls him into a hug. As soon as his head makes contact with her shoulder, he begins to sob.

21

AMANDA

Maundy Thursday, 2025

Amanda is exhausted. She's spent the whole day getting ready for Luke and Julia's first visit to Hallows Abbey. Her labours began with a huge shop at the supermarket, followed by a thorough clean of the whole flat, making sure to make room in the lounge for the airbed she's bought. They'll have to fight over the spare single bed, she thinks, remembering childhood wrestling matches in the lounge, which Luke had persisted with even when he'd grown more than a foot taller than his sister. Julia had always been impressive in these bouts, using her short stature and powerful legs as a weapon against her gangly brother.

When it's all done, she sinks into the sofa and looks out of the window. It's a glorious spring day. There's a gentle breeze and a flock of seagulls is dancing overhead, ducking and diving on thermals rising from the sea. She leans over and pulls the window open a crack, inhaling the salty air. She can't wait to share this place with her children.

Amanda pulls out her phone and sends messages to both of them, saying how much she's looking forward to seeing them tomorrow afternoon. She doesn't want to appear needy, but it doesn't hurt, she decides, to remind them she's expecting them for dinner. She's actually paid for their rail fares for this trip. She offered, in fact. Without checking with Mike, who's been too distracted to talk about anything that isn't about the school, anyway. She'd decided that he'd have agreed if she'd asked him.

She hears Mike's keys in the lock at 4 p.m. Father Paul's continued ill health has meant he's worked every day of the holidays so far, trying to reassure parents and plug any holes in the school's processes, some of which had only come to light after the Ofsted inspection. She knows he's very worried about how things are, even though he's barely spoken about it. She knows, because he's been having nightmares every night, nightmares where he's shouted out, thrashed about in bed and even sat up, talking to someone who isn't there. 'Hi,' she calls out from the living room, expecting him to walk through the door any moment. But he doesn't. There's a worrying silence. She decides to go and see what's up. She finds Mike sitting on their bed with his back to her, staring out of the window towards the sea. 'Mike?' He doesn't reply. 'Mike?' she says, with gentle kindness. She walks around the bed and sits down next to him. 'What's going on? Are you ill?'

'No, I'm not ill,' he says in one long sigh. 'At least I don't think so.'

'Then what?'

'The Ofsted report has come in.'

'Oh?'

'Inadequate. This school is inadequate. That's what it says.'

She would have expected him to have emotion in his voice as he delivers this awful news, but he doesn't. He sounds strangely flat, as if his voice has detached itself from his mind.

'Just because of that night at the cove...?'

'Partly that. But it also turns out old Bede hasn't been doing his pastoral job very well. There were lots of untied ends to lots of very tangled threads. The inspectors are right to question it. I think... I think this could be the beginning of the end for the school.'

'Oh, Mike. Surely parents will see through the admin stuff. They'll see how much effort's being put into educating their kids...'

'I doubt it. I mean, it's incredibly expensive to send them here, isn't it? And with the VAT on school fees now, it's even more pricey than it was before. And boarding schools are dying out in the UK. No one wants to send their kids away any more. I don't blame them, to be honest...'

'But you've done such good work here. I know it's made a difference. Perhaps not obviously, so far, but it will do. Parents will see it, see you're offering something different...'

Mike turns to face her, his face still startlingly blank.

'I doubt it,' he says. 'But thank you, Mandy. Thank you for trying to support me through this. I know it's been... really hard for you.'

'It has,' she says, startled at this sudden attempt to communicate with her. She's been craving a conversation like this for months. 'It's been difficult, but—' *But, she's about to say, but actually I'm growing to like this place. It feels more like home than London now.*

'But it won't last much longer,' he says, interrupting her. 'We've had ten parents serving notice on us just this week. And that's even before this Ofsted rating becomes public knowledge. That'll be the final nail in the coffin.'

Normally, she'd pull him in for a hug now. She'd comfort him. But she looks at his expression and knows instinctively that such an approach would be unwelcome.

'Surely it's not that bad. You have kids here whose families have been attending Hallows for generations. This school is a well-respected centre for Catholic education. And as I said, you've done so much already to turn it around.'

Mike rubs his eyes, which remain dry and blank.

'I know what you're trying to do, Mandy, and I love you for it, but really. It is that bad. It just is. But the good thing is, at least our time here will be over soon. I know you've hated it.'

'As I was going to say, I...'

'Look, given what's going on, I've decided Julia and Luke shouldn't come and visit tomorrow. I'm just about to message them to let them know.'

Amanda is blindsided.

'What?'

'I'm just... distracted. I'll have to work. And the whole place is in disarray.'

'But we've planned it. We're supposed to be having a family time, over Easter...'

'Mandy, we can't now. Surely you see that. Everything here is falling apart. There's no point getting them here to see it, anyway. It's OK. We won't be here much longer.'

'Hang on...' Amanda can barely speak. Anger is rising rapidly from her toes, ripping through her core. 'I've been looking forward to them coming for months. Since we first arrived, in fact. I so want to show them the life we've built for ourselves here...'

'But we haven't built a life here,' Mike replies, still seeming calm. 'It was a mistake. It was all a mistake. I should never have done it. The sooner it's all over, the better.'

'I don't understand.'

'I know.'

The rage reaches Amanda's brain.

'There you go again, treating me like an idiot.'

'Mandy...'

'No. Just don't. I can't bear it. You don't care how I feel, do you? You haven't cared, ever since you saw this job advertised. You've been like a dog with a bone, determined to get it, whatever gets chucked away in the process. And in this case, it's us you've chucked away, isn't it? And for what? A job you are now quite likely to lose. You've been so busy doing the big *I am* that you've failed to notice me battling my own body. I'm not sleeping well, I'm a ball of anxiety and I can barely remember my own name some days. And by the way, you've also missed me settling here, making friends, finding peace. You haven't seen me, I mean *really* seen me, for a long time.'

Mike looks like he's been slapped. Amanda is glad that at least she's managed to provoke a reaction from him. His blank expression was infuriating.

'Mand...'

'No. I don't want to hear it. I can't bear listening to you trying to make it right. Because so much is wrong, isn't it? And you can't fix all this with words. They aren't enough. Oh, and I'll tell the children about your decision. OK?'

Amanda's last few words are choked. She knows she's going to cry, so she needs to get moving. She grabs a few things from her bedside table and chest of drawers – underwear, a book, her moisturiser – before heading into the bathroom to find the rest of the essentials. Then she throws them in a small bag, grabs her phone and heads for the door.

Rosie will have things I can borrow, she thinks, slamming the door behind her, noting with sadness and anger that Mike didn't make any effort to stop her leaving.

* * *

'I'm so sorry to land on you like this, again,' says Amanda, sitting down on a stool in Rosie's kitchen. Her hastily packed bag of belongings is by the front door. 'I just didn't know where else to go. I can barely think.'

'It's absolutely fine. I don't have any plans, well, except some wild swimming tomorrow, but you can borrow one of my cossies for that.' Rosie smiles, and Amanda is suddenly immensely grateful for her friend's warmth. It's such a contrast to Mike's apparent heart of steel.

'Thank you.'

'Would you like some wine?'

Amanda nods. 'Yep. I think that would be very helpful.'

'So he unilaterally cancelled your children's visit? He didn't consult with you at all?' says Rosie, pulling a chilled bottle of white from the fridge and carrying it over to the table.

'Yep.'

'Why do you think that is?' Rosie reaches for two wine glasses from a glass-fronted cabinet to her left.

'Honestly, I don't know. I suppose he's just got incredibly selfish? I don't know really... it feels...' Rosie pours wine into the glasses and hands Amanda one. 'Thanks,' she says, receiving it. 'It feels... like he's done it deliberately, to spite me.'

Rosie raises an eyebrow. 'Why would he do that?'

'I don't know,' says Amanda, tears threatening to return. She gulps down some wine to try to keep them at bay. 'I just wonder if... if we've reached the end of the line?'

'That's a big thing to say, and to feel,' says Rosie, sitting down on a stool next to her.

'Yes...' Amanda stares into her glass.

'Do you really mean it?'

Amanda thinks about that brief moment of togetherness at Christmas, when they'd been swimming in the freezing sea. That was the last time, she decides, that Mike had felt like the man she loves. Then she thinks about the silences, the distance, even in the bed they share. Their different priorities. What amounts, she thinks, to the gradual dissolution of their partnership. Because despite the fact they're still married, they no longer feel like two people pulling in the same direction.

'I... don't know,' she replies. 'We've been together for such a long time.'

'Where did you meet?'

'Oh, university. We were both in the rowing squad. He was tall and handsome, and I had a thing for men in Lycra.' She manages a brief smile. 'When we graduated, he decided to do a PGCE, but I wasn't sure. I faffed around for a bit with various temping jobs, then tried working as a teaching assistant for a bit to see if I'd like it, but I didn't. Then we got married, had kids young... and I've just worked in and around the schools he's been at ever since.'

'So you've never really had your own career.'

Amanda is about to take a sip, but stops. She knows this about her life, of course she does, but she's never really considered this before.

'Yes, I suppose you're right. I never really got started. To be honest, I haven't really minded it much. I was never very ambitious and when the kids came along, they were my world.'

'But do you mind now, now that the kids have left home and have their own lives?'

Amanda nods. 'Yes. Yes, I do. I think that's definitely part of it. I've felt quite lost. But actually, working with you, in the medical room, has been a highlight of my time here. I've felt... useful.'

'Yes, you're a natural with the boys. And they really like you. You have a lovely warm, calm demeanour about you.'

Amanda feels herself glow with what she realises is pride.

'Thank you. It has felt good. And I've also loved getting to know you and your friends. Even if it has meant freezing my bits off in the sea.'

'Ah yes. Well, no pain, no gain,' says Rosie, topping up Amanda's glass.

'True,' says Amanda, taking a sip. 'So, what do you think? Is it over? You've had your own break-ups. Did they happen... like this?' As she says this, she feels like she's leaning over an abyss, staring into the darkness. An abyss she'd previously been blissfully unaware of. It has never occurred to her that her marriage might not go the distance.

Rosie stares into her wine glass.

'Honestly, only you have the answer for that. But I'd say, for what it's worth, that the perimenopause is a pretty terrible time to be trying to make any major decisions. You're not yourself at the moment. And Mike isn't either, is he? And men go through their own mid-life struggles. If I were you, I wouldn't leap to any quick decisions. Has he been in touch, by the way? Asking where you are?'

'I don't know. I turned my phone off when I left. I didn't want to talk.'

And also, she thinks, she didn't want to be staring at her phone, willing him to call. She doubts he's tried. He didn't seem at all bothered when she left.

'Why don't you turn it on and see?'

'I will, later. When I can face it.'

'Fair enough. Did you message Julia and Luke yourself about their visit? Before you turned your phone off?'

'Yes, I dropped them a message. I lied and told them their dad wasn't feeling well, and that we'd postpone until next week. But I don't think we'll be able to do that. They're probably busy, and I'm not sure whether I'll be able to move their train reservations...'

'Cross that bridge when you come to it. Why, out of interest, didn't you tell them the truth? That it was Mike's idea to cancel?'

Amanda ponders this.

'I suppose... I suppose I just don't want them to worry. And to think badly of him, and our marriage...'

'Because it might blow over?'

Amanda puts her wine glass down and sits back into the seat.

'Yes. I suppose so.'

'I think, if you're still feeling like that, then it may not be over,' says Rosie. 'When I left my husband, I wanted to burn every bridge known to man. Nothing was dragging me back into that hell.'

22

THERESA

15 July 1966

The lunch bell rings on the final day of term. In normal times, this would herald a cacophony of joy which would ricochet around Hallows' corridors, as hundreds of boys are released from classroom captivity into more than two months of freedom. But not today. Not this term. Not just five days after the annual prize-winner's boat trip ended in tragedy.

Instead, the boys' conversations are muted as they head outside to be reunited with their parents, who have been pulling up in the car park for the past hour, putting seats down and rearranging boots to accommodate trunks, school bags and hockey sticks. Some didn't wait until today. Theresa knows that several parents defied the headmaster's instructions and picked up their children as soon as the full horror of the missing boat became public knowledge. She understands why. Hallows Abbey has not been a happy place to be this past week.

England are due to play Argentina in the quarter-finals tomorrow, but World Cup fever has deserted the school. The annual prize-giving has been cancelled. Cups and certificates were instead given out in a very sombre assembly after breakfast. And the traditional church service which usually sends the boys out, complete with the school orchestra and choir, was instead replaced with a prayer vigil for the missing. Theresa had been required to attend, and the muffled sobs and shocked faces of the boys were almost too much to bear.

Theresa gets up from her desk and walks over to her window. Several cars have parked around this side of the school building, and she watches as a mother, beautifully turned-out in a dandelion-yellow short sundress and white sandals, runs to her son, a second year called Billy, and gathers him up in her arms. Then his father, a stiff-looking man with a tidy moustache, walks forwards and pats him on the back. His son and his wife can't see his face, but Theresa can; this trussed-up Briton is holding back tears. Then they turn and walk together, hands and arms still touching, towards their car. Theresa watches as they close the door, fasten their seat belts and drive away out of view. Then she sits down on her upright wooden chair and weeps as quietly as she can: for the lost boys, for the lost teachers, for Trystan. Even though John's revelations have left her with a terrible guilt about her relationship with him, she still feels smothered by her grief. Finally, she weeps for her own family. She wishes her father and mother had been capable of the sort of affection she's just witnessed.

When they've gone, Theresa tidies the room, locks the medicine cabinet and shuts the door behind her. Then she heads upstairs to the headmaster's office.

She arrives at Father Crispin's door and knocks hard, twice. Instead of telling her to come in, however, she hears footsteps, and the door opens.

'Ah, Miss Murphy. Could you please wait for a few minutes? I have someone with me.'

Theresa nods, and retreats to a chair positioned on the opposite wall, usually the unhappy home of a boy who's been sent out of class for bad behaviour and is awaiting his punishment. Theresa spends the next few minutes examining the framed portraits of various monks on panelled walls and listening to the chatter of the secretaries in the room next door. Even these conversations, normally so bright at the end of term, sound muted.

The headmaster's door opens suddenly, and John is standing in the doorway. He has tears rolling down his face.

'John...' Theresa says, but he doesn't stop to talk to her. Instead, he starts to walk down the corridor, before breaking into a run. Father Crispin looks pained.

'He's just told me he's leaving the school,' he says. 'Such a waste. Such an intelligent boy. His family will be so disappointed, given his scholarship.'

Theresa thinks about John's mother. What will she do? she wonders. John said that Trystan had left them. She assumes – hopes – that he was still supporting them financially. If so, how will she cope financially now?

'I can't believe it. He's such a good student...'

'Yes, but troubled,' says Father Crispin, before retreating to let her inside. 'Very troubled.'

'Did he say why he wants to go?' she says, walking in and accepting the chair he's offered, opposite his desk. The room is large, with two sash windows to her right letting in the summer light and offering a view of the windswept coast and the deceptively benign sea beyond.

'Oh, he feels like a duck out of water, I think. He has ever since he came. It's difficult, you know, giving scholarships to local boys. So often, they struggle to fit in, no matter how bright they are. And then there is survivor's guilt. It's a real phenomenon, you know. That poor, poor boy.' He pauses. 'Now, Miss Murphy... What can I do for you?'

Theresa nods and inhales sharply.

'I'm afraid I'm also here to hand in my notice,' she says quickly, getting the words out before she can change her mind.

The old man raises an eyebrow.

'Goodness,' he says, sitting forward in his seat. 'That is unexpected. I'm so sorry to hear you will be leaving us. I hope you haven't been unhappy here? When we spoke coming up to Christmas, you seemed very content.'

Theresa thinks of how innocent she'd been at Christmas. She hadn't yet met Trystan, hadn't yet discovered the addictive and yet destructive nature of desire, and hadn't realised the dreadful implications of her own desperation, coupled with naivety.

'Oh, yes. I was. I am. I like the job, very much. But...' She pauses. 'But I miss my family in Ireland.' She cannot, *will not*, tell him that she is leaving because she has had an illicit, shameful affair with a married, older man, and she cannot bear to stay here now he's dead. She hasn't the energy to hide her immense grief or her immense stupidity from everyone here, and more than that, she realises her father was right all along. She was never capable of making a go of it in England. She should never have been stupid enough to believe she could.

'Are you sure, Miss Murphy?'

'Yes,' she says, swallowing hard.

'I know it's been... very sombre here, since the accident. Actually, I meant to speak to you. I have heard you will be needed as a witness at the inquest next week. But it's just a formality, my dear. I understand from our receptionist that you suggested the boating company involved?'

Theresa is shocked. She'd known there was going to be an inquest, but it had never occurred to her she might be called to give evidence.

'Oh... I didn't...'

'Don't worry, it will be very brief, I'm sure, and we are very happy to accommodate you until it's over. But what I meant to say is... I hope the accident isn't why you're heading home? That you don't blame yourself in any way? It was terrible, unexpected weather. No one could know that was going to happen.'

'No. Of course, the accident is... simply dreadful,' she says, tears welling in her eyes. 'But no... the fact remains that I miss my family,' she says, knowing that she's so unconvincing, she probably sounds like she's auditioning for a minor part in amateur dramatics.

'If that's the case, my dear, I obviously will not and cannot stop you leaving us,' says the kind old monk. 'But we shall miss you.'

* * *

Theresa is on her way back to her room when she hears shouting coming from the boys' toilets. It doesn't sound even remotely playful, and so she pushes the door open without hesitation.

'What on earth...' Theresa has been greeted by a scene she had never anticipated. Because a boy is lying on the floor, blood pouring from his nose. She recognises him as Harry, one of a group of classically naughty boys, the type who talk during class and stick whoopee cushions on teachers' chairs. His home is in the Channel Islands, and he's probably still at school because he's heading home on a long train and boat journey tomorrow. And kneeling next to him on the floor, his fists locked like grenades and his face like thunder, is John.

Harry takes her entrance as an opportunity to flee. He springs up and runs past her, not giving her any opportunity to examine him.

'John?' she asks, glaring at him. 'What on earth just happened?'

'He called me a faggot,' he says, his voice defiant.

'Well that's... That's not on, John,' she says, shocked at hearing this derogatory language come from John, of all people.

'So I hit him.'

She can almost see the anger rising from him. His expression is as hard as metal.

'You mustn't hit people...' she says, knowing as soon as she says this that it's pointless. She knows from her own experience that when a red mist descends on a man, nothing but time will cause it to abate.

'I don't care. I don't care any more,' he says, his head held high. 'Because I'm leaving.'

'Yes, I wanted to talk to you about that,' she says, gently, hoping to help him calm down. 'Will you reconsider? Honestly, John... none of it is your fault. You couldn't have stopped the accident, even if you'd spoken up. It was just the storm. Just the weather. You are not to blame.'

John stands up swiftly.

'I'm going now, Miss Murphy,' he says, brushing past her.

'John?'

'*I said, I'm going,*' he says, more firmly, as he sets off down the dark corridor, not looking back.

23

AMANDA

Good Friday, 2025

There are storm clouds on the horizon as Amanda drives through the gates of Hallows Abbey. It had been a clear spring day at first light, when she'd woken early after a fitful night, made herself a cafetiere of coffee in Rosie's kitchen, and stood at the window looking out to sea.

It was then she'd turned on her phone for the first time since she'd walked out of their flat yesterday and discovered Mike's messages.

The first one was sent about half an hour after she'd left Hallows Abbey. It had been simple. Brief. To the point.

> Are you OK, Mand?

And then, half an hour later:

> Mand? I'm worried about you. Are you OK?

And then, an hour later:

> I'm so sorry.

And then ten minutes later:

> I mean that. I really am so sorry.

An hour after that, he'd sent a message begging her to come home. Then there had been nothing more until 5 a.m., when she'd received a flurry of messages.

> I'm so worried.
>
> And I know I said I was sorry yesterday, but I don't think it was enough.
>
> Please forgive me.

It was this last message that had shaken her out of her stupor. Until this point, her anger had allowed her to brush his apparent knee-jerk apology aside. But the final one didn't sound like Mike. She'd never heard him using that phrase in all of the years they've been together. And suddenly, what happened to his brother had thrown itself into her consciousness, and she hasn't been able to shake it since. That message had made her throw a few things in a bag, leave a note for Rosie and jump in the car.

During the short drive back to Hallows she'd wondered exactly what he was seeking forgiveness for. Because there was definitely a difference, she'd decided, between saying sorry and seeking forgiveness. The former, you do when you've said something in the heat of the moment that you didn't mean. The latter hints at something far more serious, she thought. Something far more profound.

The school car park is deserted when she arrives. It's early, and the school is still closed for the Easter break. The only other cars she can see belong to the monks. Their shared vehicles are kept on the far side, under a small carport with a corrugated plastic roof. Most of the live-in staff, meanwhile, have taken the opportunity to go on holiday or visit friends and family.

Amanda grabs her bag, coat and phone and locks the car. She's about to head to their flat via the door at the bottom of their staircase when something makes her pause. Despite the incoming bad weather, a solitary ray of sunlight is lighting up the bell at the top of the abbey tower. It's momentarily so bright, in fact, that it seems like someone is standing up there shining a torch. On impulse, she decides to walk over to the old church instead of heading straight back home.

When she reaches the abbey, its heavy external oak door is slightly open. This is surprising. The monks access the abbey from a covered walkway that leads to their living quarters which has its own door. They only usually open the main one for public services on Sundays. She pushes and it swings open with surprising ease.

It's dark inside. The murky daylight outside is doing little to lift the gloom. However, a single candle is burning in a glass case on the altar, and Amanda is drawn to it. She walks down the aisle and sits in one of the pews near the front, placing her coat and bag on the floor by her feet. She takes a minute to absorb the sights and sounds of the space she's in: the hint of incense; the gentle crackle of the candle; the distant whistle of wind forcing its way through the small gaps under the doors. She looks above the altar, at the stained-glass window, which depicts the life of Jesus, from innocent, nurtured boy to a hounded and frightened man.

It was a similar view that she had taken in weekly as a child, sitting with her parents in the pews of their local parish church. Her mother and father had been regular attendees, more, she thinks now, for the social network and comfort it provided, than for their own personal faiths, which were rarely spoken of. Her own faith had waxed briefly in her questioning teenage years and then waned as she'd entered her twenties – ironically, around the time she'd undergone a conversion to Catholicism, so she could marry Mike in church.

She rarely prays now, but today, she feels like she should. After all, there's a great deal for her to pray about: her marriage is in the worst state it has ever been in; the school, her husband's employer, might close; she's grieving her parental role; and, last but not least, she seems to no longer be in control of her body or her mind. Oh, for a return to the relative hormonal stability of her twenties and thirties, she thinks, as she leans over and puts her head in her hands. *Oh, for those days when I felt like I knew who I was.*

Please God, she thinks, *please help Mike. Please help him find a solution to the school's problems, one which brings him peace and also brings him back to me.*

Please help him see that it's not the location that's wrong, but the situation we're in. Please help him see things from my perspective.

And please help me, she adds, fighting the feeling that this is a selfish ask. *Please help me deal with these changing times, with the changes in my body and in my brain, with the fact that Julia and Luke are leaving us, bit by bit. Please help me rediscover who I really am, and help me find happiness again.*

When she's run out of miracles to ask for, Amanda remains leaning over for a few more moments with her eyes closed, revelling in the unusual opportunity to reflect on her worries and feelings in silence.

When she does sit back and open her eyes, she's startled to find she's no longer alone. A monk is standing in front of the altar, just a few metres away from her.

'Oh, I'm sorry. Did I disturb you?' he asks, clearly alerted by the creak of the pew as she returns to an upright sitting position. He's an elderly man with a kind face and a warm voice. She doesn't recognise him, but then, she's only really met the small group of monks who are involved with the school.

'Oh, no. Thank you,' she says, smiling at him.

'It's wonderful in here, isn't it?' he says.

'Yes. I rarely come in here, outside of services. But something made me come in today, and I'm glad it did. It's making me feel better.'

'I find that, too,' says the old man, walking a few steps closer to her. His proximity makes her feel like she needs to engage him in conversation.

'Do you still feel that, even though you have to come in here so often?' she asks, wondering afterwards whether this is an impudent thing to ask a man who has pledged his life to God.

'Yes. Although I usually feel more at harmony in it when I'm able to pray by myself. But don't tell my brothers that,' he says, in a tone that threatens laughter.

'Oh, I won't.'

'Are you seeking something in particular today?'

She looks at him in surprise. This is a personal question, she thinks. She doesn't know this man. And yet there's a benefit to that, of course; if he doesn't know her, he has no preconceived ideas about her. He also doesn't know who she is. And this makes her bold.

'Yes. I need... I need some advice. About my... relationships.'

That's all she wants to say, just in case he has recognised her and realises who her husband is.

'I see,' he says, before pausing and looking intently at his own hands for a moment, as if he's trying not to unsettle her by looking at her directly. 'Well, I'm far from an expert on families, but I do know what it's like to cohabit with my fellow men. And for what it's worth,' he says, before taking a deep breath. 'For what it's worth, I believe that we always know what we need, even if we haven't reconciled ourselves with that yet. And that things are always better if we are honest with ourselves about this, and with others.'

Amanda thinks about how much she has been tiptoeing around Mike, worrying that if she tells him how she's really feeling, she'll upset him, or ruin his concentration, or cause an argument. She decides that as soon as she walks back through their front door, she's going to be completely honest with him. Because it can't hurt, can it?

'Yes,' she replies. 'Yes, I agree.'

'And also… When someone apologises… They are asking for help, as well as for forgiveness,' he adds, before turning to look at the altar and its wide, tall, solitary candle.

'Yes,' she says, deciding at that moment that she needs to go and find Mike. 'Yes. Thank you.'

'Not at all, my dear,' replies the monk as she grabs her things and makes her way back up the aisle at speed. 'Not at all.'

* * *

Amanda walks back to the flat so quickly, she's almost breaking into a run. She arrives at their front door in less than two minutes and drops the house keys in her haste to get inside. She picks them up, inhales deeply to try to calm herself and turns the key in the lock. Once in, she heads straight for the lounge, ready to have a proper talk with her husband, who has taken to working at the dining table in there, rather than in his office, during the Easter holidays. But he's not there. There's evidence he has been, however – his laptop is on the table, plugged in, and there's a half-drunk cup of coffee sitting beside it. She turns and heads back into their bedroom. He might be having a nap, she thinks.

'Mike?' she says, pushing the door open wider. But he's not here, either. He must have been called into his office, she thinks, before deciding to check the spare room, just in case he's in there, sorting the boxes she's been nagging him to sort ever since she moved to Hallows. Chance would be a fine thing, she thinks, as she pushes at the door.

What greets her on the other side of it makes her gasp in surprise.

Because he *has* been sorting through the boxes. Two of them are open on the bed. She walks over to them, keen to see how far he's got with it. She's hoping there's a bin bag somewhere, and that it's been filled with at least some of the contents.

Yes, there is one, she thinks, spotting a bag on the floor beneath the window. A wave of warmth washes over her. Mike has been listening to her after all.

And then she sees it.

Lying on the bed next to the smaller box is an old school photo. At first she thinks it's one of Mike's, but then she realises the school name underneath is unfamiliar. It's definitely not where her husband went to school. She wonders why he has it. Perhaps it has one of his childhood friends in it. Her eyes scan the teenage faces, keen to see if she can spot anyone she knows. Then she finds him.

Olly, Mike's brother. He must have been about fifteen here, she thinks. Two years before his suicide. *Oh Mike. You never talk about him, but here you are, keeping his school photo all of these years. Why don't you talk about him?*

And then she spots someone else in the photo. Someone else she knows.

Her blood runs cold.

24

THERESA

30 July 1966

'I'd like a cup of tea, please.'

'Milk? Sugar?'

'Milk, please. One sugar. Oh, and a toasted tea cake, please, with butter.'

Theresa is in the cafe at Bodmin railway station. It smells of strong, stewed tea, buttered toast, and a faint but distinctive tang of diesel. There is red and white bunting strung behind the counter, a nod to the impending final of the World Cup, which is tonight. It's the same everywhere. Newspaper headlines shout about it, conversations are dominated by it and plans are being made around it.

Theresa couldn't care less. She wishes she could hop on a long-distance train right at this moment and head back to Ireland, but the letter from the coroner had been unequivocal. She doesn't have a choice. She has to get through today before she can leave.

'That'll be one shilling and sixpence, please.' Theresa pulls out her purse and finds the change she needs. She hands it over. 'Thanks, love,' says the woman behind the till, who's wearing a yellow gingham pinny around her waist, and whose wiry hair is swept back into a bun. 'Go and find a seat. I'll bring it over when it's ready.'

Theresa turns and wends her way between a sea of Formica tables towards a vacant table for two in the far corner. She passes a menu hanging crookedly on the wall, listing 'Tea – 8d' and 'Cakes – 1/-' in smudged handwriting. A middle-aged woman in a navy-blue dress with a prim collar sits near the window, her gloved hands clasped around a chipped china cup. Beside her, a young couple share a pot of tea, the man's grey flannel trousers slightly baggy at the knee. His girlfriend – or fiancée, more likely, Theresa thinks, spotting a ring – has her hair set in soft waves. She's wearing a sleeveless floral dress and white sandals, and her cardigan is draped neatly over the back of her chair. Lucky them, she thinks, as she sits down. Lucky them, having an ordinary day, doing ordinary things. She's still numb with her unspoken grief. It's hard to imagine when she'll be able to live the ordinary world again.

The Beatles' 'Yellow Submarine' is playing from a radio set in the corner, by the till. She finds herself humming it. It's been playing in her head in a loop ever since it was released a fortnight ago, along with its B side, 'Eleanor Rigby'. And then she stops humming. For this lovely song is far too jolly, far too nonchalant, for today's business.

The waitress brings her cake and tea and she drinks and eats with speed, consuming for nourishment and not enjoyment. When she's finished, she picks up her handbag and walks out of the cafe and down to the taxi rank. She's pleased there isn't a queue.

'The Shire Hall, please,' she says to the driver of the cab at the front. He nods, smiles, and she climbs into the back. It's a short journey from the railway station to Mount Folly Square. She pays the driver and climbs out, taking in the imposing Georgian building in front of her. Built from pale grey stone, its frontage has three open archways, giving it the feel of a temple or a university. Quite fitting, she thinks, for what she's here to do today. It's a day for questions, she knows that. She wonders whether there will be any answers.

The taxi drives away, and she walks the short distance across the square and into the building, through the middle of the three arches, and then up a flight of stone steps. There's a desk to the right at the top. A small queue of people are waiting to have their enquiry dealt with.

'I'm here for the Walker trial,' says a man at the front. He's wearing a trilby hat.

'Court six, starting in half an hour,' says the woman behind the desk.

'The robbery? The Constantine robbery?' says the woman in front of Theresa, whose hair has been backcombed into a huge beehive.

'Court three.'

'The inquest?' says Theresa, as the woman in front of her clears.

'Coroner's court. Third door down that corridor, to the left,' says the receptionist, already transferring her attention to the man who's standing behind Theresa. She takes her cue, and heads in this direction, checking her watch as she goes. It's midday. Only half an hour to go. She feels her heartbeat quicken as she walks. Not long to wait now. *Better*, she thinks, rehearsing the words her mother said to her several times before she left, *better to get it over with*.

She's been worried about this moment ever since she received the letter inviting her to give evidence. She's thought long and hard about what she's going to say. She has no intention of declaring her relationship with a married man to the assembled crowd. She thinks she's worked out a suitable half-truth which will not obstruct justice, but not ruin her reputation, either. Not to mention the fact that talking about him is likely to make her cry. All that matters, she's decided, is that the families of the missing know why their loved ones died.

She finds the coroner's court and pushes a heavy wooden door. It opens into a large room, with wooden benches that look like church pews on three of its sides. She recognises some of the bereaved parents sitting on them, their faces ashen. She's relieved that John doesn't appear to be here, and neither does his mother. On the fourth side is a dais, on top of which is a large, ornately carved desk and a chair. Behind this is wood panelling, with the British royal coat of arms carved above. Theresa's stomach churns. This is a courtroom, she thinks. This is a trial. And she feels like her guilt is etched on her forehead.

'Theresa Murphy,' she says, introducing herself with a quivering voice to a man with a clipboard who's just inside.

'Ah, Miss Murphy. Thank you for coming. You are one of the first to be called, I believe. Please head through this door here, to the witness waiting room. I'll come and get you when it's your turn.'

'Thank you,' answers Theresa, her mouth dry. She follows his instructions and enters a smaller room, which is panelled on all sides, with windows well above eye level. It feels claustrophobic. Wooden chairs are lined up around its edges, and in the middle is a large glass-topped coffee table covered in well-thumbed newspapers and magazines, obviously to help witnesses pass the time.

There are several people in the room already, all male. She doesn't recognise any of them. Neither the headmaster nor the secretary who actually booked Trystan's services are here yet, she notices, although she is sure they must also have been called to appear. She takes a seat as far away from the men as is possible in such a confined space, puts her handbag down on the floor beside her and picks up a women's magazine, flicking through it idly. As she does so, she runs over the answers she's prepared to the questions she knows they might ask. She's been doing this almost constantly since the letter arrived. 'Can you tell us how you came to know Trystan Trevelyan, Miss Murphy?' 'Can you tell us why you felt he was the right person for the job, Miss Murphy?' 'Can you tell us why you fell for his charm and his good looks, and didn't twig he was cheating on his wife, Miss Murphy?'

Obviously she knows they won't ask the last one, but it's one she's been asking herself on repeat. It's been haunting her dreams. *Why?* she thinks. *Why was I such a fool?* Then her thoughts are interrupted, because a woman has just walked in. It's a woman she recognises, the landlady of The King's Head in Porthgerran. *What a fool she must have thought I was,* thinks Theresa, cringing at the memory of her clumsy attempt at finding out the address for 'her boyfriend'. The older woman must have known Trystan was married. Theresa tries to avoid her gaze, but she sees her clock her as she enters. And then she realises with a panic what the arrival of this woman means. She *knows*. She knows Theresa was in a relationship with Trystan. And so, she'll know she's lying if she tries to pretend otherwise in front of the court. And suddenly, all of Theresa's well-rehearsed excuses evaporate. She realises she's going to have to tell the truth. And oddly, this realisation doesn't make her fearful, as she'd thought it would. In a way, she thinks, it's a relief to have to be honest.

The next hour passes slowly. Theresa watches the hand of the large clock on the opposite wall. She can hear muffled voices and she can see the court is full whenever the clerk comes into the room to call another witness. Two men have been called through so far. She doesn't know who they are, but she surmises they may be involved in the boat trade in some way. Then, finally, it's her turn. The clerk calls her name and she gets up and walks across the room so quickly, her brain takes a while to realise she's doing it. She's desperate to get this over and done with.

The room is now packed. Theresa estimates that at least fifty people have entered and taken a seat since she went into the anteroom. And then she spots John sitting in the far corner, and her stomach lurches. He deserves to know that it was her who was responsible for his father getting the job, but she didn't want him to find out like this. She wishes she'd been brave enough to tell him when they were alone.

She is directed to three steps leading to a desk, which reminds Theresa of the lectern in church.

'Please place your hand on this Bible,' says the clerk, who's followed her up there. 'And read the words written on the card.' Theresa sees there's a small card stuck on the desk, with a phrase typed on it.

'"I swear by Almighty God that the evidence I shall give shall be the truth, the whole truth, and nothing but the truth",' she says, noticing that she seems to have swallowed her voice. She clears her throat.

'Thank you, Miss Murphy,' says the coroner, who's sitting at roughly the same level as her on the other side of the room. He is in his mid-sixties, wearing a well-cut black suit. His white hair is combed over the crown of his head and slicked down with Brylcreem. 'Now, I have a few questions for you. Take your time in answering them. I know this is a strange environment, but please try to relax. Our purpose here is simply to ascertain facts.' Theresa nods. 'Now, the first question I have is this. Until recently, you were the school nurse at Hallows Abbey. Mrs Pascoe, the school's receptionist and one of the administrators, has told us that you came to see her shortly after the school's usual contractor fell through, to recommend a local boat captain, Mr Trystan Trevelyan. Can you please tell us how that came about?'

Theresa picks up the cup of water that's been placed on the lectern next to her and takes a sip. Then she puts it down and looks straight ahead, deliberately avoiding John's gaze. He'll be shocked. In fact, he won't be just that, she thinks. He'll be angry as hell.

'I... I knew Trystan... Mr Trevelyan needed work. He's... he was,' she corrects herself, 'an experienced captain of fishing boats. He'd heard that Hallows Abbey was seeking to commission a crew to take the boys out, apparently from a conversation in the pub, The King's Head, in Porthgerran. And he knew me, so he asked me to put in a good word for him. So, I gave Mrs Pascoe his address.'

'How did you know him, Miss Murphy?'

Here we go, thinks Theresa, saying a silent prayer for forgiveness, even though she knows she doesn't deserve it. From here on, her reputation will be sullied. She's certain they'll report it in the newspaper. Perhaps it will even make the Irish press?

'We were... he was... we were in a relationship,' she says firmly, trying to keep her grief out of her voice. She doesn't deserve to publicly mourn a man who was never really hers.

A little bit of whispering follows. Theresa stiffens.

'I see. And how much did you know about Mr Trevelyan's work history?'

Theresa is surprised not to be questioned more on their relationship.

'Only what he told me.'

'And what was that?'

'He told me he'd captained lots of fishing boats, mostly out of Porthgerran, the nearest village to the school.'

'Were you aware that he was unemployed at the time the school was seeking a boat and crew for their trip?'

'Yes. I felt... sorry for him. I wanted to help.'

'When you agreed to put in a good word for him, Miss Murphy, was that something you were happy to do?'

Theresa remembers how desperate she'd been to please him.

'Yes.'

'What sort of man was Mr Trevelyan, Miss Murphy? In your experience, and your opinion?'

An unbidden memory of the dark heat of their meetings flashes into Theresa's mind. She blushes and is sure the whole of the room can see it.

'He was...' A whole host of adjectives come to mind – witty, powerful, confident. But then she realises in a flash of awareness how much his behaviour resembled that of her father's. She starts again. 'I thought, when I first met him, that he was an admirable man. I thought he was reliable, strong and just out of luck. But now, I think... I think he was angry.'

'And what makes you say that?'

'He was unemployed, and it made him angry. I know... I know about angry men,' she says, looking directly at the coroner. She thinks for a moment that he might be about to ask her a follow-up question, but if he is, he thinks better of it.

'Thank you, Miss Murphy, for your time. That will be all.'

And with that, Theresa is released. She descends the steps from the witness box in a daze and then makes a snap decision. Her original plan had been to walk straight out of the coroner's court and not look back. But she doesn't do that. Perhaps it's the unusually subdued reaction to her revelation, or a desire to assuage guilt, but she decides to dip into a spare seat at the end of one of the long pews. Or perhaps, like everyone else here, she simply wants to hear some answers.

The next person to be called is Mrs Pearce, the landlady of The King's Head – the woman Theresa had recognised in the waiting room. She walks up to the witness box with the confidence of a woman who's used to staring down rowdy male customers.

'You are Mrs Andrea Pearce, publican of The King's Head in Porthgerran, I understand?'

She answers in the affirmative, before swearing on a Bible, just as Theresa had.

'Mrs Pearce – you own and run a pub by the harbourside in Porthgerran. I understand that it was in your pub that Mr Trevelyan first heard about the planned boat trip from the cove beneath Hallows Abbey.'

'Yes, it was.'

'How did that come about?'

'Quite a few of the staff from the school come to drink in the pub, particularly at weekends. It was one of the groundsmen, I think, who first mentioned it. He said he'd been asked to spread the word in the village, as the school wanted to use a local vessel and crew.'

'What was the name of the groundsman in question?'

'I believe he's called Colin. I'm afraid I don't know his surname.'

'Yes, Colin Wilson. He will be appearing later.'

Andrea Pearce nods.

'That sounds right. Yes, he started talking about it and Trystan Trevelyan bit his ear off. He was desperate for work. Lord knows he'd drunk away most of his money... Not just in my pub, you understand. I would turf him out when he had too much. In fact, I've had to do that more times than I can count.'

'Would you describe Mr Trevelyan as a habitual drinker, then, Mrs Pearce?'

'Oh, yes. In fact, I'd describe him as an addict. Some days, he'd be hammering on our door before opening time.'

'You said he was desperate for work. Do you know why? Porthgerran is a well-known fishing town. Men with his level of experience are usually in demand, I understand.'

'He was a drunk. He had a reputation for being unreliable.'

Theresa starts to feel nauseous.

'I see. So, in your opinion, was he the sort of person you'd hire to take you out to sea on a boat trip?'

'Absolutely not.'

This is all Theresa can bear. She bolts out of the room before the coroner has the opportunity to ask his next question. Once in the hallway, she leans against the opposite wall and takes several deep breaths, because she feels like she might vomit. Several people walk past and shoot her a strange look, but she doesn't care.

He was a drunk. He was a drunk, and he had stopped getting jobs because of it. How could she not have seen that? And what had she done? She'd only gone and got him a job skippering a boat again, a boat full of precious boys and teachers from Hallows. If she hadn't done that, she's certain they'd have looked harder, and chosen someone else. But they hadn't. They hired him, and it would be likely, wouldn't it, that he would have been intoxicated when he took those boys out.

I need to get out of here, she thinks. *I need to get out of here, away from these people who know about my guilt.*

She turns and walks as fast as she can out of the court complex and back into the square. Then she realises she's left her handbag in the witness waiting room. She'll have to go back there for it at some point. For now, though, she needs to be alone. She needs somewhere she can think. She spots a small park off to the right. That'll do, she thinks. She'll find somewhere to sit and try to calm down. She walks towards it, still fighting the feeling of bile rising from her stomach. She's glad when she spots a wooden bench beside a hawthorn tree. She sits down and puts her head in her hands, instinctively making herself look as small as she can. Ideally, she'd be invisible. She doesn't want anyone to see her like this. Especially anyone connected with the inquest.

She closes her eyes and immediately sees the faces of the lost boys. They are bright, happy, excited; and they're on a boat. And then Trystan moves into the frame, and she opens her eyes to break the spell. Seeing him in her memories feels like torture.

Then she realises she's not alone in the park after all.

'Hello,' says Andrea Pearce, the landlady of The King's Arms.

'Hi,' replies Theresa, wishing desperately she was anywhere but here, with this woman who knows too much.

'Can I sit down?'

'Of course.' She can't say no, can she? Theresa was bred to be polite – and anyway, she can't think of any possible reason why she should say no to this woman, who was so nice to her, even though she'd originally suspected her of sleeping with her husband.

'I saw you were upset. And I couldn't just leave you here by yourself, in the state you're in. I can imagine how you feel.'

'Can you?' Theresa sits up and examines Andrea, whose face is hard to read. She looks... resigned.

'Yes. I suspect that uncomfortable exchange we had when we first met in my pub told you all you need to know about my relationship with my husband.'

Theresa remembers how Andrea had assumed she'd need an abortion, the inference being that she'd got pregnant by Andrea's husband. Theresa hadn't really thought about it much at the time, because she'd been so caught up with her own shame about her relationship with Trystan.

'But it's him that's in the wrong, not you,' says Theresa. 'He shouldn't be... going out and meeting... other women.'

'Girls. They're usually girls,' says Andrea. 'Make no mistake, they're over the age of consent – he's not that much of a fool – but they're not that old, either. They're your age and younger.'

'I'm sorry,' replied Theresa.

'Oh, goodness, it's not your fault and it's certainly not mine. But I do know how it feels, being lied to. Feeling like a fool for ever believing the lies you were told.'

The older woman's sympathy makes Theresa's tears return. She realises Andrea reminds her of her mother.

'I feel like such a fool,' she says, reaching into her pocket for a handkerchief, and then wiping her nose and eyes with it. 'I knew he drank. But I just didn't... I didn't think he was a *drunk*, you know? And I had no idea that's why he'd lost his job. I would never have recommended him if I'd known...'

'Why would you know, love? He didn't tell you, and it's not as if you know any of the fisherfolk in Porthgerran. You're young, and when young people fall in love, they fall hard. They fall blindly. I should know.' The bitterness in her voice is undeniable.

'But he's married... he had children. And we were... having sex. I am so ashamed.'

'Oh, goodness. I know you're from Ireland and things are different there, but this is the sixties, Theresa. Times are changing, even in Cornwall. This is all on him, you know. These men prey on women like you. They know you're impressionable and they'll be able to get away with whatever they like. I'm sorry, I know that's probably hard to hear, but it's the truth.'

Her words are shocking, but Theresa realises she's right. He'd seen her need for love and pounced on the opportunity it had presented to him. This realisation is both upsetting and freeing. But there's something else, another thought that's dragging her down.

'I know. Thank you,' Theresa answers, sniffing. 'But how do I rid myself of this awful guilt, that it was my stupidity, my lack of curiosity and wilful blindness, that led me to recommend the man who took them all out to sea, to their deaths?'

'We don't really know what happened yet. That's what the inquest is for.'

'But the coroner clearly thinks his drinking is an issue. Otherwise they wouldn't have called you, would they?'

'It's obviously one line of inquiry, I grant you, but they've got loads of people left to question. The school's headmaster, the harbour master, former colleagues of Trystan's, the RNLI, and the people who last maintained the boat... All sorts. Are you going to come back in to listen? I think I'll stay for a bit.'

Theresa absolutely does not want to do this. She doesn't want to have people's eyes boring into her, and she really doesn't want to have to talk to or be confronted by any of the relatives of the dead, who she's convinced will hold her responsible, even if Andrea says they won't. But then she remembers she's got to collect her handbag from the witness waiting room.

'I actually don't think I can cope with hearing more of the inquiry, but I've left my stuff in there.'

'Ah, I see. Fine, then. Shall we walk back in together?'

'Yes,' says Theresa, getting up with reluctance. She really doesn't want to go back into the courtroom, but then, she doesn't have a choice. She has to go through it to get her bag. But once she's done that, she can go. She'll get a cab or walk to the station, whichever is quickest, and as soon as she can she'll make the journey back to Dublin, back to the rest of her life. A life where she'll hopefully be able to forget her grief and her guilt. And maybe in time, even forget Trystan.

As she walks back with Andrea, however, she acknowledges that the latter hope is highly unlikely to come true. She knows she'll never be able to forget him, for reasons both good and bad. You never forget your first love, even if it all turns out to be a sham.

'Shall we wait for someone to come out before we go in?' Theresa asks, as they arrive at the door to the coroner's court. She's hoping to catch a noisy moment, so she can dash in and out without anyone really noticing.

'Nah, we'll be here all day,' says Andrea, pushing the door open before Theresa can stop her. Theresa has a split second to decide whether to wait or to go, but in the end she decides to go in behind Andrea, hoping that the other woman's taller stature will help her hide.

And it does, for about three seconds, until Andrea ducks into a nearby pew and Theresa is left without any cover. Even though most of the people in the room are paying attention to the current witness, a man in his fifties who's wearing a smart black suit, she feels like the eyes of everyone assembled are burning her. She strides over to the door of the witness waiting room, pulls it open and surges through, but makes sure she stops it slamming behind her, her theory being that she'll be in and gone so quickly, no one will really pay any heed. She exhales with relief as soon as she's on the other side and is relieved also to see her handbag is still where she left it, beside the chair she'd been sitting on. She grabs it and heads straight back to the door, ignoring the clerk, who she can see out of the corner of her eye may be about to try to talk to her. Theresa is determined not to stop. Instead, she pulls the door handle down, pulls it towards her and walks through it, back into the courtroom, where the witness is still venting forth, and immediately towards the door that leads to the corridor. She's relieved to find no one is standing in front of it. Just a few seconds later, she's through that door and back into the hallway, her heart hammering in her chest.

She stands still for a moment and takes some deep breaths, absorbing the relative calm of the hallway, where people she doesn't know, and who thankfully also don't know her, are going about their entirely separate, unknown business. When she feels like she won't scare the receptionist with her flushed face and clammy hands, she heads towards the entrance. She is almost out of the reception, almost out of the whole court complex, when she hears his voice.

'Miss Murphy,' he calls out. She carries on walking. She's not Miss Murphy to anyone here now. She'll go home and be Miss Murphy there instead. '*Miss Murphy*,' he repeats, much closer this time. She can hear that he's running. She realises, with a sinking feeling, that she will have to face him. She turns around.

John is about six feet behind her, and he's panting, his face red. He's never been an athlete, she thinks, and the memory of the cruel bullying the boys subjected him to comes back to her strongly.

'Yes, John?'

'I'm so glad to see you again.'

She's been worrying that once he knew the truth, he might rage at her, perhaps even hit her. What she doesn't expect is for him to be pleased.

'Are you?' she says, wondering if she's walking into a trap.

'Yes. I want to talk to you,' he says, still panting.

'Oh.'

'Will you give me a few minutes, please? Before you go?'

Unable to deny this young, damaged boy anything, Theresa agrees. She leads him back to the bench she'd escaped to earlier, and they both sit.

For a while, neither of them says anything. It's time they both need, she thinks, to catch their breath, both literally and metaphorically. Theresa listens to the buzzing of bees gorging on nectar from a flower, children playing in a park, a train whistling in the distance. This normality calms her. And then she feels a little bit brave.

'I'm sorry I didn't tell you that I recommended your father for the trip,' she says, before she can back out of doing so. 'I didn't know how to.'

'It's all right. I didn't tell you I knew him before the accident, either. I didn't tell anyone, and if I had, the school probably wouldn't have let him take them all out to sea. We are both equally to blame for that part of it, I think. Although actually, I don't think it's on either of us,' he says, stroking the petals of the tiny flower. 'The RNLI were just giving evidence. They said that the storm the boat was caught in was unforeseeable and potentially deadly to vessels. They used those exact words. And they also questioned a guy from the Falmouth boatyard, the place *The Towan* was last taken to for a service. His opinion is that it was unseaworthy. The owner had rejected his quote for remedial work.'

Theresa sits back in her seat, letting this news sink in.

'I see,' she says, although her brain is going to take a lot longer than a minute or two to really process what this means.

'It'll be interesting to see what they conclude,' John continues.

'Yes,' she says, knowing that this is a huge understatement. 'So, are you really not going back to school? Now that you know it wasn't your fault?'

'I know it might not have been my fault,' he says, correcting her. 'But yes, I can't go back. I hit Harry, didn't I? I was so angry... And I said I was going, so I think it's for the best. I'll just go to the local school. And then I'll need to get a job.'

'You should do that if you think it's best, of course, but I really do think you should ask for your place back. I suspect Harry won't even have told anyone who hit him. His ego won't have been able to cope with it being you who did it.' This raises a small smile, the first she's seen from John for a long time. 'And it's not too late. Term doesn't even start until September. Father Crispin will understand, once he knows who your father was. He's a kind man.'

'Yes.'

'You really should, John.'

'I'll consider it.'

'Do.'

'I'll consider it, if you promise to do something for me.'

'What do you want me to do?'

'I want you to come back, too. Come back to Hallows Abbey.'

Theresa looks at John in horror.

'I can't do that, John. The court may not have gasped at me carrying on a relationship with a married man, but the Catholic Church sure as hell will care. They won't want me caring for impressionable young boys.'

'All right then,' says John, agitated. 'All right. I get it. How about this, then. How about you just stay in Cornwall? There are hospitals here, other boarding schools, nursing homes... We need nurses here. Good ones. Why can't you stay?'

She realises he's pleading with her.

'Why on earth do you want me to stay here, John? I failed you. I kept seeing Trystan, even when you warned me not to, and I didn't tell you about the part I played in him being hired.'

'Well, because you and I share something. We both feel guilty, don't we? And we understand why. No one else does. I need you around, so I can talk to you about it, whenever I need to.'

'Oh... I see.'

'And the other thing is... this might sound ridiculous to you, but... You seem to understand me. And no-one else does. I've felt so alone, but you make me feel... safe. Please, Miss Murphy. Please don't leave me again.'

Theresa puts her left arm around John's shoulders. He leans into her and starts to sob.

'You can call me Theresa,' she says, rubbing his back as he cries. 'It's Theresa, from now on.'

25

AMANDA

Good Friday 2025

Amanda is still staring at the school photo when her phone rings. She looks to see if it's Mike calling her, perhaps wondering where she is. But it isn't. In fact, it's a mobile number she doesn't recognise.

'Hello?' she says while looking out of the window. The weather's turned quickly, as it often does on this exposed part of the coast. Rain is now lashing at the window.

'Is that Mrs Chapman?'

'Yes.'

'It's Bede here.' Amanda wonders briefly how the deputy head pastoral got hold of her phone number, and why he's calling her. She has met him a few times in the walled garden, but he's a man of few words. With her, anyway. 'I'm sorry to bother you. I know it's the holidays. But I wondered if you know where Mike is? He was due to meet with me to go over communications we plan to send out to parents. You know, while the headmaster is still... off work. But he's an hour late. Is he with you, by any chance?'

It takes Amanda a millisecond to decide what to do.

'Oh, goodness, I'm so sorry, he's ill,' she says. 'I didn't know he had any meetings this morning. He's been sick as a dog since the early hours.'

'Oh, right. Thank you. Do give him my good wishes,' says Bede, his tone not at all matching his words.

'Thanks. I will,' she replies, cutting him off swiftly. As soon as she's sure the call is closed, she stands up quickly and calls Mike's mobile. She needs answers from him.

But then she realises she won't be getting them any time soon, because his phone is ringing inside the flat. She follows the sound and discovers it's in the pocket of Mike's coat, which is hanging from a peg in the hallway. Why on earth has he gone out and left his phone? she wonders. That's unlike him. And he obviously didn't take his coat, either, despite the terrible weather outside. Well, let's hope he's somewhere dry, she thinks, grabbing her own raincoat and pulling on her shoes. She needs to find him. They need to talk.

It takes Amanda about fifteen minutes to establish that Mike isn't in the main school building. The majority of it is locked up, anyway, so there are very few open rooms to search. Next, she checks the administration offices, but finds these empty, too. Then she walks across the car park to the abbey, pulling her hood up to shield her face from the pouring rain. However, when she gets there, she finds the door locked. Someone must have done that after I left this morning, she thinks. Perhaps that monk I bumped into.

Amanda stands with her back to the door for a moment, grateful for the slight overhang of the roof, which is shielding her from the worst of the rain. She's trying to think where Mike might be. And then it comes to her. Perhaps he's at the mine? Perhaps he went for a walk and decided to shelter there from the rain? This seems possible, at least, so she turns and heads in the direction of the coastal path.

The rain is coming down in sheets now, soaking her trousers and her trainers. She wishes she'd worn better shoes and clothing, but of course, she hadn't imagined she'd be searching the headland for Mike. She'd thought she'd find him in his office, or in the abbey. Not out here, in the wild weather. *When I find you, I'll be having words*, she thinks angrily, as she surges on towards the old mine buildings, which she can just make out through the murk. *Making me worry like this.*

She reaches the door that leads into the engine house with relief. She yanks it open, noting that it's even more off its hinges now than it was when she was last there. Inside, it's dark. She takes her phone out of her pocket and switches on the torch. There's no sign of him. She shines it into every corner, but there's nothing there but old sacking, some sundry rubbish, dust and a few old boxes.

'Mike?' she calls out into the twilight. 'Mike? I'm worried. Where are you?'

No one answers. The only things she can hear are rain hammering on the roof, and dripping – she realises that the tiles above are cracked and dislodged, and they are no longer capable of keeping the weather at bay in several places. She stands still for a moment, listening to this atmospheric orchestra, before another possibility occurs to her. It's not a good possibility, she realises. In fact, it's a frightening prospect. But maybe, just maybe, she thinks, he's *there*.

She pulls her hood back up and exits back into the weather, shoving the door closed behind her. The wind is surging in, and she has to lean forward into it to be able to make headway. The rain is now testing her coat's waterproofing. A cold sensation at her elbows suggests it may have been breached. A few minutes later, she arrives at the top of the steps down to the cove. She remembers the beautiful summer's day when she first descended them, and the magical, chilly Christmas Day when she and Mike had joined Rosie's festive swim in the Atlantic.

Then she thinks of the memorial to those lost boys and teachers, just a few metres away. Had they set out to sea on a day like this? she wonders. A day which started off clear and fine, and then became, almost without warning, a tumultuous tempest? Amanda shivers, and not just because of the damp and the wind. She's lived by the sea for long enough now to realise that it's an unpredictable wild animal; benign and beautiful one minute, vicious and deadly the next. It should be respected at all costs. She pulls her hood more tightly around her face and begins to walk down the steps. As she does so, the wind pushes her towards the cliff. It feels like an unseen hand, preventing her from falling.

When she reaches the bottom, she's glad that the tide isn't high. There's still sand to walk on. She's about to turn right and head for the cave, when she sees it.

At first, the rain is coming in so fast and so directly that it's almost blinding her. She shields her eyes with her hand and scans the beach, left to right. But then she spots something. An object, a seal, a bird, it's impossible to tell, but there's definitely *something* in the water. She sprints towards it, not caring about the sand she's sending flying or the very real risk of falling.

When she gets closer, she sees it is neither a seal nor a bird.

It's Mike.

He's standing with his back to her, knee deep in water, the waves crashing over his thighs.

She doesn't hesitate. She wrenches her shoes off, throws them behind her on the beach and wades to where he is.

'Mike!' she shouts as the freezing water makes contact with her ankles, and then her thighs. She doesn't notice how cold it is. 'Mike!'

He doesn't turn, even though she knows he must be able to hear her. When she's close enough, she reaches out to touch his shoulder. He flinches slightly, but he doesn't move his head. He's still gazing out to sea.

'Mike? Why are you out here? Come back to the beach. You'll get hypothermia.'

His lips are blue, and he still doesn't answer her. There is something really wrong. She's never seen him like this before. She chastises herself for not realising earlier. Because his strange behaviour, over the last few months, and the distance between them – it must, she knows, have been leading them to this. And then what did she do? She walked out on him. She left and didn't say where she was going. *What a fool I am*, she thinks. *What. A. Fool.*

'Mike?'

There's still no response, so she does the only thing she can. She puts her arms around his waist and pulls hard.

'No,' he says, finally, as she succeeds to move him a few inches backwards.

'Why?' she says, her teeth chattering.

'Because... it's over. Between us. Isn't it?' Mike seems to be struggling to speak. 'I've ruined...' He tails off, and for one dreadful moment she thinks he might be about to dive face first into the sea. She reaches out to grab him again, and he doesn't resist this time.

'No,' she says, trying his hand, rather than his waist. '*No*. I love you, Mike. Now come back with me, please. Let's go home. Let's get you warm.'

And then she tugs gently at his hand, and to her immense relief, he follows.

26

THERESA

31 July 1966

Theresa is awoken by her alarm clock. She's packed most of her things already ahead of her imminent return to Ireland, but she's left out the bare essentials.

She feels surprisingly well rested, having slept reasonably, given the emotional nature of the inquest. Perhaps, she thinks, her mind was just so exhausted from reliving horrible memories, after that surge of adrenaline and the resulting dip afterwards when it was no longer needed, that it simply had to shut itself off.

What John had said to her yesterday, about needing her to stay around in Cornwall, had come as a shock. However, she has come to realise how fond she is of him. She'd been devastated at the thought of him being on that boat, hadn't she? And so relieved to find he'd survived, too, even while she'd been in the darkest hours of her grief. She is prepared now to acknowledge they have a special bond, and she also knows he's been through hell. So, she has made him a promise. A compromise. She intends to remain in his life, albeit at a distance. She will keep in touch with him, to help him follow the right path.

Theresa swings out of bed, visits the bathroom to freshen up and pulls on a denim skirt and a crisp white shirt. She checks the mirror. A smart, well put together young woman stares back at her, and this is also something of a surprise. She had expected yesterday to wring her out, but oddly, it has made her feel lighter. Perhaps, she thinks, *it's because I've aired my shame, and it hasn't defeated me?*

Her stomach rumbles. Some tempting smells are wafting up from the school kitchen, which is still busy feeding the monks and remaining staff, even though the school is closed. She realises she's incredibly hungry. She walks down the stairs and into the dining room. It's empty save for a young man behind the serving hatch. She pours herself some water, collects some scrambled eggs and some toast from the servery, and notices newspapers lined up neatly on a sideboard. She decides to pick up a couple. It feels strange to her, being in the dining room by herself. Having something to read will pass the time. She picks up a copy of the *West Briton* and one of *The Times* and takes a seat on one of the benches.

The Times is dominated by England's victory last night at Wembley. She'd gone to bed early, before the match had ended, but had known of the win all the same. The Hallows Abbey kitchen staff had made such a racket, there could be no doubt. She has no stomach to read about the win. Those boys, she thinks, will never get to know of it, and the thought of this, and of so many other future events they will never experience, makes her heart break.

She moves her attention to the *West Briton*. She's keen to immerse herself once more in stories about the touring productions visiting Truro City Hall, complaints about new developments and reports from village shows.

But then she sees what's splashed on the cover, and she freezes.

Coroner: 'Unsafe' boat and sudden storm caused *Towan* tragedy

Theresa is glad she's sitting down. Her heart is thudding, and even though this headline suggests her worst fears may not have been realised, she feels compelled to read every single word of the news story, which takes up half the page. The story reads:

A packed coroner's court has heard that *The Towan* tragedy, in which fourteen lives were lost just off Porthgerran during a pleasure trip in July,

was likely to have been caused by an 'unstable' boat caught in an 'unexpected' storm.

Ten students and two teachers from Hallows Abbey, a Catholic boarding school near Porthgerran, perished in the accident on the 10th of July, along with two crew members. None of their bodies have been recovered, and the boat has also not been found.

Coroner Michael Wight, sitting in Redruth yesterday, said in his summary of findings: '*The Towan* was not adequately equipped with life jackets for all passengers on board. Furthermore, evidence presented at the inquest indicates that the boat had undergone conversion from a merchant vessel to a pleasure craft in recent years. I heard expert testimony which highlighted concerns that this conversion process was not conducted to the necessary standards, potentially compromising the vessel's stability.' The court also heard that *The Towan* may have only been carrying one small inflatable lifeboat.

Commenting on the weather on the day of the accident, Wight stated that the vessel had encountered 'a sudden and unexpected summer storm of considerable violence'.

Responding to rumours that one of the teachers on the trip might have been feeling suicidal following a diagnosis of a terminal illness, the coroner said they were 'scurrilous and without a single element of truth'.

The coroner also heard concerns about the reliability of *The Towan*'s captain, Trystan Trevelyan, during the session. However, Wight concluded that there was no evidence to suggest that Trevelyan's ability to captain the ship had been compromised on the day in question. In addition, the court heard that the ship's first mate, Andrew Lane, was a very reliable and respected sailor.

'Would you like tea, madam?' the man behind the service hatch, calls out across the room.

'Yes please,' she says, and he emerges from the kitchen immediately, placing a steel teapot and cup and saucer in front of Theresa.

'Thank you,' says Theresa, desperate for him to leave so she can immerse herself back in this story, which feels like it has a magnetic pull. When he leaves, she picks up where she left off.

In his concluding statements, the coroner wanted to reiterate the importance of ensuring pleasure craft meet strict safety standards following conversion. He recommended that all pleasure boats carry an adequate number of life jackets and conduct regular safety checks.

While coroners' courts do not apportion blame, Coroner Michael Wight said his findings suggested that the fatal accident occurred due to a combination of severe weather conditions and the inadequate state of the boat following its conversion. These factors, he said, were compounded by a lack of sufficient safety equipment. The captain's habitual alcohol consumption, while concerning, was not considered to have materially contributed to the tragedy, he added.

Theresa reads the article three times. She wants to digest every word. And as she processes each one, an atom of her guilt detaches from her mind and her memory. Not every atom, mind you; she knows that whatever the coroner has said, she will feel guilt about her idiocy and complicity for the rest of her days. But seeing it in black and white, printed for the whole world to see, does help a little. Perhaps it would have happened anyway, she thinks, even if they'd hired a different person to skipper that boat. Maybe. Possibly. For the first time since the accident, a small part of her is a little bit prepared to consider this possibility, and that's definitely progress.

And then she realises what she needs to do, and where she needs to go.

***

The sun is already high in the sky when she leaves the main school building and heads towards the abbey. There's hardly any breeze, and even the ever-present seagulls appear to be taking siestas. It's so quiet, in fact, that her footsteps seem to be echoing off the buildings. This isolation suits her, however. She hasn't come here to talk to the living.

She turns right and walks up to the large door that marks the entrance to the abbey and is relieved to find it unlocked. Inside the church, the temperature is at least ten degrees cooler, which comes as a relief. And it's darker, of course, although sunlight is beaming in through several of the stained-glass windows, projecting a rainbow just to the left of the altar. Theresa's steps generate an echo in here too, as her heels strike the cold tile flooring down the aisle. When she reaches the front, she genuflects and dips into one of the pews and sits for a moment, staring at the frieze behind the altar, with its depiction of Jesus on the Cross. It's an image she'd seen so often during her upbringing, both at church and at school, that she had grown almost immune to it. She didn't really see it, she thinks, not really; she'd almost ignored it, to save herself thinking about the agony He must have gone through at that moment. In fact, she reflects, she'd learned to ignore a lot of the dogma she'd grown up with, pretending the rules didn't exist, so that she could be *free*. And that freedom that she'd embraced with so much ecstasy, that freedom to fall in love, to enjoy love – or what she had thought was love, she reminds herself – that had come at such a cost. *I'm so sorry*, she thinks, hoping that despite everything, God is listening. *I'm so sorry for what I've done.*

Then she sees that she is not alone in the church. One of the monks is just off to her right, sweeping.

'Oh, I'm so sorry. Please don't let me disturb you,' he says, and smiles. He's quite tall, with white hair in a side parting, and he has quite striking blue eyes. She doesn't recognise him, although this doesn't surprise her. Not all of the monks attend the school's service every Sunday, preferring to hold more private services away from prying eyes and whispering, bored boys.

'You're not.' She smiles back. He has a warm, friendly face, and she's relieved he doesn't know who she is.

'Are you a regular here?' he asks, moving gradually towards her as he sweeps.

'I used to be,' she says.

'It's a beautiful place,' he says, coming to a stop just in front of her. 'A wonderful place to come to talk to God.'

'Yes.'

He smiles again and resumes his sweeping.

'Do you think He listens?' she asks, surprising even herself with this question. She's not even sure where it's come from, except there's something about this man, about his open face and kind eyes, that makes her feel she can ask this.

'God? Oh, yes. But He doesn't just listen here. He listens everywhere. You don't need to be in a church. Sorry. I expect that's an unacceptable thing for a monk to say. I should report myself to the abbot.'

Theresa smiles.

'But what about forgiving us? Is that...' She finds she can't finish the sentence.

'Oh, yes. He forgives.'

'I know we are *taught* that He will forgive us. The nuns taught me that as a child. If we are really sorry. But what if...' She pauses, wondering if she dares say it. 'But what if, you've wilfully broken his rules? What if you've sinned outrageously, dreadfully? What if you have gone so far off the tracks, you might never find your way back again?' Tears form in Theresa's eyes as she acknowledges, *announces* out loud, her guilt and her shame. It had been difficult to do it yesterday, in front of the coroner's court, but it feels even harder today, in front of God. A God she has been taught to fear since she was a tiny child. 'I'm so sorry. You must think me a terrible Catholic. I shouldn't even be asking these questions.'

'Goodness me, child. Everyone is allowed to question. I do so all the time.'

'Do you?'

'Oh, yes,' he says, placing his brush against the pew. 'May I sit down?'

'Of course.'

He takes a seat a few feet away from her on the pew.

'If you are sincerely sorry, you are always forgiven.'

Theresa sniffs.

'Thank you. That is... that is wonderful to hear.'

He smiles again.

'Is there anything else I can answer for you, while I'm here?'

She ponders this, and then decides she'll risk it. After all, he has no idea who she is.

'Do you think it's possible to redeem yourself? Do you think people around will forgive you? I know God will, but will... people around here? If I stay?' This is what Theresa is worried about; that if she stays in Cornwall, she'll forever be haunted by her reputation as a 'loose woman', with loose morals.

'In my experience, most people are far too caught up in their own business to give much thought to what's going on elsewhere,' he says. 'I suspect whatever it is you're worried about will be old news in a few weeks.'

Theresa nods.

'Thank you. Yes, I suppose you're right.'

'And may I say something else, my dear?'

'Yes, of course.'

'Your heart always knows the way. Not that bit of you that reacts to your senses – I mean the core of you, your soul. Your soul always knows the way. It pays to follow its lead.'

She thinks of the connection she felt talking to John yesterday, and the love she feels for her sisters. She knows exactly what he means.

'Thank you,' she says, smiling. 'Thank you.'

The monk resumes his sweeping, gradually making his way towards the back of the church. She spends a further ten minutes sitting in front of the altar in silent contemplation and prayer. She prays for guidance; that her next move, whatever it is, will be the right one, both for her and the people she loves. When she's finished, she gets up and genuflects in front of the cross, as she has done so many times in her life without really thinking. This time, however, she does so with meaning, and as she walks back up the aisle, she feels a new sense of purpose. It feels like she's just donned a special kind of shield.

She's very glad of this feeling when she sees a very familiar face straight ahead of her. It's Father Crispin, the headmaster.

'Miss Murphy,' he says, smiling. Theresa feels awkward. Crispin had also been called to give evidence to the coroner. Which means, of course, that he knows the truth now about her relationship with Trystan. She aches to get away, to avoid the desperately awkward conversation that's bound to follow. She needs to book her ferry crossing. She plans to leave first thing tomorrow.

'I... wanted to drop by before I go,' she says, her voice faltering. 'I'm just going to the cove now, actually... I wanted to...' She begins to walk away.

'Please, don't leave on my account. You are always welcome here.'

She turns and looks at him in surprise.

'I know I have sinned dreadfully,' she says. 'I apologise for doing so while I lived here. I know it's not the standard of behaviour expected by members of staff.'

'No, it isn't. But we all sin, Theresa,' he says, using her first name for the first time. *Well, I'm not an employee now, am I?* she thinks. 'And if we seek forgiveness, we are always forgiven.'

'That's what the monk I was talking to just said,' she says, smiling. 'I didn't ask his name, but he was so lovely. The monk who was just cleaning the church.'

'Which one was that? Can you describe him?' asks the abbot.

'He was tall, with blue eyes and white hair in a side parting. He was so lovely. So reassuring to talk to.'

The abbot doesn't reply for a moment. She wonders if she's said something wrong.

'Oh, I'm sorry. Was he supposed to be working in silence? I don't want to get him in trouble.'

'No, child. No. But the monks don't clean the abbey. We have female cleaning staff from the village who do that.'

'Oh.' Theresa is confused. 'Was he breaking the rules, then? By being here?'

'No, I rather think he was doing God's work,' says Crispin.

'Yes.'

'I believe you've been speaking to Brother Volmar.'

'Ah. Volmar. Yes. He was lovely.'

'Volmar died a year ago,' says Crispin, still smiling.

It takes Theresa a few seconds to realise what he's just said. 'He... died?'

'He was one of the kindest men I have ever met. He provided me with a great deal of solace and reassurance, and a gentle ear, for all the years I knew him. It is as you would expect, I think, that he could continue to do so, even in the afterlife.'

'I'm sorry... are you saying I've just been talking to a ghost, Father Crispin?' she asks, incredulously. That man she spoke to, she thinks, cannot have been a ghost. He was as solid, as real as Crispin or her.

'I rather think I am,' says Crispin. 'And you are not the first person to report seeing him, either. He seems to appear when he is needed.'

'I... I don't know what to say.' Theresa looks around her, expecting to see this monk, this Volmar, floating by or jumping out from behind a pillar.

'I'm sorry, Theresa. Please don't be frightened. He cannot harm you. He certainly would never wish to do so. If you can, I would try to see it as a blessing. That's how I saw it.'

'You've seen him, too? Since he died?'

'Oh, yes,' says Crispin. 'I certainly have.'

'And did he help you?'

'Oh, yes.'

27

AMANDA

Good Friday, 2025

'Just come inside, my love,' says Amanda, coaxing Mike inside their flat like a child. She's praying no one saw them make their slow, sodden walk from the coastal path to the residential block. As far as Bede and the rest of the management team are concerned, Mike is just laid low with food poisoning or norovirus, and that's how she's determined it will stay.

She is relieved when he crosses the threshold and she's able to shut the front door behind them.

'Let's go into the bathroom first. We can take your wet things off and warm you up in the shower.' He's still impassive, his face blank, like a ventriloquist's dummy. She tries not to panic. It won't achieve anything, anyway, even if she does. She cajoles him into the bathroom and peels off his clothes, like she used to do for the kids when they were toddlers. He's shaking with cold, and his skin is grey. She chucks his wet clothes in the direction of the corridor and then turns on the shower, and the room fills with steam. 'In you go, my love,' she says, gently. He does as she asks. She wonders for a moment whether she's going to have to wash him, but she's relieved when he picks up the shower gel from the ledge, squirts some on his hand and washes himself methodically, four decades of muscle memory kicking in.

She sits on the toilet to wait. His expression, when he's turning to face her, is no longer blank. It's more... pained, she thinks. Yes, pained. In pain. She wonders whether his frozen limbs are aching as they thaw, or whether his pain is more of the emotional kind. Both, she thinks, most likely.

When he's done, she hands him a towel and watches him dry himself. Then she lifts his dressing gown from a hook on the back of the door and helps him put it on.

'How about I set you up on the lounge with a blanket, and I'll make us a hot drink,' she says, sounding like a relentlessly cheerful Guide leader on a long, rainy hike. He makes a noise that sounds like 'hmmm' and follows her into the living room. He sits down with a loud sigh, and she pulls one of the blankets they keep in a pile in the corner over his lap. Then she walks into the kitchen, flicks on the kettle and sets about making two cups of tea. She's grateful for the fact that she could do this particular activity in her sleep, because she needs to think carefully about what she's going to say to him. She's not a trained psychotherapist, and that's what he really needs, of course. That, she thinks, will have to happen later. Whether he wants to do it or not, and she already knows that the answer will be not. He's that sort of man.

When she's decided what she's going to say first, she dumps the tea bags in the bin and carries the mugs into the lounge, where Mike is now staring straight ahead, apparently into space. She sits down next to him, puts the mugs on a side table, and says, 'I'm here.'

She could have said any number of profound things or asked any of the myriad questions she's got swirling around her head, particularly about that photo, but in the end, she'd thought the best thing was reassurance. He'll need that more than anything, she thinks, knowing that, frankly, that's what she needs most of all, too.

And then he does something unexpected. He starts to cry. Not just a few tears running down his face, but huge, body-wracking sobs. He's never cried before in her presence, not really, except for a few happy tears shed after the children's births. She's taken aback. She instinctively drapes her arms around him and gathers him close. She wonders if, given their recent arguments, he might shrink from her, but he doesn't. In fact, he leans in more. She feels his warm body on hers, and the rawness of his emotion, and she instinctively just wants to provide comfort. That doesn't mean that all is forgiven, of course. Life and feelings are never that simple. But for now, she knows that the man she loves needs her help, and that's enough.

'I don't deserve you,' he says, into her shoulder.

'Don't be silly,' she says, incredibly relieved he's able to speak.

'I don't. I realised that, yesterday, after you left. I realised that I've been taking you for granted for so long, and I've put you through so much. I've been so selfish.'

After an intense minute, Mike pulls away. Amanda picks up one of the mugs of tea and hands it to him, before picking up her own.

'That's not true,' she says, taking a sip. He has a point, of course, but she's not going to ram that point home now, not when he's so down. And after all, she could have refused to come to Hallows, couldn't she? She could have, if she'd really not wanted to do it. And in the end, she's almost grateful that he forced her out of her comfort zone, out here to the beautiful countryside, by the wild sea. 'I mean, you getting a promotion here was about us, wasn't it? More money, a better pension for our retirement...'

'No. Coming here was... one of the worst ideas I've ever had,' he says, lifting his mug to his mouth with trembling hands.

'Oh, Mike. You've been so busy and so I think you haven't really noticed, but honestly, I've grown to really like this place. It took me a while to realise that the troubles I've been having were more about what's going on in my body and mind than they are about where I am. And I love my new friends. I like my new job. I think it could work here. But I know your job here has been much harder and more exhausting than you'd hoped...'

Mike doesn't say anything immediately. But instead of staring straight ahead, he looks at Amanda for the first time since she persuaded him to leave the beach.

'Like I said,' he says, his eyes fixed on her, 'I don't deserve you.'

'No... It's not like that.'

'*It is.*' Mike's manner has changed, and Amanda feels unsettled by it. He seems like he's being powered by a force she's never noticed before.

'What is it, Mike? What is it that you need to tell me?'

'It's... Oh God, it's too much,' he says, putting his tea down and closing his eyes. 'I don't even know where to begin.'

'Does it have something to do with Father Paul teaching your brother?' she asks, with trepidation. Because it was his face, the face of Hallows Abbey's headmaster, that she'd recognised in that school photo.

Mike's steely expression wavers.

'You saw it, then?' he says. 'I should have put it away. I was trying to sort things, finally, as you'd asked. In case you came back. So I could show you I was trying to make an effort, to try to make you happy... And then I just... I just... I couldn't. I can't. I can't do it any more.'

'Tell me. Tell me why that photo made you feel so upset. And why you never told me that you knew Paul, from before.'

'I didn't know Paul. Not really. He taught Olly, not me.' Of course, she thinks. Olly and Mike went to different schools. 'After Olly... did what he did, there was no way in hell Mum and Dad were going to send me to the same place. Because it was that school that sent him into a spiral. He was bullied there, you see. Badly bullied. And Paul was his form teacher. Olly went to him for help when it got really bad, but all Paul did was give him useless advice about standing up for himself. And that made Olly feel like it was all his fault. He committed suicide not long after. Paul could have saved Olly then, if he'd got him the right help. I really think he could. But he did nothing. The inquest let him off any sort of blame, but I've never forgiven him for what he said to Olly, and what he didn't do.'

'So why on earth did you take a role at a school where he'd just been made headmaster, if you disliked him so much?'

He takes a large gulp of tea and swallows hard.

'I didn't know it *was* him, at first. I saw the deputy headship advertised and you know I'd always been itching for a promotion. God knows why, given what it's been like, but anyway... I wanted a change, and I saw this place and obviously given my experience with Catholic education, I thought I'd stand a good chance of getting it. And I also thought, given our happy holidays in this area, that you might like it, too. I thought it might give us a new start, after your mum's passing, and now the kids have left. God, I'm a fool.' He says, shaking his head. 'So, yes... I applied. It was only when I'd been invited for interview that I discovered who'd just been brought on board as the new headmaster.'

'And that didn't put you off?'

'It did, at first. But then I realised it might be an opportunity.'

'An opportunity for what?' Mike looks pained. '*What*?' she repeats, determined to find out what's going on in his head.

'Revenge.'

28

THERESA

2 August 1966

'Fishguard Harbour! All change, please.'

Theresa steps off the train, the heels of her black knee-high boots clicking on the platform as she adjusts her handbag's shoulder strap and picks up her suitcase. She takes in her surroundings. The station is a mix of old and new, the Victorian architecture of the ticket offices and waiting rooms contrasting with the diesel engine lining the platform. The last steam service departed from this platform just a few years previously. The main building's brickwork has been darkened by decades of soot and salt. A large clock, its numbers roman numerals and edged in gold, hangs from the main station building, its hands ticking steadily towards eleven.

Theresa stands still for a moment, trying to calm her anxiety, which has been prompted by the hive of motion around her. Porters in navy uniforms push trolleys loaded with luggage, and passengers surge for the exit, except for one couple who are sharing a passionate embrace before the sea divides them.

She wonders for about the fifth time today whether she's doing the right thing, leaving England. But then she thinks about Trystan. The man she'd loved, the man she is still grieving for, despite his lies, who has now gone forever, doing a job she recommended him for. A man who is now unable to support his family, John included. *No,* she thinks. *No. I made a terrible mess of my time at Hallows Abbey. Daddy was right. I will never make anything of myself over here.*

She needs to get moving, or she'll risk missing the ferry she's spent a whole day, a night stop, and then several hours this morning, travelling to meet. She walks out of the station and follows signs to the port, passing a kiosk selling newspapers and sweets. As she approaches the ferry terminal, she sees its concrete walls are plastered with posters advertising trips to Ireland, promising adventure and a warm welcome. The irony of that, she thinks, is extreme.

Up on deck, the air is thick with the scent of saltwater and diesel. Above her, seagulls cry, their calls piercing the hum of the boat's engines as it pulls away from port. She remembers how she'd felt when she'd first set eyes on the small town of Fishguard. She'd never been to Wales before, or England, for that matter. She'd felt excited, nervous, when she'd first seen it from the ferry. She'd absolutely been a fish out of water, there had been no doubt about that. She'd been an Irish Catholic convent schoolgirl with a childhood not entirely dissimilar to the nuns who'd taught her. She'd had no idea about anything, anything at all. But also, she'd felt a huge sense of relief at finally gaining her independence. Independence, of course, which has led her down a terrible path.

She wishes she could go back and never meet Trystan at all. If she hadn't, she'd still be at Hallows. The thought of that beautiful, barren place tugs at her heart. She had enjoyed her work there. She'd loved helping the homesick boys with their complicated lives, just like her own.

The ferry's horn blasts, and the noise brings her back to her senses. Nothing good will come of thinking like this, she decides. Nothing at all.

The journey to Rosslare takes four hours. Theresa spends most of the trip on deck. She isn't a good traveller, and she doesn't trust her stomach.

As the ferry pulls into Rosslare, Theresa doesn't want to leave the boat with the first surge of passengers. Instead, she stays on deck and watches the harbour workers engaging in what seems to be the precarious task of winching several cars off the ferry and onto the pier. She's so interested in this activity, in fact, that one of the stewards has to attract her attention.

'Miss? It's time to disembark, miss,' says a young Welshman with an earnest expression.

'Oh, I'm sorry. Of course,' she replies.

'Shall I carry your bag?'

'Oh. How kind. But I'll be fine. It's very light.' She picks it up.

'Were you in England for the World Cup, miss?' 'Oh, yes. It was hard to miss,' she replies, trying to smile convincingly. The truth is, she can hardly bear to remember John's wonderful words that had summed up the boys' excitement so well: 'the thought that for once, we might be more than we are.' She sees the faces of those lovely lost boys in her mind, and she fights the urge to cry.

'Must have been something,' he says.

She nods and walks slowly down the steps towards the gangway, the man trailing her; checking, no doubt, that she's actually going to leave. In fact, a small part of her, maybe not even that small a part, wishes to stay on the boat, to let it take her right back to Fishguard without ever setting foot in Ireland again. The rational part of her brain knows this is ridiculous, of course. She has to get off. She has to keep moving. She has to go home.

* * *

Theresa manages to snatch a small amount of sleep on the bus to Dublin. Her accommodation the night before, a very cheap bed and breakfast in Cardiff, had been both noisy and dirty. When she wakes – feet swollen, mouth dry – she sees they've entered Dublin. The roads are wider here, and the traffic thicker. Georgian buildings, blackened by soot, compete with modern high-rise offices and flats, adorned with plastic panels giving splashes of colour, and angular concrete roofs. The River Liffey glistens under muted sunlight.

Finally, the bus pulls into Áras Mhic Dhiarmada on Store Street. The building, opened in 1953, had been dismissed by critics as a 'pile' and 'like a factory', but most Dubliners are now quite fond of it. She disembarks from the bus and waits patiently for her bag to be handed to her by the driver. It's certainly got the hint of the exotic, what with the pillars at its entrance, wood panelling and its Venetian glass mosaics. If only the rest of Dublin was this modern, she thinks, receiving her bag and walking, with no particular urgency, to the stands which host the local buses. She searches the timetables for the next bus to Tallaght, walks over to the required stand, and sits and waits.

As she does so, she looks about her. *These should be my people*, she thinks. *I'm from here.* Born and bred in what was once a tiny village on the outskirts, but which is now rapidly becoming a town. But why, then, do they seem so unfamiliar? Their accents should be the same as hers, shouldn't they? But she finds she's unable to immediately understand the conversation two young women are having next to her on a bench. *Can local slang have changed this much since I left?* she thinks. *Or have I forgotten?* And their clothes – well, the hemlines mostly seem to be lower here, she thinks, tugging her miniskirt down towards her knees. She's now doubting this clothing choice, which had seemed perfectly fine in Cornwall. *What will Daddy think of it?* She considers changing in the ladies' toilet, but this thought is disregarded when she sees her bus approaching. Better to get this over with, she thinks. She gets into the queue to board.

She knows the initial explanations will be the hardest. She'll have to tell them she hadn't settled at Hallows. She'll have to say that last part without looking at anyone, because she's a dreadful liar.

She won't be here long. Only until she can find herself another job in Dublin, and somewhere else to live. Although she's decided she needs to come back to Ireland, she's not prepared to remain in the family home. Even her love for her sisters is not enough to make her do that.

Theresa reaches the front of the queue and digs in her pocket for the change she needs to pay her fare. She's had it in a purse in her bedside table ever since she arrived at Hallows. It feels odd to be back using Irish pounds again, she thinks, handing it over to the driver.

Theresa sits on a worn leather seat and looks out as the bus navigates the bustling streets of central Dublin. Theresa hears snippets of gossip, plans for evening dances, and the occasional burst of laughter. She's keen not to be drawn into conversation with her fellow passengers, however, because she's too anxious about what's to follow. So instead, she eyes the men hustling on the pavements; the shops selling polished red apples and pyramids of potatoes; the lengthy queue for the public baths; young women in vibrantly patterned sundresses; men in sharp suits and linen shirts; and babies being pushed along in gleaming prams.

As the bus nears Tallaght, the cityscape begins to dissolve into sporadic fields and ever-growing clusters of houses. The government has designated it an area for growth, prompting a building boom the likes of which none of the locals could ever have imagined. You can see the construction dust in the air, Theresa thinks, looking up at the sky, which definitely has a yellow tint to it.

Then the bus passes a sign proudly announcing their arrival in Tallaght, and despite her long journey, Theresa's heart starts to beat faster. There's the post office; the bar, with several men sitting outside, chain smoking; the streets of terraced cottages. The bus stops, and lots of passengers disembark. But not Theresa – not yet. She sits on the bus as it drives to an area where the road widens, and the homes become gradually larger, with bigger and bigger gardens. Finally, she presses the stop request button and feels the bus slow.

She is the only person getting off here. She lugs her suitcase onto the pavement and pauses as the bus restarts and trundles off to the next village along. She fantasises for a brief moment about picking up her bags and running after it, and taking it to the end of the route, wherever that might be. But she doesn't, of course. Instead, when she can no longer see it, she picks up her bag and walks to the left, down a lane which forks to the right and goes up a small hill. Halfway up, she opens a large, ornate metal gate. She stops for a moment, inhaling the heady scent of cut grass and honeysuckle, a glorious cocktail for a summer's day. Then she takes a deep breath and walks about fifty feet up a paved path towards a solid, square, elegant Georgian house, which sits at the top of the hill, its rural view disappearing daily as housing stock grows. It's still the most beautiful house in the village, though, she thinks. Everyone agrees upon that fact. And everyone knows about this house, of course, because it's the home of the area's new Teachta Dála – their Irish Assembly member, the Irish equivalent of an MP.

The new Teachta Dála for this area of south-western Dublin is Morris Murphy.

Daddy.

29

AMANDA

Good Friday, 2025

'Revenge? How?' Amanda locks her eyes on Mike's, even though he's currently looking down into his lap, avoiding her gaze. She can't quite believe what she's just heard. It feels like her husband has been possessed. And even though she knows he's in a very vulnerable state at the moment, she feels her hackles rise, because he has clearly been keeping something from her. Something big.

'I thought... I thought... I could make his life miserable, just like Olly's life had been miserable. Make him feel some of that mental torture.'

'I see.' Amanda can imagine how Mike must have felt, coming face to face with the man who he blames for not saving Olly from his terrible fate. For being culpable through neglect. How angry he would have been that such a man could have been promoted to headteacher, given this painful piece of family history. And she also knows – but has never said so out loud – that Mike's relationship with his parents nosedived after Olly's death. They were both destroyed by it, absolutely destroyed, and were apparently unable to support their surviving son emotionally. So it's quite likely, she reasons, that at least some of this rage at Father Paul is a projection of Mike's deep, unacknowledged pain about that. 'But if you wanted to do that, you've been going about it a funny way. I mean, it seems to me that you've just been working yourself to death making this school better. That rewilding session I attended... It was good, Mike. Those boys were really responding to you. How has that made things worse for Father Paul? Did you... did you change your mind, after you arrived?'

Mike looks directly at her for a brief moment. He looks hunted.

'I never wanted to take the school down. If anything, since arriving and seeing how things are, I've wanted to make the school better, to save it. And you know that, of course. You've put up with so much, Mandy. I haven't been around for you.' This is an understatement, and they both know it. Amanda nods, because she doesn't think it's the right time to have a serious conversation about the dreadful state of their relationship. 'I know I've neglected you. Us. But I'm a teacher. It's a job I love and I want to do it well. I care about the boys, about improving things for them. But I still wanted to skewer Paul. The only way I could cope, working in such close proximity with him, was to know that eventually I'd be able to bring him down.'

And then something occurs to Amanda. Something extraordinary.

'And you succeeded, didn't you?' she says, remembering the headmaster's unexplained breakdown, after the incident at the mine. *Suddenly*, she thinks with a jolt, *suddenly things are making sense*. 'You knew those boys were going to be at the cove that night.'

'Yes,' he says, shuffling around so that he can look out of the window. 'Or at least, I had an inkling.'

'Was it your idea?'

'Partly.'

Who is this man? Amanda thinks. *I don't know him at all.*

'You put those boys in danger, and caused a huge scandal for the school, just because you were angry at the headmaster?'

'The boys were never in danger. I knew the tide would be out.'

'Hang on. When you say you had an inkling they'd be there – what do you mean?' Mike takes another sip of his tea, which Amanda thinks must be getting quite cold by now. 'Tell me. How did it happen?'

'They are curious, those boys. Interested in the world, in history, in me, in each other. We've built a good rapport at the rewilding club. We got talking about the boat accident in the sixties and they asked me more about it.

They'd come across a podcast about it which featured all kinds of conspiracy theories, most of which were based on the fact that none of the bodies were ever found.' Amanda tries to keep her face straight. This isn't the time to tell him how well acquainted she is with it. 'Some of them became obsessed with it and wanted to find out more about the boys who were lost. Then someone mentioned the ghost stories that swirl about this place – you'll have heard the one about the friendly monk.' Amanda feels a shiver run down her spine, when she thinks about the conversation she'd had with the monk in the abbey. But she shakes it off. He was definitely real. 'And anyway, I told them about Ouija boards, and they became obsessed. And I said I'd help them do it.'

'But they could have done it in a dormitory, couldn't they? But instead, they went out to the cove. Why?'

'Oh, they go there all the time to vape. It was one of them who suggested it. It wasn't me. They wanted to go there because it was where the boat set off from.'

'So you knew it was going to happen? And you did nothing about it?'

'Yes. I decided to let it pan out.'

'And they got in trouble for it, didn't they?'

'That bunch are always in trouble for something. It was water off a duck's back. I made sure their punishments were slight.'

'You made sure they were caught?'

Mike shakes his head. 'No. I knew they'd never forgive me for that. I just... didn't stop them. And I crossed my fingers, I suppose, that it might blow up in Paul's face.'

'I don't get it, Mike. I just don't. Ofsted were called after that incident. The reputation of the school was thrown into question. Why would you risk that? Why would you risk your job?'

Mike turns back round and puts his half-finished mug of tea on a small table next to the sofa.

'It was me that sent the tip-off to Ofsted.'

'You... You did what?'

Amanda's eyes flare. She can't believe this. She can't believe this at all.

'The safeguarding set-up here is terrible. I knew if Ofsted came, they'd find Father Paul and probably Bede culpable for those policies, or lack of them, and they'd probably lose their jobs.'

'And the risk of the school closing was one that was worth taking? After that huge move, that move I did for you... you were prepared to risk it?'

'It will be fine, Mandy. I'm in charge now. Paul's out of the picture. And the parents trust me. I've got a plan to turn this place around...'

'And what about Father Paul? I know you don't like him, and he behaved really badly where Olly is concerned... but the poor man seems to have completely broken down... Did you know that would happen?'

Mike inhales and exhales through his nose before he answers. 'All alcoholics remain alcoholics. Some of them just don't drink.'

'What are you saying?'

There's a short pause.

'Olly told me years ago that Father Paul had a booze problem. That sort of thing is impossible to hide from a bunch of boys who see you every day. He said he used to stink of it. He obviously dried out afterwards, otherwise the Church wouldn't have let him take a leadership role like this one here. But I wondered what might happen, you know, if I left some alcohol around. Nothing too obvious. I didn't pour him a glass of vodka, or anything. But I've kept a bottle of whisky in my office, in a cupboard we use to store stationery, ever since I arrived. He has the keys to my office, and we both use the cupboard. I noticed the level go down a couple of months ago, and then it would go up again. He was topping it up, hoping I wouldn't notice. I let him. I said nothing.'

'Oh my God.'

'I didn't make him drink it, Mand. He was stealing it from my office. That's not great, is it?'

'But you left it there deliberately.'

'I put temptation in his way, yes. But it's his own fault for giving in. He's a monk. He's supposed to be able to cope with temptation.'

'But he's an alcoholic.'

'Yes.'

Mike's anger at the headmaster is obvious. His nostrils flare. Amanda is surprised she hasn't suspected he felt this way about Paul before. Had there been signs she'd missed? Possibly, she thinks. She's been so busy dealing with her own crisis, and of course, Mike has been so busy and so tired. She'd put his strange behaviour down to stress, when she should have been asking more questions.

'So you think he's been going downhill for a while, and the incident at the cove had nothing to do with it?'

He shrugs.

'I expect it didn't help. But you know, I didn't mean for him to get ill. I thought he'd have to leave his post due to his addiction – you know, quietly retire once the monks realised he was back on the booze. And if that didn't work, I thought he'd just panic about the reaction from parents after the incident at the cove and stand down anyway, and with luck, Bede, too. But I didn't foresee him having a crisis and withdrawing completely. I contacted Ofsted before I really understood how badly he'd reacted to it all. I promise you that. I would never do that to someone. Especially after Olly. No, his breakdown was... entirely unforeseen.'

Amanda stares down at her empty mug of tea.

'I'm going to put the kettle on again,' she says, deciding that she needs time to think. She gets up and walks into the kitchen before Mike can say anything more. She's not even sure if he has anything more to say, but she needs time to process what she's heard already. He's never kept secrets from her before. Not that she knows of, anyway. And discovering that he's done so, and that he's done something so out of character, is unsettling, to put it mildly.

She fills the kettle on autopilot and flicks the switch to on. While she waits, she wonders why he didn't follow her. And then she realises that he might still be too cold to follow her. And then she thinks about how she found him, standing in the freezing water, staring out to sea, and she realises with a start how close she came to losing him. And then the tears come, slowly at first, then in torrents. She's glad of the noise of the boiling kettle, which masks them. Or at least, she'd thought it was masking them. Because within a few seconds, Mike is wrapping his arms around her, and she is sobbing into his shoulder.

'I'm so sorry, Mand,' he says, over and over again. 'I'm so, so sorry.'

30

THERESA

Evening, 2 August 1966

It's 7 p.m. when Theresa finally arrives at the front door of her childhood home. The sun won't set for a few hours yet, but it's been baking the front elevation of the house all day, and she can feel its warmth emanating from the walls and the paving beneath her feet. She is about to raise her hand to grasp the large silver knocker on the glossy black door but stops just before she makes contact with it.

She knows she needs to do it, of course. She can't stay here all night. But the issue is, she knows that once she's done it, she'll also have to absorb the shock of their wonderful housekeeper Fionnuala, who will no doubt answer the door, and her mother and four siblings, who will probably be in the dining room eating their supper. And once that's done with, she'll then have to start the painful process of explaining the reasons for her return.

In practice this means deploying the lies she's prepared. But it's not really the lies that are giving her pause. It's the fact that she will have to see her father again. She knows she will have to tolerate him gloating.

She turns towards the door and knocks twice, hard, before she can change her mind. It isn't long before she hears footsteps clicking on the tiles in the hall, and the door opens. As expected, it's Fionnuala who opens the door. Despite the fact it's the sixties and most households that can afford help only have a daily cleaner, her father insists on retaining a full-time member of staff. Although she's embarrassed by this ostentation, she is fond of Fionnuala, a woman who brought a great deal of much-needed warmth and reassurance to her childhood.

'Miss Theresa! Goodness, we didn't know you were coming home for the holidays. What a treat.'

Fionnuala opens her arms wide, and Theresa melts into her embrace. When they part, she sees the housekeeper's face is full of joy, and in that moment she decides she's not going to explain everything, not just yet. Later, she thinks. Later tonight, or tomorrow, at breakfast. After all, she's tired. She needs to sleep and think things over. She also needs to have a solid plan about what she's going to do next before she tells them she's left her job at Hallows. Particularly when she tells her father. This thought almost stops her crossing the threshold, but it's lovely Nula's expression that persuades her to do so.

'Thank you, Nula. What a wonderful welcome.'

'Well, come in, come in,' says the housekeeper. 'They're in the parlour. And you're in luck. I haven't served dinner yet.'

Theresa's mother and sisters are sitting just a matter of feet away, but something is holding her back.

'Is Daddy home?' She feels anxious just saying it.

'Oh, no, miss. He's away in Dublin until tomorrow. Parliamentary business.'

'Oh. I see,' says Theresa, a weight lifting from her shoulders. 'Well, that's great,' she says, walking in with purpose, placing her bag down by the bottom of the stairs and striding up to the dining room door, which she throws open for dramatic effect.

There are squeals and shrieks, and Theresa braces herself against a whirlwind of siblings: Fiona, fourteen, who seems to have shot up in height; Mary, twelve, her hair in gleaming brown bunches; Patricia, nine, with her gappy smile; and little Anne, four, who is no longer a podgy toddler but an agile, spritely little girl.

'Goodness,' says a voice from the other side of the room. It's the voice of Theresa's mother, Elizabeth. 'You're back.' She's doing well to mask her dismay, thinks Theresa, who eyes her closely. She made a promise, you see, and she hasn't honoured it.

* * *

It's several hours later, and Elizabeth and Theresa are sitting on a bench in the front garden, making the most of the cooler air. They are alone. Her younger siblings have been packed off to bed with great reluctance, and Nula has clocked off for the day. Theresa is both relieved and nervous that they will now be able to have an honest conversation, away from the others.

'Why didn't you phone, to let us know you were coming home?'

'You'd have tried to persuade me not to.'

Her mother doesn't reply immediately. Theresa watches the sheep that are grazing in the field further down the hill and listens to the sparrows and the finches singing in the trees that border the house. This is a view she has always loved. She missed it dreadfully. And she will miss it again, when she goes. Because she knows she must.

'Yes. I would.'

'I'm sorry. I'm sorry I came back.'

Elizabeth inhales sharply through her nose. 'Don't be.'

'But I promised.'

'I know. But I shouldn't have made you promise.'

Now it's Theresa who is lost for words. Elizabeth had been so firm with her about going. She wonders whether something has changed, whether things are better now. There are so many things she wants to ask, in fact, but she isn't sure she wants to know the answers.

'It was for the best,' says Theresa, after a pause.

'It wasn't. I put too much pressure on you. You are so... young. I shouldn't have expected...'

Theresa is startled by this. Her mother is not usually given to talking about feelings. Keeping your own counsel is very much the Murphy way.

'I know I shouldn't have come back. But I had to, Mammy. I had to.'

'Why? Were you unhappy in your job?'

'No. Yes. Sort of...' Part of her really wants to tell her about Trystan, because she's grieving and confused. But then the shame overwhelms her, and she just can't do it. Having a sexual relationship outside of marriage is a terrible sin on its own in the eyes of the Catholic Church, even without it being with a married man. A man with children. And her mother has always been so emotionally absent. She's never felt able to confide in her about anything.

'I made a mess of things. A terrible mess.'

'I'm sure it's nothing that can't be fixed.' This is the sort of thing Elizabeth used to say when Theresa had fallen out with her friends at school, or got in trouble with a teacher. It had been soothing then, and mostly correct. But it can't be now. Theresa knows she can't undo the things she did with Trystan. Or bring him back from the depths... A lump forms in her throat, and she swallows hard to try to clear it, to try to dismiss her grief. So instead of replying, she nods in response, because she can't think of something to say that won't give her away. And then she decides to tell her mother half the truth. *It will make things easier while I stay here*, she thinks, *while I look for another job*.

'There was an accident at school.'

'And you were somehow involved in it?'

Theresa shakes her head.

'No. No. It was... dreadful. A group of boys, really talented lads, the best of the school, academically – they went out on an annual boat trip with some teachers and there was a storm and... the boat was lost. They're all gone.'

'How absolutely dreadful.'

'Yes.' Theresa starts to feel tears rising, remembering the raw grief that had surged through the school like a virus in the hours and days afterwards. She wonders for a moment whether Elizabeth may be about to embrace her, but this doesn't happen. She's not surprised. It hasn't happened for years.

'But how can that be your fault?'

Here we go, thinks Theresa. The lie. The necessary lie.

'I handled things badly with a set of parents. The parents of one of the boys who was lost. I was insensitive. It was a difficult time for everyone at school, and I... I was struggling. But I behaved badly. Unacceptably. And so I resigned.'

'They didn't ask you to leave?'

Theresa shakes her head.

'Oh, no. No, they were happy for me to stay.' She thinks of the kindly headmaster, bewildered by her decision to go. She thinks of John, desperate for her to stay around, even though she'd known she had to go. 'But I just couldn't stay. Not after... that.'

'I see. Well, if you think it's for the best, I'm sure it is,' says Elizabeth.

'I'll find another job, Mammy. Maybe one in Ireland. Definitely not around here, of course. And when I'm settled, I'll find somewhere with enough room for... well, Fiona, at least. At first. She's old enough, I think.' Then she sniffs, and asks the questions she's been burning to ask, ever since she arrived home. 'Is he still... doing it?'

Neither of them says anything for a moment. Instead, they listen to the sounds of high summer which are all around them. The sheep bleating, the birds singing, and somewhere, a farmer driving a tractor around a field.

In the end, her mother replies not with words, but with a gesture. She nods. Slowly and painfully. And then she takes a deep breath, and says, 'Sometimes. But only when he's... tired. Or drunk. Or he's had a bad day at work. It's been very difficult, you know. The opposition have used the collapse of his business as ammunition during debates. He's found it difficult to take.'

Theresa's heart sinks. She had hoped that her father's election to public office might have quelled his anger and shame at the loss of the family firm which he'd inherited from his father. It had been a seismic moment in his life, and he had reacted very badly to it. Not that he'd shown that to anyone outside the home. Outside, he was still a fine, upstanding member of Irish society. But at home, behind the front door and always after Nula had gone home, her mother had borne the brunt of his rage.

Theresa had only discovered this by accident.

They'd thought she was upstairs in her room. She'd gone to bed early that night, preferring to read and listen to the wireless by herself rather than spend time with her father, who generally refused to let her watch the television, because he preferred to read the papers in silence in the evening with a large glass of whisky. However, on this particular night she'd grown restless and had decided to fetch a glass of milk from the kitchen.

It was then she'd heard them – the muffled cries and the sharp, whispered words. Confused, and wondering if her mother had fallen and hurt herself, she'd walked straight up to the closed parlour door and opened it, to be greeted by a hideous tableau which is etched in her memory: Elizabeth, collapsed in a chair, her arms up in front of her face; and her father, looming over his wife, the poker for the fire in his right hand, raised up like a jockey about to crack a whip.

Most men would have been deeply ashamed to be caught in the process of beating their wife. They would perhaps have pretended there had been a misunderstanding. But not Morris Murphy. No, Morris Murphy had simply turned towards his daughter, and shouted, 'And you! You're as useless as her. Your mother can barely bring herself to dress up nicely and turn out in town with me. And you have your training but haven't shown an ounce of interest in actually working to support yourself. You're all limpets. Pathetic limpets.'

Theresa had been paralysed with rage. Elizabeth's most recent and please God her last pregnancy, with Anne, had taken everything that remained of her mother's mental fortitude. Mammy had been struggling with her nerves and her energy levels ever since. She had seemed, on occasion, to be simply blank and numb, her responses minimal. She couldn't believe her father hadn't noticed and understood that. And as for Theresa, well, she'd only recently qualified and had postponed applying for jobs so that she could keep an eye on her mother and the other children, while Elizabeth got herself back on her feet. It had felt like the right thing to do. Her father, however, clearly felt differently.

She'd been about to argue back, to give Morris a piece of her mind, when he'd lunged at her with the poker, hitting her on the shoulder. It had still been warm from the fire. And when she'd stood her ground, rigid with shock, he'd hit her again, this time across her legs. She'd cried out in pain. This had apparently been the cue he needed to stop. He'd left the room swiftly, without even looking back.

When he'd left, she'd pulled herself back up to standing, wincing in pain, and gone to check on Elizabeth, who was still in the chair, still guarding her face with her hands. When she'd got close, she'd seen her mother was shaking.

'It's all right, Mammy,' she'd said, kneeling down in front of her and placing her hands around Elizabeth's, guiding them back down into her lap. As she'd done so, she'd seen what looked like scorch marks on her mother's right arm, and a red stripe on her skin where her dress sleeve had ended. 'It'll be all right,' she said then, feeling the ache in her legs and the pain in her shoulder.

'Will it?' Elizabeth had said, finally.

'Yes, it will. I will make it right.'

'No, you won't, my girl,' she'd said. 'What you'll do is leave. He has never hit the children. But now you're a grown woman, he won't spare the rod.'

They had argued about that for some time that night, and over the days that followed. Theresa's every instinct had been to protect her mother, but in the end, Elizabeth's dogged insistence had won the day. Theresa had agreed to her wishes because she realised her ability to get a good, stable job brought with it the possibility of escape not just for her, but for her siblings and, if she could persuade her to leave, her mother, too.

She had left Ireland with the aim of making enough money for her own place, with room for as many refugees from her family home as she could fit. And this is one of the reasons she feels ashamed. Instead of doing that, she had allowed herself to be distracted by lust and that strange addiction to being needed, and so she'd taken her eye off the prize. The savings she's managed to put away from Hallows aren't enough to fund anything more than a rented room for a month at most.

I must do better, Theresa thinks. *In my next job, wherever it is, I will work harder. Next time, I absolutely will not allow my selfish thoughts to distract me from my mission.*

* * *

Morris Murphy returns from parliament after supper the following evening, after Nula has finished her working day. His arrival is marked by the slamming of the door and what looks like an electric shock running through Elizabeth's body. Theresa is glad that neither Fiona nor Mary, who are both nearby reading magazines, seems to have noticed.

'Oh,' he says, entering the room where the family is gathered, spying Theresa sitting in an armchair in the corner, reading. He doesn't greet either of her siblings or his wife. Instead, he walks over to where Theresa is sitting.

'I didn't know you were coming back for a holiday.'

She examines him. She can't smell alcohol, but it's hard to tell at this distance. He looks relatively calm, however. Even so, she fights to control the serpent of fear that's wriggling in her stomach.

'I'm back for a little while, actually, Daddy. I've decided to find a new job.'

'You didn't like your old one after all?' he says, walking towards a small table in the corner which houses a decanter of whisky and some crystal glasses. He takes out the stopper and pours himself one.

'Yes, that's right.'

'Hmm,' he says, taking a sip of the whisky.

'Why don't you girls go and see if the little ones are in bed yet?' says Elizabeth to Fiona and Mary, her voice a strange monotone.

'OK,' say the girls, almost in chorus. They appear glad to be allowed to leave and are running upstairs within a few seconds of their mother's suggestion.

'So your great adventure in England wasn't so great after all, eh?' Morris takes a seat in a chair a few feet away from Elizabeth.

'I really enjoyed the role, but I want something a little closer to home, so I can be near my sisters.' Theresa doesn't even look at her mother as she says this. She does observe her father's face, however, to see how he takes it.

'I see,' he says, sipping his whisky. 'They sacked you, then?'

Before, this would have made her shrink back into the chair. To cower. To acquiesce. But now, after all she's been through, she feels her hackles rise.

'No. I left.'

'Did they make you?'

'That's enough, Daddy.'

Out of the corner of her eye, she sees her mother flinch.

'I'm sorry, child?'

'I'm not a child. And I was not sacked. They wanted me to stay. But I've come home, for a while at least, until I can find something else, closer to here. I want to be around to help Mammy...'

'Ah, yes, well, there we could be doing with some help, couldn't we, Elizabeth?' he says, smirking at his wife. 'Given how pathetic you're being at the moment. Perhaps Theresa can show you how to behave.'

Theresa is about to hit back with angry words. She has them ready formed, ready to come out, to defend her mother. But Elizabeth gets there first.

'How. Dare. You,' she says, low but loud. Firm. Determined. She hasn't looked this determined, in fact, as far back as Theresa can remember.

'Sorry. What the what now?' Morris is chuckling. He knocks back his whisky.

'How dare you speak to my daughter like that,' she says, just as determined. 'Or me.'

'You're my wife. I'll speak to you how I damn well like,' he says, his voice so loud, Theresa thinks the girls upstairs will be able to hear. She remembers hearing similar arguments as a child, muffled, through the floor. She'd felt sick with worry every time, and she'd stayed awake until late making sure her mother had made it into bed, still alive.

Morris stands up. Given that he must have been drinking before he came home, he's surprisingly steady on his feet. Theresa knows what he's about to do. She jumps up, determined to get between him and the poker, which is hanging by the fireplace.

She succeeds but then finds herself inches away from her father. He's at least five inches taller, and as she looks up, she sees his nostrils flare.

'What the hell do you think you're doing?' he says, glaring down at her.

'You will not hit her again.'

She remembers those words Father Volmar – if that's who it really was she'd been talking to – had said to her in the abbey. *Your heart always knows the way. It pays to follow its lead.*

And tonight, Theresa's heart knows that she came back to Ireland not just to escape her sins, but because she loves her sisters, and her damaged, desperate mother needs her help. She'd left home because Elizabeth had told her to do it, but she's known all this time that she had unfinished business here. She's come back to deal with it.

'I will do as I like.'

Morris lunges past her. She sticks out her foot on instinct, and he stumbles, but doesn't fall. The fact she'd nearly felled him enrages Morris. He doesn't bother reaching for the poker. Instead, he raises his fist.

Everything then happens very quickly.

Theresa is preparing to duck, hoping that her youthful speed will work in her favour, when Elizabeth springs up and throws herself between them, so it's her face that he hits, not Theresa's.

Elizabeth yelps and falls to the floor. Morris stands over her, hyperventilating. Theresa sinks down to try to help her mother. And Nula, the housekeeper they've employed for decades, pushes the door open wider and enters. She doesn't come as far as the hideous tableau on the floor, but far enough that Morris can see her.

'Thank you for staying late, Nula,' Theresa calls out, still tending to her mother.

'That's all right, miss,' says Fionnuala, her shock clear in the tone of her voice. 'I'm always happy to help.'

'I'm all right,' says Elizabeth, sitting up slowly, with her head in her hands. 'I'll be fine.'

Theresa stands up, noting that her father appears to have been struck dumb.

'What did you see, Nula?' she asks.

'I saw Mr Murphy hit Mrs Murphy through the gap in the door,' she says, her head high and proud. Theresa is convinced she can hear Morris snarl.

'And are you prepared to stand by what you saw in court?' she asks.

'Yes.'

'She's my wife. I can treat her how I like. There's no law against it,' says Morris.

This is, unfortunately, mostly true. Divorce is illegal, of course, and the Gardaí often view domestic violence as a private matter. But when you're in high office and there's a potential for prosecution under the Offences Against the Person Act, things look rather different. This is the calculation Theresa made when she asked Nula to stay behind this evening, and it's the one undoubtedly running through Morris's mind, too. He can't risk a public scandal, not now his only source of income is his government job.

'Even if the police don't take things further, mud sticks in politics,' she says. 'It wouldn't do for a man who espouses Christian values to be suspected of abusing his wife, would it?'

'You are the very devil,' says Morris, retreating to his chair and his whisky.

'Perhaps,' says Theresa. 'Thank you, Nula. You can go home now. I'll look after Mammy. We'll see you tomorrow.'

'No we won't,' snarls Morris, just as she turns to leave. 'You're sacked.'

'People talk, Daddy,' says Theresa. 'They talk a lot. If you sack Nula, I reckon they will ask why. And she won't have a reason not to tell them, will she?'

'Fine. How much do you want?' he asks the housekeeper.

She turns and faces him. 'I will take no payment, Mr Murphy. My father hit my mother too, until she was near dead. I'll be damned if I'll take your hush money.'

Silence descends on the room, which is filled with pain, rage, defiance and bravery.

'Damned nest of vipers.'

These are Morris's only words before he gets up and storms out of the room. A minute or so later, they hear the front door slam, and another minute later, a car engine starts and her father's car roars away.

'I'm so grateful to you, Nula,' says Theresa, returning to check on Elizabeth. 'I hope Daddy will keep you in post. He should do. He won't be able to cope with the shame if this gets out.'

'If he does, I will be happy to keep working here,' replies the housekeeper. 'I care for you all too much, and he's hardly home, at any rate. And if I do lose my job, so be it. I'll find another. I can't stand bullies. I wish I'd thought to do this myself. Now, let me go and see if I can rustle up some ice for that bruise. You poor thing, Mrs Murphy. You poor, poor thing.'

* * *

The next morning, Theresa rises early. When she reaches the bottom of the stairs, she notices her father's car keys are missing from their usual spot. He probably stayed out at his club, she thinks, or in an hotel. It doesn't matter. All that matters, really, is that he didn't come home. She hopes that Elizabeth has had a peaceful night.

She walks through to the kitchen and makes herself some toast and tea, before carrying it to the dining table. Then she hears the letter box clatter and realises the newspaper must just have been delivered. She walks back into the hallway and is surprised to see it isn't the local paper, but a handwritten letter. She picks it up and sees it's from England. She tears the envelope open as she walks back to the table and pulls it out as she sits down.

It's written on one side of lined paper torn out of a notebook, and it begins 'Dear Theresa', with 'Miss Murphy' written and then crossed out before it.

It continues:

I know this letter will arrive almost as soon as you do and for that I apologise. I just wanted to reiterate what I said when we met. I think I was very emotional that day, and I may not have made much sense, but I wanted you to be absolutely certain of my meaning. I do think we have a link, you and I, and I would greatly appreciate your support. I understand you have your reasons for returning home and I respect those, but if there is any chance of you coming back to Cornwall, please be assured I will be very happy to see you.
Yours sincerely,
John

She is reading the letter for the second time when her mother enters the room.

'Who's that from?' she says, coming to sit down at the table opposite Theresa.

'Oh, one of my former students,' she answers, folding it back up quickly, before turning her attention to her mother's face. As expected, her right eye is so swollen it's almost closed. 'You're up early,' she adds, gathering from her mother's opening statement that she'd like to pretend, at least for a moment, that what happened last night didn't actually occur.

'Yes. I heard you get out of bed.'

'Oh, I'm sorry. I didn't mean to disturb you.'

'That's quite all right. Look, Theresa… I wanted to speak to you, alone, before the children awake. About…' she pauses '…about last night, but also about what's happened in the past, and what happens now.'

'What do you mean? I don't think Daddy will try anything stupid. He'll be too worried about people finding out. I think you'll be fine for a while. I'm going to find a job in Ireland, and in time, you can all come and live with me. I told you I'd make it right.'

'I should have stood up to him a long time ago,' says Elizabeth.

'Mammy, it's all right. I know you were put in an impossible situation...'

'I wasn't. I'm a grown woman and I should have realised he'd go for you too. And for your sisters, in time. I've been a fool. And not just that. I've been... absent. I've been so busy struggling with my own demons that I've failed to be there for you, and for your sisters. You haven't had a mother, have you, for far too long. And I am deeply ashamed about that.'

Theresa wishes she could hug her mother, but experience tells her that Elizabeth would shrink from it. So instead, she uses words to convey how she feels.

'You have been so down since Anne's birth. I know it's been hard for you.'

'That's no excuse.' Elizabeth is shaking her head.

'It is. You aren't well.'

'That's as may be. But it's time. It's time I sorted myself out. I can't live like this any more. And you shouldn't have to, either.'

'But like I said, you won't have to. I know you can't divorce him but you can live apart from him. I'll get a job and...'

'I am going to leave him.' Theresa's eyes widen. This is entirely unexpected. 'I'm going to call my sister today. As you know, she and Martin have a large house and there's room for all of us. Truth be told, she's offered to take us before now, and I've been too proud to agree. So we will go there, and your father will, I suspect, send me with some money, because his pride and the fear he'll have about losing his post will make him do it.'

'Oh, Mammy.' A tear has formed in the corner of Theresa's left eye. She wipes it away with the sleeve of her nightdress.

'I missed you, when you went,' says Elizabeth. 'I missed you. I know I didn't write and we hardly exchanged words before you set sail, but I did miss you, Theresa. You mean a great deal to me. More than you can...' And now it's Elizabeth's turn to cry. This woman, formerly so blank, so numb, is starting to feel again, and the tears rain down like torrents. 'More than you can imagine. And I'm so sorry. So sorry about everything.' She holds out her hand across the table, and Theresa takes it, startled. 'What you did last night... I was in awe. Persuading Nula to stay and bear witness, and standing up to him... That was an act of courage and ingenuity. You are an amazing young woman.'

'I don't know what to say.' And she really doesn't. Theresa is speechless.

'You don't need to. But what I want to say, before I go and make myself some tea and begin this blessed day, is that you don't need to worry about me or your sisters any more. You mustn't feel you have to be here to protect us. I am going to do it from now on.'

'But Mammy...'

'I mean it. Please go and follow your star, wherever it leads you. I will always be around, holding the fort, when you want to come and visit.'

Elizabeth gets up and pats Theresa on the shoulder, briefly, as she leaves the room. When she's gone, Theresa stares at the envelope she's holding, deep in thought.

31

AMANDA

Late May 2025

April has given way to May. The hedgerows that line the twisting lanes around Hallows Abbey are alive with bees, making the most of the plentiful blossom and the warmth of early summer.

Inside Hallows Abbey, things are changing too. Slowly. Mike returned to work after a week off for 'flu'. Amanda had agreed to this on the understanding that he go to see the GP, which he did, with some reluctance. She knows it must have felt difficult for a man who had made it his life's mission to always appear unshakeable and unbreakable. He was prescribed antidepressants and he has also started counselling, not with Frances, but with a male counsellor they'd found in Redruth. Early signs suggest this combination may be helping him. He seems a lot calmer, and he's listening to her more. Which is vital, because she's still processing what he told her. She still can't quite believe how much he lied to her, and that he laid a deliberate trap for Father Paul, who is still nowhere to be seen. They've talked a lot about this since his revelations. He's told her a lot more about Olly, too, and about the terrible time he'd had after his brother's death. Particularly, about how he eventually came to blame himself for not spotting signs he was suicidal. He'd never told her any of this before. She is beginning to understand how those dreadful years long ago have been hanging around him like invisible chains ever since, weighing him down.

She hasn't forgiven him for any of it. Not yet. That will take time. But at least, she thinks, they're actually talking. They are actually telling each other how they really feel. That's a huge improvement.

'Shall we lock up?' asks Rosie. It's half past four on Friday, and all classes are over for not only the day, but also the weekend.

'Sure.'

'Are you OK, Mandy? You seem... on edge.'

Amanda hasn't told her friend about Mike's secret. She can't tell her. It would be the end of her husband's career. So she's forged on, trying to paste a happy face on every day, to pretend everything is fine. Rosie knows Mike has been finding work hard and is a bit stressed, but that's as far as it goes.

'Oh, sorry. I'm constantly thinking of one hundred and one things at the moment. I'm not on edge. I'm just distracted.'

'Hormones causing you trouble, huh?'

'Always.'

This is true, of course. She'd turned her alarm off that morning and forgotten she'd done it. She'd stared at her phone for quite some time, wondering why it hadn't gone off.

'Do you know what you need?'

'What?'

'A swim.'

'I need to go and think about dinner...'

'No you don't. Mike won't be finished for two hours, will he? Come on, come with me. Let's have a dip.'

Amanda looks out of the window at the golden afternoon light.

'You're a very persuasive woman, Rosie.'

'I know this.'

* * *

'Is Father Paul coming back, do you know? He's been ill for a while now.'

'The honest answer is, I don't know,' Amanda replies, floating on her back, looking up at the azure sky. The sea is so calm today, it could be taken for a lake. 'We keep being told he will return, but we don't know when.'

'Well, Bede is clearly loving his moment in the sun.'

'Yes, he's certainly getting to grips with paperwork now, after the criticisms from Ofsted. He seems to be at least coping, which is good.'

'How's he taken to Mike's new rules?'

Mike recently took the decision to ban student access to mobile phones each weekday, except for a couple of hours in the evening for family phone calls, and chats with friends elsewhere. They must leave their phones in a safe for the rest of the time.

'You know, after initial resistance, the boys seem to have adapted, and so has Bede, even though it was Mike's idea. He never liked the phones anyway.'

'Talking of Mike's ideas, I popped into the walled garden the other day and saw that new student garden project you've been helping with. It looks great.'

'Yes, I missed my allotment a lot, so it feels good to be teaching them some important life skills, outside. And Mike's been talking to the local gig club about getting the boys involved in sea rowing, you know. He's also persuaded the art department to set up an art and nature club...'

'I'm beginning to think I want to attend this school,' says Rosie, chuckling. 'Art and nature! Sign me up.'

'I know, right. Where was that when I was at school?'

'Do you think he's done enough to be... safe? For the school to keep going?'

This question makes Amanda's stomach turn. She knows this is something Mike thinks about all day, every day. And her, too. Because his risky decision to alert Ofsted to the incident in the cave could still come back to haunt him. There's a meeting of the governors next week. It's possible they might tell him he's out of a job. And also, she thinks, that the Church has taken the decision to close Hallows entirely. It feels absurd, given how long the school has existed, but she knows it really might happen. Hallows runs on tight margins, and just a small dip in enrolments for next year could be catastrophic.

'I really hope so, Rosie,' she says, righting herself and swimming towards the shore. 'I really do hope so.'

* * *

It's nearly six in the evening when Rosie and Amanda part at the entrance to the school grounds.

'I'll see you Monday,' says her friend, as she walks away in the direction of the car park.

'Yes, have a lovely weekend,' replies Amanda, waving as she disappears around the corner of the school building. She loiters for a moment, enjoying what's left of the day's sun on her face. She's about to enter the school when she spots something unusual out of the corner of her eye. It looks like smoke, and it's coming from the direction of the garden.

Despite the fact she's still damp from the sea, she decides to investigate. There's no official reason for there to be a fire in the walled garden at the moment. The caretaker certainly wouldn't have lit one. She wonders if one of the boys has managed to get in there after hours and lit an unauthorised fire in the fire pit. She uses the school wifi to message Mike to tell him what she's seen before walking at speed in the direction of the smoke.

As she gets closer, she can see it's definitely coming from inside the garden. She reaches the gate and is not surprised to find it open. She walks inside and sees smoke billowing from the far corner. And then she realises, with horror, that it seems to be coming from the chicken coop. She runs.

When she reaches the corner, she finds the right-hand side of the coop well alight, and it seems like the whole structure is leaning at a funny angle. *I need to save the chickens*, she thinks. She can see them cowering on the far left, as far away from the seat of the flames as they can manage. She looks around desperately and spots a discarded spade a few feet away. She snatches it up, approaches the left side of the coop, shoves the spade in the door frame, and heaves. At first she thinks it's not going to budge, but then the flimsy lock gives way and it springs open. The chickens run out in panic and disappear behind her, to safety. She breathes a sigh of relief. Then she looks back at the coop and assesses her options. There's a tap halfway along this side of the garden wall, with a hose attached. She runs up to it and turns it on. She's hauling the hose back towards the coop when Mike appears.

'The coop's on fire! Help me,' she says. He does so, without question. He sprints with the hose to the far corner of the garden and aims it at what looks to be the seat of the fire, which is the rear right corner of the coop.

'How long have you been here?' he shouts.

'Just a few minutes. But long enough to let the chickens out,' she says, checking they are still free ranging behind them.

'Oh God, you went that close to the fire? Mand. That was dangerous.'

'I wanted to save them.'

'I know,' he said, putting his arm around her. 'I know.'

'Shall I call the fire brigade?' she asks, now she has time to think.

'I reckon we might be all right, actually. It's dying down.' Mike's right. There are no flames now, just smoke, and it hasn't spread to the left-hand side of the coop. 'You got here just in time, I think.'

'I'm so glad. I just saw it, you know, and thought I'd come and check it out.'

'How on earth did this happen? Do you reckon one of the boys has been smoking in here again?'

This is when Amanda realises why she thought the coop was at a funny angle. Because it *is* at a strange angle. Someone, she realises, has pulled it out from the wall.

'Oh God, they didn't go behind to smoke, did they?' she says, the horror of what might have happened suddenly occurring to her. Mike realises instantly what she means. He throws the hose down, and they both run round to the back of the coop.

It's been pulled out a good couple of feet from the wall. The evening shadows and the smouldering planks make it hard to see what's there, but Mike gets his phone out and turns on its torch.

Amanda gasps at what the light has just illuminated.

32

THERESA

Late August 1966

'Truro! Passengers for Truro, alight here.'

Theresa steps off the train with her suitcase, leaves it at the left luggage kiosk and sets off to explore Cornwall's only city. It's a glorious sunny day, and she has a spring in her step. She feels like a different woman to the one who left Cornwall almost a month ago with her tail between her legs. This time, she has a different plan, and not only that – her mother and sisters are safe. She no longer has the weight of their suffering on her shoulders. She feels free.

Today, she thinks, as she walks down Lemon Street, today is the beginning of everything else. And it will begin, she has decided, with an apology. She knows she has to do this to be able to move forward. This is a scary thing to do, that's true, but there's something about the new her that is able to cope with it. To rationalise it. To see beyond it.

She takes in the scene around her. Seagulls wheel overhead, their cries echoing against the elegant Georgian buildings that line the road. The scent of honeysuckle at the height of its power drifts from a nearby front garden, mingling with the tang of fish and chips from a takeaway on the corner. Theresa's mouth waters. She's missed Cornish fish and chips.

She pulls out the map of the city she picked up at the station. Theresa checks the address against the map one final time, puts it back in her pocket and sets off. It's a location in the north of the city, near Victoria Gardens.

Twenty minutes later, she's standing outside a row of terraced houses. They're mostly two rooms up, two rooms down. Children are playing out in the street, and outside number twelve, the address she's seeking, a red trike is balanced against the front wall and a partially deflated football rests beside an empty plant pot.

Theresa takes a deep breath and knocks. There's the sound of footsteps and a baby crying, and then the door is opened slowly, on the chain. A woman in her late twenties peers at Theresa through the gap.

'Who are you?' she asks. Theresa can see she has a baby in her arms, and that she looks exhausted. Theresa almost backs out, because of what this baby means. But she can't. She has to do this.

'Hello. This is really awkward.' Theresa squirms. 'But are you... Trystan Trevelyan's sister?'

The woman looks her up and down and then laughs bitterly.

'He told you that, did he?' She had known, as soon as she'd discovered that he had a family, that the address he'd given for his 'sister' was likely to be for his wife, instead. But what she hadn't expected is the look of pity she is receiving. After her confession at the inquest, she'd expected his wife to be furious with her. But she doesn't seem to be. 'You too, huh?' is all she says. 'You'd better come in.'

Theresa walks into a small front room, which is sparsely furnished with a threadbare sofa, a battered armchair, a wooden coffee table and two mismatched upright wooden chairs. A new television set sits incongruously in the corner.

'Take a seat over there,' she says, pointing to the sofa. She places the baby down on the floor next to assorted metal toys, which he immediately picks up and starts mouthing. 'I'm Katie. Can I get you anything to drink?'

'Theresa. And no. It's OK. I can see you have your hands full. Look, I'm so sorry to bother you. I won't take long. I'm just here to apologise.' She takes a deep breath. 'I... had a relationship with your late husband. You probably know all about that from the papers. But you must know I had no idea he was married and if I had I'd never have gone near him, I swear. I am absolutely mortified... And if there's anything I can do...'

The woman sits down in the armchair next to the baby. Theresa braces for her rage.

It doesn't come.

'Seriously, I should probably be thanking you, if I'm honest. I was pregnant while he was with you and frankly, him seeing you meant I had a break. He was, how shall I put this... persistent? Determined? He loved women, did Trys. Especially ones he wasn't married to.'

'Oh.' Theresa is shocked.

'Did you think you were the only one?' Theresa can feel herself shrinking. Now her shame is mingling with embarrassment. She is even more of a fool than she'd thought.

'I'm sorry. That's unfair of me. He was a charmer. How old are you? Early twenties? I met him when I was about your age, and back then, I thought he was the bee's knees. It took me far too long to realise he wasn't. I can't expect you to be any different.'

'I... He... he was charming, yes. And I wanted... to be wanted. But that's no excuse. I just came to say how sorry I am.'

'Don't be. Don't get me wrong, I didn't wish him dead, but... him having affairs is the least of my troubles.'

'I'm so sorry. How will you cope, now that he's gone?'

'I'll manage. The Seafarers' Mission are helping. They gave us that TV—' her eyes dart over to the gleaming new box in the corner '—and his state pension will help. We'll get by.'

'I wish I had something I could...'

'Don't be daft, girl. You're just starting out. Save your money.'

Theresa finds she has no idea what to say, so she decides to leave.

'You don't need me here. I can't be helping. But I am so grateful for your time.'

She stands up. Katie follows her.

'Before you go, Theresa... just one piece of advice,' the older woman says, reaching to open the door.

'Yes?' says Theresa, stuck between her arm and the outside world.

'Beware charming men who promise you the world. Don't make the same mistake I did.'

'I... Thank you,' she replies, and Katie removes her arm and opens the door.

Theresa sets off down the street at pace, waving an awkward goodbye.

* * *

Half an hour later, Theresa returns to the station. She retrieves her suitcase, checks the boards and walks to platform two to await her next train.

She sits down on a wooden bench and considers the encounter she's just had. In some ways, it was devastating. She's found out that Trystan had had a pregnant wife the entire time she'd been with him. She thinks about those friends of his in the pub, who probably knew about it. But then she thinks about Katie's apparent absence of anger about Theresa's role in the affair, and her determined advice, which has now taken up residency in her mind.

Because there was an important truth in what Katie said. Theresa is coming to realise that she's actually had a rather narrow escape. In fact, it might have been far worse for her if Trystan *had* been single, and in need of a wife.

When the train to Falmouth is called, Theresa springs up from the bench and experiences a strange sensation: a weight she's been carrying around for months has just left her. She opens a door to a carriage and enters in what feels like a dream. She spends the short journey staring out of the window, absorbing the ancient hedgerows, the grazing cattle, and the sunburnt heath – all sights of a county she thought she would never return to, but one that feels, nevertheless, like home.

When her stop is called, she alights, visits the ladies' to check her appearance in the mirror, leaves her bag at another left luggage counter – soon, she hopes she'll have somewhere proper to leave it – and heads to the taxi rank. She asks the driver to take her to Castle Hill.

When the cab pulls up outside a grand Victorian building with sweeping lawns overlooking the sea, Theresa says a little silent prayer for wisdom and confidence and walks up the drive with her head held high.

* * *

John is waiting for her when she comes out. She'd written to him before she left Dublin and told him about the interview, and he'd insisted on meeting her afterwards. She pulls him in for a brief hug, and she feels him relax as she does so.

'So what was it like?' asks John, as they head towards the town centre.

Theresa recounts what she's just seen: the children's home's grand Victorian proportions, its sweeping lawns, its view of the sea and the little apartment that comes with the role of live-in nurse. And then she thinks of the many faces of the children there: questioning; resignation; loneliness; fear. Their faces reminded her of the boys at Hallows Abbey, even though of course there is a huge gulf in their circumstances. But they are all children, she thinks. All in need of love and care.

'It's... a decent home, I think,' she replies. 'There are fourteen boys there. There are two of them to a room. All ages.'

'And you'd be there all the time?'

'Yes. I'd have days off, obviously, but yes, I'd live there.'

'Lucky kids.'

Theresa almost replies that she thinks the children there are the opposite of lucky, but then she considers John's awful childhood, and she realises he'd probably have preferred a children's home over living with Trystan.

'I haven't got the job yet.'

'They'll offer it to you. You're good at what you do.'

'I hope so. I'd like it, I think.'

'And you'll have a spare room?'

Oh, goodness, thinks Theresa. *He wants to live with me, doesn't he?*

'Yes. But John, I...'

'It's all right. I know you want to offer a room to one of your sisters. I don't expect to move in with you and become your son. You just being close is... good. It's enough. It's more than I expected, actually, if I'm honest.'

Theresa stops walking for a moment.

'Oh, John. I'm here for you, of course I am. You're a large part of the reason I came back. I feel better, being here.'

'That's wonderful,' says John. 'It really is.'

'How are you feeling now?'

John looks thoughtful. 'Do you mean, do I miss my father? Because the answer, of course, is no.'

'I know that. I meant to ask, actually. How did your mother take it? I know Trystan left her, but still... him dying must have been a terrible shock.'

'I didn't realise you didn't know. My mother's dead.'

'Oh my goodness.'

'She killed herself...'

'I'm so sorry. I wish I hadn't asked. I had no idea...'

'It was almost seven years ago now,' he says, his voice oddly detached. 'My mother killed herself just after he left. She loved him, despite everything. He drank, he failed to contribute enough financially, and he played away with other women. And in the end, she simply couldn't take the grief of it any more.'

'I'm so sorry.'

'That could have been you, you know. He was dangerous around women.'

Theresa nods. She knows now that this is true.

'So did Katie bring you up? I... met her earlier. She was... very kind,' she says, as they resume walking.

John shakes his head.

'No. When Mum died, my aunt and uncle took me in. They live here, in Falmouth. They don't have much money and they're confused by what they refer to as my bookish nature, but they're a darn sight more pleasant to live with than my father ever was.'

'I'm glad about that, at least. So where have you got in mind for our dinner, then?' She's agreed to meet him for a meal, before heading to her hotel.

'I rather hoped you'd come and meet my guardians, actually. If that's OK?'

'Of course.' She's surprised by this, but delighted. She'd been meaning to talk to his mother about her ideas, but now she knows this is sadly impossible. Meeting his guardians will work out well.

'How far is it?' she asks, as they wend their way through the town's backstreets.

'Not far. Ten minutes, maybe.'

They walk along in companionable silence until they come to a row of terraced cottages, all braced against the hillside. 'Here is it. Number six,' he says, knocking at the door.

'Are they expecting us?' she asks. John looks shifty. She's about to remonstrate with him when there's a shuffling sound, and the door begins to open.

'Hello?' says the woman who's answered the door. She's got striking auburn hair pulled back into a low bun, and she's wearing a knee-length floral house dress and a pinafore. Then she spots who's standing next to Theresa. 'Oh, it's you, John. Why didn't you use your key?'

'I have a guest with me. You always want a warning when there's a guest.'

'Oh, yes,' says the woman. 'Sorry. Yes.'

'This is Miss Murphy, Auntie. She was my school nurse at Hallows.'

The woman's eyes soften. 'Ah, I see. Well, come in, both of you. I don't want you making the doorstep look untidy.'

Theresa walks through the door straight into the front room. About ten feet square, it contains a brown cord sofa, a small wooden table, a fireplace with a mantelpiece topped with a framed drawing of the Virgin Mary, and a single, worn armchair. Through a door to the rear, Theresa can see a kitchen, and stairs leading upwards. 'Take a seat. I'll bring tea.'

Theresa and John sit on opposite ends of the sofa. She looks about her as John's aunt clatters about next door, opening cupboards and turning on the kettle. Despite its simple furnishings, the room is spotless. It's cleaner in here than their front room in Ireland, she thinks, and her family pays someone to keep house.

'How old were you when you came to live with your aunt and uncle, John?' Theresa asks, realising she doesn't know this detail.

'Oh. Eight.'

Theresa imagines an eight-year-old, grieving his mother and deeply afraid of his father, walking into this house, and fights the urge to gather John into her arms in an attempt to console that little boy.

'Goodness,' is all she can think of to say.

'Here we go,' says John's aunt, walking back into the lounge and placing a tray on the table. 'Would you like milk?' she asks Theresa.

'Yes please. No sugar.'

The woman nods, pours the tea and hands it to Theresa.

'Thank you. You have a lovely house here. Mrs...'

'Oh, I'm so sorry, I should have introduced myself. Or John should have! I'm Annette. Annette Evans. My husband Joe is out at work.'

'Nice to meet you, Annette.'

'And you. John's told me a lot about you.'

'Has he?' Theresa is surprised, yet again, about the importance she seems to have had in John's life.

'Yes. He said you were the nicest thing about his school,' she says, passing John a cup of tea, and then serving herself.

'Actually, I've been wanting to talk about his schooling,' says Theresa, deciding that there's no time like the present.

'It's been concerning us a great deal, too,' says Annette, sitting down in the armchair. 'Throwing away that scholarship to that school... It's sacrilege. Your mother would be turning in her grave, John.'

Theresa feels John bristle. She knows how angry he is, beneath the well-behaved surface he's currently managing to maintain. She remembers only too well the impact of his fists on that school bully. She doesn't want him to snap at his aunt, who he's told her has been kind and caring towards him ever since she took him in.

'If I may... I think it's important you should know how unhappy John was at Hallows,' says Theresa, shooting a glance at John, who simply nods. 'Some of the boys were horrible to him.'

'I see,' says Annette. 'He didn't say. Why didn't you say, John? We were so shocked, when we heard you wanted to leave. It just came out of the blue.'

The teenager shrugs.

'I just didn't want to bother you,' he says, finally.

'I wouldn't have been bothered. My sister would have wanted me to have been bothered, anyway. And Joe and I care. Of course we do.'

'I know that. But I also know that the schooling at Hallows was free, and it's such a good school. I didn't want you to be disappointed in me.'

'John, for the last time, we are never disappointed in you,' she says. 'We're just worried. Your father has just died. I know you didn't have much of a relationship with him, but that's a lot to take in. And then you just came home from school and announced you wanted to leave Hallows, and we have no idea what to do with you next. You're so clever. Joe and I love you, you know we do, but we don't know what's what, on the academic side of things. It was never my strong suit, anyway,' she says, looking at Theresa apologetically.

'I've been giving it some thought,' says Theresa, sipping her tea. 'I've been worried about his education, too. But we've been talking, John and I, and I've also spoken to the headmaster of Hallows, Father Crispin, and I think we may have come up with a plan.'

'Oh,' replies Annette. 'What is it?'

'I don't want to go back,' says John.

'Oh, no, it's not that.' John visibly relaxes. 'Father Crispin is good friends with the priest at St Piran's, in the centre of Truro. He has agreed to continue providing John with a religious education, outside of schooling, which I propose should be at the grammar school. He's very academic and I'm certain he will be offered a place.'

'So he'll attend school as normal, and have extra classes at St Piran's?'

'Yes, exactly.'

'Would you like this, John?' asks Annette. Theresa is struck by how considerate this woman is of her charge. It must be tough, Theresa thinks, to take on someone else's child, particularly when, for whatever reason, you haven't had one of your own. But just in this small window into their relationship, Theresa discerns that John's aunt has vastly more genuine affection for him than he has given her credit for.

'Yes,' replies John, fervently.

'Well, if it's what you want,' says Annette, sipping her tea. 'Then that's what you should do.'

'You don't mind that I'm leaving Hallows Abbey?' John asks, wide-eyed. 'You were so pleased when I got in there. I thought...'

'You silly boy,' she says, playfully leaning over and patting his knee. 'I don't care where you go to school. My sister just wanted the best for you. And so do we.'

And then for just the second time since she's met him, Theresa witnesses John cry.

33

AMANDA

Late May 2025

'Oh my God,' says Amanda. 'What the hell is that?'

Amanda and Mike are staring at what looks to be a hole in the ground.

'I think it's exactly what it looks like.'

'What is it? A sinkhole? Did the monks put the chicken coop there to cover it up?'

Mike squats down and shines his torch into it.

'I don't think this is natural,' he says, coughing because smoke is drifting in their direction. 'In fact, I know it isn't. There are steps down here.'

They exchange quizzical glances.

'We should go and tell the abbot…'

Amanda doesn't manage to finish her sentence, because they both hear a noise coming from the hole. Coughing.

'Hello?' she calls out. 'Hello? Is someone there? Are you hurt?'

She wonders whether one of the staff came to try to fight the fire and fell down there, or perhaps someone was doing maintenance to the coop, and tumbled down the hole accidentally. But then she sees a pool of wax near the top of the hole, and she starts to doubt her theories.

There's more coughing, but no response to her cries.

'I'm going to go down there,' says Mike.

'You can't. It might not be safe.'

'It sounds like someone needs help.'

'Should I call for an ambulance?'

'Good idea.'

Amanda gets out her phone, but sees it has no signal. She calls 999 anyway, hoping her phone will connect to another network, but the school's isolation means the call goes unconnected.

'Damn it. I'll have to go and find some wifi...' She trails off, because Mike is already lowering himself into the hole. There's absolutely no way she's going to let him go down there alone. She shelves the call for now.

'I'm coming too,' she says, following him.

'The ladder's quite sturdy,' calls out Mike, his torchlight flashing as he moves downwards. She turns around and descends backwards, clinging on to the wooden ladder as she descends into the darkness.

'I've reached the bottom.'

Amanda is relieved to hear he's down safely. She is too, a few seconds later.

It takes a few moments for her eyes to acclimatise to the darkness beyond their limited phone torches and the daylight coming through the hole above them. It's then that they see it. Another source of light – a round circle in the distance.

'That must be the exit,' says Mike.

'What is this?' asks Amanda. 'A smugglers' tunnel, or something?'

Amanda is well aware of Cornwall's history of smuggling, and of far worse – deliberate wrecking of boats. Some terrible men had lured boats onto rocks by pretending their hand-held lanterns were lighthouses.

'It might be. But I wonder if it's part of the tin mine, actually,' says Mike.

'I thought all the tunnels were blocked up?'

'They are, by the mine buildings,' he says, shining his torch back and forth. The tunnel behind them, the one that would have gone inland, is blocked by solid earth. Only the other direction, the one that appears to lead slightly downhill towards the light, is open. 'Maybe they left a few open further out?'

'Maybe. Hello?' Amanda calls out again, mindful that they came down here to try to find the person in need of help. There's still no answer.

'Shall we go and see if they're down there?' asks Mike.

'Yes, OK.'

They walk slowly down the tunnel, which smells of earth, damp and salt. The ground beneath their feet is rocky and uneven, and Amanda stumbles, only saving herself by bracing against the wall to her right. It feels damp.

'You OK?' Mike calls back, from several feet ahead.

'Yes, fine,' she says, righting herself. 'Any sign of the person we heard?'

'Not yet.'

And then the singing starts. It's a man's voice, she thinks, someone with a beautiful voice, and the song is echoing down the tunnel walls.

> The first time I met you, my darling
> Your face was as fair as the rose,
> But now your dear face has grown paler
> As pale as the lily white rose.

'Where's that coming from?' she says, speeding up to join Mike. The white circle at the end of the tunnel is now about ten times bigger. It's clear now that it's daylight, and she thinks she can make out blue sky.

'Here,' says Mike. Her eyes are dazzled by the light for a moment, but she can see that he's reached the end of the tunnel. She joins him and sees that she's looking out over the cove. The familiar rock faces are to her left and right, and the little quay that leads out from the beach is below. She realises that the tunnel's exit is hidden from below by a rocky outcrop straight in front of it, which she and Mike are currently standing behind. And atop it, perilously close to what must be a sheer drop off the edge, is Father Paul, singing.

> Love the White Rose in its splendour
> I love the White Rose in its bloom...

'Paul? Can you hear me? *Father Paul?*' Mike is shouting, but the headmaster isn't responding. Amanda moves to the right as far as she dares and peers around the rock Paul is standing on. It's about a fifty metre drop from here to the beach, she reckons, and straight down. There's a small ledge that juts out on her side, and she shuffles onto it, clinging to the rock.

'Father Paul?' she says, wondering if he might respond better to someone who isn't one of his senior colleagues. And perhaps, she thinks, being a woman, and therefore definitely not a fellow monk, might help too.

It works. He turns his head.

> I love the White Rose so fair as she grows.
> It's the rose that reminds me of you.

She sees he's holding a bottle of supermarket own-brand vodka in his left hand.

'Why don't you come down, Paul, and you can tell me more about your song?' she says, smiling.

Paul's nose twitches.

'It's "The White Rose",' he says, his gaze unfocused. 'One of my favourites.'

'I like it. Why don't you come down? It looks dangerous up there?'

Paul laughs.

Out of the corner of her eye, she sees Mike finding footholds in the rock – presumably the ones Paul had used to get up there – and he starts to climb. She understands what he's going to try to do, and she also understands her part in it.

'What's it about?' she asks, keeping her tone light.

'They sing it at funerals in these parts. It's about loss. About death. About grief.'

'That sounds depressing, for such a beautiful tune.'

'Life's like that, isn't it. All beautiful things…'

He doesn't get to finish his sentence, because Mike has just pulled hard at his waist. For one heart-stopping moment she thinks they both might fall forwards, but then Mike's relative youth and fitness win the day. Paul falls backwards, but Mike clings to him, and his own feet land back on the ground behind the rock outcrop with a thud, Paul tumbling down beside him.

Amanda rushes over, concerned that one or both of them may be seriously injured. She's relieved to see Mike is already pulling himself up and brushing dust off his clothes.

'Oh my God, I thought you'd both...' she says, but there isn't time to tell Mike how she feels, because Paul is scrabbling about and yelling in pain. She looks down and sees his ankle is lying at an odd angle. 'I think he might have broken it.'

'Better that than breaking everything in a fall down there,' says Mike, and the thought of what that would do to a body makes her feel queasy. She nods. 'Let's help him get back to the Abbey,' he says. 'They must be wondering where he's gone.'

* * *

When they reach the steps that lead up to the walled garden, they both realise they're going to need help to get the elderly monk up the steps and through the hole.

'I'll stay here with him,' says Mike. 'You go and get help.'

Amanda emerges from the darkness into the garden, with the still smouldering chicken coop on her right. She yells down into the hole that she'll be back very soon and then sprints out of the garden and towards the monastery. She'd considered going to the school, but it's after teaching hours, and most staff will have left. She doesn't want to go to one of the boarding houses, as the boys there might find out what state Paul is in. Even though he clearly has terrible failings, he's a human being and she doesn't want to see him humiliated. And anyway, his injuries aren't life threatening. She has the time to go to the other monks for help. She runs around the main school building, across the roundabout and to the right of the abbey, to a door for visitors to the monastery. She presses the doorbell several times and hears its shrill bell ring deep inside the two-storey Gothic building.

She waits for a couple of minutes, shifting her weight from foot to foot to give her nervous energy an outlet, until she hears someone turning a key in the lock. Seconds later, the door opens. It's Bede. Oh God, she thinks. It had to be Bede, didn't it? He'll love witnessing Paul's downfall. She decides to ask for the abbot.

'Is Father Anthony around?'

'Hello, Mrs Chapman. Yes, he's definitely here, although compline starts in ten minutes. Could you perhaps come back tomorrow morning?'

'It's very urgent. An emergency, really...'

'I see. Is it relating to the school?' he says, concern etched on his face.

'No. Well, sort of. It's Father Paul. Please, can you get Father Anthony?'

'Has he gone wandering again?' says Bede, raising his eyes to heaven. 'I'll come and bring him back.'

Amanda is surprised at his nonchalance.

'Yes, although I suspect he's broken his ankle. He's in a lot of pain and he's down a hole in the walled garden and we will need several people to help him up.'

Now it's Bede's turn to be surprised.

'Goodness. All right. I'll just go and rally the youngest and strongest of my brethren, and we'll be with you momentarily.'

Amanda is amazed how quickly the septuagenarian monk moves. Within a few minutes she is walking back towards the walled garden flanked by three monks: Bede, Albert, who she knows from her work in the walled garden, and Simeon, who occasionally teaches Latin at the school.

'You said he was down a hole of some sort?' says Bede, slightly out of breath due to the pace Amanda is setting.

'Yes. With Mike. It's an old mining tunnel, in the walled garden.'

'I thought we'd covered that entrance up,' says Albert, and it becomes clear immediately that although the staff at the school seem to have had no idea about this tunnel, the monks certainly do.

'I think Paul brought a candle down with him to light his way – heaven knows why, I'm sure he must have a torch – but he left it above the entrance, lit. It got too close to the hen coop and well... there was a fire. You'll see,' she says, pushing open the door to the walled garden and leading them to the far corner.

'What a mess,' says Albert. 'Are the chickens...'

'They're fine. I let them out.'

He looks relieved.

'Mike and Paul are down here,' says Amanda, leading them over to the hole. '*I've come back, Mike,*' she shouts. She hears a murmured response.

'I'll go down first,' volunteers Simeon. 'Can you follow me, Albert? And if one of you could shine a torch down?'

'I've got my phone,' says Amanda, pulling it out.

'Thanks,' he says, and lowers himself down into the darkness.

Five minutes later, Father Paul is pushed out of the hole with extreme inelegance. He looks pale and confused, and he retches into the earth. Amanda is relieved when Mike makes it back up the ladder, and then the group makes the slow and awkward return journey to the monastery.

When they reach the side door, Bede turns to them both and says, 'Thank you so much for your help with this, but I think you'd better leave him with us now. We don't allow visitors to the monastery at this hour.'

The door is shut before they can argue.

PART III

PART III

34

AMANDA

Early June 2025

Amanda is hot. It's not a hot flush – despite it being the most talked about menopausal symptom, she hasn't been graced by one of these yet. No, she's absolutely baking because the room allocated for the meeting of the Hallows Abbey school governors is too small for the assembled crowd of twenty people, and it has windows which don't open. She wonders whether this is deliberate, to try to persuade the governors – a mix of parents, local professionals, a member of the humanities teaching staff and representatives from the Catholic diocese – to make the meeting as brief as possible. If so, it hasn't worked. They've been at it for almost two hours now.

She wishes she'd said no when Mike had asked her to attend for moral support, because he'd thought he was going to be running this session with just Bede. None of them had expected Father Paul to make an appearance, on crutches, his face pale but his expression determined, his manner sober.

They haven't seen him since they rescued him from the mine the previous week, and all of their efforts to find out about his recovery since have been rebuffed. Even Father Anthony had ducked questions. He'd merely thanked them for their role in saving him and also for their discretion in the matter. But that's been it.

They've spoken about what happened many times since, however, just between themselves. It was an extraordinary thing, to see Mike literally saving the life of the man he'd blamed, rightly or wrongly, for his own brother's death. It was certainly a turning point for Mike. He'd seen Paul not as a controlling, humourless, cold teacher but as a human being with human failings and emotions. Mike had told her that in the time he'd been alone with Paul in the darkness, waiting for help, he had sounded, in his alcoholic stupor, as if he was talking to his mother. He'd cried like a child.

Amanda pulls out a tissue and mops her face. Surely this meeting must be nearly over, she thinks. It *needs* to be over soon. Mike looks exhausted. He's feeling so much better but she knows he has limits, and the grilling he, Bede and Father Paul have been subjected to so far would dent anyone's armour.

They've fielded myriad questions on safeguarding, on discipline, on their new mobile phone policy, their financial status and their continuing close working relationship with the monks in the abbey.

The representative from the Catholic diocese, a senior priest who's come all the way from Plymouth, has been particularly difficult. Amanda thinks about Mike's concerns that the Church might decide to close the school down. She can see why he's worried about that, having heard the way the diocese refers to the school as 'financially weak', with 'an uncertain future'. The representative has just told everyone present that it is the Church's view that Catholic monks should be moving away from direct, governing roles in schools. Father Paul's face had been impassive when he said this, which Amanda had admired. She'd have scowled.

Given what she knows about his current state, Paul has put up a good fight during this session, batting back questions, insisting that the school has the right safeguards in place to protect its students and that its future remains bright.

And then there is poor Bede. Ever the hopeful leader. Ever the bridesmaid, and never the bride. He has also put on a good show. Better than she'd expected. Probably better, in fact, than everyone had expected. He eschewed criticism of Mike or Paul, which is, she thinks, a sign of personal growth. She's glad. She has grown to quite like him during their chats at the allotment and the chicken coop, despite his offhand manner and his undoubtedly difficult working relationship with her husband.

'Last question,' says the chairman of the governors, a GP from Redruth. 'Mrs Mitchell?' He points to a slight woman who Amanda reckons is at least seventy-five. She must be a grandparent governor.

'Thank you, Mr Chairman,' she says, standing up with some difficulty. 'As you all know, I've been a governor of this school for more than two decades. I care deeply about its future. I know that it will take a great deal of work to put it back on the right course. With the greatest of respect, I want to enquire about your health, Father Paul. It is no secret that you have been absent for some time. Is your job here worth damaging your health further? No one wants you to drive yourself into the ground over this. Least of all, me.'

Father Paul stares intently at the woman and doesn't reply for a moment. The room holds its breath.

'I would be the first to acknowledge that I haven't been well,' he says, finally. 'As you'll see, I'm carrying an injury at the moment, but I have also had a more... general illness which has seen me be laid low. I am deeply grateful for both Mike Chapman and Brother Bede for holding the fort. Both of them have done an excellent job. As you've heard throughout, neither Mike nor I have been in post long enough yet to overhaul the systems in place at Hallows Abbey. But we have a solid plan, and, thanks to Ofsted, we are fully aware of any weaknesses now, and we have put them right.' Bede is looking a bit sheepish as he speaks. Well he might be, thinks Amanda. As deputy head pastoral for the past five years, the errors are, she thinks, largely to be laid at his door. 'I am entirely confident that Hallows Abbey will continue to be one of the most highly regarded Catholic schools in the country, and that your children will be safe and nurtured here.'

'Thank you, Headmaster,' says the chair of the governors. 'Now, I'd like to bring this extraordinary meeting to a close.'

Amanda sees a brief flash of relief pass over Mike's face, before his professional visage returns. She is much less concerned about how she appears. She needs to get out of this room before she melts. She is about to stand up when someone shouts, 'Stop.'

It's Bede.

He stands up and scans the room silently. The attendees note this and sit back down again, no doubt with some reluctance. Amanda wonders what on earth he's got left to say.

'Sorry. I wanted to say something before you all go.' A ripple of concern washes through the assembled crowd. This is certainly not in the agenda. 'I have been past retirement age for several years now, and of late I've been increasingly aware that I am no longer able to keep up with the workload required for my role. Indeed, I'm not sure I even *want* to keep up with it. And lately my brothers in the abbey have been asking me to take on more of a supervisory role over there, and I have decided that I wish to do so. So, I will be retiring from the school. I will stay, of course, as long as is necessary to replace me. But yes,' he says, looking, Amanda thinks, a little tearful, 'yes, I am going to retire.'

'Thank you for sharing that with us,' says the chair of the governors, not even missing a beat. Amanda is impressed. She's feeling quite stunned. 'We will of course be very sad to see you go.'

'Thank you,' replies Bede, smiling weakly, and sitting down.

Even though Amanda suspects this moment will be one that Bede will remember until his dying breath, the impact of his life-changing announcement on everyone else present is almost cruelly brief. The governors begin gathering their belongings and the process of getting out of their allocated seats within a few seconds.

Amanda takes her cue. She pulls her top away from the skin it's stuck to on her back and makes for the exit. She's relieved to find Mike by her side.

He whispers, 'Let's get out of here. I don't want to have to talk to anybody.'

'Good plan.'

They are through the door in seconds and already walking back in the direction of their flat when Father Paul calls out, 'Mike. *Mike!*'

Amanda's husband stops and turns around, and so does she. 'Sorry to shout,' says Father Paul, moving as fast as he can on his crutches. 'But I wanted to ask you if you have time to come back to my office for a chat. I know I haven't been around much... and I wanted to talk to you, after... last week.'

'I...' says Mike, clearly rather blindsided.

'It's important,' says Father Paul. 'And please, come too, Amanda.'

'OK. When?' replies Mike.

'Now?'

'All right,' Mike replies, and Amanda follows him.

When they reach Father Paul's office door, Mike pushes it open for him, and once he's in and settled, Mike and Amanda follow.

'Do come and take a seat,' says Father Paul, pointing to two chairs on the other side of his desk. They do as he asks. 'I want to start by expressing my sincere thanks. I was in... a very dark place and there is no doubt that you saved me from a very terrible fate.' Neither of them knows what to say. Mike mumbles something about doing what anyone would do. 'And I understand that neither of you has told any of the other staff about my obvious inebriation, which is quite remarkable, and totally undeserved. Or my dreadful foolishness with that candle.'

There's a knock on the door.

'Excuse me,' he says, hobbling over on his crutches and opening it.

In walks the elderly school governor who'd asked Father Paul the piercing question about his health and its impact on his ability to do his job. Why on earth is she here? Amanda wonders.

'I'd like to re-introduce you to Theresa Mitchell. She's the longest-serving school governor of Hallows Abbey. She's also a very dear friend of mine,' he says, showing her to a comfortable armchair near the window.

'Oh,' says Amanda, unable to hide her surprise.

'Hello,' says Theresa, in her lilting Irish accent. 'It's wonderful to meet you.'

'I wanted her here, because there's something I must tell you. It's Theresa that persuaded me to do so. She's been my confidante ever since I was a teenager. She was a school nurse here, in fact, when I was a pupil.'

'You were a student here?' says Mike. 'I had no idea.'

'Only briefly. I had a full scholarship and attended for one very miserable year.'

'I'm sorry to hear that.'

'It was... largely my fault,' says the headmaster.

'John, that's simply not true,' says Theresa, and suddenly every pair of eyes in the room is focused on the white-haired woman with the air of calm.

'John?'

'That was my name before I took holy orders. All Credans take a saint's name when they become monks. I took Paul. But before that, I was John.'

'I see,' says Mike. 'Yes, I suppose I knew that.'

'It doesn't really matter,' says Father Paul. 'I'm still me, whatever name you call me. I'm still...' He shoots a glance at Theresa. 'I'm still the oddball, awkward boy who didn't fit in anywhere. I was insecure about where I'd come from. I came from poverty, you see. And despite my above average academic brain, I could never be accepted. It enraged me. I so desperately wanted to be someone else. So desperately, in fact, that when my wastrel father was paid to take a group of boys on a boat trip, I didn't step in and tell the school he was an alcoholic who should not be trusted with other people's lives.'

'*The Towan*...' says Mike. 'You're talking about *The Towan* tragedy?'

'Yes.'

'It wasn't your fault, John. It was never your fault. The coroner said as much.' Theresa is sitting forward in her chair, staring at the headmaster, who is avoiding her gaze and staring at the floor.

'I know that. But even though the coroner found that it was the weather and the condition of the boat that caused it, I never forgave myself. Because nobody will ever know what really caused them to sink. The coroner was using an educated guess. What if they'd used another company? They'd have used another boat. A better boat, maybe.' He pauses, but none of them say anything. Amanda is thinking about the podcast she'd listened to, and the headmaster's dismissal of its contents. That student's decision to dig it all up and turn it into entertainment must have felt like a terrible blow. 'I watched them leave, you know. I went down that tunnel from the garden and watched them leave on their final journey.' Father Paul rubs his eyes, as if he's trying to disguise tears. 'And after... after he died, and he took all those boys with him to the bottom of the sea... after that, I was haunted. Both when I was asleep, and when I was awake.'

'I see,' says Mike, although Amanda suspects, like her, he has no idea why Father Paul is telling them this.

'I never really... I never really recovered from it. The guilt. It drove me. I channelled the anger into my faith and my studies. I was determined to rise to the top of the Church, to be someone people looked up to. Whatever the cost. And not just people – God. I wanted God to be proud of me, to approve of me, despite everything. Getting the job here, as headmaster, felt like a victory. I felt I could finally soothe that damaged boy, that poor angry, damaged boy I used to be at this school. And so I pushed. I know I drove both you and Bede too hard...' he says, looking at Mike.

'You pushed my brother too hard, too,' says Mike, and Amanda has to swallow to stop herself gasping out loud. They had agreed that no good would ever come of Mike confronting Father Paul about his bullying of his brother. *But here we are*, she thinks. *Here we are. There's no going back now.*

'I know who your brother was, Mike. Chapman's a common enough name, but you're quite alike. I knew as soon as I met you whose brother you were. I see Oliver's face, too, sometimes, in my nightmares. I just prayed you didn't know who *I* was. *What* I was, to your family. I've prayed about that every night, in fact.'

'I... why didn't you say?' asks Mike.

'You didn't seem to know, and I... I was too lacking in humility to want to invite your justified rage into my life. I was too consumed with my ambition. I was using it to push away my guilt. My ambition was useful cloud cover for that. But my God, Mike... I'm so sorry. I am so sorry that I didn't see how Oliver felt, how badly he was feeling. If I could go back and act differently, to go easier on him, I would. I so desperately wish I could.'

Amanda is dumbfounded, and she can see that Mike is, too. This is not at all how either of them thought things would play out.

'Tell them, John. Tell them what happened, down at the cove,' urges Theresa.

'Yes. *Yes*. That terrible night when we all went out in the storm, I thought we'd lost those boys. I thought, like that dreadful day in 1966, that they'd drowned. That history was repeating itself. And when we found them in the cave, it was so dark. Just candlelight. But I thought, just for a moment, for the briefest moment, that they had the faces of... faces of the lost boys. I could see them all so clearly. They were back from the dead. Only a flicker, a flash, really. But it was enough. Everything I'd constructed around me came crashing down. Psychologists would say I'd been "triggered", that long-suppressed emotions came to the surface. All I can tell you is that I descended immediately into a very dark place. I was incapable of functioning. I stayed with Theresa for a long time afterwards but returned to the abbey a fortnight ago. Too early, I think.'

'I've been a nurse all of my life,' Theresa says, by way of explanation. 'And later, I qualified as a social worker, too, after I married and had my family. I have looked after many troubled children...'

'Including me,' says the headmaster.

'Including you,' says Theresa, smiling.

'I didn't realise,' says Mike. 'I had no idea.'

Please, Amanda thinks, realising what he might be about to say. *Please don't tell him about your role in what happened that night. He doesn't need to know. He really doesn't need to know.*

'You can't have, Mike,' says the headmaster. 'I didn't tell you anything. I pretended I was a bulletproof leader, full of good ideas and strict rules. I never told you how wounded I was, underneath.'

'I don't know what to say,' says Mike.

'You don't have to say anything. But now I've told you, I need to tell you about my plan. I didn't tell the governors in there, because I wanted to have a calm conversation with you both, and I also wanted to know if Bede wanted to stay on. Now that I know he doesn't, I feel the time's right to talk to you about things. Things that I hope will happen.'

'Go on,' says Mike. Amanda sees his hand is shaking. She can't even imagine how he must feel, hearing the teacher who bullied Olly express his heartfelt regret. Does he feel glad? she wonders. Relieved? Or is he still angry?

'The diocese is determined to separate the abbey from this school.'

'I got that vibe during the governors' meeting.'

'Yes. It's been a common theme across the country in recent years. Not surprising, given the horrific cases of abuse that have come to light. Some monks were... should not ever have been left in charge of children. Let's put it that way.' He swirls his glass and stares into it, as if he's reading tea runes. 'But yes, it's actually an approach I agree with. There should be a lay headmaster at Hallows Abbey. A monk should not be in charge of this school.'

Amanda is astonished. Is he actually putting himself out of a job?

'I don't understand. It's Bede who just announced his resignation. Not you,' says Mike.

'Not yet. Despite the dreadful time I had at this school when I was a boy, I have grown to love it since returning here. To understand the special kind of education it offers. And I do not want it to fail. If I resign now, the parents will lose all confidence in us. The numbers on our rolls are already too low. We won't survive if even more leave.'

'No, that's true,' says Mike.

'Despite what I've said to you... despite how difficult I may have made your job... I do like your plans, Mike. I like the ideas you have. And I think you have the right vision to lead this school in a new direction.'

'Like... what?' Mike asks.

'Well, we could consider, for example, whether the time has come to open our doors to girls. And to day pupils, perhaps? Traditional boarding schools are on the out. Flexi-boarding is something to consider. I think this school could be so much more, so much more relevant and so much more valuable, if we change it. And I think you are the person to do it.'

'You're going to... resign?'

'Not yet. But I will. When I can be certain the governors will back your appointment. Theresa will talk to them. She has a lot of sway.'

'I *am* planning on retiring from my governor role,' says Theresa, looking at Amanda and Mike. 'I'm in my eighties, I've got a new great-grandchild to enjoy, and my husband Bob would like me to be at home more. Frankly, I've been at this business for too long. But yes, I've told John I'll stay long enough to see these changes through. I owe it to him.' Theresa has a steely look in her eye, Amanda thinks. She wonders why this woman who's apparently made a career out of caring for vulnerable children has remained so loyal to a man who's developed a reputation as a bully.

'I realise that you may not want to stay on,' says Father Paul, finally sitting down on his chair. 'I can imagine that working with the man who is going to be trying to, once again, recover from his addiction to alcohol will be difficult. Not to mention that you, quite rightly, blame me for my role in your brother's death. I'm surprised you haven't resigned before now, in fact. But I suppose what I'm saying is that if you are prepared to stay, I will only be here for a short while longer. And I'll be very hands off. To be frank, I think it will be better that way. I'm a lot better than I was, but I'm still... not well enough. Not nearly well enough. No, I won't give you any trouble, I can promise you that.' Father Paul – John – looks tired as he says this. Amanda realises that the governors' meeting took a lot out of him, and this burst of honesty, of baring his soul, has clearly stolen the rest of his energy away. 'Anyway, if you could think about it, and let me know... We can begin making plans, either way. If you want to leave, I'd appreciate you letting me know soon, so we can recruit a suitable replacement. But if not... Yes, please do let me know.'

'I'll do that,' says Mike, taking his cue from his grey-faced colleague. 'Mandy and I will talk it over. I'll let you know as soon as I can.'

Mike stands up, and Amanda follows suit. She's actually surprised she can still stand, given how shocked she is by this turn of events. Mike, she sees, is doing a better job of hiding how he feels. That's one of his strengths, she thinks, although as they both know, it's also a weakness.

'Thank you... thanks,' says Father Paul.

'I hope you feel better soon,' says Amanda, instinctively.

Paul's head rises slowly. 'Thank you, my dear. Thank you,' he says, managing a weak smile.

'It was nice to meet you, Mrs Mitchell,' she says, as Mike walks to the door and opens it.

'And you too, Mrs Chapman,' answers Theresa.

35

THERESA

Early June 2025

'John? Oh, goodness, John. Let me get you some water.'

Theresa pushes on the arms of her chair and hauls herself up to standing. All her joints creak these days, and every action takes far longer than it used to. She's grateful, however, to make it this far. A privilege denied to many, she thinks, as she walks over to the water cooler in the corner of the room and fills one of the water glasses on the sideboard. She places it in front of John.

'Drink it. Little sips,' she says, as she would have said to a homesick boy in this very building, all those decades ago. 'Do you have any food in here?'

John nods. 'Yes. In the cupboard. Biscuits.'

Theresa rummages inside the cupboard, pulls out a pack of custard creams, and rips it open. She finds a small plate and lays three out for him and takes two for herself. They are a favourite of hers, after all. And she has learned never to deny herself her joys. That's one of the key lessons she's learned in life. She bites into one of them and a ripple of pleasure passes through her. It took her years to get over the guilt, but yes. Never, *never* deny yourself joy, she thinks. *Never*.

'Here you go. I recommend eating all three of them.'

John smiles weakly.

He picks one up and nibbles it.

'Don't gnaw at it, John. Eat the bloody thing.'

'All right, all right,' he says, biting a bigger chunk off and chewing it.

'That's better,' she says, listening to his jaw chewing and his throat swallowing. She's glad he's eating something, at least. This evening was the equivalent of a marathon for him, given his frail mental health. And physical health too, actually. His drinking, a terrible inheritance from his father, is a huge concern. He needs to spend some serious time getting that back under control. He's done it before, so she knows he can do it again. 'You did the right thing, telling them, you know. I know you took some persuading, but it was the right thing to do. There aren't any secrets now. That always feels better. I remember how I felt after the inquest. I felt relief, knowing you knew I'd recommended your father for that job. Everybody knowing, in fact. Once it was out in the open, the impact was so much less than I'd feared. I'm sure you'll find the same. Although, there was one bit of that you hadn't told me about.'

'Which bit?'

'You said you'd watched *The Towan* leave, from the tunnel.'

'It's not important really, but yes, I did.'

'How did you know about the tunnel?'

'Oh, I'm a local boy. My father's family were all involved in smuggling. I know all of the tunnels and caves around here.'

'I see.'

'You know, I think I'm the reason one of those conspiracy theories about *The Towan* started. I've always enjoyed singing. My mother Morwenna sang beautifully, and she taught me her favourite songs as a child. I've always sung them ever since her death, as a sort of talisman, I suppose. As a kind of protection. I was singing them in the tunnel above the cove that day in 1966, when I watched them set out to sea. I always felt that it was sacrilege, in a way. Singing while my drunken father took them out to their deaths.'

'You couldn't have known.'

'No. I suppose not.'

'It'll be fine from hereon in, John. You'll be able to retire quietly, and get well, and live out the rest of your life in peace. I am sure of it.'

'I hope so. There's every chance Mike will tell everyone that I'm off my rocker, hallucinating... He could have me removed overnight, if he wants.'

'And if he does? What's the worst that could happen?'

John picks up his glass and sips.

'I'll go back to the abbey, I suppose. Pray five times a day, work in the gardens, read...'

'That's what you're planning to do anyway, isn't it.'

'But I'll be disgraced.'

'Don't be ridiculous. Mental illness isn't disgraceful.'

'I'd be pitied, then.'

'You're mistaking pity for sympathy. They are not the same thing, John, and you know it.' John picks up his second biscuit and bites into it. 'I wanted to ask you something, actually. In our meeting just now, you told Mike and Amanda that you were haunted after the tragedy. Not in your dreams, but when you were awake. What did you mean by that?'

'You never miss a trick, do you? Look, can we just pretend it was a metaphor?' he says, trying to avoid looking at her. 'It was a long time ago.'

'What did you see?'

'Stop it.'

'What was it?' she asks.

He sits back in his seat and glares at her. 'Are you going to really make me tell you?'

'Yes.'

'I saw... a demon.'

'A demon?'

'Yes. After the accident, I went to the abbey late one night, after lights out. I felt so guilty that I hadn't warned the school about my dad's reputation and I wanted to pray, to beg for forgiveness. So I let myself in there and while I was there, a... demon approached me. Tempted me. He was clearly feeding off my guilt.'

'What do you mean, he was a demon? What did he look like?'

John fixes his gaze on her. 'He looked human. But all demons do. They disguise themselves.'

'What did he look like? What was he wearing?'

John shrugs. 'He was dressed like a monk. I thought he was one of the monks from the abbey.'

Theresa's heart quickens. 'How did you know he wasn't?'

'Because he disappeared into thin air. And appeared out of thin air, too. Without making a sound. He came and went in an instant. No human can do that.'

'What did he say to you?'

'I barely remember. Something about everyone being welcome in God's church.'

'That doesn't sound very demonic.'

'No, but...'

'I think I've met this monk too, John.'

His eyes widen.

'Did he have white hair?'

'Possibly.'

'And blue eyes?'

'It was too dark to tell.'

'Look, John. Let me level with you. I've never told anyone this, but yes, I spoke to this monk once. He was called Brother Volmar.'

'He was a real man? A real monk?'

'He was, once.'

'Once? Come on, Theresa. You don't believe those silly ghost stories the boys spread around the school, do you?'

'If you don't believe the boys, then try believing Father Crispin. He was your headmaster, wasn't he?'

'Yes. He was a fair man. A good man, I think.'

'He told me it was Brother Volmar I'd seen. He said that he'd died six months before I met him, in the abbey. Just like you did.'

'When did this happen?'

'Just after the inquest, in 1966. That would be just after you saw him, wouldn't it?'

'Yes. If he's the same person... I mean ghost. Oh, Theresa, this is madness.'

'What's more mad? Believing you saw the benevolent spirit of a recently deceased monk, or a demon sent to drag you down to hell?'

'Benevolent?'

'Oh, yes. Father Crispin said he always comes to people in need. He was very reassuring to me. He set me off on the right path, in fact.' She sees something pass across John's face. Is it relief? she wonders. Or regret, at years lived in fear and anger? 'Whoever it was you saw, I do not believe it was evil,' she adds, walking over to him and putting an arm on his shoulder. 'You have been troubled for a very long time, John, but I don't believe you're evil. Not in your heart. And neither does God. And he knows who you are. I promise you that.'

36

AMANDA

August 2025

'Did we really have to bring this enormous hamper?'

'I don't want any of us to feel hungry when we're at sea.'

'We're going to be hugging the coast, Mandy. Not heading off to Ireland.'

'Yes. I know. But I want it to be nice. I want everyone to have a lovely time. I mean, the kids are finally here! I want them to be... happy.'

'They *are* happy,' says Mike, stopping for a moment and turning round to see Julia, Luke and his boyfriend Ben. They're supposed to be carrying a cooler with the drinks, but at the moment Luke is lying in the tall grass, apparently paralysed with laughter, while the other two look on in amusement. 'But they're not actually kids any more, Mand.'

'I know,' she says, as they get going once more. 'I know. But it's hard to let that bit go, isn't it?'

'They'll always need us, you know. And they'll always be ours.'

'Yes.' Amanda thinks about the tiny babies who'd sat in the crook of her arm; the little hands which had clutched hers on walks; the children she'd swung in the air at the school gate. 'I suppose one of the hardest things about being menopausal is knowing that you will never have more children. That your usefulness is... done.'

'Don't be ridiculous. You are more useful now than ever. Don't you remember how exhausted we were when we had young kids? How little time we had for anything else, and even each other? We've *had* children, Mand. We were so lucky to be able to have them. But they've grown now, and we can enjoy the fact they can wipe their own bottoms and even make their own money. One fine day, at least, when they've finished this endless studying.'

'Yes, talking of that,' says Amanda, as they arrive at the top of the steps to the cove. 'What do you think Julia is going to do now her MA's over? She hasn't been in touch much lately. I thought she and Tom had all sorts of plans. But she's been a bit quiet. Have you heard about any jobs, or anything?'

'Nope.'

'I'll ask her, when we get going,' says Amanda.

'Yes, sounds like a plan. Talking of plans... What time are Sandra and Rosie bringing the boat up to the jetty?'

Amanda glances at her watch as they begin the descent to the beach below.

'She said midday. She should be here any minute.'

'Good. To be honest, I'm so hungry at the moment, I might break this hamper open on the beach.'

'Well, if you will keep doing this intermittent fasting, Mike. It's just making you more ravenous at lunch, I reckon.'

'I need to do something to retain my youthful good looks,' he says with a wink. 'How else will I keep you?' She laughs, but she can see he's partly serious. 'I don't deserve you,' he says.

'We made a promise when we married, didn't we?' she says. 'We promised to be with each other, in good times and in bad. And we have been, for more than two decades. I'm not going to run screaming for the hills, just because you're struggling with your mental health, am I? That's daft.'

'You've put up with all sorts of stupid stuff on my behalf.'

'Yeah, well, I found the car keys in the fridge this morning. I think I thought I was putting the milk away. You've got years of this crap to deal with, you know. I won't be out on the other side of menopause for a while. Oh, and my bottom will soon start to eclipse the sun. I am a comfort eater, as you know.'

Mike manages a smile.

'We'll be OK, won't we?' he asks, as if he's pleading with her.

'Yes, of course we will. We're us.'

Amanda smiles, and so does Mike. And then for a brief moment she remembers how desperate he'd been, how low when she'd found him knee-deep in the water in this very cove, and she acknowledges how far they've come. It feels good to be here today; a celebration of recovery. Or the beginnings of it, anyway.

It has been an interesting summer. After Bede's shock resignation and Father Paul's even more shocking revelations about his past and his addiction to alcohol, they limped along to the end of term. After the last trunk had been loaded and its owner driven away, they'd spent a good couple of weeks talking through options. They did discuss moving but finding Mike a new job at the end of the summer term, especially a leadership role, was highly unlikely. Most of these roles recruit in spring. And of course, Paul's offer to back Mike for the headship, while not a cert, was and is a very tempting prospect. It'll come with just the same level of stress, of course, and perhaps even more. This much they both know.

However, Mike is excited about being able to drive the sort of change that he's been dreaming about, and of course, staying here, on this little promontory on the northern coast of Cornwall, is something that she wants to do. After a difficult start, she has grown to love this windswept, barren landscape: the rhythm of the waves and the cries of the seagulls are now her lullaby; the huge sky is an ever-changing, living piece of art. It suits the new version of herself that she's adjusting to. No longer defined by who needs her, and increasingly at the mercy of unpredictable hormones, she has found unexpected solace in the natural world, and in her job, looking after the students.

She has definitely moved on. She's stopped listening to *The Towan Conspiracy* podcast, ceased pondering on abductions to strange utopian communities or suicidal teachers. She realises that indulging in these theories had allowed her to disconnect from reality, from the far more prosaic reasons for the things she was experiencing. She had been wrestling with painful change, processing emotions and seeking answers to important questions in her life. Most of which, she thinks she's now found answers to.

She now accepts that the tragedy was just that: an awful accident brought about by a perfect storm of bad weather and insufficient safety regulations. The kind that happens every day around the world and yet causes those involved such pain that its impact ricochets through generations.

They reach the bottom of the steps. Amanda shades her face from the sun with her right hand and sees a small black object just below the horizon.

'Boat's coming in,' she says. 'Right on time.'

'Got to hand it to Rosie,' says Mike. 'She's one of my most reliable members of staff.'

'Surely that would be me?' says Amanda, teasing him. 'I've slaved away for you for more than twenty years.'

'A labour of love, Mandy. A labour of love.' He smiles and takes her hand.

'I can see the boat!' shouts Luke, who's just reached the bottom of the steps with his partner and sister.

'Seriously, Mand,' says Mike, his voice quiet, no doubt aware that the echo in the cove could mean the others could hear him. 'You don't feel like that about our marriage, do you? Because if I thought you really felt like being married to me was a chore, I'd feel... very bad about you having to be here with me. I mean, I haven't been easy to be with for quite some time. I just...'

'Shhh,' she says, putting a finger to his lips. 'Don't be silly. I'm joking. I'm a grown woman, and one of the unexpected joys of this phase of my life is that I am prepared to put up with much, much less. If I didn't want to be here, Mike, I wouldn't be. I'd be gone. But I'm here. Because I love you.'

'I love you too,' he says, and he kisses her, lingering on her lips for just a second longer than needed.

'Eurgh, you two, get a room,' says Luke as he, Ben and Julia arrive at the end of the jetty.

'I refuse to apologise,' says Mike. 'We're not dead yet.'

'Enough, Dad, I just can't bear to think about this.' Julia looks like she's smelled something rotten.

'They're pulling into the cove,' says Luke, giving them all the distraction they need. They stand and watch as a thirty-foot cabin cruiser nears them, with a waving Rosie at its bow. She's holding a bunch of helium-filled balloons.

'Ahoy there,' she shouts, her voice echoing around the cove. 'How's the birthday girl?'

Amanda grins broadly. She'd been a little reluctant when Rosie had proposed a boat trip for her forty-seventh birthday, given the terrible history enshrined on the plaque on the cliff above, but Rosie had pointed out that the boat's owner, Sandra, was a skipper for the RNLI and frankly, who could you go out with who would be a safer bet? Amanda couldn't disagree with this, of course. And also, she has decided she will not let fear control her. She'd spent so long being afraid of losing her identity as soon as the children left, of losing her marriage, and she's realised it was pointless. The only direction now for her is forwards, she's decided. And with freedom, not fear.

'Feeling good,' she replies as the boat pulls in, and Rosie throws her a rope.

'Can you wrap that round the post there and give it back to me? Then we'll do the rope at the back.'

'Sure.' Amanda does as she's asked, and twenty minutes later, they are all on board and preparing to cast off. She's positioned herself on the padded seat at the back, a few metres behind Rosie's steering position. Mike and the boys are round the front, doing something with the ropes. The sun has just come round onto the cove and Amanda has closed her eyes, enjoying the warmth on her face.

'Hi, Mum,' says Julia, sitting down next to her.

'Hello, you.'

'Are you having a nice birthday?'

'I am.'

'Did you like the perfume I got you?'

'I did. But the best present is having you all here with me. I miss you, you know.' As she says this, Sandra calls for the boys to cast off, and the engine begins to hum beneath their feet.

'Yes, I was going to ask you about that, actually,' she says, leaning her head on Amanda's shoulder.

'Oh?'

The boat starts to pull away from the jetty.

'He's gone, Mum,' says Julia, her voice muffled as she speaks into Amanda's shirt. 'Tom's gone, back to his parents. It's over.'

'Oh darling. I'm so sorry.'

'I thought... I thought we might get married,' says Julia, quietly. 'And now I feel like a complete idiot.'

'You're not an idiot, darling. Of course you're not. Some relationships just don't work out. People change.'

'Yes. Well. Clearly.'

'What are you doing about the flat?' asks Amanda.

Julia looks pained. 'I don't know, in all honesty. It's only a one bedroom. I can hardly get a flatmate.'

'Any chance of getting out of the lease?'

'I'm going to ask. Tom's paying his share of the rent, at least. He's living rent-free with his parents up in Walthamstow.'

'I see.'

'I was wondering if you and Dad might have room in this new cottage you're renting.'

They'd signed the lease the previous week. It's a three-bedroom ex-fishermen's cottage with a little garden and a view of the sea. It's a stopgap while they put their flat in Bristol on the market. They've decided to try to buy somewhere near the school. In the area, but far enough away to give them both the space they need.

'You want to come and live with us?' Amanda can't contain her surprise.

'Yes. Not forever, but... I've finished the MA and I'm not at all sure I really want to work in film. To be honest, I'm not sure what I want to do. And living in London is so expensive. I wondered if I could live with you guys for a bit, while I work things out?'

Amanda has to stop herself from laughing. She's spent so long mourning their empty nest, and had almost adjusted to it, almost acknowledged its potential joys – and now this! Her daughter wants to come home again.

'You are always welcome here with us,' she says, smiling. 'You never need to ask.'

'Oh, thanks, Mum. I'm so relieved,' says Julia, hugging her.

'Can we all join in this hug?' says Luke, as he, Ben and Mike join them at the stern of the boat, which turns and makes its way out of the cove.

Julia springs back, wiping away a tear.

'This old bird always welcomes hugs,' says Amanda, and Luke embraces her warmly before going off to find the cool box and the chilled beer that's within. He hands one to Mike, who sits down next to Amanda.

'Julia and Tom have broken up. She wants to move in with us for a bit,' she says.

'Ah,' he says. 'That'll be nice.'

They sit in silence for a while, their years of love and friendship doing the talking for them. They know how they both feel about this turn of events. There is no need to say it.

The boat pulls further away from land and is about to turn left to hug the coast, when Amanda spots a figure on the coastal path at the top of the cliff. They're not walking along it, but standing still, looking out to sea. At them, she thinks. And then she realises they're wearing what looks like a monk's habit. And then the monk waves. Quite clearly, quite deliberately, at the boat.

'Did you tell Father Paul we were coming on this trip today?' she asks Mike.

'Oh, no. Why?'

'Because there's a monk up there on the cliffs,' she says, looking back in the same direction. But he's not there now. He's disappeared.

'Where?' Mike asks, scanning the cliff path.

'Oh, don't worry,' says Amanda. 'It must have just been a walker. My mistake.'

As the assembled group of her loved ones open drinks and try to decide where they should stop to eat lunch, Amanda sits and stares at where the monk had been standing. She *knows* she saw him there. She wasn't mistaken. And then she feels a strange sensation of calm pass over her, a feeling of love and warmth, and she decides not to ask any more questions.

'Right, who's for champagne?' she says, heading to the cooler. 'I think it's time for a celebration.'

* * *

MORE FROM VICTORIA SCOTT

Victoria Scott's next enchanting historical story, is available to order now: https://mybook.to/VictoriaScottBackAd

AUTHOR'S NOTE

Cornwall is a county I know very well. I've been holidaying there since I was a child and have been an even more regular visitor since I met my husband in 2004, because his parents chose to retire to a village near Falmouth.

Over the years we've stayed not only at their place but in cottages, apartments and campsites all over Cornwall. The inspiration for the entirely fictional Hallows Abbey and the similarly fictional fishing village of Porthgerran came from a week we spent near Chapel Porth. It's an area made famous by Winston Graham's *Poldark* series, which chronicles the lives and loves of the Poldark family, who became wealthy from tin mining. Although the county's last tin mine closed in the late 1990s, the industry's decline began a long time before that, with most closing by the early twentieth century. The engine houses and chimneys that once powered these mines now lie in ruin along the coast, with their tunnels stretching for miles both inland and out to sea.

The Towan is a fictional boat. Thus, its sinking never happened, and its crew, passengers and fate come entirely from my own imagination. However, while writing it I had in mind a very real tragedy in Cornwall in 1966: the sinking of the MV Darlwyne, in which two crew and all twenty-nine passengers died. We have stayed near the boat's setting off point in Mylor on several occasions and visited the memorial at the church. A Board of Trade enquiry concluded that the Darlwyne had gone to sea in a storm, was in poor condition, and didn't have enough lifesaving aids on board.

Incidentally, I named the boat in this novel after Towan Beach near Newquay, which is also home to the Headland Hotel, where Roald Dahl's *The Witches* was filmed. Its architecture and position inspired the design of Hallows Abbey in my mind's eye, along with my old school, Malvern Girls' College, which is another example of classic red brick Victoriana. My experiences as both a day girl and later a boarder there also came in useful when writing about the boarding school experience.

Talking of experiences – I was going through the perimenopause when I wrote this novel. In fact, I still am. It lasts years and its impact is only now really being spoken about widely and openly. It was important to me when writing Amanda's story to give an authentic portrayal of this difficult period in many women's lives. Like Amanda, I have often struggled to remember words and names (which is tricky when you're a novelist and university lecturer!) and on occasion the unexpected, overwhelming anxiety has been crippling. I hope readers who are also struggling in perimenopause will feel my solidarity with them leaping off the page.

Further inspiration for this novel came from the fabulous BBC podcast Uncanny, which is brilliantly crafted audio featuring real people talking about their encounters with the supernatural. One of my favourite episodes featured a woman who'd got a job at a boarding school in Yorkshire, only to find herself being woken up every night by the sound of a child crying in an empty room next door. It sent a real shiver down my spine (and I'm sure everyone else's who listened to it – it was very creepy!) Afterwards, it got me thinking about the deep unhappiness I'd witnessed in some of my boarding friends and how that might, if you subscribe to 'stone tape theory' – the idea that emotional events somehow embed themselves into buildings to be replayed again and again – result in places like boarding schools being a location for these phenomena.

One of the things I love about Uncanny is that it always includes a sceptical point of view, inviting listeners to decide whether they do believe in ghosts or whether there is a rational explanation for the story being told. I'm still firmly on the fence, I must say, although a large part of me desperately wants ghosts to be real. I certainly enjoyed writing about a benevolent ghost monk, because my optimistic soul loves the idea that some spirits might actually be angels in disguise.

Finally, while Theresa Murphy is a fictional woman, I took inspiration for her from my late mother-in-law Anne Scott, who travelled from Ireland to England as a young woman in the 1960s, studied nursing in London, and then made the country her home. She met my father-in-law Bill, married, had a very successful nursing career and amongst it all gave birth to my husband, for which I am of course eternally grateful. She was a wonderful, warm woman with a wicked sense of humour and she is terribly missed.

If you'd like to find out more about me or my five other novels, just visit my website, www.toryscott.com, or follow me on one of my many and varied social media accounts. (I spend far too much time on them. Do come and say hi.)

ACKNOWLEDGEMENTS

Astonishingly, this is my sixth novel. I'm not quite sure how I've managed this in the four giddy years since the publication of *Patience*, my debut, except that I simply can't not write, and also that I've had excellent support along the way.

Firstly, a huge thank you goes, as ever, to my husband Teil for giving me the space and time to write, and for making me excellent coffee to keep me going. Similarly to my wonderful children Raphie and Ella who have to put up with Mummy spending a lot of time thinking deeply about the fates of fictional people. I'd also like to thank my dad, Chris Milne, who was at boarding school in the sixties, for checking my period detail, and one of my oldest friends, Catherine, for making sure I was getting all the Catholic references right. And while I'm at it, I'd like to send out a big virtual hug to my writer friends, particularly Marion Todd, for brainstorming plots with me and generally providing free therapy.

This is the fourth novel I've written with Rachel Faulkner-Willcocks as editor. The first, *The Women Who Wouldn't Leave*, was published when she was working at Head of Zeus, and my most recent three at the excellent and innovative Boldwood Books. She continues to be an absolute powerhouse, full of great insights and killer instincts. We are a very happy partnership and I consider it an honour to continue working with her.

Last but definitely not least, I'd like to thank my agent Hannah Weatherill at Watson, Little for her consistently wise advice, her industry savvy, her belief in me since the very beginning, and for always having my back.

Book credits

Editor: Rachel Faulkner-Willcocks
Agents: Hannah Weatherill at Watson, Little (literary agent and book to screen)
Gabrielle Deblon at Watson, Little (foreign rights)
Cover design: Jane Dixon-Smith
Copy editing: Sandra Ferguson
Marketing: Niamh Wallace and team
Sales: Wendy Neale, Isabelle Flynn and Amanda Ridout
Proofreading: Arbaiah Aird

ABOUT THE AUTHOR

Victoria Scott has been a journalist for many media outlets including the BBC and *The Telegraph*. She is the author of three novels as Victoria Scott, including her Gothic timeslip novel *The House in the Water*.

Sign up to Victoria Scott's mailing list here for news, competitions and updates on future books.

Visit Victoria's website: www.toryscott.com

Follow Victoria on social media:

- x.com/Toryscott
- facebook.com/VictoriaScottJournalist
- instagram.com/victoriascottauthor
- tiktok.com/@victoriascottauthor

ALSO BY VICTORIA SCOTT

The House in the Water

The Storyteller's Daughter

The House on the Cliff

Letters from
the past

Discover page-turning historical novels from your favourite authors and be transported back in time

Join our book club Facebook group

https://bit.ly/SixpenceGroup

Sign up to our newsletter

https://bit.ly/LettersFromPastNews

Boldwood

Boldwood Books is an award-winning fiction publishing company seeking out the best stories from around the world.

Find out more at www.boldwoodbooks.com

Join our reader community for brilliant books, competitions and offers!

Follow us
@BoldwoodBooks
@TheBoldBookClub

Sign up to our weekly deals newsletter

https://bit.ly/BoldwoodBNewsletter

www.ingramcontent.com/pod-product-compliance
Ingram Content Group UK Ltd.
Pitfield, Milton Keynes, MK11 3LW, UK
UKHW040042180925
7956UKWH00001B/2